She

Taught

Me

Everything

She

Taught

Me

Everything

by Amy Smith Linton

Lifted Board Press, LLC

Published by Lifted Board Press, LLC
7901 4th Street North Suite 4000
St. Petersburg, FL 33702

Cover design by Paul Utr

ISBN: 979-8-9879092-0-1
Library of Congress Control Number: 2023916998

For my favorite skipper

Chapter 1: The North Country

STARTING when we were little, my sister made a habit of waking me in the middle of the night.

"Get up!" she'd hiss, the ends of her long hair tickling my face as she leaned over me. "Wake up, sleepyhead! It's time to go. Right now." She'd yank the covers away and push a gym bag at me, her voice quiet and urgent in the dark. "Get your things."

Five minutes later, the time exact by her watch, I'd be in the field behind the house.

She'd examine what I was wearing: blue jeans, a chambray shirt, a windbreaker. She'd ask me about what I had packed. The meager list—my pencils and a sketchbook, a piggy bank, a jack-knife, my birth certificate, some underwear, a sweater, photographs, a flashlight, socks—was never quite right.

"You don't need the flashlight," she'd tell me. "And just pick a small sketchbook if you have to bring one at all. It's not essential. You can always make more pictures."

Her voice was hushed but full of excitement.

"How much money do you have? Did you remember your birth certificate? What would you eat? Next time make sure to pack something to keep you going, like candy or raisins."

That was my sister, Vivian Marguerite Jones, at twelve, at fifteen, standing tall in the moonlight, with an army-surplus rucksack slung over one shoulder. "Alright then, if we had to make a run for it right now—where would you go first?"

I went through the drill again: where we would meet, what we would do if we got separated, if our parents got arrested, if someone were chasing us, if things got really bad.

After a few minutes, I'd tiptoe back up the kitchen stairs while Viv climbed hand-over-hand up the rope she'd rigged out her window. She went up fast, as quiet as smoke.

IN THOSE days before our parents left for good, we stayed in rented farmhouses in Vermont, New Hampshire, New York. We moved often, usually without much warning. Viv and I changed schools at least once a year. We packed up one April and I never finished second grade at all.

My sister and I weren't permitted to go to sleepovers or birthday parties. We couldn't invite friends over to visit, and when we moved, we were not allowed to write to anyone.

Viv and I wore homemade gingham dresses to school because our father thought girls should look like girls. We talked funny and we didn't make friends easily. We rarely had access to television. People thought we were stuck up.

Our parents left us alone in the houses, traveling for weeks at a time for my father's work. On cold evenings when we were left alone in a creaking old farmhouse, Viv would lead the way down the wooden staircase to the kitchen and tell me to make hot cocoa. She'd check my measurements, police my technique, and remind me to wash the pan before leaving the kitchen. When she was impatient, she'd make the cocoa herself and bring a cup to me.

One night, she stalked into my room unannounced, two mugs steaming in the chilly upstairs air. "Here," she said, thumping the cocoa down on the dresser next to my bed. She never seemed to spill no matter how she crashed dishes around. She never scalded the milk when it heated, even over a wood stove. On her, a flannel nightgown looked long and elegant.

Viv perched on the sagging mattress and pulled the sketchbook out of my hands. "What if Magda and Jahn don't make it back this time?" She always referred to our parents by name.

"They'll come back!" I said, even as I wondered whether her saying so might make disaster strike.

"What if they don't?" she persisted, her eyes squinting to mean little slits. "What if Jahn's truck runs off the road and they get killed dead?"

I felt a prickling deep inside my nose, a panicky burn in the pit of my stomach. I didn't dare to blink in case the tears started.

"Well?" she said. "Figure it out, Nicky."

After a moment she relented, sipping her cocoa and pulling a face at me. "Better to think about it now when it hasn't happened than to be surprised later."

My sister taught me everything I knew back then. She taught me how to tie my shoes and she made sure I finished my homework. When she shook me awake in the middle of the night and said, "It's time to get out of here," I got up and went because it was how she helped me get ready for the world.

Chapter 2: Sarasota, Florida, October 1993

WHEN the telephone rang in the middle of the night, I knew.

The Tennessee state trooper on the other end said, "Your sister's been hurt pretty bad."

In my haste to get to Nashville I didn't ask a single question.

There had been a car accident. What else did I need to know?

I'd been dreading a call like that my whole life.

Yes, I was Nicola Jones.

Yes, my sister was Dr. Vivian Jones Rowan. Yes, I would come right away. Of course.

I was in Sarasota then, renting a room from some artist friends. A nomadic twenty-six-year-old, I was a successful painter, in my way. I had been painting decorative murals for a couple of years and was in the middle of a big commission with an up-and-coming architect. I had part-time jobs lined up to make the rest of the ends meet for the winter. I'd started a class at New School in Sarasota and a gallery owner had offered me a solo show of watercolors that coming March. I was as settled as I'd ever been.

Scrambling to the airport, trying not to imagine that it was too late already, I never spared a thought for Viv's husband, George. *Dear George*, she always called him. It should have been Dear George on the phone.

George wouldn't have let a stranger call. He should have been the one to tell me that I needed to come to Tennessee. If he were okay, it would have been him on the phone, not the state police.

Each time my thoughts traveled this path, I stopped and tried to think of something else.

Long before anyone else was starting the day, I was pacing through the airport. I stood with my charge-card in hand as the dim nighttime lights of the airport gave way to flat white Florida daylight. I waited at the end of the vinyl-rope maze with my duffel—packed in less than five minutes in the dark of my room—bumping against the point of my hip as I shifted my weight from foot to foot.

The ticket agent sipped from a steaming mug as she emerged from behind the baggage conveyer. After a moment, she waved me to the tall counter.

The Tennessee state trooper's accent stuck with me as I tried to explain, *there's been an automobile wreck. My sister has bin in a bad wreck. In Tinnassee.* I had to clamp my teeth together to keep from repeating it over and over again.

Nashville?

I nodded.

A flight left in a couple of hours. She couldn't give me a discount, but the airline would reimburse some percentage of the ticket price within two weeks if I presented written proof of my hardship, she explained.

A doctor's note, say. And here was a reimbursement form to fill out if I wanted.

Of course there was a form. There was always a form. That was how the Tennessee state police found me. Viv had created an emergency contact form of her own, ages ago, with my name and address and phone number. She'd kept copies in the glovebox of her car and her husband's car and in both of their wallets, just in case.

As I slouched on a bench in the echoing waiting area, this idea made my toes scrunch up inside my shoes. I stood up to walk. My address had changed every six months or so, but I never doubted that my sister had updated every one of those emergency contact forms each time.

Viv was always ready for things. After our parents left us, she was the one who came up with the plan of how the two of us would get by on our own until she turned eighteen. She knew all about forms.

It was Viv who filled out the permission slips, signed the report cards, completed the inoculation records and college applications and credit histories, until our past was a series of overlapped forms, with the *no parents* card buried deep.

Still, all the preparation Viv could dream up, all those escape routes and contingency plans, the rendezvous points and the code-words, all the excuses and cover-stories she had created, all the forms she had filled out and the thousand what-ifs she had anticipated—none of it seemed to help as I stood outside the door of my sister's room in the hospital.

My sister the doctor was now a patient in a glass-walled room in the intensive care unit of her own hospital. The same hospital she used to stride through wearing surgical scrubs and flower-printed plastic clogs, calling out orders, remembering everyone's name, a flotilla of residents and nurses bobbing in her wake.

My sister's surgical partner was telling me that the good news was that there was plenty of brain activity.

"Which means she's probably alive in there," he said, with a push of hope in his voice. It was an obvious struggle for him to think of Viv as a patient rather than a colleague.

He'd introduced himself with an improbable series of syllables: Dr. Petrikis-Melonakos. He let a beat pass before telling me that everyone called him Dr. Pete. He and Viv had been working together since residency. Though Viv had spoken of him for years, I'd never met him before.

"Why don't I finish some things and in about fifteen minutes—" The doctor frowned at the spot on his arm where a watch might normally appear. He rubbed the bony knob of his wrist. "Maybe half an hour? I'll stop by and we'll get a cup of coffee. Okay?"

He closed the door of Viv's room behind him as he left. I pulled the chair closer to Viv's bed and sat down.

The air smelled of iodine and paper. My chair squeaked. The artificial light and machine noises were almost peaceful. Something—a respirator?—kept a steady pace, slower than my own breathing. Another machine went *brush-brush, hum, brush-brush.*

Gritting my teeth against panic, I looked at Viv, perfectly still under the covers. Or rather, imperfectly still—she had never been so motionless before.

Viv was always a restless sleeper, a kicker, a talker, a prodigious snorer. Awake, she was constantly in motion—waving her long hands, cocking her head to one side, swinging a leg, raising an eyebrow, crossing her eyes.

It was hard to look at her wrecked face. A terrible chiaroscuro, dark and light. On the less damaged side,

7

she looked young—and maybe even chubby, for her, even allowing for the swelling of injury. Her cheeks were rounded, her stubborn chin the only sharp spot along her jaw. The hair that hadn't been shaved was ponytailed to the side. Viv always had twice as much hair as anyone else, and even now, compressed by a thin yellow rubber band, the dark auburn tangles made a respectable mass. I wanted to smooth the ponytail, bundle it around my palm the way she always did before tucking it into the back of her collar at the nape of her neck. She often pushed her hair out of her face as if she were impatient with it, but she knew it was great hair.

The bad side of her face frightened me. Her bare white scalp looked as defenseless as an egg in a nest. The delicate cheekbone was puffed and shiny with injury. Stiff black stitches pulled swollen skin together in a curving line of dried blood that started under her bruised cheek, snaked up her bald temple and vanished under an ominous gauze patch. The left side of her mouth was huge, her lips smashed and dark as a plum, with blood pooling below the skin.

From the shoulders down, Viv formed a sizable line of lumps under the thin covers. Three blue foam pillows on top of the white cotton blanket wedged up against her, holding her on her side, so that both feet pointed to the left.

The right middle finger—the one she so loved to flash—was blue and swollen, taped onto an aluminum cast. An intravenous drip fed into the back of her other hand.

Nurse after nurse bustled in to attend to Viv while I waited. One tidy dark-haired woman with the clear red cheeks of a Mary Cassatt painting introduced herself, but I forgot her name immediately. She explained what she was doing as she emptied the catheter bag and hefted the bags dripping into Viv's arm. "And as for you,

Dr. Rowan," the nurse said, wrapping a blood-pressure sleeve around Viv's free arm and looking at Viv's face, "fluids look good. I'm going to check your pressure now."

With a theatrical roll of her eyes, the Mary Cassatt nurse told me, "She can probably hear everything we say, so don't let's talk about the new hairdo." She smiled at me while she pumped the sleeve. Her lips moved as she watched the gauge. Finished, she unwrapped the sleeve and put Viv's arm gently down on top of the covers. She picked up the clipboard that hung from the foot of the bed and jotted some notes. "Alright, Dr. Rowan, that's it for now. See you later."

As she closed the door behind her, the nurse smiled and wiggled her fingers in a small wave at me.

Nurses came and went.

Dr. Pete eventually returned. He patted Viv's leaning feet when he stood next to the bed and invited me to walk with him.

We made our way along the fluorescent-lit green hallways in silence. He walked quickly without seeming to hurry. Like most people, Dr. Pete stood a little shorter than me. He had a thin, clever face and rimless eyeglasses. He held doors open for me and nodded to people we passed.

In the nearly empty hospital cafeteria, he helped us both to Styrofoam cups of coffee and carried them to a table near the window. He clasped his long fingers around his cup as he explained what they knew in his careful, lightly accented English.

"Your sister and her husband were in the car late last night. Your brother-in-law was behind the wheel. Sometime after midnight, the car left the road. The highway police will know those details. The car struck a tree."

He didn't pause or look away as he continued.

"Your sister's husband died at the scene, instantly, from what we call blunt force head trauma. It must have been very quick."

Dr. Pete waited for me to acknowledge him before continuing. My neck felt like wood. My face felt like wood. I wiped my palms against my jeans. I nodded.

"Your sister, also, was struck here and here, during the crash."

As he described the damage, he indicated the side of his own head, his ear, the point of his jaw, the molars on the left side of his mouth. After each injury, he paused and asked, "Are you with me?"

I was.

"It was some time before another car drove past that same spot. They called for help at around three in the morning. The ambulance with your sister arrived here shortly after that." He pushed his fingers against his left temple. The tips of his fingers whitened with the pressure. "Because the skull injuries were compressive, she went right into surgery." He rubbed his head for a moment.

Behind the glass cases of the cafeteria, an aqua-capped woman dropped her mop with a tremendous clatter. A burst of laughter and applause came from behind the half-wall to the kitchen. I kept my attention on Dr. Pete's slow and careful words.

"In surgery we were able to remove the pieces of bone that had dented in. Do you follow?"

I did.

"With an injury like this, we worry about inflammation—swelling of the brain and spinal tissues—and so your sister has had a series of CT scans to monitor that."

I didn't ask what a CT scan was.

"The surgery—Nicola?" Dr. Pete was staring at me through his bright-edged glasses. "Do you need to cry?"

My eyes were burning.

He scooted his chair around the corner of the table and put a palm on my arm. His hand was warm even through the sweater. I knew it would be a comfort to put my head down on his bony shoulder. I couldn't move.

"If I start—" Taking a deep breath against the tightness gripping my chest, I finished the thought. "I don't think I'll stop."

Dr. Pete shrugged but didn't slide his chair away.

After a moment or two, I said, "What else?"

Dr. Pete spoke clearly, explaining terms like *concussion, cerebrospinal fluid, inter-cranial pressure, blood flow.*

I let him finish, and then I asked the one question that mattered to me.

"Will she be okay?"

He took a long pause before answering. He was gazing out the window. I smelled a ghostly puff of coffee as he exhaled.

"I wish I could tell you. But with serious head injuries like this, nothing's for sure." He seemed to stop himself with an effort. Looking into my face, he smiled and added, "We've had patients recover from worse."

He had some cheerful things to say about the success rate of the surgery, and about how the first few days were the most critical with brain damage.

"She has brain damage?" I asked.

Dr. Pete froze for a moment. Then he spoke with exaggerated slowness. "Yes. That's why we operated."

I understood then. Of course her brain was damaged. It wasn't her scalp or some innocuous flesh *near* the head wound that had swelled and was draining. It was her brain. Her skull had cracked like an egg. The dangerous swelling was *in* her brain.

After a long moment, Dr. Pete squeezed my arm. "You are her only family, yes?"

I nodded.

"What about your sister's husband's family?"

Viv and Dear George had eloped. They had taken themselves down to the courthouse in Manhattan the week after Viv graduated from medical school. I was in Italy that spring. None of their friends knew about the wedding until afterwards. They had announced the news at George's softball game—his company team played every Tuesday in Central Park—and the team had toasted them with cheap champagne from a Korean place around the corner. Viv had called me in Rome to tell me the news.

They had driven up to New England for their honeymoon, visiting his parents—Mother and Dad Rowan—and an aunt, or maybe a godmother he called *aunt.* There were no other kids in George's family. They made a lot of stops with friends from his college and prep-school days. They spent a week in a cottage in Ogunquit Beach.

Then they had relocated to Atlanta, where Viv began her surgical residency and George went to work for the brokerage house. George's mother had died a few years ago and Dad Rowan had moved someplace warm—Arizona. Viv and George, who were always going on adventures together, had squeezed a hike of the Grand Canyon into a recent visit with Dad Rowan.

Dr. Pete waited while I remembered these bits of history. I told him what I knew.

"Yes," Dr. Pete said. "I don't know if George's father has been notified yet."

We both reached for our cups.

"The good news," he said, his brown eyes brightening behind the lenses of his glasses, "is that

Viv's—your sister's—pregnancy has not been affected, and overall, she seems to be in good physical condition."

"Her pregnancy?" My voice came out very loud.

Dr. Pete looked, if possible, more alert behind his shiny little glasses. His voice was very even.

"Your sister is twenty-five weeks pregnant."

In months, that would be five—six?—months pregnant. The kick of shock sent air out of my lungs in a rush.

Not chubby. Pregnant.

"This is a surprise to you?" Dr. Pete said. "But you have been in touch with your sister, right? She talks often about what her sister the artist is doing."

Viv and I talked on the phone once a week. Usually Sunday afternoons because of the cheaper long-distance rates. As adults, we had never lived in the same state, but I usually stopped to visit her as my travels took me. I'd spent a long weekend with her the previous spring on my way back north from Florida.

Viv had moved to Nashville after her surgical residency in Atlanta, but I'd never wanted to settle into a single hometown. I relocated as often as the whim struck me.

It was a point of pride for me, back then, to be able to load all my worldly possessions into my little pick-up truck and drive away.

Still, my sister and I never skipped more than a week or two between calls. We talked politics, stupid television shows, clothes, music, my painting gigs, her surgical practice in Nashville. We talked nearly every Sunday. But babies were one of the things we never discussed.

"No," I said, trying to smother the feeling of vertigo. "She didn't tell me."

Chapter 3

THE INTERCOM blared, asking for Dr. Pete to take himself to radiology. "I must go," he said as he stood. "I think I should make a couple of calls for you. You'll be needing some help."

I nodded.

He looked wryly into his full cup of coffee and then back at me. "She and the baby are getting the best care possible."

I hadn't thought to worry about that.

He fidgeted a moment and added, with a wince, "She's a fighter."

As if I didn't know. It had been the two of us against the world for a long time, and Viv was the reason we had made it.

He shook my hand with both of his before hurrying away.

I sat as the clashing of pans and the rattle of carts rolling in the kitchen grew louder. Aqua-capped workers moved in the recesses of the cafeteria. They shouted to one another as they worked.

THE DAY our parents left us, I was browning beef and onions for chili con carne for supper, working my way through the oil-splattered pages of the *Farm Journal's Cookbook* because my sister refused to let Magda teach her how to cook. ("I'll be damned if I'll slave my life away in the kitchen," was Viv's standard response, which invariably made our soft-spoken mother wince).

I was in the seventh grade, and I was happy cooking. The cookbook had vivid off-tone color plate pictures of heaping harvest feasts. I was trying a recipe for a *hearty crowd-pleasing chili* made with white beans. Viv was upstairs doing schoolwork.

Our parents had been gone for just a day or two. I suppose the signs were everywhere, had I stopped to pay attention.

They'd left an envelope for Viv, instead of just slipping a few bills under the sugar-bowl. We'd lived in this house on Star School Road for nearly a year — probably a record for us—but firewood for the next year was already piled high.

The house itself must have felt different, with noise echoing around in the open space from what they had taken away. Jahn never took his tools out of the truck, but he'd taken the second muddy pair of work-boots and his winter coat from the back porch when they'd left this time. He'd removed his shaving things from the bathroom, leaving behind only a soapy ring on the sink.

Magda often brought her sewing machine with her when she traveled with Jahn, but she never packed the little china salt-and-pepper shakers and the heavy seasoned cast-iron skillet unless we were moving. I couldn't have failed to notice, and perhaps that's why their departure was less a surprise after all than it might have been.

When Viv and I ventured into their bedroom later, we found the room stripped. Magda's wind-up alarm clock and the little milk-glass pitcher she used to hold bouquets of flowers were gone. The thin wedding-band quilt and the heavy quilt with the green stars had been packed and taken away. The bureau drawers yawned bare down to the flowered paper liners. Even the scent of rosewater and English Leather shaving cream had faded into the motionless, empty air.

Still, when the black wall phone rang in the kitchen, I picked it up without a moment of suspicion. I listened to our mother's soft lisp on the other end of the line. *Were we okay?* Yes. *Was my sister there?* She was—did she want to talk to Viv? *No.*

It was unusual for my mother to telephone and check on us. She and Jahn had been leaving us alone for years. They didn't jot down a contact number, as I later learned parents always do. They never told us what they were doing or when to expect them back. As a habit, they left some money before driving off. They'd be back when they came back. It was understood that Viv was in charge. Viv knew what to do in case of various emergencies.

For the life of me, I'd like to remember that Magda said more to me that last time she called. I know she didn't explain or make anything that sounded like an excuse. The one thing I really remember was this: "Honey, we have to go now."

She didn't mean us, *we* have to go, she meant *them— they* had to go.

"Be good," she said. Automatically I answered that we would. There was a crackling silence, and then she whispered, "We love you."

The line went flat before I could get the word "Wait," out of my mouth. I stood with the heavy receiver in my hand and then I thought: this was it. It was the end of everything.

I turned off the stove-burner, carefully, and removed the apron and hung it on the nail beside the stove. Then I sprinted up the stairs, shouting, "Viv! Viv! Viv!"

She looked up from her book and I saw the color fall from her face, until she looked as shocked and scared as I felt.

"They are gone," I told her. And then in case she thought I wasn't serious, I added, "No joke."

We were frozen there, looking at one another for a very long time. Then Viv snorted loudly, slapped her textbook shut, and said, "Well, we're going to need to get a car."

I started to laugh—from relief or surprise, I don't know which—but a sob came out instead. I put my hands over my eyes and took a deep, shaky breath.

"That's not going to help," Viv told me, getting up from the bed and thumping her book down on the side table. "Crying is useless. Come on, let's figure out how much money we have."

She started rummaging around in her dresser, giving me a minute to pull myself together.

"Nicky?"

I sniffed and wiped my eyes.

"First, you know this means we can read during dinner, right?" Viv's eyes were shining, maybe from excitement. "And we can eat what we want."

"No more lima beans?" I asked, half serious.

"Only if there is nothing else to eat. But never liver. Definitely never liver."

"Viv, what about curfew?"

"What about what?"

"Curfew, you know, eight o'clock every night, rain or shine, no excuses, no exceptions. Remember?" Jahn was a stickler for us being home by curfew.

She frowned at me, one eyebrow pulling down harder than the other, the way it did when she was teasing. "Cure flu? Curlew? Is that French or something? Whatever it is, it sounds dreadful."

We smiled at each other. Then Viv turned back to her dresser.

"I've got my waitressing money and the emergency fund. Go get your piggy bank and then we'll scrounge around and see how much they left."

After I got to my room, Viv called out, her voice sounding distracted, as if she were doing math in her head already, "Nicky? You can start baby-sitting now."

Viv was a junior in high school then. She waited tables after school at The Pit Stop, a greasy restaurant full of chrome and thick ceramic dishes and cigarette smoke. Our father opposed the idea of Viv working.

"You will neglect your studies to buy clothes?" he'd shouted. "You will have strangers look at you and give you money for smiling?"

"No sir, I'll be saving up for college." Viv had ended the argument, coolly, as if he were a boy being fresh at school.

There was no arguing college with Viv. Our parents never spoke more than a few weeks into the future. Later, after I spent time with other families, I realized the advantages of this perspective. There was very little *we'll see* or *maybe next year* in our family. The answer was almost always *yes* or *no*.

But my sister looked farther ahead and talked about the future without fear. She'd made up her mind. She was going to be a doctor. That meant college after she finished high school, and medical school after that. So she had to take the SATs. She was going to get scholarships and student loans.

When Viv started to bring home college prospectuses, our father was silent. Our slender little mother, pale and quiet as a tree in winter, looked at Viv with pleading in her eyes.

But Viv just stuck out her pointed chin and kept going to The Pit Stop after school, getting a ride home before eight o'clock curfew with the quiet neighbor-lady down the road, saving her money, making her plans.

My sister and I ate chili and cornbread that first night when it was just the two of us. We sat at the kitchen table, with the back door open to the spring air and a little pile of coins and paper money and the file of house accounts stacked in front of us. We'd found the half-dozen or so niches where our mother had squirreled away cash. A hundred dollars in an envelope, ninety-two dollars in tinfoil under the neat packages of frozen beef in the freezer, two hundred and thirty-three dollars tucked into the photo box.

They'd left deposits with the gas company and the electric company. They had leased the house for two more years, all paid up. The woodpile was stocked. We had just under fifteen hundred dollars in cash. On the other hand, we had no car, no bank account, no health insurance. I was thirteen. Viv was not quite seventeen. We lived six miles from the nearest store and there was no one we knew to go to for help.

"Brush your teeth," Viv told me that night. "Brush them twice as long, because I don't know when we'll get to the dentist."

Chapter 4

ARTIE SLATE was waiting for me when I got back to Viv's room. He called my name from an open door, and I didn't recognize him at first. His dark skin looked yellow. His startling grey eyes were hooded and bloodshot. He held out his long arms and engulfed me in a corduroy-jacketed hug.

I felt the muscles of his back straining against tears, tensioning like a bowstring. He straightened after a moment and sniffed savagely. His face was wet. I felt my own eyes fill. I stretched my jaw, steadied my breathing, and told Artie that I was sorry.

He said, "Oh Jesus, Nicky. George. Oh God."

I didn't know Artie very well. At any other time, I would have said I didn't like him. We didn't connect. He seemed shallow, too smooth, a player. He was very handsome—pretty even, with those bright grey eyes— but he seemed too used to the attention.

My opinion, but once, while talking about something—funding for music education, maybe?—he'd dismissed the topic by saying, "People like that need to get a real job." I'd laughed, thinking he was being ironic, but he hadn't been joking. A successful lawyer, he said it was his business to keep an eye on dollars and sense. He tolerated me and my Bohemian ways, I was pretty sure, only because I was related to Viv. Perhaps I was too sensitive; some people just didn't care about the arts.

But he was George's best friend, a running buddy from college who went to law school when George went to business school. Viv and George spent a lot of time with Artie and his wife Leora, so I had seen them dozens of times over the years.

"Sorry," he said, honking into a handful of tissues. "I just can't believe it. I mean—I'm a mess."

He folded the tissues and then pressed them to the outside corner of each eye. A delicate gesture for such a big man.

"We were going to play ball and go out for breakfast Sunday morning. The state police knocked on the door and I thought it was him." Artie's face crumpled for a second. He recovered and said, "Then I thought he was messing with me. Like he got some good old boys to dress up like troopers. Or maybe he convinced some troopers to go along with him. You know."

I did know.

It wouldn't have been the first time George had talked strangers into playing along in an elaborate prank on a friend.

"They came to the house because Viv indicated that—as their lawyer—I should be contacted." Artie's voice took on a deeper, courtroom tone. "Apparently, Vivian carried some paperwork in her wallet. "

"Yeah, me too," I said. "They called me."

His jaw muscles pulled tight before he spoke again. "They told me they reached you. They said you were coming. They, ah—" His voice cracked. "They need to get an identification of the body. Of George. They prefer to have family."

"Me?"

"George's dad is out of the country."

In all my life, I had never considered the idea of identifying a body. My leg made contact with Viv's bed. I'd backed away from Artie without even realizing it.

Artie brushed at a pinprick hole in his faded black sweatpants, his fingertips sweeping over the nub of fleece that mushroomed through the fabric. He didn't look up as he shrugged. "I know, it sucks."

We both looked at the shiny floor under our feet.

I thought about Viv's bruised, half-bald head, her tender neck. My sister, pregnant and broken. I took a breath and let it go. Viv wouldn't have hesitated. Whatever I felt, whatever fear it was that made me want to say no to this—it didn't matter.

I felt myself nodding. "Okay," I said.

Artie squared his shoulders and said, "So the coroner? Tomorrow—?"

I kept nodding.

"Nicky, there's more."

I stopped nodding. My stomach lurched, as if something had unexpectedly shifted. It was possible to feel worse yet, even after everything else.

Artie looked at me from under his swollen brows. "You know I am Viv's and George's lawyer? Right? Well, we can discuss the details, but Viv named you, specifically, as her medical guardian. And she's given you power of attorney."

I probably looked as puzzled as I felt.

Artie continued. "That means that until she's able to care for herself, you're the person she designated to look after her and the house and everything."

Muscles I hadn't even noticed unknotted in my shoulders. Just the house. Just the house and the dogs— not some other awful fountain of grief.

Reminded of George's dogs, I asked Artie if anyone had stopped by to check on them.

After a moment of confusion, Artie pulled a face and shook his head. "I never thought about them till this minute."

"It's okay," I said. "I'll stay there tonight."

Artie looked relieved. "You're—ah—welcome to stay with Leora and myself, if, well—"

I told him it was okay, that I'd be fine at Viv and George's house.

"You'll have dinner with us? Leora's cooking."

"I tell you what," I said, growing impatient. "If you telephone Leora, I'll go talk to the nurses and tell them where we can be reached."

He agreed, asking if we might meet back here in the waiting room in fifteen minutes.

I suggested he come find me in Viv's room when he was finished talking with his wife.

"Fine," he said. "I'll just go and make that call." He stood up and plucked at his sweatpants as if adjusting a crease in a pair of dress trousers before striding off.

IT WAS closer to thirty minutes before Artie returned. The dark-haired nurse with the Mary Cassatt complexion had been back with another nurse. Together they'd gently re-positioned Viv's body.

I held Viv's hand, the one with the splinted middle finger. I looked at the shape of Viv under the covers, at the bump where a baby would be. A baby? She and George had always seemed complete, just the two of them. They went camping and climbed caves and did winery tours and scheduled their next adventure.

I looked away, studied Viv's hand instead. Her fingers were smooth, dry, and the skin was warm. Her fingertips and palms were flushed rosy red around the purple bruising.

From the doorway, Artie cleared his throat and began talking in his peculiar way, with an introductory nasal honk. "Ah—ah, Leora will be here in twenty minutes or so to pick us up. She wants you to have dinner with us."

I was tired and felt a spark of irritation. I didn't want to speak as loudly as Artie had, to be heard over the machine noises in that small room. I didn't want to disturb my sister.

"She's cooking chicken," he added, shuffling his big sneakers and putting his hands into his jacket pockets and then taking them out again.

He looked at me for a moment and I saw him very nearly look at Viv. His gaze skittered away. He peered intently at the metal doorframe.

"Nicole?"

"Nicola."

He looked up and blinked several times at me.

"My name is actually Nicola, not Nicole," I repeated.

"Right. The—"

The Mary Cassatt nurse came to the door. Artie jumped aside to allow her through.

"I should give you a moment." He lurched between the hallway and the room.

"Don't leave on my account," the nurse told him, though he had already turned away.

He stuck his head back in the doorway. "I'm—ah. I'll be in the waiting room when you're ready." And he was gone.

This is Viv, I wanted to say, staring after him. You two argue about the red wine at dinner. She claims to hate the subject, but she always ends up talking politics anyway, remember? Spinach gets caught in her eyeteeth and Dear George never thinks to tell her.

I might have muttered something as I looked at the empty doorway, because the nurse looked at me. I rolled my eyes toward where Artie had been.

"Everyone has a thing," the nurse commented, leaning over Viv. She nodded at the empty doorway.

"Beg pardon?"

"Seems like everyone gets the heebie-jeebies from something. Maybe it's hospitals for your friend there."

"I guess," I said, not meaning it.

"Uh-huh." She drew the word into a sassy curve, like a kid practicing sarcasm.

I looked at her. The nametag on her badge read: Lisa. She was examining an almost-flat plastic envelope at the side of Viv's bed.

I wanted to snap at Lisa. "Heebie-jeebies?" Artie was a grown man. He could just brace up and deal.

But the nurse smoothed Viv's hair aside for the ear thermometer with such matter-of-fact tenderness that I felt ashamed. I wasn't irritated with *her*, after all.

After Lisa left, I sat down in the squeaky chair next to Viv and matched my breathing to the calm, constant machine noise. I tried to make my mind a blank. I listened to the intercom and the rattle of metal wheels from the hallway, voices down the hall, footsteps, beeping. A hospital is never quiet, really.

When she was doing her residency in Atlanta, I'd visited my sister at work a few times. She was on call for days at a stretch, so if I wanted to spend any time with her, I'd have to catch her at the hospital. We ate meals together at the cafeteria and I'd follow her around. She showed me the little rooms where the residents sometimes bunked for a nap: dark little closets with bare walls and a hospital bed and an alarm clock on a side-table and not much else.

"Glamorous," I'd commented.

"It's about getting away from the light and the noise," she said. But she was grinning as she spoke, clearly excited about even this aspect of her job. "Sometimes I'm here so long I forget what day it is!"

My sister was always going to be a doctor.

VIV was maybe seven the first time she performed surgery. Probably not her first operation, but it's the one I remember. I would have been almost four, holding a heavy chrome flashlight while we knelt at an upholstered footstool. Afternoon light filtered through the curtains of the living room.

I think we were alone. Our mother might have been asleep upstairs, but I don't remember. She spent a lot of time sleeping when Viv and I were little. I have no other memories set in that house.

Viv had draped a white pillowcase over the operating table. She directed me to use a cotton ball dabbed in witch hazel to sterilize the steak knife, a pair of round-tipped paper-scissors, and a needle that she had already threaded.

I don't know how it happened that it was my most beloved baby-doll, Baby Vinnia, on the table, but Viv insisted that the toy needed to have her appendix removed. To be fair, Viv never kept dolls herself, so perhaps it *had* to be my Vinnia on the surgical table.

The bumpy point of the steak knife made a dimple in the fabric belly of the doll as Viv pressed down.

"Hold that light steady, nurse." My sister frowned at me over the patient. "Crying is not going to help. If we don't operate right now, I won't be able to save her."

My sister set the knife down and gave me a considering look. "Sniff really hard and stretch your jaw like this."

I sniffed and did as she suggested, baring my lower teeth and flexing the muscles of my jaw, drawing the cords of my neck tight and then releasing them a couple of times.

"Better?"

I nodded.

"Good," she said, taking the knife up again, "Because we need to finish this operation. Baby Vinnia needs you to be brave. Okay?"

After surgery, when my sister tucked a tissue-paper bandage over the short, crooked row of stitches, she said, "You were great."

She handed the doll over and said, "Baby Vinnia is going to be just fine. As good as new."

Chapter 5

ARTIE stood at the edge of the overhanging roof at the front entrance to the hospital. The rain speared down like tiny arrows, gold against the light. We were waiting for Leora. He shivered, hunching his broad shoulders from the damp with his hands shoved deep into the pockets of his jacket.

Leora Slate left the door open on her red BMW as she hurried toward us. She wore a brown velour tracksuit, a flattering few shades darker than her skin. She had to stand on tiptoe to pull me into a matronly embrace and we stood like that for a long while, just barely rocking back and forth. A stack of wooden bangles clunked from her wrist to her forearm, one after another, tapping on my back. She carried with her the faint smell of Jergens lotion.

"I've been praying for Vivian and her baby all day, Nicky," she said into my ear. "The Lord's will is not for us to know."

Vivian and her baby, I thought. Vivian with a child? The idea seemed preposterous. I felt almost woozy with the strangeness of it.

Leora continued to half-hold me. We were standing just that extra bit too close for comfort. She gave me a final pat and announced that supper was waiting at home. She said something about biscuits and gravy, but I couldn't pay attention.

Artie held the door open so that I could clamber into the back of the BMW. Dark circles under his eyes cut into the smooth curve of his face. He looked terrible. He hadn't said a single word to his wife. Leora hadn't so much as touched his arm. I switched my duffel bag from one shoulder to the other.

"Put her bag in the trunk," Leora said to Artie.

"No," I said. "I—I think I have to stay." What had possessed me to leave my sister? I had no business going home with them—never mind how itchy and uncomfortable their silence made me feel.

What if Viv had already woken up? As soon as I thought it, I could barely keep from rushing back to my sister's room. It was like being at the train station when you realize you should already be running if you were going to catch your train.

"I'm just going to stay with Viv a while longer."

Leora turned back from her car with a puzzled frown. "But I've made supper."

"I appreciate the offer—really—it's just—" My heart jumped with the urgency to return to Viv. "I have to go."

"Sure, hon. We'll do this another time."

I was nearly dancing with impatience. "I'll see you tomorrow," I said to Artie.

"We'll be praying for her!" Leora called after me.

MY SISTER hadn't woken up. Nothing had changed in her room, aside from me being damp and out of breath. As the panic faded, I felt a slow roll of nausea.

I ducked into the bathroom and drank five tiny paper cups of water. I took out my barrette and gathered my hair back into a clump. I washed my face with a squirt of the anti-bacterial soap from the dispenser and frowned into my reflection until the feeling of sickness faded.

I thought about Leora's offer of prayer, her certainty.

AT ONE of the schools where I attended fifth grade, I was fascinated by the way a pale, shrimpy town girl spoke a blessing over her lunch tray. "Thank you, Lord, for that bounty which I am about to receive." She had spoken without self-consciousness in the noisy cafeteria. Every day without fail she would breathe this small thank-you over her food and then tuck in.

I often thought about it that year: Bounty. Lord. Receive. Was it like salt, sprinkled on everything to make it better? Did it change the flavor of food? Did it keep her safe as she ate?

"Some people believe in God," Viv had explained. "Some people believe that God made everything, and he looks after everyone."

"Do you believe in God?"

"Yep," she answered, as if it were as simple as putting on socks.

"How come?"

My sister gave me a long look down her nose. "Because it made sense to me. I made up my mind. Magda used to take us to church."

"Really? Honest Injun?"

"Don't say that. It sounds ignorant. "

"But you mean for real we used to go to church?"

"No, I'm lying." Viv oozed sarcasm. She continued after a moment. "You were too little for church. You went to Sunday baby-school and ate cookies or something."

"What about Dad?"

She laughed. "Yeah, right. Can you imagine Jahn listening to a sermon?"

Our father wasn't good about being told anything. An irritable man who looked and sounded a bit like Boris Badenov, he sometimes bragged that he never put up with anyone telling him how to do his job. This trait probably helped explain why we moved so often. He kept having to find new jobs.

"No, this was before they had that really big fight about church. You remember—the night we spent in the truck? At the place in Vergennes?"

I didn't, but I nodded anyway. My sister had taken me away from the house often enough when our parents started arguing. I remembered her leading me by the hand to the old tree fort in the maple tree one snowy afternoon, boosting me up the rungs, bundling us up in an old wool blanket, and then reading aloud until the sun went down.

She fixed up a little nest in the hay in the old barn in Rossie where we could escape the noise of shouting and Jahn knocking things over. In the summertime, when it was warm, the truck was always a good place to go.

"No one is ever going to boss me around like that. Ever. No matter what," Viv said.

"So what about the night in the truck?" I said.

"He threw a chair through the window that time. He was pretty drunk," Viv said. "He cut his hand. It was a scrape, really, didn't even need stitches, but what a fuss she made! Such a sheep. She promised him she would never talk about religion again."

Viv nodded at my expression.

"Yeah, and I don't think Magda ever said another word about church or God or anything like that ever again."

DESPITE my sister's explanation, I kept wondering about prayer that winter of my fifth grade in school. I kept thinking about what it meant to pray and why people did it. Did it make people feel safer, or was it like a magic spell that *did* keep them safer?

At about this same time, one of the dairy cows at the nearest of the local farms slipped on the concrete aisle of the milking parlor and broke a leg. The farmer had the cow slaughtered and each of the families who bought milk from the farmer—it was cheaper and fresher straight from the agitator tank and the dairy farmers welcomed even a little extra cash—got a portion of the elderly creature.

The beef was barely edible, even as hamburger. Loins, chops, brisket, all ground into the chewiest, least flavorful meat imaginable. Hamburger so tough there was no forming patties. It made muffiny meatloaves and spaghetti sauce orange as daylilies, and it floated like the drowned in mulligan stew.

Wanting to explore the possible power of blessing a meal with prayer, I tried it one night over another dreadful meal of ancient cow.

Before picking up a fork, I repeated the words silently. My father, of course, was quick to notice, his pouched and bloodshot eyes narrowing at me.

"What is this one doing, eh?" His accent added menace as it thickened the words.

"She's probably just gathering her strength," Viv broke in.

"Do you mean to criticize the beef again?" Even he had to find the humor in the situation, but his tolerance for what our mother called *backchat* was thin. He was quick to slap.

"No, sir, I wouldn't make fun of the hamburger." My sister kept her expression blank. "I mean, we're not *allowed* to have chewing gum at school."

The joke had seemed funny when Viv told it to me as we washed our hands in the little upstairs bathroom before supper. My father just waved his hand impatiently at her and hunched over his food.

Bounty. Receive. Lord. I tried saying it, but nothing changed.

I DIDN'T know the right words to say in prayer over my injured sister. Viv had taught me *Now I lay me down to sleep*, but it hadn't stuck with me. I'd never felt that certainty, and though I tried from time to time, I had never picked up the habit of praying.

Where to start? I didn't know if there *were* right words for anything like this. I didn't know if I believed in God. I didn't know if he listened when people prayed. I didn't know whether he cared about the words or the thoughts behind the words, or the intentions underneath the thoughts. But I prayed.

I prayed to God to make my sister be okay. I prayed that God would let her be okay. I asked God to let her wake soon and to let her wake up healthy. Please, oh please, over and over, please, please. Then, after some time, it was please, Viv, please, Viv, as if I could pray to Vivian to bring herself back.

Chapter 6

IT TOOK ages to get to Viv's house. The taxi driver and I sat in the car at the gatehouse, listening to the metallic clank of the meter racking up 20-cent increments of time while the tinny voice of the dispatcher called out coded messages to other drivers. The security guard at Viv's gated community picked slowly through an index file and found that Viv had listed me as an approved visitor. He held the card by a corner and came back outside to apologize for keeping us. Then he asked for my identification and took another century to copy information from my driver's license.

I could barely remember the turnings to Viv's house. Past the gatehouse and the clubhouse, nothing looked like a landmark. The development was too new, the large, bland houses set too far back from the road. At every corner, like cowboys roping a mustang, a handful of cross-stakes held a spindly young sapling straight.

The taxi had to turn around twice, and we backtracked until we found Viv's street.

The driver, still aglow with the camaraderie of our having not really been lost after all, got out and offered to walk through the house for me, but at the sound of the dogs he retreated to his cab. I waved until he drove off and then groped around for the spare key that Viv kept hidden under a loose stone in the walkway.

Dear George, a Tolkien fan, had trained the mastiffs—Balin, Dwalin, and Tomkin—to stand down with the Elvish word for "friend." The mastiffs were huge dogs, colored brindle and fawn like wild beasts. They had heads as big as basketballs and legs like young tree-trunks. The dogs were not great barkers, but their low rumbling growls were thoroughly convincing.

I unlocked the heavy door, opened it a crack, and spoke the word ("*mellon*") into the dark room. The growling stopped. I called each of the dogs by name as I reached in to flip the light-switch.

They stood in a half-circle a few feet away from the doormat, their feet planted wide, and their heads raised high. Balin, the smallest and oldest of them, blinked painfully against the glare of the recessed lighting. White hairs grew along the tops of her eyes, like reverse eyebrows. It occurred to me that the dogs had been locked indoors since sometime the day before.

"Do you want to go outside?" I asked them. My voice sounded stupidly loud, like an adult asking a third grader how old he was this year. The dogs responded with guarded enthusiasm. I walked ahead of them to the door that led to the back yard, and they hurried outside, grumbling. Even as they squatted and lifted legs, they kept looking back at the house over their shoulders. Suspicious creatures.

I refilled their water dishes first. Then, knowing it would only get worse, I tracked down and cleaned up their gigantic craps from the garage floor. Dear George kept a flat shovel in the mud room for just such a purpose. He had explained the first time I visited, "They are big dogs, and you know, you can't ask them to do the impossible." Surveying their mess then, he'd giggled and added, "Or not doo-doo the impossible."

VIV was never fond of dogs. She had a faint, crooked scar on her left arm, the result of an attack by a Cocker spaniel that came after us when we were little. I didn't remember the event myself.

"That dog came running out of its house and I didn't even feel this happen," Viv would say, rubbing the scar. "For a minute I thought he was going to get you, but I chased him right back up his driveway. I got sixteen stitches and a tetanus shot."

Viv retold this story to me so many times when we were growing up, I'd created a montage of it in my mind's eye. There was the dog, a brown blur with crazed whites showing around its eyes, and my sister standing guard in front of me with her leg pulled back to kick, and then the sixteen stitches on her arm.

Dear George's mastiffs, the size of goats or young calves, didn't seem to count as dogs to Viv. She'd called them "George's livestock." They didn't go to her for petting. When she and George sat together on the couch, her sock feet too would rest on the dogs' warm sides, but if she strode through a room, they'd watch her calmly and stay out of her way.

AS KIDS, we'd never kept pets of any kind. When we lived in the country, Viv had made a habit of rescuing baby birds and injured rabbits. She discouraged me from handling the animals, though she let me help clean their shoebox cages. She knew I longed for a pet, so she reminded me that it would be unfair to tame a wild animal only to have to abandon it later. Her missions were strictly scientific: she would rescue the injured animals, nurse them, and if they survived, she'd return them to the wild.

The closest I came to a pet was when Magda and Jahn had been away. One of the barn-cats slipped into the house, and when the plush grey creature jumped purring onto my bed, I was tempted to give in to the powers of fate and animal wisdom. This cat, I thought, wanted to be *my* cat. It had chosen me.

The cat made a den in the bottom of my closet and proceeded to have a litter of kittens. I got Viv and we watched in the half-light as the cat neatly delivered and cleaned her kits. One of the squirming little things rolled out of the safety of the towels and Viv gently placed it back at its mother's side.

The grey cat seemed relaxed and competent as the kittens settled in to nurse. Having expected something more dramatic, I asked Viv why the mother cat had bothered to come into the house to give birth.

My sister laughed at me. "Duh. If you were a mother cat, where's the safest, coziest place to have your babies? Not just inside—but in whose closet? This cat is no fool."

We hid them until the kittens' eyes began to open, though I think Magda—with her country wisdom and observant eye—must have known the mama-cat was in and out of the house. Not that she was likely to say anything.

Eventually, Viv and I transplanted the whole batch of kittens back to the barn. Viv let me make up a cardboard box lined with towels, and we carried the kittens by hand to the hayloft. They were plump but light, with flat little faces full of milky blue eyes and pink tongues. Their needle-sharp claws caught hold of everything once they were picked up and they mewed as if their world was ending until they were back with the rest of the kits.

"It's cruel to keep an animal for a pet if you can't take care of it," Viv explained. "And we don't have the money for vet bills or cat food."

She looked at my face for a moment and added, "Plus, you know—them."

I knew. Or rather, if neither of us knew for sure how Jahn and Magda would react to our bringing home a pet, we didn't dare to test them.

Jahn had once deliberately run his truck over the neighbor's dog. It was a car-chaser and an incessant barker, a big, smelly, rusty-black dog that spent most days trotting along after the bachelor farmer who lived on the other side of the common driveway. Jahn complained to us about the dog's noise and about the inevitable yellow snow and piles of dog crap on our side of the driveway.

When their trucks passed, Jahn smiled and tipped his hat to the bachelor farmer and muttered about filthy animals, vermin, and the moral responsibilities of ownership, but he never spoke to the dog's owner.

It was not unusual for Jahn to stew on a slight like this. Viv said he didn't want to attract the attention of the authorities—she had a lot of theories about our parents—but I sometimes thought our father simply enjoyed keeping his anger wrapped around him like a steel-wool shirt. He held onto grudges and acted as if everyone did the same.

When driving, Jahn wanted his passengers to be quiet. He said he couldn't tolerate the distraction. Even though he didn't like listening to anyone, he himself often complained bitterly about things as he drove, using both hands to gesture if he worked himself up to a real lather. But this weekend morning as he piloted the truck down the road, he was silent. The dog barked as it ran alongside.

The motor noise never changed, but Jahn let the truck drift left over the centerline and then swerve right, willful and smooth as a dive into deep water. Even Magda gasped at the bump, the yelp, and the second thud as the back wheel of the truck bucked over the black dog's body.

Jahn gazed in the rearview mirror and said, "That dog will never shit in your flowers again, Magda."

After the briefest of pauses, Magda patted his leg.

My sister's grip on my shoulder had tightened. She always grabbed me if the vehicle veered. Jahn was not exactly drunk when he drove us all to the library and the laundromat, but by lunchtime his driving grew more careless. The truck would weave from one side of the road to the other. With a few beers in his belly, he tended to over-correct an error in steering so that we swayed like people on a carnival ride.

Temper lent an even more spirited style to his driving as he muttered and swore, steering with a knee as he gimbaled his beer-can through a series of swoops across those narrow country roads.

In the shocked moments after Jahn hit the dog, Viv's grip on my shoulder softened into a hug. She bent her head over mine and squeezed me with both arms, the layers of winter clothes squeaking between us. I closed my eyes tight and took quick, shallow breaths to keep myself from crying.

Perhaps he had planned how he might kill the dog, or maybe he was taken with the impulse in the moment, but we understood then that Jahn could do this kind of thing. And that Magda wouldn't say a word to stop him.

DEAR George's dogs were whining at the door before I finished cleaning up, so I let them back in. They watched me from the mudroom entryway and seemed fractionally less suspicious of a home invader who tidied up after them. In the kitchen, Balin ambled over to her stainless-steel food dish and lowered herself to the dark tiled floor with a clumsy thump. The dish was empty. She glanced into the shiny depths of the bowl between her outstretched legs and then looked me straight in the eye. The sensation of a smile stretching the tired skin of my face surprised me. The dog food— marked "KIBBLE" in George's very tidy handwriting— waited in an aluminum garbage bin inside the pantry. Tomkin and Dwalin followed me into the pantry and backed out in front of me as I carried scoops of food to the three dishes. They stood by their full bowls looking at me for an expectant moment before I remembered that they were waiting for permission. "Have at!" I told them, and they immediately began to gobble.

The sound of their eating reminded me of my own stomach. I didn't feel so much hungry as simply hollow. The last thing I had eaten was dinner the day before in Florida after beach-volleyball practice. It seemed like a month or more ago.

I found the refrigerator—a professional-looking Subzero camouflaged with a dark wood front that matched the cabinets—and pondered my options. It was well stocked with eggs, beer, a carton of heavy cream, take-out boxes, milk, a vegetable bin stuffed with leafy greens and apples. The meat drawer held deli packages and hunks of cheese.

I cracked open a Rolling Rock and took a long pull. The dogs were still crunching and smacking over their stainless food bowls. Tomkin stopped eating to look up at me. A surplus roll or two of skin had slid to his brow, giving him an extra-anxious look. A thick line of brown-flecked slobber slid back into the dish. "Good dog!" I told him. His tail waved uncertainly a few times, and he bent back to his meal.

"Mastiffs drool," Dear George had explained to me. "It's just part of the package. They are sensitive. Their feelings get hurt. You have to consider their dignity."

I put down the beer and opened drawers until I found a stack of terry-cloth hand towels. It was good to have a chore, to keep me from thinking how still Viv's house seemed. I pulled out three towels and went back to my beer. The dogs knew the drill. After finishing, they stood still as I wiped their wet black faces, their slobber-striped chests. A scattering of white hairs on Balin's dark muzzle gave her a sparse beard to go with the white eyebrows. I tossed the towels into the laundry room.

We all returned to the foyer where I had left my bag.

"Well, dogs," I said. "Here we are then." They looked back at me without enthusiasm. "Are you ready to call it a day?"

I trudged upstairs to the guest room I'd used in the spring. Tomkin and Dwalin, the younger dogs, followed me. Balin stood silently at the bottom of the stair runner and looked up after us. She swayed slightly on her big bony legs. Her brown eyes shone blue in the light, as if she were growing cataracts. Dear George probably carried all one hundred and thirty lumpy pounds of her up the stairs every night. And back down in the morning. I couldn't carry her, but it seemed cruel to leave her standing unsteadily at the foot of the stairs.

There was another bedroom on the ground floor. I turned around and started back down. From the hallway above, Dwalin and Tomkin looked put-upon for a moment. Then they came down past me in a rush of huge paws thumping and a whipping about of iron-hard tails.

The downstairs bedroom was tucked around the side of the kitchen right next to the laundry room. I suppose it might have been designed for a maid. Or, the thought came to me like a jab in the belly: this could be a room for the nanny.

My thoughts coiled around the fact of Viv keeping her pregnancy secret from me. Why? She *had* taken a vial of blood from me the previous spring. Was that related? She'd brushed aside my questions then and it hadn't seemed worthwhile to press her for answers.

There were so many questions. Not a single one I could answer. It made me restless and full of feelings I couldn't define.

As I was standing still with my uncomfortable thoughts, Balin must have decided this was the time to get her ears rubbed, because she nudged her big square head into my thigh.

"Right you are," I said. "Focus on the now, big dog."

Chapter 7

I OPENED my eyes in the dark and listened to Dear George's dogs breathing. It was what my best friend Trisha called the *wee smalls*. Trisha and I had stayed up together until the wee small hours of the night many times, starting when we were roommates at college.

Trisha traveled for work and claimed that there was a special strangeness that happened in the wee smalls when you were alone in an unfamiliar hotel room. The furniture looked odd, as if it had slid out of a Salvador Dali picture. Distances multiplied, so that you were not just alone, but alone by a long way.

Trisha slept very little while on the road, so she always gave me the number of her hotel. That way I could call if I happened to be up this time of night, because she would surely be awake. But Trisha was home, no doubt snoozing like a rock next to her boyfriend in his cheesy bachelor pad in Jersey City. I'd call her in the morning.

I'd have to tell her that pets didn't make much difference in the wee smalls. Their heavy breathing did not soothe. I tried to fall back to sleep in the darkness, but my mind was full of images I didn't want to see, ideas I didn't want to think about. I tried closing my eyes, but it was useless. I was awake. I heard the minuscule click of my eyelids parting and reclosing as I blinked. It was going to drive me crazy.

I threw back the covers and swung my legs out of bed. I turned the bedside lamp on and saw that Tomkin's eyes were open.

"Don't get up," I told him. "Everything is fine. I just can't sleep."

Tomkin kept his muzzle tucked under his flank. His tail curved to meet his front paws. He looked like a brown jade netsuke carving, sized for the pocket of a giant. I'd unpacked my sketchbook earlier and put it on the bare bedside table. I kept the flat metal box of drawing pencils glued to the inside cover of the sketchbook. I didn't even have to stand up to reach it.

I wanted to use a single line to express the strong curve of Tomkin's spine, the rabbity bones of those long tucked-up hind legs, and the set of his ears on his square head. He was not a fat dog, but his considerable mass looked squished to fit on the rug. I tried to reproduce the slightly uncomfortable expression in his eyes as he looked up at me but had to start over. Tomkin sighed at me, and I told him he was a very good dog. He closed his eyes as if deliberately shutting me out.

I flipped the notebook closed and looked at the other dogs. They were curled up too, each on a throw rug in various parts of the room, like big kids perched on small inner tubes floating on a quiet lake. They were asleep, or at least they looked asleep.

I tried to put my head back on the pillow, but it was no good pretending. I needed to get up.

Tomkin padded along with me to the kitchen, stopping twice to stretch, taking his own unhurried time to work all the kinks out of his long back.

I unhooked a gleaming copper kettle from the pan rack above the stove. Dear George loved to cook. This was his spotless industrial-flavored kitchen with the copper pots and bare black granite countertops.

I poked through the cupboards until I found the mugs, honey, and some herbal teabags. There was also a baggie of some surprisingly good-smelling weed in with the teas. George liked to twist one now and again. Not that Viv ever joined him, as far as I knew. Too much to lose, she'd told me, long before anyone had offered me any.

"ONE single joint." She'd summed it up as we sat at the kitchen table that first spring when our parents were gone for good. "And we get put in foster care. You know what that means—"

I did know. There were lots of stories about how bad it could be, but we had *known* Michelle Aigner. A shy girl with eyes as green as grass in a pale, doughy face who rode the bus with us. On the long ride home the half-dozen or so of us—not friends, since we were in different grades and the country distances between houses kept us from playing together after school, but still—exchanged stories as the school bus bounced along the narrow roads. Michelle Aigner with her green eyes and her soft, sad face offered up details about the foster system. She didn't complain, though it had been one grim thing after another, even before she stopped riding the bus.

Rumor said that the foster dad broke Michelle's arm and both collarbones. Teachers whispered together about mysterious "internal injuries" that were going to keep her in the hospital for weeks. As far as I knew,

Michelle never returned to school. We moved away, and I never learned what happened next for her.

"Until I turn eighteen," Viv said. "It's essential that we stay invisible. We can't afford even one mistake this year."

DEAR George was different, of course. He was an only child, born late to wealthy parents. He had gone to Philips Exeter and then to Dartmouth. I met him the summer I was au-pairing on Long Island in 1986. He'd come out to stay at the Hamptons most weekends to visit friends from school. He was flying through a summer internship in Wall Street and was scheduled to finish business school in New York the next year.

At first impression I had been ready to dislike George Rowan. Yes, he was tall and funny. He had the comfortable good looks that seem to come with the prep-school package: straight teeth, shiny hair, the lanky grace of an athlete. He wore expensive clothes without seeming self-conscious of the pricey, preppy logos.

He was an organizer: he put together beach volleyball games most weekends and hosted at least one actual clambake. But he included not just his hosts and his handsome buddies from the city, but au pair girls, lifeguards, locals he met in town. He made social connections without discrimination. He had a way of noticing people, and he was fearless about talking with anyone.

Technically, George and I never went out. Not on an actual date, anyhow. My sister had warned me about people like him and I stayed on my guard. Even when I wanted to ignore her precautions, it was hard to dismiss Viv's advice. She always seemed to know so much.

"Rich boys—especially good-looking rich boys—are the worst. They think they already own the world. And sometimes, the ones that seem the nicest? They can be the meanest of all."

I was babysitting for the Oliver family in East Quoque after my freshman year in college. All that summer George came out to the Hamptons early on Friday afternoons, piling out of his battered old Volvo with his floppy head of hair, his funny giggle, and his handsome friends. They played endless games of volleyball and lounged around Tiana Beach.

Over an ice-cream cone he told me he'd done some downhill ski racing until he realized he didn't like his own odds. He was funny and self-deprecating.

He told me about wringing six months' worth of adventure out of the three-week-long trip to Europe his parents had given him for college graduation. (Hostels and dishwashing played a big role.) His perspective was like looking around with van Gogh goggles on—the world bright and clear in broad brushstrokes.

Everything seemed so easy for him. All the things that had kept Viv and me on the straight and narrow were alien to George.

He made me laugh, yet when he asked me to go to the movies or for dinner that summer, I parried. I thought there would be a ton of time to decide if I wanted more.

"Remember, for boys, it's all about the chase," Viv told me. "I'm not saying don't have a boyfriend. Nothing wrong with the chase. Just, you know, figure it out and go slow. Don't get trapped into anything."

At the end of the summer, I told George about how I was going into Manhattan to visit Viv. George said, "Why not let me take both of you to lunch? A real Manhattan lunch."

So, the week before school started, I met Viv outside Lincoln Center. We walked along Central Park, chattering a mile a minute about our summer adventures.

George was waiting by the marquee entrance to Tavern on the Green, a sportscoat slung casually over a wide shoulder, a quizzical expression on his face.

When I got close enough to make the introductions, I put a hand on my sister's arm and held the other out toward George. I said, "Viv, I'd like you to meet George Rowan."

They looked at each other and it was like someone taking a photograph with a flashbulb. I saw it happen.

They shook hands, and then I was just a bystander, following them as the hostess ushered us into the restaurant. They talked as if they had known each other for years.

My sister never asked me if I minded. How could I mind? From that lunch on, George and Viv were inseparable. I imagine she never thought twice about why I had brought him around. .

THE kettle began to whistle, and as I made my tea, I noticed Tomkin sitting next to the refrigerator, as straight and alert as an Egyptian statue. He gave me a heavy look.

I hurried over to the refrigerator. I unwrapped a slice of pre-packaged yellow cheese and gave half of it to the dog.

"These guys will do just about anything for cheese," George had bragged to me. He had put a tiny triangle of cheese on the very end of Dwalin's quivering black nose and told him to wait, *wait*, wait. The dog had stayed frozen, drooling, until George had told him to "Have at!"

Afterwards, George leaned down and shook the jowly skin of the dog's face in an ecstasy of praise. It surprised me that the dogs never seemed to resent this treatment. Instead, they trotted in place on their big feet, eyes glowing, tails flailing, ears folded against heavy necks, seeming just as pleased as George that they had waited and gotten their treat like good dogs.

Tomkin was looking at me. I realized I had taken a bite of the remaining cheese slice myself, the bland, sour taste of it lingering across my tongue. I gave the rest to the dog, who wolfed it down and left a small puddle of drool on the gleaming tile floor.

I got one of the towels out of the dirty laundry. Tomkin stood patiently waiting for me to wipe his face. His skin moved loosely on the big bones of his jaw, his lumpy skull. His ears flopped limply.

He leaned into the towel with a happy little groan as I rubbed, and it came to me in a rush how much the dogs would miss Dear George. That George would never again tell the dogs how good they had been as they danced in place. The dogs would never know what had happened to him.

And it occurred to me that George was gone, really gone. I would never see him. Viv would never see him.

His silly, high-pitched giggle and his lanky walk, and the proud way he looked at my sister were all gone forever. George was dead. My nose clogged and my eyes filled, and I was on my knees, hanging onto the dog's neck, crying into the dog-scented towel.

Chapter 8

THE STATE TROOPER had a smooth, fresh pink face, as if he had never been exposed to cold air or bare sunshine. He was tall but soft, a ring of baby fat cushioning his belt. He removed his stiff hat and called me "ma'am" and Artie "sir."

He asked us to wait outside a pair of swinging doors. The word *Morgue* was printed on the frosted glass windows of the right-hand door. The State of Tennessee required our help during this difficult time, the trooper informed us.

After a moment, a slight woman wearing blue scrubs emerged from behind the doors. She asked us if we were ready and then led us in.

I hadn't let myself anticipate what it would be like, but I hadn't expected so small a room with so much natural light. Not a basement. No stainless-steel drawers set into the wall. Not like on television. It was chilly and there was an odor that I didn't want to think about.

It took only a few hard moments for Artie and me to look at the body, identify it as George, and be led back through the door marked *Morgue.* Artie carried the plastic shopping bag of George's personal effects.

Leaving that room, I tried to fill my mind's eye with enormous peony flowers, Georgia-O'Keefe-scale blossoms, to keep from thinking about what handsome Dear George had looked like on the metal gurney.

It wasn't working. *Poor broken George*, I thought, and my stomach clenched at the thought of the damage done to him. Outside the building, Artie lit a cigarette, but wasn't smoking it. I had taken one from the pack when he offered but hadn't lit it.

I fiddled with the cigarette and the disposable lighter in one hand. To keep from feeling my fingers shake, I pressed the fingertips of the other hand against the jagged edges of the crumbs lodged deep in my pocket seam. The air was damp and cool, the wind sneaking around the corner of the brick building.

"I'm the executor of George's will," Artie announced. His voice seemed loud after our silence. He swung his arm back and forth, leaving a feathery trail of cigarette smoke. He seemed to take up a lot of space in his immaculate suit and elegant camel overcoat.

"Uh. Okay," I said. I didn't say that Viv had mentioned more than once how convenient it was to have Artie—a lawyer—practically family.

"He wanted to be cremated."

Cremation. The word seemed alien. I'd never known anyone who had died. I'd never attended a funeral. I'd honestly never thought about these things. I'd studied scores of death masks and memorial carvings in museums, but it didn't connect. I'd never thought what it was like when the person who died was someone you knew. Another thing I wasn't prepared for.

Artie repeated, "George wanted to be cremated."

"How—?" I couldn't finish the question.

"He told me. Oh, you mean how do you go about the—ah—process?"

I flicked at the lighter, working to light the cigarette, and nodded, my eyes down.

"The funeral people arrange that kind of thing." Artie paused and, seeming a little reluctant, he asked if I was sure I was okay.

I told him I was.

"As their executor, of course, I am prepared to handle the funeral arrangements and all that."

"I wouldn't even know where to begin," I admitted, tobacco smoke coming out with my words.

"That's alright. You don't have to." Artie's voice deepened theatrically as he spoke. I suppose he was trying to be kind, but it sounded staged. It sounded patronizing. Next he would be telling me, in an octave lower yet, not to bother my pretty little head about it.

"It's really *not*," I snapped, and then shut my mouth with a click. He was probably trying to be kind, in his own way. He couldn't help sounding pompous.

Truth be told, I felt relieved that someone else could do this. I was glad to have someone else handle the details of burying a person, even though it meant Artie would be burying his best friend. The relief made me feel guilty. It was irritating, and I saw myself taking it out on Artie. And yet, truly, I didn't *want* to learn how to bury someone.

"Sorry," I said.

Artie shrugged and flicked his cigarette butt into the wet grass. Did he even know he was littering? He said, "I just meant that this part—talking with the funeral director, submitting the newspaper notices—is something I can do."

At my nod, he returned to explaining in that deep, stagey voice, "My point is, it's often difficult for family members to—"

I interrupted, knowing I was being rude. "I get it, Artie. So what comes first?"

Artie outlined the process of getting a person buried in the state of Tennessee. Artie would talk with the funeral director and the pastor at Viv and George's church.

"They had a regular church?"

Artie looked surprised. "Yeah, they went to St. Bart's most Sunday mornings, unless Viv was on call. George and I play—ah, we used to play—basketball before church."

"I didn't know that," I said, more to myself than to Artie.

Artie continued to describe what needed to be done. He would contact George's friends and colleagues and start to organize a memorial service.

"If you feel up to it, perhaps you could start calling Viv's—" Artie checked himself. He had been pacing and he spun on a shiny heel to face me. "Maybe you could prepare a list of people who need to know about the situation?"

"I'll make the calls for Viv," I said.

"Good." Artie turned again, thinking on his feet. "Ah—you might find it's best to keep the conversations short and to the point."

I felt my eyebrows rise, but I mumbled a quick agreement. Did Artie imagine I needed to be told this? Did he think I was that clueless? Well, I reminded myself, I'd *said* I didn't know where to begin.

Artie continued, frowning. "I'll leave the information about the funeral home and so forth on the answering machine at the house. People will want to know."

I agreed and he continued the explanation. It sounded as if he'd said these sentences more than once. He was careful to make everything clear, and when he finished, I thanked him.

"Can I drop you off anyplace?"

"No, I'll stay with Viv. I'm driving her car."

"Ah—that's fine," Artie said. "Do you need anything for the house? As guardian, you know that you will be reimbursed—"

"No," I interrupted him. "I have money."

"Yes, well, Nicole, with a house as big as—there are expenses—"

"Artie, I get it. And if Viv is not awake when I get the phone bill, believe me, I'll call you."

I didn't correct his version of my name again. People often got it wrong. Still, hearing him say it with such sincerity felt like sandpaper.

Artie faced me, holding his palms up in peace. "Nicole, I don't want to be the bad guy here. Nevertheless, your sister has entrusted you to do everything that's needed. For someone not accustomed to this kind of responsibility—there are considerable assets to manage. Uh, not just the house—"

Responsibility? What kind of flake did he think I was? I ran my own business. All my bills were paid; I had happy clients and work waiting in Florida. I pushed down the annoyance and said, "Let's do this: next week, if we still need to tackle these details, we can meet then. Okay?"

"If that's what you think is right," Artie answered, his face set. It couldn't have been plainer if he said it aloud: he thought I was wrong.

I tried to explain. "Look. It's too soon. It hasn't even been two whole days." I made an effort to smile. "Viv's not going to thank me for poking around in her business."

I stuck the cigarette butt into the gravel-filled tray next to the door.

"You know Viv," I said. "She'll understand if something urgent comes up, but she'd hate it if she thought I was prying."

Artie unclenched his jaw, clearly weighing my words.

"And believe me, I'd do a lot *not* to make her mad at me," I added, making a face of mock fear.

Artie had witnessed my sister lose her temper a time or two. He nodded with a faint smirk. "Fine," he said. "Understood."

He pulled a leather card case from his jacket and extracted a thick business card. He fished out a gold pen and jotted something on the card. "I'm writing Leora's number at work and the house number for you. Call for anything."

As he whisked off, coat billowing, I had a fleeting wish that I had snagged another cigarette from him. The bitter flavor stayed in my mouth, a reminder of how people pass the time waiting outside a hospital.

Without wanting to, I remembered the muddy, ambered, unnatural color of Dear George's skin. I shivered and took a long look around at the crisp autumn morning, trying to gulp in the clear russet and yellow glow of the leaves. After a moment, I went to my sister.

Chapter 9

A PAIR of nurses was just leaving when I got to my sister's hospital room.

"Is she awake yet?" I said, peering past them.

One stood aside, shaking her head. "No, there's no change," she said. "The OB/GYN should be by after a bit," she said.

A knock on the doorframe came just as I'd decided to fetch myself a hot tea. Viv's OB/GYN was a striking woman who might have posed for an aging Renaissance Madonna, her expression both serene and concerned. She shook my hand and introduced herself. She turned to Viv and took a long look into Viv's face.

"Vivian," she said. "Hi. It's Marilyn Wilsey."

She looked at Viv's chart, flipping pages back to read, as she explained, the on-call OB/GYN's notes. She pointed to one of the machines ranged next to Viv's bed.

"That's the fetal monitor," she said. "It looks fine, but I like to listen for myself." She pulled her stethoscope from a jacket pocket and held it briefly against her palm before bunching the covers aside and listening to Viv's abdomen. She moved the scope over Viv's belly, intent on whatever she was hearing or not hearing. Finally she straightened and, with a smile, asked if I wanted to listen.

I did.

The earpieces were warm and they blocked out the noises of the room, as if I were ducking underwater. After a moment I heard gurgling and a faint, thrumming *fu-fu-fu* sound, rapid as a rabbit's heartbeat.

"Is it supposed to be so quick?" I asked Dr. Wilsey.

"Yes, it's fine." Her voice was kind. "The average heart rate at this stage is around one hundred and twenty beats per minute." She pointed to the monitor, which, obligingly, read, *122 bpm.*

"Can you tell me about the pregnancy?" I asked, still listening to Viv's aquatic inner workings.

Dr. Wilsey shot me a shrewd look. "Her pregnancy has been as normal as any. Your sister has gained exactly the amount of weight I suggested. Her blood pressure has been low. Healthy low, I mean. The baby has tested out perfectly normal. Right now I'm going to do a quick exam." She herded me from the room. "Would you send in one of the nurses?"

In front of the nurse's station, I flagged down the nurse who'd spoken to me earlier, Charise, and asked her to help Dr. Wilsey. I went to the cafeteria and then wandered back to the uncomfortable molded fiberglass chair outside of Viv's room, sipping from a Styrofoam cup of dusty-tasting tea. After a few minutes, Dr. Wilsey opened the door and invited me back in. Charise gave me an encouraging smile as she left.

Dr. Wilsey's oval face was smooth, expressionless but pleasant as she announced, "I'm glad to tell you that the car accident does not seem to have adversely affected the health of the fetus."

"Good," I said.

"It's very good. We don't like to see anyone get into a car crash, least of all someone like your sister, with her reproductive history." She went on to say something about how amazing the uterus was at protecting a fetus, even through an event like this.

I looked at the undamaged half of my sister's face. My lungs seemed empty, so the question started at a whisper.

"But. Her reproductive history—?"

"You are the medical guardian, as I understand?" She was fiddling with my sister's IV as she spoke.

I nodded, then managed a faint, "Yes."

"Excellent." She turned to me. "Let me tell you what I am thinking: our first priority is to be sure Viv's condition is stable. Her blood pressure, blood sugar, and liver enzymes all look very good. That's excellent news."

I nodded.

"Right now, she's getting her nutrition through the IV, but unless your sister's condition improves dramatically, we'll need to think about a feeding tube. That baby is going to need a lot more nutrition than we can deliver through an IV. I think it would be wise to prepare for every eventuality."

"What do you think will happen?" I asked, finally catching my breath.

"Well," the doctor said with a smile. "In the best case, Vivian wakes up and is ready to walk out of here in a few days." She looked away and her smile dried up. "In the worst case, we manage the pregnancy as best we can."

My voice came out oddly normal, a little loud, even. "How do we do that?"

Dr. Wilsey clasped her hands together, a series of papery crinkles forming between her brows as she started to speak. "As I'm sure you know, your sister would want us to do everything we can to make sure her baby has the best chance possible."

She began pushing at her cuticles without looking down at her scrubbed fingers.

"Premature babies tend to have a host of medical problems and complications. I think we should do what we can to help your sister hold on for the next ten weeks—"

I interrupted her, "*Help her hold on*? What are you saying?"

"In the worst case, is what I mean here." The doctor spoke slowly, each word coming out careful and reasonable, but she was pinching the nail bed of her ring finger. The tip had turned scarlet. "At the moment, there's no conflict between what is good for your sister and what is good for her baby. I think if the situation changes medically, we will need to consider the options very carefully."

"What options?" I asked.

"To be honest with you, I don't know. I think it's better to keep focused on the situation at hand. And—" She anticipated my question. "At the moment, your sister is stable, the pregnancy looks good and, well, we'll see how things go."

I nodded. "So what do we do?"

The doctor unclasped her hands and spread her palms wide. "For now, our strategy will be to make sure your sister and the baby are getting the nutrition they need. We'll keep a close eye on Vivian's blood pressure and anything that could indicate a problem with the baby." Her forehead was smooth again as she straightened the covers over Viv's legs. "As it stands, I think we just wait and keep a watchful eye on your sister."

She wrote her phone number down for me and told me to call anytime. From the doorway, she turned with a smile and said, "If I know your sister, she'll probably be up and about before long. She's one tough lady."

I followed Dr. Wilsey to the doorway. "Excuse me, but what you said about Viv's history, what did you mean?"

Her forehead crinkled. She seemed to be considering my question too carefully.

I rephrased it. "Is there anything I should know about my sister's history?"

By her expression, I could see she was making up her mind not to tell me anything. She took a deep breath, but I broke in again.

"In order to make a good decision about her and the baby, is there anything I should know?"

She put her head to the side and gave me a long look. "That's not unreasonable, I think. Shall I summarize?"

At my nod, she folded her hands again and leaned against the doorway.

"Your sister has had several early miscarriages in the past three years, and naturally, she was concerned."

The doctor gazed at me.

"Miscarriages are not as uncommon as you might think. Many early pregnancies end that way. If there's a serious defect with the fetus, the pregnancy may terminate itself, often in the first month or two. Mother Nature's way, but it can be devastating. As I told your sister, I saw no reason to think she would have a problem with this pregnancy. She's been the picture of health, really, and she's in her sixth month. Nevertheless, she was anxious about the pregnancy. She was more than willing to take whatever precautions I suggested."

"I see," I said. I couldn't imagine my sister being willing to take anyone else's precautions. But I also couldn't imagine her wanting children—and here we were. Not only was she pregnant, but she'd been trying. For years.

"I can give you additional details," she said unclasping her hands. "But I think I've covered the highlights. She was willing to make considerable sacrifices to have this child." She patted my arm.

I put her card, which I had been pinching in the crook of my thumb as she spoke, into my jeans pocket. She said she'd be back in a day or so, to telephone if I had any questions or concerns, and I thanked her.

I sat down on the squeaky visitor's chair and thought about what *considerable sacrifices* might have meant to Viv. My sister's skull was cracked, her clever brain had sprung leaks, and her left eardrum was ruptured. Those were her same chapped hands, with an IV tube and a finger splint, and those were her long legs and her bony knees. At the edge of the capped sleeve of her hospital gown, there was the old dog-bite scar, white on the pale skin of her bicep. And she had a baby floating inside that formerly flat stomach.

A baby. Looking at her, I couldn't understand how I hadn't seen it when I first saw her.

Viv had never gone gaga over infants, never made kooky faces at kids or gushed, "Aw, look how cute!" when we passed a storefront of tiny clothes. Unlike me, she'd never been a babysitter as a kid.

She was intolerant of parents who kept their noisy children inside the movie theatre. She'd ask to be seated away from a cranky baby at a restaurant. I remember more than once when she had slapped me to stop me crying when we were little. She hated crying, never cried herself. She said it never helped anything to cry.

I tried to imagine my sister and a newborn. She must have done a residency rotation in pediatrics, not that we would have talked about it. A swaddling bundle in my sister's elegant arms? Did she even know how to change a diaper? Maybe George had wanted a baby.

For a moment I'd forgotten about the morgue.

His face had been transformed in death. The skin had the streaky coloration of paving marble: pale greenish white, with yellow and a mottled, horrible mahogany. I wanted to erase that memory.

Looking at my sister in her bed, I mixed an imaginary palate of titian white, cadmium yellow, and raw sienna that would capture the subtle tints of her pale skin, the copper gleam of her hair, the quality of light that breath gave her. The bruising was coming up purple and scarlet on her jaw to match her lip. Along the line of stitches, the skin was stained with orange, and it looked too tight.

Despite the damage, however, it was possible to almost see life running through my sister's body. Her swollen lips looked dry, but not bloodless. She was pale, but she looked alive. When I touched her arm, it was limp as pasta, but it was warm and springy. A spot at her collarbone pulsed to the rhythm of her heart.

I concentrated on seeing the vitality in Viv's quiet body, hoping to overlay the image of Dear George with this example of life breathing in front of me. It reminded me of the anatomy book my sister had brought home in high school, in which the illustrations started with a base picture of the skeleton. A series of separate acetate sheets covered the skeleton: the digestive organs, blood vessels, nerves, muscles, and finally, like a smooth bedspread, the skin. But the thought came back to me: there was a baby under that bedspread. And she hadn't told me anything about it.

MY sister had a masterful way with truth and partial truth from as long as I could remember. I knew how to lie, of course—who doesn't by age six or seven? But Viv was very good at it.

She would ask me, "What's the story? What's the truth?" and I would waver. Was it true that I had lost my lunch-money? Or was it true that Viv had *told* me to say that I had lost it while she put the money into our emergency piggy bank?

"It's lost," I'd say, not certain of the mechanics of how those quarters had moved from my pocket to hers.

"Right!" she'd tell me. "That's great. Because you *did* lose your lunch money. Even if we know where it is."

"But—"

"But nothing. You don't have to tell every bit of the truth all of the time."

The lesson really sank in when I spilled ink on the hearth in the big house in Rossie. Jahn and Magda rented houses that were furnished, so each time we moved, settling in felt like a kind of scavenger hunt. The previous tenants usually left behind odd loot: dishes and board-games, jars of old buttons and blanket chests full of winter coats, and—treasure of treasure—books.

In Rossie, the house was especially well furnished, with vivid old Oriental carpets and nice pictures on the walls. Sheets and blankets were still on the beds and old people's clothes were still hanging in the closet—Magda had us push the clothing to the back and stack the linens in a hall closet. Jahn warned us against damaging anything in the house, but when I found a little box of metal quill-pens and a bottle of India ink in the big desk drawer, I could not resist.

Jahn and Magda were away again and at first, I was very cautious. I used the bottle of ink only at the kitchen table, protecting the Formica tabletop with a layer of newspaper. Then I got the idea of picking one of my best sketches—a view of the genteel front of the house—and inking over my pencil lines so that it would look like an illustration from a book. I was proud of how well it was turning out, the way the pencil drawing was transformed by my steady lines of black ink into something more certain and more true.

But at the kitchen table, my hands turned purplish from cold. I was worried I'd ruin the sketch with fingers grown slow and stiff. I kept having to take a break to warm my hands by the fire in the other room.

So I carried the sketch and the ink into the living room and set myself up in front of the fireplace. I don't know how, but inevitably, of course, one big fat black drop of ink fell onto the parquet floor in front of the fireplace. At my wail, my sister came running and assessed the situation in a glance.

"Shush," she said. "Here, move that stuff back into the kitchen and wash your hands."

"Jahn is going to kill me," I said.

"No, he's not."

I pointed to the spot. "It's indelible ink. It doesn't wash off."

"Put that stuff back in the kitchen," Viv repeated. "Nobody's getting punished for this. Go!"

When I returned to the living room, my sister was poking through the embers under the grate. She gently lifted a lozenge of coal with the long-handled tongs and then carefully placed the red cinder on top of the ink spot. I saw her lips move as she counted, one-two-three, and then she dashed the ember back toward the fireplace where it flared and faded to gray on the field-stone hearth.

"Viv!"

"What? There was a big pop and it's just a good thing you happened to see the cinder. It could have been so much worse."

"But—"

"It's not a bad lie," she told me. "It's hardly like lying at all. We will just tell a different part of the truth. Ink-stain or burn-mark—they are both there, right?"

My sister waited until I said yes, and then continued.

"But it's easier on everybody if it was a cinder that left the mark, right?"

I nodded.

"Can you picture it in your mind?"

I could. I could visualize the crackling of the firewood, the loud pop and the spark streaking across to the wood floor. It glowed orange even in the sunlight. I felt the hurried sweep of my hand—no, my foot—to send the coal back into the fire. I nodded again.

"Now, just forget about the ink."

I smoothed my face and said, "What ink?"

She rolled her eyes at me. "Too much."

"Oh, *that* ink. I forgot about *that* ink."

My sister gave me a look that was both exasperated and proud. "You have to be able to lie. Believe me, everybody lies, so it's essential that you can do a half-decent job of it."

We both looked at the black scar on the chestnut floor.

"When?"

She looked at me.

"How do you know when to lie?" I said.

Viv grinned. "Always know *why* you are lying. Magda and Jahn need to know about the cinder. It could have been dangerous."

"But I did spill ink, didn't I?" I said, for a moment almost unsure.

"Yes, and that was clumsy and stupid. But still, it's not really your fault. Jahn and Magda are just asking for this kind of accident. You are too young to be playing around a fireplace."

"Pioneer kids did," I said, thinking of the *Little House* books. "And I'm not that young. I'm nine."

"Duh, newsflash: nine *is* young. And don't say *nine* like that, like a North Country hick. And by the way, in case you can't tell—Jahn and Magda aren't pioneers, they are just lazy and mean. To save us all the fight, *this* is a good time to lie."

She peered into my face and sighed.

"Fine," Viv said. "Here are the rules: lie to keep us out of trouble. Lie to keep us safe. Don't tell a lie just for fun and don't lie to make someone like you. Okay?"

"Okay." But it was a long time before I was able to fool her.

Chapter 10

WITH no more tests or doctors scheduled for Viv, I left
to get a start on calling her friends.

The garage door opened to reveal the three dogs
crowded in the mudroom doorway. They stood
shoulder to shoulder to shoulder, their dark, saggy faces
worried even while their tails wagged wildly. Tomkin
let out a single, deep *woof!* as I shut off the Saab's
engine. They leaped to the car door, but when I stepped
out, their joyful welcome scaled down a notch. They
were not unhappy to see me, but, frankly, I was a
disappointment. Dwalin slipped past me and stuck his
head into the car. He backed out with his head hung as
low as a cartoon caricature of sadness.

I let them out and refilled their water bowls and got
three drool towels. I stood at the back door watching the
two younger dogs gallop around the grass lawn while
Balin took an unhurried sniff around the post-and-rail
fence. Trios of young pines and skimpy maples marked
the back corners of the property. Lush, mossy green

growth spilled over the gaps between the flags. Damp fallen leaves on the cold stone scented the air.

Balin ambled up the terrace steps and stood leaning against my leg. I rubbed her bony head, and when I stopped, she pushed her face against me. I gave her a couple of gentle thumps on the ribs and stepped back inside.

I perched on the uncomfortable chrome chair at the little kitchen nook where they kept the answering machine and telephone. Opening the drawer to get something to write on, I found a striking tableau: the drawer contained at least a dozen unused yellow pencils honed to needle sharpness, a portfolio folder marked *Take-Out Menus*, a pristine pad of note paper, a nested bundle of three thick broccoli-stalk rubber-bands, a perfectly aligned stack of twenty-dollar bills, and nothing else. Not even dust. I had a dizzying impulse to call my sister and tell her about this vision of neatness— a stark modern still-life with pencils.

It took only a moment to realize my stupidity. Viv knew all about it; she was married to the man. This was the way Dear George organized things. He squared corners and couldn't bear clutter. At the start of Viv's residency in Atlanta, he'd thrown away all of her case notes because he thought the scraps of folded, odd-shaped paper must be trash. My sister had told that story about him for years.

I pressed the blinking red light of the answering machine and heard the unearthly voice announce that I had seven messages. Two hang-ups, one reminder from Dr. Lisle's office about a teeth-cleaning appointment for George, two loud wake-up calls for "Fat Boy" to get up and get his ass to the gym, a curt message—"Vivian, hey, give me a call when you have the chance"—from a man who left neither name nor number, and, finally, Artie's deep voice announcing the details about the funeral parlor and the memorial service.

The dogs returned while the machine was still playing, and I told them I had to find Viv's address-book.

The dogs followed me into the study, sniffing around the room as if reading important messages in the glossy floorboards. Viv and Dear George had shared the space, which looked like an advertisement for Ethan Allen furniture: a big, formal desk, cabinets, and bookshelves in matching dark wood. The shelves were full of textbooks and binders and mismatched framed photographs of George's family.

I plunked into the leather desk chair and started looking for Viv's address book, shuffling through neatly organized office supplies. Clearly the work of tidy Dear George.

He had filed house bills, bank statements, and other financial stuff in alphabetical order by company name. George's handwriting looked like the print found on architectural plans or mechanical drawings. I didn't find any files with Viv's distinctive backwards-slanting script.

It made me think about my own filing system. I kept a metal milk crate (clearly labeled "Property of Northfield Farms") under the bed or at the back of a closet. I poured all my check stubs, receipts, and bills into the crate. At tax time, I simply went through everything and tossed what I didn't need.

I stopped to think where Viv might keep her things. Balin looked up at me from where she and Tomkin had settled down for a nap. I told her she was a good dog, and she flattened her ears against her head and thumped her tail once.

My sister rarely carried a purse. The nurse-supervisor at the hospital had given me Viv's wallet, pager, and the jewelry she had been wearing. The watch—the one I had sent to her from Italy as a graduation present—was still running. When I had called to congratulate her on finishing medical school, Viv had put on a dreadful Italian accent and told me the wristwatch was, "Fabulosa, bella! Takes-a licking, keeps-a ticking!" Turned out she was right.

The thought came to me sideways: bedside table. At the bottom of the stairs, I told Balin to stay. The other two dogs galloped up with me. The pale carpet was thick and cushy, deep enough to muffle the dogs' noisy progress. Viv and Dear George's bedroom was a roomy cool space with two sets of clothes draped across the arms of the loveseat. A pair of bedside tables framed the king-sized bed.

It was easy to see whose side was which. Dear George's table held a clock radio, a half-full glass of water centered on a coaster, and a copy of *The One-Minute Manager* stacked squarely under an Isaac Asimov science-fiction novel with a bookmark. On Viv's table, the folding travel alarm clock was tipped on its face, while an opened manicure kit and box of tissues perched with the telephone on top of a leaning pile of medical magazines.

I opened the top drawer of Viv's bedside table and found her battered silk address book under a handful of lip balms, a pink stick of cocoa-butter, and a plain black book, which I guessed was probably her journal. She'd kept a diary as long as I could remember, first in black-and-white composition notebooks, then later in black ledgers like this.

Back downstairs, I settled into the kitchen nook with Viv's address book. The fabric had faded to a pale blue along the spine, but the scarlet and gold of the pagodas and bamboo still popped on the bright turquoise cover. I'd bought the book in high school for Viv's birthday.

The pages were well thumbed, with scraps of paper adding to the bulk. Viv had a habit of tearing the return address off an envelope and taping it into the book, which saved her the energy of transcribing it. She jotted telephone numbers on the reverse side of those slips of paper and tore out the paper when the address needed to be updated.

I rehearsed what I would have to tell Viv's friends, and then I started with the As.

Ackerman, Alverado, Ayers. There were a lot of names in Viv's book. I remembered her few high school pals and most of the crowd from college. I didn't know many of her med school buddies, but I noticed she had inked a small green triangle next to some names. It came to me that this was a stylized pine tree. My sister must have used it to mark her Christmas-card list. If I ever got around to sending out Christmas cards, I'd probably do something similar. I figured these were the people who mattered most.

The first call was the hardest.

"Hi, can I speak with Charlotte Ackerman? Thanks. Charlotte? This is Nicola Jones, Vivian's sister. I am calling to tell you that Viv has been in a car accident."

By the third call, it fell into a rhythm. At first, I started to say that Viv was not awake, but that sounded wrong. So I just announced that she was in intensive care. I gave them the details about George's funeral parlor, the hospital. They asked if they could do anything, and I told them it would be a big help if they would pass the word to Viv's other friends.

After an hour or so, I took a break and tried to phone my friend Trisha. We'd stayed close even after I dropped out and took off to Europe. Later, after Trisha settled into a corporate routine and I kept moving from place to place, we ran up crazy long-distance phone bills reading *Cosmo* magazine together and keeping tabs on each other's love lives.

I reached Trisha's answering machine, and her message—"Yeah, Yeah, wait for the beep"—made me smile. I told her to give me a ring when she got around to it and left the number.

I put the kettle on for tea and flipped to the Js, where I had my very own page. Viv wrote down each of my addresses and then crossed them out with a single line. After I took up a whole page, she'd taped in a piece of lined paper that folded out. It was already half filled with Viv's strong left-handed handwriting.

I looked over the list: freshman year at 207 Barnes Hall, and my summer with the Oliver family in East Quogue. An arrow pointed back to Barnes Hall for sophomore year.

Then came the "in care of" years after I quit school: in care of Cutillo in Brooklyn Heights, in care of the au pair agency, in care of the Collogia family on Via Bonchi Vecchi in Rome, the Amanzi family in Florence.

When I had come back and worked at the temp agency, I'd shared that Hudson Street loft with all those girls and taken a plein-air class at the New York Academy of Art. A quick stay with the Cutillos, and to the big apartment in Crown Heights when I spent the semester at the Educational Alliance Art School. The two house-sitting gigs in Florida last year. The address of the bone-cold flat in London—I'd spent day after day at the Tate wrapped in wool and a down-filled jacket, looking at the Turners—and back again to Florida.

The list finished with the Cutillos last summer, followed by my current address in Sarasota. More than a dozen places in less than ten years. It seemed excessive, laid out like this. But there was so much see in the world, I wanted to explain. No one was asking, but for a moment it felt as if I was in the middle of an argument.

I took a gulp of tea and turned pages until I found my spot and began calling again. I left more messages and talked to people until I reached the one Z in her book (Steve Zemenian, whom Viv had dated in college and who had ended up marrying her friend Marie Chou). I was starving and it felt like I had been carrying boxes of books up and down steps rather than just talking on the phone.

I investigated the leftovers. A chicken pasta something or other looked edible, so I heated it up and cracked open a Rolling Rock.

I put the dogs outside and thought about the things no one had said on the phone. Viv's friends had been shocked, upset, some offered to pray, and almost everyone wanted to help somehow, but not one of them had asked about the pregnancy. There was some consolation in knowing I wasn't the very last person to get the news.

I flipped through the calendar Viv and George kept on the shelf above the telephone nook. Viv's on-call schedule was color-coded in the tidy penmanship of Dear George. Viv had noted two appointments with a check mark and the word *up* next to it. She hadn't written a location or doctor's name. She jotted details about social events—DG's Charity Auction for Bosnia @The Drake—but nothing about baby showers or Lamaze classes. She had drawn a small red star next to a date in December but hadn't mentioned what would happen that day.

I threw the Styrofoam container away and thought some more about what I didn't know.

My sister had not told me she was going to have a baby, and she apparently hadn't told any of her old friends about it either. Maybe nobody knew about it.

Except for George, Leora, and Artie, and people she worked with at the hospital. It was as if she wasn't even pregnant. For all I could tell, she hadn't even planned to bring a baby home. Maybe George didn't know. Could that be possible?

Could you be six months along and keep it from your own husband?

I took the stairs two at a time. The upstairs guest room was spotless, unchanged from my last visit. No bassinet, no crib, no rocking chair, no crates full of baby gear in the closet. The spare room, the one with the daybed, still held the same sparse collection of leftover lamps and a few cardboard boxes marked *Upstairs Misc.* The guest bathroom was pristine, the dark teal tiles gleaming.

The master bathroom looked as if they had run late in leaving. Goopy toothpaste marked both sinks and the towels hung bunched over the rails. I'd need to change the towels and do some straightening up in here before Viv came home. Come to think of it, they probably had a cleaning service. I almost remembered her saying something about it.

I poked through the drawers in the sink vanity—I didn't recognize the brand names of the make-up. They looked expensive. The plain white jar of Pond's cold cream in the back of the drawer looked like an old friend.

Sticking my head into the two walk-in closets, I didn't spot anything worth investigating. Dear George evidently stacked his blue jeans by degree of fadedness: light to dark in a stack above his blue shirts and white shirts and grey suits. They smelled faintly of George's piney aftershave. Viv's things—not nearly as well organized—had the ticklish, talcum scent of shoes and perfume and clean laundry.

I returned to the bedside table on Viv's side. Under a *Vogue* magazine, I found an oversized paperback entitled *What to Expect When You're Expecting*. Under it was a book of baby names with little slips of paper stuck into the pages. The relief was intoxicating.

A ghostly single *woof* rose from the backyard. I jammed everything back into the drawer and ran downstairs to let the dogs in. Their fur was cold and smelled of autumn. They looked at me as if I'd forgotten something important.

I asked them, "What? What is it, dogs?" but they just kept looking at me attentively, their ears up and the wrinkles twice as deep between their eyes. I looked out the back door, but the lawn was empty. "What?"

Then I remembered that it was their dinnertime too. Way to be a good dog-sitter.

Chapter 11

I WAS in the shower when the phone rang. I let the machine get it. It was past 10:30. I'd had enough of the telephone for one day.

Hot water was pouring over me and the conditioner was chasing through my hair and down my skin when a jolt of adrenaline kicked through me. What if it was the hospital? I bolted out of the glass bath-enclosure, leaving a trail of water to the kitchen. The dogs jumped up and raced along with me, nearly tangling with my legs.

I punched the blinking red light.

"Vivian? It's me. Hey, if you're there, pick up." The man had waited for a count of ten. "Call me when you get in. I've got something for you."

It was the same guy who'd called before. He still hadn't left a name or a number.

ONE full year after our parents left, I twisted my ankle badly during an indoor field-hockey game in gym class.

When Mr. Greveau, the vice principal, couldn't reach anybody on the telephone at home, he had me wait in his office. Still in my gym shorts, I sat on one chair with my fattening ankle iced and wrapped and propped up on another hard wooden chair while he perched on his desk above me.

Mr. Greveau was almost handsome. Younger than most of the other teachers, he had a thick head of wavy hair and a constant five o'clock shadow. He wore sweater-vests with short-sleeve polyester-blend shirts that revealed muscular arms and a pudgy middle. His glasses darkened automatically in the sun. They always had a slight tint, which made it hard to be sure what he was looking at.

Among the junior-high girls, he had a reputation for being "kind of creepy." He often fiddled with his mustache as he patrolled the school, petting it with his fingers or smoothing it with his lower lip.

After trying the home number a couple of times—I told him, quite sincerely, that that's where my mother *should* be—Mr. Greveau asked me how to reach my father. Only he said, "Where's Dad?" which startled me somehow and made me wish I'd been allowed to wait in the nurse's office. I told him that my father worked construction and that I didn't know where the jobsite was.

Mr. Greveau knelt to look at my ankle and held a hand three or four inches away from my bare leg, as if he would brush my shin with the palms of his hands. "Are you comfortable?" he asked, in a strange, too-smooth voice. He didn't touch my skin, so I tried to tell myself it was my imagination, but it was definitely creepy.

The clacking of high heels sounded outside the door. A secretary, probably, passing by on her way someplace.

He stood and propped one haunch against his desk. "I'd drive you home myself so your parents could take care of you," he said, idly sliding a piece of paper back and forth across the bare surface of his desk. "But if no one is home, I can't very well just leave you there. All by yourself."

"I can take the bus."

"I think your folks would want you to get home."

"Maybe my sister can take me," I said. "She's got her own car."

Mr. Greveau looked up from his papers suddenly. "Your sister?"

"She's a senior," I said.

"Maybe she knows where your mother is."

"I told you, Mom's probably just out doing some shopping. Or maybe visiting Aunt Nan at Brown Manor. She's there when we get home from school."

Mr. Greveau walked around to the proper side of his desk. He picked up the telephone. I tried to look bored.

Within twenty minutes, Viv was standing in the doorway of Mr. Greveau's office. Her face was flushed, and she hurried over to lift the ice pack from my foot. "Are you okay?"

"Yeah," I said. "But nobody is home to answer the phone—"

"And we thought your baby sister might need to go to the doctor," Mr. Greveau said, rising from the desk. He put out a hand to shake hers. "Miss Jones?"

Viv barely glanced at him. She was looking at my leg. I could tell she was itching to get her hands on my injured foot.

Mr. Greveau took a long look at my sister. He mouthed the edge of his mustache with his lower lip. He stepped closer and his voice was smooth, sing-songy. "Miss Jones, Miss Jones, Miss Jones."

Viv lowered the icepack gently onto my ankle. Her eyes met mine before she turned to face the vice principal.

Mr. Greveau took a step closer, his hand still extended in greeting.

Viv shook his hand.

"Do you know where your mom is?" He leaned toward her as he spoke, not letting go of her hand. Despite the tinted glasses, we both could tell that he was eyeing her body.

Viv never hesitated. "If she's not in Watertown shopping or at the assisted living place where our aunt stays, she might be at Mrs. Humphrey's."

She lifted her hand and he released it from the handshake. She turned to address me, an expression of disbelief and disgust passing rapidly across her face. "Did you try that number, Nicola?"

I shook my head.

"Can I use the phone?" Viv asked the vice principal. She tossed her hair and stretched a little farther than she needed to reach the telephone. Mr. Greveau nodded, his attention on my sister.

"Dial nine first?" she asked, with an arch look. He nodded again and then pretended to look for something on his desk, staying too near Viv.

My sister pressed a series of numbers quickly and then she waited, drumming her fingers and sighing with showy feigned impatience. She even plucked her sweater away from her side, arching her back as she did. Mr. Greveau couldn't look away.

In the quiet of the office, I heard the intonation of someone saying "Hello?" at the other end, and Viv started bubbling away. "Mrs. Humphrey? Hi. It's Vivian. Hey, is Mom there?"

The voice on the other end of the telephone spoke at length.

Viv answered, "Oh. She did?"

Viv looked at me and sent me an exaggerated look of mock annoyance.

"Okay—No, that's all right. I'll call her—No? Oh. Huh. Well, then. Okay. Okay. Bye-Bye." Viv hung up. She shook her head ruefully at me. "Mom's on her way home, but she was going to the Manor first."

Mr. Greveau looked up at Viv's face for a moment, then gazed expectantly at me.

"I told you before, Aunt Nan is at Brown Manor Assisted Living," I said. It was one of the "facts" that Viv had come up with that year: our mother shopped a lot, we had an aunt in the nursing home in the next town over, and our father was always just about to get back from his construction job.

Viv bit her lip as if she was concentrating very hard. Then she gave a start—evidently, a thought had just come to her. "If we leave now, we can catch Mom at the Manor and then *she* can decide if Nicola needs to go to the emergency room."

I swung my foot off the chair and stood. Viv half-turned and bent at the waist to pick up her rucksack from the floor. Her legs were very long, and she took her time. She must have been practicing this move in front of a mirror.

Mr. Greveau opened and closed his mouth without saying anything.

"I'll have Mom give you a call, all right?" Viv said, pirouetting around to face him.

He cleared his throat.

Viv gave him her widest smile and nodded. She waved at him. Her voice was loud and cheerful. "Nice meeting you, Mr. Greveau!"

My sister helped me hobble down the hall and out the big doors. Outside, she made extravagant pretend vomit faces, silently acking up hairballs while I tried not to laugh out loud. She helped me into the Datsun and reached across my torso to fasten my seatbelt for me. "Here, little girl," she said breathing on me, imitating Mr. Greveau's smarmy voice, "let me get that for you."

I slapped her hand and said, with broad girlish charm, "Oh, Mr. Greveau, so *nice* meeting you!"

She slammed my door and strode around to the driver's side. She popped the key into the ignition, but before turning on the engine, she looked at me, sobering. "Are you okay? He didn't scare you, did he?"

"No," I said. "He was just—creepy."

"Yeah," she said, and started the car. "Eww."

She left the visitor's parking at a sedate pace.

"Who did you call?" I said as we left the parking lot, Viv's turn-indicator flashing dutifully after our one-Mississippi-two-Mississippi-three-Mississippi stop in view of the school windows.

"Mrs. Humphrey."

"Who's that?"

"I have no earthly idea," she said. "I just switched the last two digits for our house and got some poor, confused lady who is probably still scratching her head."

"That's luck."

"Maybe, but I had a little thing all ready to do. 'Oh, my gosh! What number did I dial?' if no one picked up." She suited action to words, pulling her shoulders back and tossing her hair. "And if that didn't work, I would have said something spacey, like, 'Jeepers, I am so worried about my sister, I must have forgotten the phone number!'"

"I can't believe he believed you."

"Believed me? He was too busy drooling to hear anything," Viv said. She made a contemptuous noise.

"Miss Jones, Miss Jones, Miss Jones," I said, leering.

My sister laughed and simpered at me. "Why Mr. Greveau, what dark glasses you have! And what a big mustache!"

"All the better to gross you out with!" I said. Then I shuddered involuntarily.

Viv gave me a worried sidelong glance. She made a quick left and right, pulling into the parking lot of the little grocery store in town. She turned off the engine and, still stamping on the brake and the clutch, frowned at me.

She said, "Are you okay? Really okay, no joke?"

Instead of answering, I asked her, "How did you know?"

"How did I know he was creepy? Or how did I know I could manage him?"

I shrugged.

"Okay, it's like this. There are plenty of creepy people out there." She absently confirmed that the gearstick was in reverse and set the parking brake. She eased her feet off the pedals. "Stay there."

She came around and opened my car door. She had me spin so that she could unwrap my ankle as she continued her lecture, "No matter how you try, you can't really avoid them. You just never know who's going to be awful. It's like fate. But you can make sure it's hard for them to catch you."

She had my bare foot in her hand. "Push against my palm. Does that hurt? Okay. Now, if you can, rotate your foot. That hurts? Hmm." She pressed her fingertips on the swollen ankle and frowned. She re-wrapped my ankle quickly.

"So, someone like Mr. Greveau? He likes being the boss and—obviously—he likes to leer at girls. Whether he would do more than just leer? Let's just say I wouldn't trust him as far as I could put my boot up his ass."

We smiled at each other. The phrase was one of Jahn's favorites. Viv closed my door and got into the driver's seat again.

"But there was two of us, we were on school property, and there was a secretary on the other side of the door." Viv ticked these points off with a fingernail on the steering wheel. "So with the flirty thing, I figured he wasn't going to put the moves on me right there in his office." She started the car and pulled back on the street. "You need to get an X-ray. I think it's just a sprain, but you'll probably need a splint."

"But—"

"How to deal with Mr. Greveau? For one thing, don't get in trouble between now and the end of the school year."

"But—"

My sister poked her finger into my knee. "Just keep your head down. Travel in a pack."

By "a pack," she meant the two girls from the babysitting class at the cooperative extension. We'd become cautious friends, the three of us not quite fitting in with the rest of the eighth graders. I'd begun talking on the telephone with them for chunks of time, though we hadn't gotten to the point of inviting one another over to our houses. Viv never remembered their names.

"If he tries to get you alone, don't go. If you start to feel weird, don't ignore the feeling. Don't get embarrassed. You're smarter than that. Just get yourself away from him. Say *no* really, really loudly."

I nodded.

My sister gave me a wicked look. "Seriously, say *no*."

"No! Non! Nein!" I shouted. "But how can we afford an X-ray?"

"We have emergency money. Plus, Dr. Carbone comes into The Pit Stop for breakfast every weekend."

My sister looked at me out of the corner of her eye. "Don't worry. I've got a plan."

Chapter 12

I OPENED my eyes in the wee smalls to the sound of the dogs' stentorian breathing. A scrap of dream eluded me, and I tried to drift along after those confused images. Then a thought came to me: I should try spelling a message into my sister's palm.

In middle school, Viv read a biography of Helen Keller. At around the same time she found a little card that illustrated the alphabet in American Sign Language. Of course, she made sure I knew it, too.

We'd used sign language for the silent alphabet game when we were in the truck with Jahn and Magda. The game was a mix of I Spy and Charades using the alphabet. The goal was to spot one thing outside the window for each letter. Not much of a game, granted, but the challenge was in getting through the alphabet without saying a word out loud, since chatter irritated Jahn. Viv said he was just a bully and a drunk, but we all tried not to rile him up.

Every trip passed with the four of us sitting in cramped silence on the slippery bench seat of the truck. Wedged between Magda and my sister, I found it easy to lose myself daydreaming, but Viv often broke into my reverie. A nudge from her knee and then her hand would form the first three letters of the alphabet: a fist for A, a wall with the fingers for B, a crooked semi-circle of C.

We took turns: Viv might fake a yawn and pretend to eat an apple when she spotted an apple tree along the road, while I chewed like a cow when I spotted green B for bales of hay dotting the field outside the windshield. We spelled the answers into one another's hands, an activity that Jahn mostly ignored unless it interfered with us handing him beer from the cooler at our feet.

C for cows was ruled out—too easy—though I sometimes called C for calf, which Viv allowed if I could imitate a calf convincingly. Once, when Viv portrayed a goose with the very slightest change of expression and a subtle arching of her neck, I laughed out loud.

Jahn couldn't, in all honesty, find much to discipline me in that, but the giggles slid out of control the way they sometimes do. I tried suppressing them, but it only made it worse.

Viv egged me on at first, giving me a haughty look from the corner of her eye, so very like a goose I imagined she would honk next.

Then, after my face was hot and the tamped-down laughter had gone into snorts and gasps and Jahn had asked me what I thought was so funny for the third or fourth time, his voice growing dangerously irritated, it was her turn. My tee-heeing was finally trailing away like a teakettle losing steam and she was just starting. She tried to cough to cover it up, but before long, *she* was shaking helplessly and making snuffling sounds.

Which made me start laughing again, which in turn egged her on.

Naturally, Jahn was not amused. "You'll think it's so funny when I drive the truck into the ditch," he said. Eventually, when we were both still leaking aimless little noises of suppressed laughter, he yanked the truck over onto the sloping gravel shoulder.

"Enough," he said. "I see the two of you cannot ride like civilized people. You'll get in the back like a pair of mangy dogs."

Jahn kept both hands clenched on the wheel. He stared straight ahead. Magda silently reached across our knees and popped the door handle. Viv hopped down and held the door for me against the blustery March weather while I slid over. I was not giggling any more. It was a long, empty stretch of road, with deep ditches and not even a bare old elm trunk to slow the wind.

Magda came out after us, bracing the door with her hip as she reached behind the seat for the wool emergency blanket. She handed this to my sister without a word and waited as Viv and I climbed over the tailgate. When we settled in, she gave us an apologetic little smile. She wouldn't stand up to Jahn for us, but she'd try to soften the punishment. As soon as she let the wind wallop the truck door shut behind her, Jahn peeled out.

Viv tucked the scratchy blanket around us both. We slouched into the shelter of the toolbox, silent for a while as we jounced along. Then, though her hair was whipping around her head and her nose was already pink with cold, Viv stretched her neck, eyeing me with the suspicious look of a big white goose, and she honked twice. I shouted with laughter and relief.

We abandoned the alphabet game and sang instead, our voices loud and happy against the big gusts of wind.

VIV didn't react to my spelling W-A-K-E-U-P into her palm. Her hand stayed limp. The machinery kept *whoosh-whooshing* and *peeping*. Disappointment was like a punch. After a rough moment, I started to untangle Viv's hair, careful not to tug her poor scalp. I spoke aloud to her as I wove a sage-green ribbon into the loose braid. I dabbed some colored lip balm around the cuts on her chapped lips.

It was a little close to playing with dolls, I told her, a practice she scorned. But on the other hand, we both knew if it were *me* holding so still and her with the makeup bag, I'd end up with a goofy ponytail on the top of my head and a handlebar mustache painted on with waterproof mascara.

IT WAS Viv who taught me how to use makeup that first summer after our parents left. She brought home a treasure trove of samples from the cosmetics counter of Empsall's department store and tried half a dozen looks on me.

Viv upended the shopping bag of miniature lipsticks, tiny packets of foundation in an array of beiges, sample tubes and flat disks of color encased in clear plastic, diminutive mascara wands and brown brow pencils. She gathered our hairbrushes and set up the bureau mirror on the kitchen table.

"This is you as Miss de Larcey," Viv said, giving me the teased hair and kittenish black eyeliner of her French teacher. "This is you as Mrs. Frandon," she announced, turning me to the mirror so I could see the perfect circles of rouge and the sharp boundary between foundation orange and my own pale skin along the jaw line, which was, sadly, the look favored by the band leader at school. Viv painted my eyelids silvery blue and clumped on the mascara and said, "This is you as Kindra

Janders, tenth-grade slut. Guess what? You *will* be flunking algebra and social studies again."

She scooped up a blob of Pond's cold cream and demonstrated how to take off the makeup. "I know you are the artist and all," she said, gently wiping my face, "but let me show you how to do this the right way." She reminded me to pat my face dry and not to pull at the skin. When both our faces were clean and dry, she told me that we were lucky not to need much liquid foundation.

"Heavy foundation tends to cause breakouts," she said with authority. "But a little blush won't hurt."

She circled pink powder onto her cheekbones and mine and then, selecting a tiny foam brush, she dabbed color along the edge of first mine and then her own long eyelids, a grayish blue that flattered her gray eyes and my blue ones.

"Just a little color, not too much, right at the edge of the lash-line, is the most subtle look." Then she feathered mascara along my lashes. "You make them darker, but not much thicker, see? You work from the inside out, like that."

A swipe of color for our lips, coral for my pale face and pink for hers. We smiled at each other in the mirror, our glamorous smoky eyes meeting over sets of identical overlapped eye-teeth in our matching and reflected mouths.

DR. PETE knocked lightly on the doorframe before coming into the room. He said hello to me as he looked at Viv's chart.

"No change," I reported.

"Well, it's early days," he said, patting Viv's feet.

"How long do 'early days' usually last?"

Dr. Pete beckoned me into the hall.

"It's never certain how much an unconscious person can understand, so I don't like to talk about your sister's condition in there." He took his glasses off and rubbed his neck for a moment. When his eyelids shut, his face slid into lines of fatigue. But when his eyes opened, he appeared perfectly awake.

Dr. Pete said, "Your sister's injuries are severe. I wish I could tell you more, but we are in a hold pattern. For perhaps a couple of weeks."

"Weeks?"

He slumped against the wall. "I know. We just have to wait and see." Then he straightened and said, "I spoke with the people at our office. News traveled pretty quickly through the hospital about Viv. Ms. Walsingham, the office manager, will leave you a message at the home phone if something comes up—with insurance, or paperwork, anything like that."

"Okay. Thanks," I said.

"I didn't contact Viv's church. I think Arthur Slate will handle that, but I did ask the hospital chaplain to check in."

"He did." The chaplain, a vague, sandy-colored man, had offered to pray for my sister and left me a handful of brochures about support services. I'd accepted both as standard hospital service and not given it a second thought.

"And that's about it. The partners and I have divided up your sister's caseload. Even if she wakes up perfectly healthy this minute, she's not scheduled to work until well after the baby is born."

"Actually, do you know when she's due?"

Dr. Pete paused before answering. "Her official due date is January 4. She said she hoped not to have a Christmas baby."

"Oh. Yes, of course."

"Excuse me, Dr. Pete?" A short, freckled doctor approached us. "Sorry to interrupt. When you get a chance?" He hooked a thumb over his shoulder and nodded at Dr. Pete.

"Duty calls," he told me, with an apologetic smile.

"And never uses the answering machine," I replied.

Dr. Pete's smile widened into a big grin. "That's what your sister always says!"

"I know!" I said, feeling my own lips stretch in a smile to echo his. It was one of the dumb jokes Viv and I had been telling each other for ages.

"I'll be back later on, with a team of other doctors and residents," Dr. Pete said, looking at his bare wrist. "After lunch."

"I'll be here," I called after him as he hurried down the hall.

Chapter 13

AFTER settling the covers over Viv's legs and then crawling around behind the bedside table to find an outlet, I started the boom-box I'd brought from Viv's house. The one cassette tape in Viv's car was Charlie Parker. I'm not a jazz fan, but Charlie Parker's sax made the room seem less like a hospital.

I had forgotten to bring my sketchbook or even a magazine to flip through. I found myself looking forward to anyone coming through the doorway. It was terrible to realize how little I could do for my sister.

"Hey, sis," I said. "How about we read a book together?"

WE'D shared every book that passed through our hands when we were little. Not just the essential titles, like the big dictionary and the *Emily Post's Etiquette* that moved with us, but anything we discovered. It was part of the ritual of moving: Viv and I would scour the new rooms for good reading material.

She resisted coddling me when I was first learning to read. "You can read that," she'd tell me, and in a very short time, I could.

Some evenings, I'd bring a book to her and ask for help. "That's too babyish," she'd tell me, dismissing the easy picture books. "Bring a harder one and I'll help you."

So I'd retrieve a thicker book—the red linen-covered volume of Grimm's fairy tales with its colorful illustrated plates, say—and settle at the foot of her bed. Before long, I'd be struggling to sound out an unfamiliar phrase. "What's this word?" I'd ask. "What does that mean?"

As often as not, she'd give in and take the book from me, reading aloud the story of Clever Hans or Hansel and Gretel. She'd go fast at first, sighing heavily when I asked for clarification, but before long she'd settle into it, her voice growing breathy and dramatic as the story turned dangerous.

"So what *should* Hansel and Gretel have done?" I would ask her at the end, to prolong the time. She relished cracking the hard shell of the old stories, picking out the lessons she thought we should know.

"Terrible things happen," she told me. "Sometimes it means that it's the children's job to take care of each other."

She suggested that Hansel and Gretel were not very bright and should have paid closer attention to the warnings they heard when they were gobbling on the witch's house. Then she admitted that the witch *had* devised the cake-cottage just so that she could capture children to eat.

When I said that it was all the fault of the woodcutter's awful wife, Viv laughed. "Who else are you going to blame?" she said. "The hungry birds that ate the breadcrumbs?"

When I persisted, saying the trouble was really started with the woodcutter, Viv gave me a long, serious look. "It's just a story about how rotten things happen. Okay? Terrible things happen and it's by luck and hard work that Hansel and Gretel survive."

As I became a better reader, Viv and I talked through all the books we read. I could always get Viv to talk by asking her what a story meant, what it *really* meant. She would put her own book down with a finger holding her place and say, "You tell me."

I would describe the three brothers who went to seek their fortune and how the first two failed but the third succeeded because he was kind to the small animals he met.

"What does that tell you?" Viv would ask.

"That being polite is better than being mean?"

"Okay, and what else?"

"That the youngest one is always luckiest?"

Viv would laugh and ask me a few more questions with her finger still marking her place in her own book until she was satisfied that I had gleaned every morsel from the story.

If she was feeling uncommonly generous, she'd let me stay with her, both of us reading silently until she was ready to turn out her light and send me to my own bed.

I BROUGHT coffee back to Viv's room and started to tell her about the cafeteria's selection of doughnuts. Not that my sister ever spent time listening to talk about food.

Trisha, on the other hand—that girl could rhapsodize about cheese fries versus gravy fries for ten minutes at a clip.

I told Viv I'd be back and made for the telephone room, which was tucked near the staff break room. A short phone booth took up one corner, the glass privacy panels on either side giving it the look of a modern triptych. No one was using the phone. I closed the door behind me, dialed the toll-free number of Trisha's company, and asked to be connected to Ms. Cutillo.

Would Miss Cutillo know what this was in reference to, Miss Jones?

Yes, *Ms.* Cutillo most definitely would.

I got a kick out of messing with the receptionist at Trisha's work. She probably recognized my voice, whether I announced myself by my own name or with one of the accented inventions Trisha and I had come up with, like frosty Brit researcher Jill Sinjin or South Indian Dr. Chitra Watanakunacorn because the receptionist never got the names right.

I waited in the echoing silence of hold, then Trisha's strong, rusty voice started without preliminaries. "Nicky! I just tried calling you and your housemate said you were in Nashville!"

"I am."

"What is it? Good grief, tell me you haven't moved again!"

I cleared my throat, but Trisha kept talking. "Are you okay?" Trisha always sounded like a cheerleader after a big game, her voice hoarse and seeming to skip a few notes as she talked.

"Yes. But there's been a car accident." I caught my breath and tried to get into the rhythm of it, as I had done with Viv's friends the night before.

"Is—is everyone all right?" Trisha asked.

"No."

"Nicky!" I pictured Trisha standing at the very end of the curly telephone cord, a hand over her mouth.

I told her Dear George had been killed. Then I told her that Viv was still unconscious in intensive care.

"When did it happen?" she asked. "How long has Viv been in the hospital?"

"Since Sunday morning. "

"This Sunday?" she asked. "The day before yesterday?" Trisha had what I like to think of as a low tolerance for chaos. She focused on facts. As a rule, she needed to know exactly how things happened, or were going to happen, step-by-step, without gaps or guesses.

"Yeah," I said.

"So it's been two days?" she asked.

It seemed longer. I nodded and then confirmed her math out loud.

"Oh my God, though," Trisha said. "What are you going to do about her husband?"

"Uh, I guess..." Trisha had me stumped there. "A funeral?"

"Very funny. But what about Viv?" She gave me a minute to think. I could tell she was pacing from one end of her desk to the other. "You aren't going to bury her husband while she's out cold, are you?"

"He wanted to be cremated, actually—" Trisha started to interrupt, but I cut her off. "You remember George's friend Arthur Slate?"

"The lawyer, the cute one? Rico Suavé?"

"That's the one. He's handling the arrangements. We're going to have a thing at the funeral home Saturday and then the actual—you know—later, but we haven't scheduled that yet."

"Good. And what about Viv? Do the doctors know how long until she wakes up? What happened?"

I didn't mention the pregnancy as I explained what I knew about the accident. We'd be needing a whole chunk of time to discuss Viv having a child. Instead, I focused on describing Viv's injuries and the surgery.

"Is there like a, I don't know, whatever, a brain specialist? Should she be at a bigger hospital?"

"Yes, there is one, but no—I think the hospital is fine."

I heard Trisha flop into her chair. "Tell me."

"The short story? They don't know. They don't know how long it's going to be until she'll wakes up, or, you know, anything, actually." I didn't say out loud that the doctors didn't how bad the brain damage was going to be. Trisha had the decency to not ask more about the injuries, which I knew was an effort for her.

"How about you? Are you okay?" she asked.

"I'm not in the hospital, so that's a plus."

"Ha, ha. But you are in the hospital. I can hear the P.A. system. Are you freaked out?"

"Can I say 'no'?" I asked.

"You can say whatever, but I'm flying down." Trisha's voice took on volume as she made her decision. "What do you need me to bring?"

"No—wait, yeah. Trisha, can you really come?"

"I'm going to stay home and do what? Of course I'm coming down. Frequent flyer miles and comp time, babe! Gotta cash 'em while you got 'em. And speaking of which, do you have a dark suit to wear at the funeral home? Do you want me to borrow one for you?"

"No, thanks. I'll get something down here."

"Okay, but—" Trisha had little faith in my sense of style.

"I know, I know," I interrupted her. "It will be something serious and tasteful and dark."

"So, what color is your hair these days?" She had helped me return my hair to normal after a one-time-only fire-engine-red experiment our sophomore year in college and she never let me forget it.

We stayed on the phone, and she answered my questions about her life, the current Mr. Boyfriend from Jersey City, the latest acquisitions for the corporate art collection she worked on, her four brothers and the rest of her big family in Brooklyn.

My shoulders relaxed as she talked. She was like a little island of certainty I hadn't realized I needed to reach. Eventually, another call buzzed in, so she hung up, promising to leave a message at the house with her flight information.

Chapter 14

AT LUNCHTIME, I walked to the parking lot where I'd left my sister's Saab. As I slid into the squeaking leather seats, I wondered how long she'd had it. The odometer showed nearly six thousand miles.

After she bought her first new car after med school—a low, ridiculously racy-looking silver Nissan sports car that George refused to ride in—she had telephoned in the middle of the week to tell me how new the car smelled and how strange it was to be the first owner. She'd even mailed a snapshot of it to me with a note on the back that said, "Everything works!"

Viv loved to drive, had always piloted her car with spirit. She'd gotten a real kick out of the sense of speed and competition even in the old orange Datsun she drove through college. She'd change gears fast and mean around corners and up inclines, pushing the gearshift casually with an open hand, her feet as precise as dancers on the pedals.

She had been stopped often when she drove the silver Nissan but had talked her way out of every speeding ticket. "Pulling the doctor card," she'd say, when she told me about it on the phone. "Because even doctors need to get to the mall in a hurry."

Had my sister outgrown the excitement of celebrating a major purchase? She didn't have to set aside dollars in an envelope for gas these days, so maybe getting herself a new car like this Saab was not such a big deal anymore.

Or maybe it was me. The thought like an icicle to the chest. Maybe she didn't want to share the excitement with *me*.

I clashed the gears trying to shift into reverse. People walking at the other end of the parking lot turned to look. I felt my face flush with embarrassment. I took a minute to breathe. I pushed the clutch all the way to the floor and made sure I'd found reverse before I tried again.

My sister had never wrecked a car, never even had a fender-bender through those icy winters of our youth. She had an athlete's reflexes and skill at gauging acceleration and convergence. And she'd been lucky, I realized, as I threaded the curves of Viv's housing development. I pulled into Viv's driveway with considerably less verve than my sister. As she told me at my very first efforts behind the wheel, I drove like an old lady.

THE dogs were not expecting me. They put in a belated appearance at the mudroom door when I pulled into the garage. I opened the back door for them, and they seemed to sleep-walk through their routine of sniffing the perimeter of the lawn and looking around suspiciously.

The answering machine had a bunch of calls: hang-ups, the minister from St. Bart's asked that I give him a jingle when I had the chance, my friend Elaine in Florida wishing me good luck, Trisha with her flight details, a woman who said, "Dr. Rowan, I'm calling to touch base about that trip in December," before reciting her number.

The rest were messages from—I assumed—friends of Viv. One said, "Call me if there's anything I can do." Another just left a number and the third was a weepy-sounding woman who said, "I'm just so, so, so, so, so sorry about your loss," without identifying herself.

I replayed the messages, imagining that Viv would have erased the last message without a second thought. But "that trip in December"? What trip? I jotted the number down, crossed it off, picked up the phone, hung up, then picked it back up and dialed the number. A few rings later, I was leaving a message of my own.

"This is Vivian Rowan's sister. Can you tell me about the trip my sister scheduled for December?" I said to the recorder, as if I had every right to ask.

The hang-up calls bothered me. I needed to change the outgoing message.

Full sunshine streaming in through the windows made the house seem even more sterile and empty. It was a relief to have the dogs back inside. They, in turn, were happy to eat the crusts from my grilled cheese sandwich.

I RETURNED to the hospital with a heavy satchel over my shoulder and a large white bakery box held in front of me like a tray. I slid the box onto the nurses' station counter and was borrowing a marker to write "Thank You, ICU" across the box when Dr. Pete stepped out of the elevator. I signed Viv's name on the box with my own in parenthesis underneath.

I opened the box and invited Dr. Pete and the crabby nurse and an older doctor in a lab coat who was walking by to have a pastry. I almost suggested that they "Have at!" as they hesitated but stopped myself.

I plucked a cherry turnover from the untidy arrangement to get them started. Dr. Pete selected a small cream puff and engulfed it in one bite. A trio of other doctors arrived, and Dr. Pete snagged and downed a second pastry without apology. He led the small group of white coats into Viv's room, introducing me as he went, explaining to me that they were part of Viv's surgical care and neurology team.

One, the chubby man with freckles who had called Dr. Pete away earlier, had a smudge of powdered sugar on his upper lip. He lifted Viv's eyelid with a thumb, his movements all economy as he shone a tiny flashlight into her eye. The whites of her eye, which I hadn't seen before, were as red as stop-signs.

"Are they supposed to be that color?" I asked.

"Hmm?" the doctor said, not glancing up from Viv's face.

"Are her eyes supposed to be red like that?"

All the doctors looked to Dr. Pete, who cleared his throat and nodded encouragement. The freckled doctor started explaining. "With injuries like this, we often see broken blood vessels in the sclera. It's caused either directly by the concussion, or as a result of contre-coup injury."

I glanced at Dr. Pete who had moved to stand at the foot of Viv's bed. "What's a contre-coup injury?" I asked.

"*Contre-coup* is a description of something that happens very commonly with head injuries. It's like in pool." The freckled doctor looked into my face then, as if seeing me for the first time. He said, "Have you played pool—billiards—at all?"

Yes, certainly I had.

"When you hit a ball, energy travels through the ball and out the opposite side from where it was struck. It's similar with the brain. The energy of a blow on one side of the skull travels through and exits or rebounds on the other side of the skull. That's the contre-coup."

"I see," I said. It was all too clear, really. The bite of cherry turnover weighed heavy in my stomach. "What are you doing now?" I asked as the doctor uncovered my sister's feet.

He looked at Dr. Pete and then continued. "The plantar reflex is a basic neurological test. We run a pen or some other sharp object on the bottom of your sister's foot. What we are watching for is a reaction, such as the toes drawing in."

My sister's foot twitched in the doctor's hand.

The freckled doctor's lips compressed for a moment. He tried her other foot. In the long pause, Dr. Pete piped up. "Well, that response is not ideal, but it's still early days, yet."

I felt my head nodding in stupid agreement. Early days.

I watched as Dr. Pete clicked his pen and wrote a few notes on the clipboard that hung from the end of Viv's bed.

Dr. Pete asked if I had any questions for the team, which I did. I might have saved my breath. I should have started by asking if *they* had any *answers*.

The team didn't know when she would wake, and they couldn't guess what she was feeling or hearing right now. They were all enthusiastic about Viv's brain activity, but they didn't know what her recovery would be like or when they might have a better idea.

Dr. Pete waited for a moment after the others had left. He seemed genuinely regretful that he couldn't give me any definite answers. "It's difficult, I know, but we must give her time."

Chapter 15

I UNLOADED the satchel I'd brought from Viv's house. A big pottery mug for tea, plus teabags. I pulled out the handful of jazz cassettes I'd found in the stereo cabinet in the living room and stowed them in my sister's bedside drawer. I traded the visitor's chair in her room for one that didn't squeak from an empty room down the hall.

I scotch-taped a photo of Viv and Dear George in goofy spelunking gear over her bed, where everyone could see it.

George used to brag to his friends about how, as a climber, Viv never panicked and never, ever quit. The two of them had bagged almost all the peaks in North Georgia and the Blue Ridge when they lived in Atlanta. During the past few years in Tennessee, they had taken up cave climbing. It was something George loved talking about, how her steadiness had brought them home through broken lights, injuries, lost paths, unexpected snow. He was so proud of my stubborn sister.

The flash from the camera gave them a startled and slightly foreshortened look, in keeping with the surreal rock formations behind them and the miner's lamps strapped to their heads.

The nurse, Lisa, smiled widely when she looked at the picture. I was still unloading things from the bag: fancy French moisturizing lotion, a sweater for me, a fluffy throw, Viv's boar-bristle hairbrush.

"It's looking very homey in here," Lisa commented.

"Might as well be comfortable," I said. "Did you get something to eat?"

She shook her head. "Watching my figure." She was bent over the clipboard as she wrote. "You don't need to bribe us to take care of her, you know." She looked up with a smile and continued, "But it's okay if it makes you feel better to feed us."

"It does," I said. And in truth, it gave me pleasure to see people enjoying food I served.

"Don't turn into a little happy homemaker," Viv used to scold when she thought I was being too domestic. "Look what good it did Magda."

AFTER our parents left in the spring of 1980, we put away the dorky gingham dresses. We cut our yardstick-long hair. We made the first independent purchases of our lives. I got a cheap watercolor set and a block of rag paper. Viv bought a rusty orange Datsun for six hundred dollars from the brother of one of the other waitresses at The Pit Stop.

While we were weeding the vegetable garden, I told Viv I'd signed up for the babysitting safety certification course at the county cooperative extension. I confessed that I wanted to take the canning class, too.

"They're free," I said.

"What else? Do they offer dish-washing lessons? Are you going to major in Home Ec?" Viv asked. "Join the Future Homemakers of America?"

"No," I said, clinging to my dignity. "But I think I can make some money anyway."

I held my breath, knowing that her disdain for Magda ("She's a sheep!") bled over into any ambition that seemed too focused on food or home. Viv frequently reminded me that "anyone can cook and clean and take care of kids. And if anyone can do it, I'll be damned if I'll waste *my* time on it."

It was a secret satisfaction to me that she was, however, quite happy to eat what I cooked.

My sister stooped over the tomato plants, plucking fat green caterpillars and flinging them into a small pitcher of water where they could drown in all their disgusting glory. She looked over her shoulder at me. "And?"

"Since I can't get a working permit until I'm fourteen—" I was thinning the row of carrots, but I saw her nodding for me to keep talking. "If I get a table at the farmer's market this summer, I can sell stuff. Strawberry jam, pickles, pictures."

Viv plopped several caterpillars into the water. "I don't know," she said. "I wonder how much jam it would take to pay the electric bill?"

I didn't answer.

After a minute, her voice took on a lecturing tone. "I don't know if it will work, but what's the worst that can happen?"

Before she began to elaborate, I interrupted, "The class is free, so the risk is around $20 dollars in supplies and the fee for the table, and we could end up with a bunch of strawberry goop in the refrigerator."

She stood straight and put both green-stained hands on her hips. She stretched and grinned at me. "A plan! I like it, Nicky."

That summer, my sister worked long hours at The Pit Stop and I babysat for days at a time. I liked kids—

loved them, actually. I watched my first hours of television with the families I was looking after, and I tagged along with Viv to see our first movies.

When not babysitting, I was picking or canning fruit. Once a week I manned a table at the farmer's market where I produced sketches to order from photos—dog portraits and architectural renderings were popular. And I sold jar after jar of preserves.

Mornings when neither of us was working, Viv drove us to rummage sales and second-hand shops, where we picked out our own clothes without the noisy disapproval of our father or the silent pressure of our mother.

At the Salvation Army thrift, we found chunky sweaters and worn men's Levi's that made me feel tall rather than just gawky. I remember catching sight of myself and briefly not recognizing the leggy, normal-looking girl in the dressing-room mirror.

Viv bought us both heavy navy-issue pea coats and then got the matching, thirteen-button wool trousers for herself. At a garage sale, Viv snapped up a pair of unworn Frye boots with stacked heels and paired them for years with long corduroy or plaid skirts.

She wore things with such assurance. She chose the neutral colors that, even now, filled her closet. Black, camel, and the charcoal gray that made her eyes look big and vivid.

I don't remember her experimenting or making the usual fashion mistakes. Her French teacher—Miss de Larcey of the kittenish eyeliner—had given her a stack of Paris-edition *Vogue* magazines, which she absorbed like water. It was as if she had suddenly grown a third arm that summer, only instead of an extra limb, she had good taste. She steered me away from home perms, prairie shirts, and the whole yellow-green family of colors that made me look ill.

Later, when she was attending med school in New York City and I was an unhappy undergraduate at SUNY Stony Brook, we sometimes met on weekends to cruise the thrift shops that used to fill Greenwich Village.

"Try this on," Viv commanded, pushing something unlikely at me—a long dress, say, or a frilly top—while I was trapped in a changing booth. I'd grumble, but it was always interesting to see what she'd pick for me. Though we were both tall and we stayed fairly thin, she never put me in an outfit that looked like one of hers.

I modeled, spinning slowly under her critical look. "Well, maybe not that length. Here, try this pink."

"Ugh." It was a boxy Pendleton suit in a nubby salmon-pink wool.

"Just try it."

It was the best color I have ever worn. The suit made me look like an elegant young Jackie O.

"It's perfect for interviews," Viv said, eyeing me.

"Interviews?"

"You'd need the right shoes. A kitten heel. Or maybe a little sling-back. Something dressy but low-key."

"Interviews?"

Viv caught my tone. "Duh. Yeah. Interviews. Like what grown-ups do when they look for work."

"Grown-ups." This was a conversation we slid into far too often.

"You know what I mean. The kind of job where you take a shower *before* you go to work, rather than needing one afterwards."

I felt my jaw clenching. "I'm not afraid of hard work."

"I'm not saying you are. I'm just saying you don't want to turn around one day at fifty and still be climbing up and down ladders."

"Maybe I do."

"Please. Spare me," Her voice grew muffled as she dressed. "We can talk about this another time. Are you ready? Do you want the suit?"

I didn't, but she bought it for me anyway and I wore it whenever I thought I needed to look adult.

I still buy things that color.

"DO YOU remember that pink Pendleton suit?" I asked, looking at my sister's battered face for some flicker of movement that might show she was listening.

After a few moments I realized I was holding my breath.

"No pressure, sis," I said, and found myself almost giggling.

One of the all-business nurses stepped into Viv's room at that moment. She didn't look at me, but I felt the weight of disapproval. How dare I find anything here amusing? She started the usual round of looking at the various bottles and bags. She read my sister's blood pressure and then extracted blood from her arm.

"Why do you need her blood?"

The nurse didn't look up from the clipboard, "Testing for anemia, electrolytes, blood sugar."

"Oh." I wondered what electrolytes were.

She departed without another word, grinding her blocky, rubber-soled white shoes into the gleaming linoleum tiles.

"Gosh, Nurse Ratched sure is friendly," I told my sister, trying to recapture whatever calm I'd felt before the nurse came. I felt off-balance. I was dreadfully sure for a moment that my sister wasn't—couldn't be—listening, but I pushed on, my voice sounding hollow. "So, sis, I wish you could tell me something. Anything, actually."

Only the *whoosh-whoosh* of the machines answered.

Chapter 16

IT WAS raining as I left the hospital that evening. At Viv's house, the dogs paused on the threshold before going into the dark yard. All three gave me an affectionate, damp bump as they came back in. I rubbed them down and checked the sleek clock above the sink before tucking myself into the phone nook.

I pressed the blinking red message light and found a pen and paper for notes.

Two hang-ups, Viv's friend Marie Chou, Trisha with her flight information, someone trying to sell some kind of legal services, a Florida friend reporting on the volleyball game I'd missed, a call from a lady at Viv's church, and then, just as I was getting ready to scavenge some supper from the fridge, a familiar male voice rang out.

"This is Ed Maynard." He gave his phone number and announced, "I'm trying to reach Dr. Rowan regarding a personal matter. Please call back at your earliest convenience."

A personal matter? What did *that* mean?

I dialed the number, a local call. My stomach rumbled as I listened to the echoing nothing between rings. I was hungry. After three rings, someone picked up the telephone.

"Hello," I said, "Ed Maynard?

"Yes."

I steeled myself. "This is Nicola Jones. I'm Dr. Rowan's sister, returning your telephone call."

"May I speak with Dr. Rowan?" His voice was light and formal. The vague drawl I'd heard on his earlier messages had nearly disappeared.

"Actually, no. Can you tell me what this is in reference to?"

I tried to gauge the silence. Finally, he spoke up, "It's a private matter, ma'am. I really need to speak to Dr. Rowan."

"Yes, I understand that. But she can't come to the telephone."

"Dr. Rowan would want to hear from me. Can you have her phone me?"

"Uh, not really."

"Has something happened to Dr. Rowan?" His voice was cautious.

"Yes," I said. I sat up straighter and looked at the wall in front of me. "The thing is, she's been in a car accident."

"Oh, no." He sounded genuinely distressed. "I'm very sorry to hear that. I hope it wasn't serious."

"She's in the hospital," I said, "and I don't know when she'll be able to return your call."

"Oh," he said. "Oh."

"I'm sorry to tell you. Were you a patient of my sister?"

I heard the stuttering clink of a Zippo lighter and the hiss of inhaled breath. Then he began, "I should explain. I'm a private detective. I'm working for Vivian."

Both my feet were on the floor, but I felt as if the chair had bucked me off.

"I'm sorry, what?"

"Vivian hired me to investigate a private matter," he said. "I'm calling to report some progress."

"She hired you to what?"

"Your sister asked me to investigate a private matter, ma'am. I was trying to reach her to discuss it."

It was my turn to be silent.

"It's important that I speak with Vivian," he continued. "Is it possible that I can talk with her at the hospital? Is she seeing visitors at all?"

"She's unconscious," I said. "You can visit, I suppose—or maybe not. It's intensive care. I don't know the rules for non-family—"

I ground my teeth together to stop the babbling.

"Can you tell me what my sister hired you for?" I asked again.

"I'm afraid I can't, ma'am. I'd really need to talk with her first."

"The thing is, she's—" I struggled with how to phrase it. "Unconscious. I'm taking care of things for her."

"Okay," he said. "But I'd like to present my findings sooner rather than later. Perhaps we can meet at the hospital?"

He suggested a time and I was answering *yes* before I had the chance to think about how awkward it was.

"But please be certain to tell her that I need to speak with her. Have her call me if she likes before then, all right?"

I clicked the receiver-cradle to end the call but waited with the phone in my hand.

I dialed Trisha's home number. At her rusty, "Hello?" I launched right into my questions.

"So, why does anyone hire a private detective? In real life, not like on television."

Trisha lived for this kind of conversation. "My aunt Sharon hired one when Uncle Tommy was fooling around."

"Okay," I said. "But I don't think Dear George was fooling around."

"*Viv* hired a private detective? For what?"

"Detecting, I guess." I gave it a beat and then added, "But that's just it—it's private. He said he wouldn't tell me until he talks to Viv."

"Is she talking?"

The question hit me hard. It took me a minute to say no.

"Oh, I'm so sorry, Nicky. Did you get my message from this afternoon? I'll be there tomorrow."

"Yeah. Thanks."

"So. Private detective?"

"Yeah. So, if George was not fooling around—actually, I think if anyone was, it'd be Viv—but why else hire one?"

Trisha took a deep breath. "Look—um. I know it's not something you want to talk about? But honest to God, Nicky, what about your parents? I mean, really, if there was ever *any* reason to hire a detective in your family, it would be to find out about them."

I didn't answer.

"Okay," Trisha sighed. "You haven't seen them since, like, the seventh grade."

"Yes."

"And you are fine with that. So you say. I get that—I don't believe it, but that's a whole other discussion." I imagined Trisha holding the phone against her shoulder with her chin, using both hands to make a point. "But what if your *sister* needed to find them for some reason?"

I heard the wind moving outside the kitchen windows. I tried to read the thermometer mounted on the window casement. Reflections from the kitchen lights blocked my view.

"Hey, hey, come on, Nicky. I'm sorry. The whole thing about your parents—it makes me crazy."

I sighed.

"Okay, look, let's talk about this all tomorrow in person. I actually have to get ready so I can cab it straight to the airport from work," Trisha said. She brushed aside my apology for having not even asked if she could talk. "Oh, and mom wants me to bring food. The cure for everything."

"Sophia's great," I said.

"Call her."

I promised to call Trisha's mom and we hung up after saying our goodbyes.

Chapter 17

I KIBBLED the dogs and watched them eat, thinking about what I knew and didn't know about our parents.

My sister had voiced so many suspicions over the years. We knew that Jahn, especially, was trying to avoid being noticed by the authorities. He went rigid behind the wheel whenever a police car appeared. He complained bitterly about lawyers and the unfairness of "the system." She thought Jahn might have done something really bad. Something criminal. Or maybe both of them had done something illegal.

She said that maybe they had been student radicals. Perhaps they were hiding out from the mob. Or maybe they were spies. She suspected that Jahn was a communist.

She'd had a dozen contradictory theories. Myself, I usually tried not to think about the two of them any more than I absolutely had to.

I toweled the faces of the dogs and pushed myself to think about Magda and Jahn.

Our mother was pale and quiet. Her name was Mary Jones, though our father called her Magda, the vowels floating long and rich in the short word.

She had sad, washed-out blue eyes that were often full of tears. She kept her light-brown hair trapped in a tight, meager ponytail. She slept a great deal, especially when we were little. When she spoke, there was a slight sibilance—not quite a lisp—that Viv could imitate to perfection on the phone or from around the corner of a room.

Despite how depressed and tired she seemed, she nearly always put in a kitchen garden as soon as we moved into a new place. And she got my father to buy flats of pansies every spring. She gathered big bouquets of lilacs in May and kept them in vases on the supper-table and on her and Jahn's bureau. She sprinkled old-fashioned rosewater on her neck every night before dinner, no matter how weepy or listless she had been during the day. I didn't know her maiden name or whether she had gone to college or how she had met our father.

I was pretty sure she was raised on a farm. She'd once told me she'd used a .22 as a girl to shoot squirrels for supper. When my father made friends with the local dairy farmers in a new neighborhood, as he always did, she slipped into the company of farmer's wives without a pause. She put up corn relish and apple butter without a recipe. She made fried chicken with a cornflake batter that my father loved. She baked her macaroni and cheese with crushed saltines and parmesan cheese on top.

She used some words differently from everyone else with her soft, lisping voice. She called wild plums "damsons" while a porch was a "stoop." She pronounced "creek" as "crick," and referred to faucets—even the ones inside the house—as "spigots." On the rare occasions when she spoke in anger, her voice took on a sharp, hillbilly twang.

She knew about cows and sheep and chickens, but she also told me about which wild animals hibernated, whether they mated for life, and how many babies they had each year. She spoke with absolute certainty and always used their full Latin scientific names.

Magda sang small scraps of old-timey songs when she cleaned the house, her voice high and brave and wavering against the air: "The river is wide, Lord, I can't swim over. Nor have I wings to fly."

She told me the facts of life without drama, in a series of declarative statements. Babies come from inside the mother. They get there from the mother and the father having intercourse. Intercourse is when the father puts sperm inside the mother so that it can fertilize the mother's ovum. Ovum is like an egg.

On bad days, she stayed in bed until Jahn came home. But when she was awake, she listened avidly to our stories about classroom squabbles and homework assignments. Maybe she was starved for news from beyond her back stoop. She didn't offer advice often, but she asked us for details and reasons behind the grudges and for explanations for why the teacher assigned various projects.

When our father went away for work, or for whatever took him from the house for more than a day or two, our mother went with him. Jahn was the center of her world and his comfort was her first and deepest concern.

She loved to read. From when we were very little, I remember her bringing my sister and me to the public library and then curling up to read in a corner while Viv and I combed the shelves for books we wanted to look at. I don't remember her ever having a library card of her own, but she would get our father to leave us at the library with her for hours.

Once I went to school, I realized that I could bring library books home. I learned that the point of a library was to let people bring books home. They were "lending" libraries, after all.

Magda read whatever books we borrowed from the school library, explaining in her diffident voice, "I don't like to bother to get myself a library card."

"She's a sheep!" my sister hissed, tossing her hair in the direction of the kitchen. "Jahn won't let her get a library card."

"But she said she didn't need one."

Viv rolled her eyes in contempt. "Duh. She said, she *said*. Do you believe everything she says? He won't *let* her get one and she goes right along with whatever he wants. What a sheep!"

I was silent.

"I'm never letting anyone tell me what to do."

I opened Dear George's Subzero fridge and rooted around until I found a bagel to toast. I melted a slice of deli cheese on top and poured a big glass of orange juice. Breakfast for supper—one of the rare treats Magda indulged us in when Jahn was away by himself.

OUR father was burly and short, with limp tan hair and snapping little black eyes. His shaven beard looked blue against his milky pale skin. He had a red puckered scar on his arm that he got, he told us once, from playing with a burning stick when he was a boy. This was perhaps the only thing he ever told Viv and me about his childhood.

He spoke with an elusive Eastern European accent that snagged on some words and shortened others. He answered to John Jones for work but introduced himself as Jahn. People often heard it as "Ian" the first time they met.

He ate with a hand resting protectively around his plate. He had a short fuse, and when he lost his temper, he slapped people, kicked things, slammed doors. He drank beer during the day and vodka or plum brandy on special occasions. He complained about the government, about taxes, about the unfairness of modern society. People at work were always "cooking up" something against him.

He refused to have a television or to subscribe to the newspaper. He allowed a radio in the house but threatened to destroy it when someone changed the dial from the classical station to pop.

He wore heavy, orange work-boots and brown coveralls. His truck rattled with toolboxes and empty beer cans. He worked construction, traveling to sites sometimes hours away. When he came home at the end of the day, his raisin eyes were bloodshot and underlined with bruised-looking pouches. He and our mother would leave us and stay nearer to the job site for days and weeks at a time.

Jahn was an enthusiastic swimmer. We often lived near big water—Lake Champlain, Lake Ontario, the St. Lawrence River—and I remember seeing him come out of the water pale and streaming during summer storms. He swam for miles, his head a steady speck between white-streaked green waves.

He taught me to swim when I was five or six. Our mother sat on shore, a wide hat protecting her face, her thin legs turning pink. She did not swim. When it was especially hot, she would wade or perhaps sit in knee-deep water while we splashed nearby.

Jahn held both my hands and towed me along until he stood in water that was over my head. The sun was bright in a blue sky and the water smelled of clean seaweed.

"First, understand that you float," my father told me. "All people float. Relax. Breathe."

To this day, it surprises me how it works: you are paddling, gasping, kicking, and then you turn over onto your back and relax, breathe, and you float. It was like discovering how to open a door or like stepping through an old door into an unexpected new room in the house you've lived in for years. The water cradled me. I squinted up at the sun. I would have been happy to float through the whole summer.

My father taught me to swim first on my back, turning the float into a splashing backstroke. "When you are swimming, you must keep moving," he explained. "Kick! Kick! Good!"

I kicked mightily and he walked alongside me, shouting to my mother, "Magda! Look at this! She is swimming!"

Of course, I swallowed a gallon of water trying to see if she looked, but my father laughed for once and hoisted me over his shoulder, thumping the coughs away. It is one of the few memories I have from that time that does not include Viv.

Later that same summer, on that same rocky beach that smelled of seaweed, my father taught me to swim properly on my front. He held a hand under my stomach, holding me halfway between blue water and blue sky. I lolled there, enjoying the feeling. It seemed to me that this part of it—being buoyed in the water— meant that swimming would be just as pleasant and as easy as floating. My father grew impatient.

"Look at your sister!" he demanded, lifting me completely from the water.

I watched the perfect bent curve of Viv's arms wheeling through the water, the powerful swishing of her kicks. She drew breath every few strokes, her face framed by moving water and auburn mermaid hair as she looked back at us.

"Be like that!" he told me, his voice harsh. "Or stay on shore forever."

By the end of the afternoon, the lesson was over. I slapped my arms as if they were logs, and half the time I forgot to move my legs, but I could swim.

Chapter 18

THE PRIVATE investigator came to Viv's room the next morning empty-handed. No flowers, no briefcase full of reports, no pad of paper at the ready. I looked up to see him standing in the doorway, a light-haired man of perhaps forty-five, in a tan canvas jacket and green denim workpants, his ears pink from cold and his hands hanging limp at his sides.

I introduced myself.

"Ma'am," he said, nodding like a cowboy from an old Western. "Ed Maynard."

He surveyed my sister from half-shaven scalp to toes and then walked to her bedside.

"Is she asleep?" he whispered.

"She's been unconscious since Saturday night," I told him, though I'd mentioned it on the phone.

"Can she hear us?"

I said I didn't know.

He pointed at the fetal monitor. "But the baby is okay?"

I nodded, but his attention had returned to my sister.

"Vivian," he said, his voice just up from a whisper. "Look at you."

I asked if he wanted to be alone with my sister.

He looked up and smiled at me. "I appreciate that, ma'am. But no. It's just such a surprise to see her like this."

I nodded, thinking, "You're telling me that?"

"Do you know how long—?" He waved at the wall of electronics and made a grimace.

"Let's talk out here a minute," I said, sliding my big mug of tea onto the bedside table.

The hallway was busy that morning, full of raised voices, a sense of urgency, and the squeaking of wheeled carts. I didn't recognize any of the nurses. I led Ed Maynard to the ICU waiting room.

One of the hospital volunteers, an antique woman in a pink sweater and harlequin glasses, was restocking the *Reader's Digest* magazines and setting out a neat fan of social services flyers. She nodded to us. Ed Maynard stood beside the door for a moment as she passed, though the door didn't need to be held.

"So," I said to him as we sat across from one another on the olive-green vinyl cushions.

There was a moment of silence.

"Boy, you look like your sister," he said.

I nodded. After a moment I added, "Thanks."

"So—" He drew the word out and then asked his question in a rush. "What happened to her?"

I told him about the accident, about George, about the phone call to Sarasota and how my sister had left me in charge. I couldn't tell what he was thinking.

"But what's wrong with her?"

"The short version," I started, and then stopped. How much would Viv want to share about her situation? Maybe she wouldn't, but here we were, and what would it serve to hold back?

I summarized. "The doctors are saying that with a head injury this serious, they don't know when she's going to wake up. Maybe soon, maybe not. And they can't say for sure how everything is going to turn out."

He held my gaze as I spoke, his hazel eyes squinting against this news. "That's a goddamned shame," he said, shaking his head. "It's just a goddamned shame."

We sat in silence for a moment. I was relieved that he didn't ask for more details.

Ed Maynard appeared to give himself a mental shake and cleared his throat.

I waited before asking, "Can you tell me what you are doing for my sister?"

He gave me a weak smile. "That's kind of an awkward question. I'm not going to lie to you—I'm not sure what I *can* tell you."

He tapped a foot several times as if sending a coded message through the floor: heel-toe, heel-toe, heel-heel-heel.

He looked up from his folded hands and grimaced. "I'm not sure where to begin," he said.

At the despairing tone of his voice, I found myself wondering if my sister had been having an affair with this man. A string of Viv's former boyfriends had sounded the same way.

Ed Maynard—he didn't look like much. He was broad through the chest. A bit of gut pushed over his belt. He seemed old to me, someone from our parent's generation. Maybe Viv found Ed's bumpy nose and those crow's-footed greenish eyes irresistible. I couldn't see it myself.

Well, I thought, as soon as he starts telling me how he didn't see the breakup coming, then I'll know another one of Viv's secrets.

"Start when you first met," I said, a little more kindly than I felt.

"My old grandma would say, 'begin at the beginning and go on from there,'" he replied with a wry smile. He peeled off his canvas coat, which had a faint, ashy smell of cigarette smoke, and settled into his seat.

"A couple of months ago, I got a call from your sister. Referred by Artie Slate. We met and discussed at length what she wanted to find out and about how to proceed if I had any success."

As he spoke, I reassessed my idea of him and Vivian. He wasn't acting like a discarded beau. I didn't think my sister would have found him attractive after all: his teeth were very large and too white, and he wore a pinkie ring and a heavy gold bracelet. Viv would have called those teeth "chompers." Plus, she despised man-jewelry.

Ed gestured with his bejeweled hand. "Your sister had very specific directions for me—"

"Directions about what, though?" I interrupted.

He continued without answering. "—and naturally, she expected my discretion on this matter."

"Naturally," I said, sarcasm giving my voice an edge.

Ed squinted at me, and I shrugged in apology. When he did not continue, I offered a short explanation.

"I didn't know she was pregnant. It's been a week full of surprises."

The private detective grinned widely, his big chompers like square white piano keys in his mouth. "People do the damnedest things, and I am here to tell you it's usually for the damnedest reasons. Excuse my language." He paused for a minute before continuing. "So I'd hoped to give Vivian my report today and see how she wanted me to proceed."

"Can you give *me* the report?"

Ed shook his head. "That's where it's kind of sticky. Since she didn't already inform you, I suspect your sister might prefer that I didn't, either."

"Look, Mr. Maynard. What are we doing here? Do you have a bill for me or something?" I heard my voice growing thinner and louder.

"Hold on there, ma'am, please. I didn't mean to add to your troubles. I just thought I could talk to Vivian." Ed took a breath. "As far as money goes, your sister wrote a sizable retainer for my services. If you like, I can give you a complete statement of my expenses right up to this very minute."

"But you can't tell me anything else."

"In short, no. It wouldn't be right."

The anger seeped back into my bones like tainted water going back into the ground. It took my energy with it. "Okay, so—?"

"I can continue the investigation. There's money for me to continue. And I guess that's what I am asking you—if I should proceed." He looked uncomfortable. "I know that's got to sound a little ack-basswards."

I nodded impatiently. "You want to know what Viv would want, if she knew what you've found out so far, right?"

"You hit the nail on the head."

I thought for a moment. "Did you find out what she wanted?"

He tapped his foot again, heel-toe, heel-toe. "There's an answer, yes, but mostly I found new questions."

"Questions that I can't answer," I said.

His crow's feet deepened. "Questions I can't ask you."

I leaned back in the chair and looked at my feet. "Do you think she'd want you to continue?"

"I don't know your sister well enough to say. In my line of work, it's a fool's game to figure how people will react to information." He pulled a card from his pants pocket and handed it to me. "'All the truth you want to pay for.' That's the motto of my agency."

He gave me a moment to look at his card before continuing.

"I tell people they can stop me any time they've heard or seen enough. I've been in this game a good long time. Made a decent living finding things out for folks. That motto there is the secret to my success."

The raised letters of his name and the agency's motto looked sharp and shiny on the heavy cream business card, even in the wavering fluorescent lighting.

I was angry that my sister had made this mess. She had no right putting me on the spot with this man with his big chompers and his apologies. She'd left me in charge and hadn't had the courtesy to tell me what was going on. I felt the accusations forming already. When she woke up, I was going to tell her a thing or two.

Still, even if I didn't want to guess what Viv wanted investigated, I couldn't picture her deliberately refusing to know something. She'd hired him and she would expect answers from him when she woke up. Furthermore, we both believed in getting our money's worth. I looked again at the business card motto. *All the truth you want to pay for.*

"Well then," I said to Ed Maynard. "If she already paid for it, I think you better get her the truth."

We shook hands on the decision, and we wandered back along the hallway to Viv's room.

I promised I'd contact him when there was any change with Viv. He said he'd phone in weekly—to report *what,* I didn't ask—and that as soon as he returned to the office, he'd send an itemized statement.

He patted Viv on the shoulder. "You hang in there," he said to her. He shrugged his coat on and was gone.

I caught up to him near the elevators. "Mr. Maynard—Ed Maynard!"

He turned, his face animated, "Is she—?"

"Did my sister hire you to find our parents?"

Ed Maynard didn't so much as blink. "Ma'am. I cannot say."

I just looked at him.

He didn't soften. He was probably very good at poker.

"I'll send that invoice along right away," he said, and pressed the elevator button.

Chapter 19

I GLANCED at the clock as I resumed my spot next to Viv. It was not even ten o'clock in the morning, and all I wanted to do was to put my head down and go back to sleep. I needed to get some exercise, but I hadn't packed running shoes. They weren't, strictly speaking, essential.

I shook it off, reaching tall to loosen my shoulders, then bending to stretch my hamstrings.

I'd have to wait until tonight to talk to Trisha about Ed Maynard.

"How about some Dickens?" I said to my sister. Settling into the visitor's chair, I opened the bumpy, tooled leather cover of *Nicholas Nickleby*. Viv had a long shelf of these double-decker novels. She didn't collect first editions, but she said she liked the heft of the 19th century editions nearly as much as she loved the long, complicated stories themselves. She refused to read paperback editions of them.

Her *Nicholas Nickleby* ran to two green leather-bound volumes with lustrous marbled endpapers and rough, deckled edges. The first reader of the book must have used a letter opener to separate the pages. The smell of age, ink, and dust came up in a faint sharp puff as I turned past the table of contents and introduction.

Before I had time to read the second page aloud, a pair of nurses came in to change the sheets and shift Viv in the bed, saying that it was for the baby.

When I asked, the older of the two explained as they worked. "As a baby grows, it takes up room in the mother's belly. We make sure to turn Dr. Rowan so gravity doesn't squish the baby into her circulation."

They bundled sheets into the hamper and were gone, closing the door behind them, leaving us alone.

Just us two, once again.

I slid the heavy book into the drawer of Viv's bedside stand. Nicholas was going to have to wait.

VIV and I had started school in the fall of 1980, minus our parents, without fuss. A high-school senior, Viv forged Magda's name on the permission slips, same as she had done for years. We went to the doctor for our physicals with the story that Mom wasn't feeling good enough to come to the appointment with us today.

Dr. Carbone's receptionist, handing over clipboards of forms to fill out, gave us a sharp look.

"Mom sent a check in case we didn't have enough cash-money," Viv assured her, giving the words a flat, North-Country intonation. She patted her handbag and said, "And she said to let you know to phone her if you need to." Viv leaned closer to the receptionist, confiding, "She was sleeping when we left the house."

The receptionist gave us an uncomfortable smile and looked away.

"She probably thinks we have a drunk mom," Viv said later. "It's fine by me. Most people get embarrassed by stuff like that, and they'll avoid looking too closely."

Classes started with the usual jumble of students with fresh haircuts, bright school-clothes, the sharp scent of newly opened packages of ball-point pens. Everyone's brown-paper book covers unmarked by the first doodle, the teachers all potentially nice and cheerful. I was excited and nervous both about the hopscotch schedule of classes and transferring students that came with eighth grade.

"Keep a low profile," Viv said. "You'll be fine. We can't afford to have the teachers wondering about us or needing to talk to Jahn and Magda."

Viv took her SATs that fall, coming home elated at having finished each section faster than everyone else. I made her a baked chicken dinner with a lopsided-but-tasty chocolate cake for dessert to celebrate.

We went to Viv's senior Homecoming football game and sat in the bleachers cheering like everyone else. When I told Viv that I liked the cheerleading outfits, she sniffed.

"They are a little—obvious. I mean, honestly, a short skirt and a tight sweater?"

"But they look cute."

Viv turned a dispassionate eye on the girls in the acid yellow and royal blue leaping at the sideline. After a moment she admitted that they did look cute.

I didn't say anything.

She eyed me with a satirical, doubting expression. "You want to be a cheerleader?"

I shrugged.

She frowned. "We aren't like them," she said, unnecessarily. "You and me—we aren't going to get caught sneaking out to party with the boys. We aren't going to flunk geometry or quit school early. Granted, we aren't going to be cute and super-popular in high school, but we also aren't going to get arrested for trespassing or for spray-painting our names on somebody's barn."

I sniggered. One of the seniors in Viv's class had done just that. Spray-painted his own name on a barn and then tried to deny it with his trigger-finger still orange with paint.

"We're going to get through this year and no one is going to find out that Jahn and Magda are gone." Viv's voice was fierce, and she paused to gulp air. She finished on a softer note. "If it means we can't go out for cheerleading or class president, that's just part of the trade-off to get what we want."

I looked at the cheerleaders again, precise as militia with their pom-poms and their bouncy hair tied back in school-color ribbons. The routine ended and the girls hugged each other like a squad of carefree sisters. From the edge of my vision, I knew Viv was watching me, her expression drawn and tense. I heaved a theatrical sigh.

"Oh, well. Maybe I'll just get the outfit."

Viv laughed, as I had meant her to.

Often that fall, I rode with my sister to The Pit Stop after school. Before Viv clocked in, the cook would grill cheese sandwiches or cheeseburgers for us, insisting that I drink a glass of milk "for my bones." From the diner, I'd wait for the bus to take me into the Square in Watertown, where I'd happily spend an evening at the library.

When we needed to know most things, my sister and I went to the library. Not the little local branch with the nosey volunteer librarian who asked about our mother and fussed over Viv if she selected too thick a book, but the big library in Watertown—the Roswell P. Flower Memorial Library—where we could get a dozen books apiece and read newspapers from all over the country.

It was easy to spend whole days looking up one thing after another, or studying the murals, or peeping up the curved stairways that led to the mysterious upstairs, or just sit reading in the airy oak-paneled rooms. Worn marble floors made the library cool and echoing even on the hottest summer day. In the winter, steam clanked in the tall, old-fashioned iron radiators and everything smelled of wet wool and old books.

The library closed at nine o'clock and I sometimes sat for fifteen minutes or so under the benign gaze of the library's small, drowsy-looking stone lions until Viv came racing to the curb in the orange Datsun.

She piloted us through the night with the windows down, both of us content in the clasp of our seatbelts, my sister driving and humming tunelessly, me skating my hand through the cottony night air with the heater pouring hot air on our feet.

Those nights it seemed as if we were getting away with something, living without parents. My sister had plans for everything. Nothing derailed her. She never seemed to be surprised by the curved road ahead in the dark. If she had doubts, I never saw them.

It was easy when we were kids: if we were separated or put into foster care or if the bomb went off and we got stranded, we would pack up the essentials and run. We always had a rendezvous-point. If we missed each other at the rendezvous, we were to leave messages at the Holiday Inn in Watertown, New York, an address I could still remember though I hadn't been back to the North Country for years.

I didn't doubt she had a plan. But how was I supposed to know what it was?

WHEN I looked up, Dr. Pete was standing with a hand raised to knock on the doorframe.

"You were a long way away," he said.

I shrugged.

"I'm glad to find you," he said, stepping in and flipping through Viv's chart. When he glanced over, he added quickly, "No, nothing bad—I just thought to check in."

I tried to steady my breath. The sense of panic had been right there, ready for a reason to leap into action.

"Are you hungry?" he asked. "I've been working for—" He glanced at his still-bare wrist and made a face. "All night, anyway. I know this diner that makes the perfect hamburger."

"It's 10:30 in the morning," I said.

"Don't be conventional. You look hungry." He put a hand on Viv's feet as he continued. "Come have a meal."

I hadn't eaten breakfast, and after checking with the nurses' station to be sure nothing was scheduled, I agreed to a hamburger for breakfast.

In the doctor's lot, Dr. Pete apologized for his car. Putting the key into his door-lock, he said, "I know it's a cliché." Grinning across the roof of the red Porsche, he said, "But it's *my* cliché."

At the diner—a dumpy mid-century chrome-plated little place next to a boarded-up office building—Dr. Pete hurried me to a corner table.

The waitress brought Dr. Pete a strawberry milkshake and menus, giving me an assessing sidelong look. "You want the usual, hon?" she asked him.

He did.

"I'll have the same," I ordered blindly on impulse, and added, "but a Coke to drink." She gave us both a world-weary look as she walked away.

"So, about Viv," I said, poking him to distract his intent gaze from the waitress' retreating form.

He looked away reluctantly, plucking a handful of paper napkins from the dispenser. "Yes. I spoke with Marilyn Wilsey. Yesterday, I think. Anyway, it looks like a team of obstetrics doctors will be assigned to support the pregnancy. You understand this?"

"Team Baby, like Team Surgical," I said.

"Yes. Having a team in place means that a doctor who is familiar with Viv's situation will be close by all the time. And because of the possible complications, well, the more the merrier."

"The more the merrier?" I said.

Dr. Pete flapped his hands in apology. "An idiom. English is not my first language. I sometimes say things stupidly."

"But—" I couldn't bear to say her name. "Everything will be okay, right?"

"I hope so," he said. After a moment, he added, "I am hopeful. Your sister is very tough, and she wants this baby."

"She never said anything about being pregnant. I mean, she never told me she even *wanted* a baby."

Dr. Pete frowned over a spoonful of pink. "It surprises me."

"Me too."

"Have some milkshake," he offered.

I shook my head, feeling tension like a hand squeezing my neck. "Not a big fan of strawberries."

"But it's your sister's—"

"Favorite. I know."

We were sitting there, smiling at each other, when the waitress brought our platters. When she said, "Enjoy," it sounded like a command.

"That's why I love this place," Dr. Pete said, his eyes once again tracking the waitress as she sashayed away.

"The waitress' butt?"

"No." Dr. Pete looked at me and grinned like a rogue. "Okay, sorry! Yes—I am a pig. Your sister also busts my chops about it."

I could imagine.

Dr. Pete continued to explain. "Anyway, it's this bossiness. It so reminds me of home."

We tucked into the fries and burgers—they were excellent—and spent the rest of early lunch talking about his childhood in Greece and the food he missed most.

Chapter 20

BACK with my sister, I took another run at *Nicholas Nickleby*. At the end of the chapter, remembering nothing of the words I'd said aloud, I put it back down again. Instead I studied my sister's bruised face. I wished she would open her eyes, Sleeping Beauty jarred from a poisoned sleep, stretching her long white arms over her head and yawning, pointing her toes, ready for breakfast.

"Wake up!" I said into the beeping quiet of the room. "Wake up like it's Christmas!"

WHEN I was turning fourteen, that first winter without our parents, Viv said, "What do you want to do for your birthday?"

"For my birthday? Really-really?"

My sister gave me a sarcastic look. "Yeah, really-really."

"There's a big art museum in Syracuse? I was thinking I could take the bus—"

"That's a wonderful idea! An eighth grader wandering around the bus station in downtown Syracuse? And you with your head in the clouds." Viv shook her head. "I'll drive you."

I took a long breath. "I was hoping to spend the whole day there."

Viv bugged her eyes at me. "So? We'll spend the whole day."

"But—"

"But, but, butter." My sister's voice was cheerful and mocking.

I understood how chancy our finances were. Each week, we counted out dollars into various envelopes for the electric bill, groceries, gas for the car. Each month, we weighed the idea of letting the phone get disconnected. Viv did some sort of juggling with the car insurance, which ended up saving us a few months' worth of premiums.

We ate a lot of oatmeal and peanut butter sandwiches. Some of our best meals were made with leftovers I brought home from babysitting —a tray of frozen chicken parmesan lasted us one entire gluttonous week. But the money was always a stretch.

I hesitated before asking my sister, "Syracuse—it's not too much?"

"Too much what? The Datsun's running fine, and we both deserve a treat." She bumped a shoulder into mine. "If I get you to the library this week, can you figure out how to get us to the museum?"

"If only they made something like—like a *drawing* of the roads!" I said. "We could use it to determine our route!"

"Dope," my sister said.

I navigated us into downtown Syracuse without mishap early on my birthday Saturday. One of the librarians had given me a quick lesson, and though I couldn't check the atlas out, I'd sketched a copy of the map and taken notes.

Viv patted the orange Datsun after we locked it in the Everson Museum parking lot. For once she was not carrying homework or a collection of medical essays. Instead she had a thick, musty, hardcover novel—*Vanity Fair* maybe, or something by Trollope—tucked under her arm.

"Are you sure you'll be okay?" I asked her.

"Duh. Worrywart. What else would I be?" Viv gave me a playful shove. "Go," she said. "Moon over each picture. I know you want to. I'll drink coffee in the café and read to my heart's content." She pointed to the modern sculptures outside of the entryway. "When the security guys chase you out at closing time, I'll be right over there."

It was my best birthday ever. I forgot about our money troubles and whether we could get by without our parents. I didn't moon over each one, but I stood so long in front of some pictures that when I took a step, the sinews in the backs of my knees snapped and crackled.

I let myself sink into the voluptuous light of the Hudson River School exhibit paintings, marveling at the smoothness of the paint, the way the brushstrokes were nearly invisible. Those enormous, elegant elms framing velvety green pastures—it was like a glamorous dream of the same sorts of fields that appeared every day out the window of the school-bus. It made me feel buoyant with possibilities, to see the world this way.

I absorbed *The Black Teapot* until I could count each vivid nasturtium and purple aster on that glorious table. I grew light-headed looking at the Andrew Wyeths and Milton Averys.

I never stopped for lunch, and though the custodians did not *quite* have to escort me, it was almost dark when I met Viv outside by the granite forms.

"Ready?" she said.

"No."

My sister guffawed. "Tell me."

I told her as we walked to the Datsun and headed home, explaining every picture by its details, the brushstrokes, the glow of color and the lack of color. Viv nodded, her eyes on the road. Back on the highway going north, I stopped to catch my breath and she pointed into the back seat.

"Hey, look in the paper bag back there."

"What is it?"

"Guess."

I opened the bag. Two cheese sandwiches and a bottle of root-beer. I was famished. When I offered her half a sandwich, she smiled. "No, I'm still full. I had three pieces of cake. It was only going to be two, but you didn't get out till now."

"Nice," I said, through a mouthful of cheese sandwich.

After a few minutes, she said, "Maybe you should be a curator at a museum. I wonder what the salary is like?"

I took a careful sip of soda, wiped my mouth. "I'm going to be an artist," I said.

"Well, yes, but in case that doesn't work out." Viv looked impatiently into her rear-view, signaled, and nipped around a slower-moving car. "You love art, right? And museums?"

I bit into the sandwich to keep from having to answer.

My sister gave me a sidelong look. "I'm just saying, for a back-up plan. It's essential to have something to fall back on. You know."

I knew, but I didn't have to agree.

SHE worked The Pit Stop on Christmas Eve that year, having heard the tips were especially good. At home, I decorated our first Christmas tree ever, a fat little pine that we had chopped down from the edge of the pasture behind the house.

While Viv waited tables, I snipped elaborate paper garlands of five-pointed stars, airy snowflakes and bands of rabbits crouching nose-to-nose and tail-to-tail. I used purloined paper-glue from school to fasten stars to rabbits to snowflakes and then draped the paper chain around and around the tree. I hung tarnished silver globes from a dusty box I'd found the attic. The house smelled of wood-smoke and cinnamon and pine-pitch.

A few days before this first Christmas, Viv had forbidden me to miss our parents. "Don't you see how lucky we are?" she said, shaking me by the upper arms. "We can do anything. Anything! They can't tell us what to do. We don't have to slink around trying not to irritate Jahn or pretend to be glad they got you another stupid set of crayons."

"Ouch!" I said, and she let go of my arms. I rubbed them and tried to blink tears back.

"It didn't hurt," Viv said. "Don't waste your time getting all gooey and sentimental. Maybe you forgot what it was like?"

I didn't answer. I had not forgotten. But sometimes, I just wanted Magda when I walked into the empty house after school. It was nice having someone cooking, and though she didn't say much, Magda was a good listener. I couldn't tell Viv, but I missed our mother sometimes.

Viv shook her head. "Just figure out what you want. Then you can make it happen. You know what I mean?"

I nodded, not trusting my voice.

My sister reached into her pocket and found a mint from The Pit Stop. "Here," she said, handing it to me.

I unwrapped the candy and popped it into my mouth.

"Nicola Maria Jones, you are one of the lucky ones," she said. "Think about it. I'm telling you: all you have to do is make a plan. Nothing—nobody—is standing in the way, saying 'Oh no you can't.' or 'How dare you?' Doing is easy as long as you know what you want to do."

I shrugged.

"Okay, look. We can do whatever we want for Christmas," my sister reminded me. "We can have a tree. We can cook a nasty old goose. We can lounge around eating cereal all day. We can go to the movies or set off fireworks. Or we can sing carols. If you want, we can stay up all night and wait for Santa."

She gave me a sly look, reminding me how excited I'd been about the jingle bells that Viv said she'd heard one Christmas. I opened my mouth to protest, but something struck us both as funny and we ended up laughing.

Despite what my sister said, I was not wallowing in sentimentality that first Christmas. Far from it. I hadn't forgotten what it was like to live under the feeling of constant storm-warning that came with Jahn being in the house. I was frightened of what might happen to my sister and me on our own—what if we were caught and put in foster care?—but it was like stepping into the sunshine not to have the constant worry and responsibility of Jahn's temper and Magda's sadness.

I had already decided this first Christmas of ours was going to be great. Far from wanting Jahn and Magda back, I was glad to know it was only Viv and me. When Jahn and Magda used to ask us what we wanted for

Christmas, there was a right answer (crayons or books) and a wrong one (anything Jahn disapproved of).

When she was in fifth grade or so, my sister answered the annual question with a request for a board game. "I would like to have *Operation* from Milton Bradley, please."

Viv must have anticipated that Jahn would refuse. Battery-operated games were one of the many kinds of toys he had banished. When he told her to pick something else, my stubborn sister said, "No thanks."

That long-ago Christmas morning, Viv smiled and thanked them as she unwrapped a skinny little paperback novel that Magda had picked out. The following year, Viv answered their question the same way: "May I have *Operation* from Milton Bradley, please?"

She told me that she liked the way the vein in Jahn's forehead bulged when she asked him politely for something he did not want to give.

For the next couple of years, Viv asked for *Operation* from Milton Bradley, please, with exactly the right degree of civility and sincerity, which meant that no matter how provoking he found it, Jahn couldn't accuse her of sass or backchat.

I was in charge this year, and I knew what I wanted for us on Christmas morning. Since kindergarten, I'd wanted a decorated tree in the house with presents under it. I wanted good things for my sister and me to eat—no greasy goose, no stringy turnips, no heavy spoonbread. And I wanted "I Saw Mommy Kissing Santa Claus" and "Jingle Bell Rock"—the silliest of Christmas songs—playing on the radio, loud.

So, as my sister was forever advising, I made a plan. When the two of us got up late and ate cookies for breakfast with the radio playing popular carols full blast, my sister would open first the small, heavy package of batteries, then the leather-bound old book I had found for her at a rummage sale, and finally, she'd tear the wrapping off the big, rattling box of *Operation* by Milton Bradley. I'd taken a trip to the Sears store in Watertown with one of my babysitting families, so I was sure she'd be completely surprised.

After presents, we'd eat more cookies and play *Operation* until we were ready for the cold sliced ham and mashed sweet-potatoes and pumpkin pie I'd made.

I was happy that night. On Christmas Eve, with the wind whispering around the corner of the house, I did not feel lonesome. I made Christmas cookies and refilled the teakettle. I brought in extra loads of firewood to save having to go outside the next morning. I snipped paper snowflakes to hang in all the windows and considered the many advantages of our solo state.

When Viv came home, I was happier yet. She kept her pea-coat buttoned when she came in and she dashed upstairs with her hands in her pockets, clutching something lumpy under her coat. From upstairs, she shouted, "Will you start me a pot of tea? Peppermint?"

I made the tea slowly, with a lot of extra scrapings and clanking so that if Viv were making any noise, she'd know I wouldn't be able to hear her. When she came downstairs, she dunked cookies into her tea and admired the tree and the decorations.

I think it snowed a little overnight that Christmas. Or anyway, it *felt* like it had snowed for that first Christmas: a light, beautiful blanket of white covering everything outside the windows. Perhaps I'm making the memory prettier than it was, but I remember the field being as picturesque as a Grandma Moses scene.

On Christmas morning we slept in, and when we made our way downstairs, we each had gifts tucked under our arms. My sister—contrary to every Paris-edition-*Vogue*-influenced particle of taste—produced an extravagantly wrapped package of pastel day-of-the-week underpants for me. In the autumn, when I told her about how all the girls in my gym-class had day-of-the-week panties, she'd said it was the tackiest thing she had ever heard. Her scorn hadn't really changed my wanting them, but I hadn't mentioned it again.

Still, sometime between then and Christmas, she'd made the trip to Woolworth's in the face of her own sense of fashion. She also got me a sleek and expensive Koh-I-Noor technical pen, which I knew for a fact I had never mentioned aloud. She must have noticed me silently fingering it at the art-supply store in Watertown and gone back for advice, because the pen came with two bottles of ink and a tin of horrible-smelling cleaning solution.

Viv and I stayed in our pajamas all morning with the woodstove pouring off heat, drinking cup after cup of hot chocolate and eating cookies. We sang along with the radio, making up a silly dance for the various versions of "The Little Drummer Boy" that kept playing.

Viv was unbeatable at *Operation*, as anyone could have predicted; she took out and replaced the breadbasket piece four times in a row before Sam's red nose lit up.

Later, when Viv had curled up on the couch and stuck her nose into the dusty old novel, I filled the ink reservoir of the technical pen and then applied its unforgiving pinpoint nib to paper. I drew my sister with her hair messy and her sock-feet drawn up to her butt on the saggy old couch and used a single scratch of ink to make each needle of the fat little Christmas tree beside her.

Chapter 21

I DROVE to the Nashville airport early, not sure how long the trip would take, but parked the Saab with more than forty minutes to spare. Inside the terminal I watched a GI and his girlfriend play cards on the floor. They sat denim kneecap to army-green kneecap, laughing at the luck the cards showed. I didn't know what the game was, but when they reached the end of something—a set? a hand?—they left the cards between them on the floor and leaned against one another, forehead to forehead, her hair a straight, shining curtain hiding their faces. Under the curtain of her hair, his dog-tags swayed between the two of them like a pendulum.

When the gate attendant announced the arrival of the flight from Newark, the GI and his girlfriend stood and faded into the crescent of people fanned out around the gate, waiting for the passengers to deplane.

Trisha emerged talking to a handsome Asian man. When she saw me, she took a moment to excuse herself from him. She hated to fly. She distracted herself by introducing herself to her seatmate. Her Filofax was crammed with phone numbers, business cards, and notes on people she'd met. She knew people everywhere.

We hugged and I lifted my eyebrows at the departing line of passengers. "Mr. Nashville?"

"Married. He works for an international training company."

"Fascinating."

"A contact. Might be useful if I want to jump ship one of these days." Trisha picked up her bag and I took it away from her. She was not especially tiny, but her stylish and manicured ways made me feel larger and stronger. I often told her that she made a lumberjack of me.

Trisha put her hands on her hips and surveyed me. "Don't hate me for saying it, but you look terrible."

"Gee, and they said a week at the spa—"

"Very funny. Okay, hag, get me out of here. I hate airports."

"Let's go find you food," I suggested, and we joined the flow of pedestrians heading for the main terminal.

TRISHA had checked a suitcase—she never traveled without her own hairdryer and economy-sized bottle of hairspray, not to mention spare handbags and matching shoes, pajamas and slippers and a bathrobe—so we waited by the baggage carousel, jostled by whole families zeroing in on their luggage.

The patchwork of other people's conversations distracted Trisha and me both. Trisha, a Brooklyn girl, found the hard, hilly accent irresistible. We started building a dialogue from the best phrases while we waited:

"Wheel, am I hayippy t'see yuh."

"He up and wint to Morgintawn."

"I niver!"

"I jist dint buleeve whut that lil chile indurd."

"What *Ah* indurd!"

IN THE car, Trisha fell asleep within minutes, her way of avoiding car sickness. She woke when we slowed and bounced over the speed bumps at the gatehouse.

"Sorry!" she said, brightly, her voice hoarser than usual from sleeping with her mouth open. "Did I snore?"

"Like a chainsaw."

She said, "Ha!" and peered out her window. "Are we there yet? Where are we?"

"We're about three minutes from Viv's place. Hey, what is your position on dogs these days?"

"Dogs? I don't mind them. Oh God. George has a huge dog, doesn't he?"

"Yeah. Actually, three of them."

"Oh, good. One probably wasn't obnoxious enough."

"Brace yourself," I said to Trisha as I pulled into the driveway and pressed the remote control for the garage door.

The dogs were waiting in the mudroom doorway, tails and heads held high, standing in descending order of height, left to right, toeing the threshold like canine Rockettes.

"They aren't dogs, they're ponies," Trisha said.

"Dincha always want a pony?"

"Not one with fangs. Wow, are they like attack dogs?"

The dogs surged toward the car, their wrinkled black faces well above the level of the car hood.

I found myself repeating Dear George's description of the dogs. "English mastiffs were bred to be protective, but they are giant cuddle-bugs. They look intimidating, but they're not very aggressive. They are like big, calm bouncers."

"Yeah, right." Trisha was staring at Dwalin, who just then began to drool against her window.

"Well, if there's a stranger, the story is they knock him down or kind of push him into a corner and hold him until the boss comes home," I told her.

"I can imagine."

Whenever I left the house, I repeated Dear George's daily command to the dogs to look after things ("*En garde, mes amis!*"). Dear George said that the dogs liked having a job. I didn't know if they were watching the house in a special way, or if they were just being their usual selves. Still, no sense taking chances. I said "*Mellon,*" as I opened the car door and called out each dog's name.

"Come on, Trisha, it's showtime."

She opened her door gingerly, nudging Dwalin out of the way to make room. She jumped when the dog stuck his head into the car behind her. "What the—?"

"I think he's looking for Dear George. He does it every time," I said, opening the trunk and lifting Trisha's luggage out. Balin had followed me around the back of the car and now joined the other dogs around Trisha.

"That's sad—Ouch! This one stepped on me." Trisha stood waist-deep in mastiffs.

"Give them a minute," I told her. "They want to be sure you're not carrying a gun."

"What?"

"Gotcha. Come on, dogs! Who wants to go outside?"

The dogs reluctantly left Trisha and everyone followed me through the mudroom into the house. I let the dogs out and found Trisha looking around the kitchen.

"Beer?" I asked Trisha.

"Do you have anything else?"

"Wine? And there's a liquor cabinet somewhere—oh yeah, over the sink."

Trisha walked to the sink and stood on tiptoe. "Like I can stretch."

I opened the cabinet for her and stood back to peruse the contents. "Looks like whiskey, tequila, pretty much the whole—"

"Just reach me down some vodka and that can of V-8 juice," Trisha told me. "Now, where is the fridge?"

I pointed to the tall panels and then opened the Subzero refrigerator.

"Cool," she said, admiring the camouflaged appliance.

"Well, Subcool, anyway." I brandished the vodka at her.

Trisha grimaced at the pun and scavenged for horseradish and Tabasco sauce in the fridge. I dished up the dog's kibble and changed their water, and before Trisha had finished her Bloody Mary alchemy, I let the dogs back in for their dinner.

Trisha perched on a tall chrome barstool by the counter, sipping her drink from a tiny straw—I didn't know where she had found the straw, although she might have produced it from her pocketbook. She carried her own Lipton teabags in there, along with gum, mints, dental floss, and a small first-aid kit.

She watched while I cleaned the dogs' faces and then offered to shake hands when I introduced the dogs to her.

"Don't be like that," I said. "They're sensitive to mockery."

She rolled her eyes, but when Tomkin plunked his large haunches down next to her, she held her hand out for him to sniff.

"It's okay," I told them both. "Pet him already. He's not about to bite you."

"He looks mean."

"Not really. Look at those sweet little brown eyes. He's just terribly concerned, that's all. Actually, doesn't he look a little like—what was his name? Turtle Boy?"

Trisha snorted. "Michael. Does not."

"Well, Tomkin *is* a handsome creature, not to mention clever." I opened the fridge. "Chicken for dinner?"

"Anything will be great," Trisha said, and began describing the horror that was airline food.

I washed greens from the crisper and blotted them in a big wooden bowl and made biscuits from a mix Dear George had in the pantry. My biscuits from scratch were never any better than Bisquick ones, anyway. As Trisha talked and I measured out cups of milk, I felt myself relax into the satisfaction of cooking for someone else.

When I started frying the chicken breasts, Trisha slid down from the stool to set places for us at the counter.

"Look at these dishes. Talk about ugly!" Trisha held two of the heavy plates up for me to admire.

I answered by wrinkling my nose.

Trisha looked at the backs of the plates. "Did your sister make these? They're homemade, right?"

I shook my head. "If you can believe it, she and George have been collecting them for years."

Trisha looked at the dishes in the cupboard and grimaced. "It's so heavy. Is this blob supposed to be something?" She flicked a spoon against the pottery. It made an unmusical clunk. She rolled her eyes. "*This* is why mass-production will win in the end. Didn't Viv register for good china when they got married?"

"She never did any of that wedding stuff."

Trisha shut the cupboard with a shudder. "No accounting for taste, I guess, but would it kill them to pick something a little less, oh—ugly?"

"Funny you should say that, actually," I said. "Well, maybe not funny-funny. But funny."

Trisha was folding paper towels into napkin triangles. She looked over at me. "What?"

I put the dogs outside. The scent of browning chicken was proving too much for them.

"The autopsy report came today," I announced.

"Autopsy?"

I flipped the chicken carefully. "They always do one here, apparently, when there's a traffic fatality."

Trisha nodded and made a hurry-up gesture with a hand, her glossy oval fingernails clicking one against the other.

I held up a plate. "Okay, so George was killed by—" I waved the plate around— "ugly pottery."

Trisha's hoarse voice went suddenly clear and musical. "Get out!"

"Yeah. They had been shopping, I guess, for another carload of this stuff." I put the plate down. "When they crashed—" I mimed something hitting my head.

"Oh my God."

"Yeah." I used tongs to tap the chicken on a piece of brown paper. I felt a smile perched on my face. "Death by pottery."

"Stop it!"

"Okay, but it's still, you know, sort of funny."

Trisha frowned at me. "It was ironic, maybe, Nicky, but funny?"

"Look, the man was driving a Volvo. Wouldn't even get into a car that didn't have airbags. He always wore his seat belt. Always used his turn indicators. He measured his tire pressure every morning before starting the car and he checked his rear-view mirrors like twelve times—always. He was the safest driver I have ever seen. Seriously. His car skids off the road and rams into a tree. He might have survived, except for the 'unsecured cargo' in the back."

I stopped to gulp my beer.

"So this ginormous, heavy pottery—which they'd just picked up from the potter—goes airborne in the crash and clobbers him and Viv from behind. And *that's* what kills him. Beyond ironic."

"Fine, then," she said. "Call it funny. But I'm not laughing."

"Me neither."

I pulled the biscuits from the oven and dropped them into a basket. I sat next to Trisha. We looked down at our food for a moment in silence. Steam rose from the biscuits.

"They are still ugly," Trisha said, flicking a nail against the heavy rim of her plate.

The phone rang.

"Oh, crap!" I said. "I never checked messages."

I snatched up the receiver and spent a second brushing off a telephone solicitor who was trying to sell time-share property in Hilton Head. The machine had three messages. I pressed play and pulled the pad and a needle-sharp pencil from the drawer. Nellie Greenspan from the Greenspan Leisure Travel, returning my call. Elaine of Elaine's Eats wondered if I might be back in Sarasota for a catering gig next weekend. And an unfamiliar woman's voice saying, "This is Maynard Investigations; Mr. Maynard asked me to pass along the message that the invoice you discussed went into today's post."

Trisha dabbed jelly onto a biscuit and said, her eyes wide, "Okay, tell me—Mr. Maynard?"

Between bites, I told her about the meeting, and about how he wouldn't—couldn't—explain why Viv had hired him.

"We can figure this out," Trisha said, putting down a fork and reaching for my hand. "So, Viv hired a detective. What's been going on with her?"

"Okay." I pushed my plate back. "Here goes. To start with, Viv is pregnant."

"What? No way! When were you planning on telling me?"

"Pretty much as soon as I heard," I said, my voice sharp, but not angry with Trisha.

"Your sister is pregnant, and she didn't tell you?" Trisha looked at me and continued with less force. "Was she just a little pregnant, maybe?"

I looked at her from the corner of my eye. "Six months."

"And she never said anything—"

"No," I said.

Trisha's rusty voice grew louder. "That woman! She's your sister, but I swear to God!"

I gave her a look.

"Okay, okay—whatever. Since when did your sister want kids?"

I shrugged.

"You don't talk about kids with her." Trisha's voice was flat.

"It's not a subject that we ever discuss."

"Of course you two don't talk about babies. It's like talking about your parents. Or the past. Why would you two talk about anything like that?"

"Trisha, be fair."

She was shaking her head. "I am being fair. She's the one—"

"That was a long time ago," I said.

"Yeah, but—" Trisha had a mouth full of words, but I stopped her.

"'Yeah, but' nothing. Look, Viv never forced me do anything I wouldn't have done myself."

Trisha looked down at her plate and then back at me.

"You *know* this." I said. "She was just—quicker. The decision was already made." Under the fabric of my shirt, I felt my shoulders tighten.

"Nicky, come on. Don't get all hunched up like that. You look like a stork—I mean crane."

It startled a laugh out of me. "Stork is right," I said.

"My big mouth," Trisha said, her expression stricken. "Just shoot me."

"If I shot you, who's going to ask me the hard questions?" I nudged my elbow into hers.

Trisha shook her head.

DURING my second year at Stony Brook, I got pregnant. I didn't think about telling anyone else. The moment I knew, I telephoned my sister.

"It's an emergency," I told Viv. "No joke."

"Okay," she answered. "Wait." I heard her carry the phone into the closet in the apartment she shared with two other medical students. "What is it?"

"I'm pregnant."

"Oh, Christ. You're positive?"

"Both sticks," I said. "I tested twice."

There was a pause, and I heard her exhale.

"I have the rainy-day money," she said. "We'll go to Planned Parenthood tomorrow—no, Friday. I'll call them and schedule you, okay?"

If I had really had doubts, I would have spoken up right then. I would have said, "Hang on, let's talk about this." I would have said, "I'm not sure about an abortion."

If I hadn't been sure, I wouldn't have called Viv. If I hadn't been sure, I'd have gone to Trisha, and we would have talked all night until I *was* sure one way or the other.

But I hadn't. My decision was already made. I barely had money to feed myself ramen noodles. At that point,

I was no more suited to having a child than to flying a jumbo jet. I wasn't ready. It wasn't an easy truth, but I'd known it then. I still knew it, though it was still difficult to think about.

Afterwards, my sister put me in a hire-car to go back to Stony Brook. Before she closed the door, she seized my hand and said, "Don't you dare cry!" She squeezed my fingers painfully tight and her eyes glittered. "Don't! You! Dare!"

I'd rested in bed on Saturday. On Sunday, Trisha had coaxed the story from me. I thought she might go all Catholic-school-guilt on me, but she had been great. In her stubborn, thorough way, she had talked me through the hard questions I probably should have asked myself before I phoned my sister.

Trisha had been the one who asked me if I had talked to the boy, if I was relieved, if—had things been different—I would have wanted to keep the baby.

The thing was, I knew my sister was good at making quick decisions and finding solutions. My sister had always preached about birth control—"If in doubt," she used to say, "double up." When I called her, I knew that she would take over, that she would figure it out, that she had a plan already. And I went ahead and let her.

"SO, okay, obviously she didn't want to tell you she was pregnant," Trisha said.

"For whatever reasons," I said.

"For whatever reasons," Trisha agreed. "But she didn't say a word to you?" Trisha carried her plate and mine to the sink and rinsed them both before loading them into the dishwasher. "No hints? Nothing about a big surprise?" She looked at me. "Sorry."

I drank the last of my beer and shrugged.

"So, what else did she not tell you?"

Chapter 22

DEAR George's service was well attended. The veteran of many such events, Trisha had explained the difference between a funeral and a memorial service to me and told me what to expect. I was grateful that she knew. As we got dressed and ate breakfast, she had a half a dozen questions I couldn't answer about the funeral home, the casket, the eventual burial. She said she would ask Rico Suavé about it all.

Dear George's co-workers were predictably respectable, handsome young brokerage guys and older management types, plus secretaries, assorted spouses. A handful of his fraternity brothers and friends from college turned up, everyone looking older and wider than I remembered.

I hadn't expected the crowd to include whole families with whom George had done volunteer work, or the knot of hard young toughs with Mohawk haircuts and ill-fitting blazers from a mentoring program he'd supported. Four Black guys in shiny blue suits introduced themselves as musicians, friends of George. They shook my hand and strolled off smelling just a little of weed and cigarette smoke, a refreshing change from the sweet odor of cut flowers.

Artie introduced me to the funeral director and then went off to attend to something.

"It's Nicola Jones," I said to the funeral director, a chubby man in a very sharp suit. His wavy hair was marcelled to his head, giving him strong resemblance to Jazz-age posters of Josephine Baker in Paris. "Not Nicole."

"Beg pardon, ma'am."

With nothing else to say, he gave me a sober nod of his sleek head before gliding on his way.

Dear George's father arrived straight from the airport. It took me a moment to recognize him, his skin tanned golden from the Caribbean cruise he'd been on. The white fuzz around his sun-freckled bald spot was trimmed short and his blue eyes turned down on the corners like a Russian icon's. He looked smaller than I remembered, thinner and more worn. He held me in a tight hug before taking a spot with Artie and the funeral director near the front of the room.

He was quickly surrounded by George's oldest friends. From what I could tell, they all called him Dad Rowan.

A trio of elderly white women introduced themselves as friends of St. Bart's. For a disoriented moment I thought of St. Bart himself, martyred and flayed, whose disturbing, rubbery face looks down from the front wall of the Sistine. It's supposed to be a self-portrait of Michelangelo and a commentary on his working conditions. I had spent more than one long afternoon staring at him when I lived in Rome.

I suppressed the urge to ask the ladies how they knew the saint. They were church ladies from St. Bart's Episcopal church. I asked if they were responsible for the stack of casseroles I had picked up from the gatehouse, and they nodded and smiled, murmured kindly about what a sweet man George had been, and told me how sorry they were that my sister was unwell. They patted my arm and moved to the row of folding chairs with tiny steps of their sensible laced shoes.

I spotted Trisha in a quiet corner with Leora Slate, near a disproportionately tall urn of white lilies. They had their heads together, cheerfully engrossed in conversation. Both were gesturing with their hands as they spoke.

The minister from Viv's church hobbled in with crutches and a toe-to-hip plaster cast on one leg. Because of the cast, he was wearing shorts with his sober collar and jacket. Not as young in person as he'd sounded on the telephone, he had a face like an Etruscan statue, all curves around an engaging, gummy grin. He apologized for his outfit as he stood next to me talking about Viv and George. He waved a crutch at the musicians when they spotted him. He introduced me to families who had brought their children, neat in miniature suits and Easter dresses, their eyes round and solemn.

Dr. Pete and the other partners from Viv's office attended, along with too many of my sister's other co-workers to keep track of. The funeral director guided them to the guest book. Dr. Pete startled me by giving me a comfortable kiss on the cheek as if we were old friends. He stood next to me until the funeral director guided me to a seat.

I recognized some residents and doctors who had stopped by my sister's hospital room. Several of Viv's colleagues left early, one by one cupping an important hand to a pager and striding out. "Pulling the doctor card," as Viv would have said, but I supposed it was polite of them to put in an appearance in the first place.

The service surprised me: Dad Rowan briefly thanked everyone for coming, his eyes bright with tears. He sat down without saying anything else, and two of Dear George's college friends came forward and talked about George's practical jokes: the time he had written a message in dandelion seed at the golf course ("Fore!"), the endless pranks involving saltshakers and sugar bowls, the chalk golf balls he slipped into the supply at the local driving range, the hoax involving three off-duty firemen and a birthday cake.

They recounted George's friends' constant attempts at retaliation: itching powder, plastic wrap, and a taxidermized badger that kept appearing as checked luggage. People were laughing and then not, as the two described the empty spot in the world left behind with George gone.

The minister from St. Bart's hobbled up the podium, blew his nose into a handkerchief and spoke a few words from the New Testament, and then the four guys in the blue suits stood up and began singing "Amazing Grace" in a raspy *a cappella*, which shifted without a hitch into a rousing version of "The Lion Sleeps Tonight," George's favorite song.

Artie and Leora had arranged for a catered late lunch at Dear George's favorite restaurant. I sent Trish ahead with them while I drove Dad Rowan back to the house.

"I never hoped to live through this day," he said in the car, looking out the window. "I never thought to see my son gone before me." He gave me a crumpled smile, the ends of his mouth pulled down by sadness.

I felt a surge of helpless pity for him, hot and useless in my guts.

At the house, he wouldn't let me carry his luggage. "I'll be better company after I get some rest," he said, leaning away from the weight of his suitcase. I'd cleared the downstairs guest room for him, and all three dogs trotted with him as he made his way along the hallway. In a moment, the house was still again, and I locked the front door behind me.

Back at the restaurant, people kept telling funny stories and drinking and talking. The din was astonishing. Platter after platter of food kept disappearing from the buffet tables. If I had ever spared a thought for it, I wouldn't have expected a memorial service to be so much like a party.

I thought how I needed to tell Viv about this, and the very idea of describing George's memorial service to Viv felt as if a tree had fallen on me.

If I were her, swimming somewhere in the dark or trying to climb up through this sleep, the last thing I would want to know was that my husband wasn't going to be waiting for me at the end of the effort.

But it was Viv. I couldn't picture her in ignorance. She would know about the car accident and about George. She would know she was unconscious. She would know she was still carrying the baby. I was convinced she would know I was waiting for her to get back.

Wherever she might be—climbing or swimming or wandering—my sister would keep moving, churning through the water, or finding tiny fissures and using leverage to pull herself up, resting calmly and catching her breath on a crumbly shale ledge until she was ready to tackle the next stretch. She had to be.

From across the room, Trisha caught my eye and walked the fingers of one hand across the palm of the other. Did I want to leave?

I did.

Chapter 23

BEHIND the wheel of the Saab, I told myself I was just going back to Viv's house to check on Dad Rowan. He'd had a long Sunday outing with Artie and some of the guys from out of town, returning to Viv's well after I'd dropped Trisha at the airport. But when I peered through the opened door of the spare room and saw him sleeping with both hands tucked under his face, I knew I had driven back because I was going to search through Viv's things until I found out why Viv had hired a private detective.

Tomkin and Dwalin circled the room as I sat on Viv's side of the bed. I pulled the drawer out from the lacquered bedside table and quietly dumped the contents onto the bedspread. I felt around the underside of the tabletop and checked the bottom of the drawer before replacing it and repeating the process with the other drawers.

The resulting pile was impressive: loose papers, bent manila folders, magazines, jars of night creams and lip moisturizers, hair clips and coated rubber bands with stray auburn hairs scribbled around them, two bank envelopes with a fat key in each, some sort of first-aid kit that included a technical-looking thermometer, and Viv's black diary. I took the diary and the paper files with me and left the other things in a jumble on the bed. The dogs followed me downstairs and stood by the back door until I let them out.

I put the papers and folders and the notebook on the kitchen counter and then brewed a pot of coffee. Not that I liked coffee. I was just killing time.

I opened the black cover of Viv's journal. The binding creaked. I flipped to the first entry and then let the cover fall shut with a thump. Ha.

I might have guessed her journal would be disappointing, one way or another. I half expected her to have written in French, or used a secret code, but I hadn't expected this: Viv had only just started this new journal, and there was exactly one entry, dated "Thursday, September 30, 1993."

I opened the book again. The message in Viv's tall, left-slanting handwriting: *"Fresh pages to fill. Abdominal surgery this morning on man w/a lariat tattooed all the way around his waist. Weird. Patient asked us not to cut the rope."*

I wondered if my sister had indeed cut the rope. Patient might still be around, since she'd written the entry less than two weeks ago. Then, sighing, I riffled through the book. Nothing else. I'd have to keep looking if I wanted to find out what was going on in her life.

SHE'D always kept a diary, as long as I remembered. In college, Viv had switched over to these unlined artists' blank books, but when we were kids, she had used old-fashioned black-and-white composition notebooks. Back then, she labeled her journal "Social Studies" or "English" to keep our parents from snooping, though I think I was the only curious one in the family.

Viv had threatened me just once, when, as a nosy eight-year-old, I snuck into her room to read her diary. Of course she caught me.

"If you ever try looking at anything of mine again, Nicola Maria Jones, I swear to God I will leave you alone. Forever." She held me by my upper arms and glared into my eyes, shaking me for emphasis.

I took her at her word and never tried to peek again.

I POURED myself a mug of coffee and let the dogs back in. Then I reached for the pile of papers and opened the top thing: a bent, reused manila folder. It held pages torn from magazines: a model wearing an ankle-length tan leather coat, a faded chintz-covered chaise lounge in a book-filled nook, an angular crystal vase with a bouquet of paintbrushes. Viv's "Idea Book." Since high school, she'd torn pictures from magazines of clothes she liked or design ideas that appealed to her taste. Sometimes she put them into a notebook. As I slotted the slippery pile back into its file, several glossy scraps of paper slid out. On top was a baby's room decorated with a mural of sunflowers and daisies.

I closed the file and leaned on my elbows.

In all honesty, we'd never mentioned the topic of babies even once since that slushy day when she had put me in the car and said, "Don't you dare cry," after the abortion.

Viv was never one to talk about a decision after it had been made, so it was not surprising that she—unlike Trisha—never asked the hard questions about regret and sadness afterwards. What was done was done—I imagine that's how she felt. I certainly didn't want to talk about the pregnancy or the abortion with her—she'd been warning me to be careful about birth control for as long as I could remember.

Plus, she had never liked children. She complained about the noise. She called them brats. She hadn't lobbied to be a godparent when her friends from college started having children.

When I flew off to Rome to au-pair, I didn't talk to my sister about the two little boys in my care. I didn't say how they smelled of chicken soup, and how the clutter of miniature soccer shoes and tiny shin-guards almost broke my heart. I told her how much money I made and what museums I went to, but I didn't talk about the youngsters I watched. I never mentioned how much affection I felt for them, or how much it wrenched to leave at the end of my time with each family.

After Viv announced that she and George had gotten married, neither one of us had approached the idea of whether they wanted to have children.

Still, this picture—these cheerful flowers painted above a curving white crib—must mean something. That she was imagining a room for this child, certainly. That she would include me in making this room, maybe. Surely she wouldn't hire someone else to paint a mural for her baby's room.

I put the file aside with a heavy sigh, which Tomkin echoed. His head was weighty on my knee.

"Aren't you glad you don't have to figure this out?" I said to the dog.

Tomkin shifted his eyes back and forth, looking more mournful than usual. He lifted his big face and nudged my forearm so that my hand fell onto his head. I patted him for a few minutes and then told him I had to get to work. He slid his front paws slowly along the floor until he reclined like a lion statue at the foot of my perch. He rested his head across his paws at such a precise and kingly angle I was tempted to get my sketchbook, but I turned back to the piles of paper.

I had finished a second mug of milky coffee by the time I worked through the mess. I organized the material into stacks: personal letters, bills and receipts, clippings and so on. There were few letters. One note from someone, "J," who could only be a former boyfriend, announcing his marriage and telling Viv—with the unmistakably spiteful tone of someone who has been spurned—how happy he was now.

I found a chatty letter on yellow legal-ruled paper from Marilyn Rowe, Viv's academic advisor at Potsdam. I didn't remember calling her to tell her about Viv. I didn't think she was in Viv's address book, but the two-page letter—all about the new crop of students and her own biology lab—was dated the previous spring and they were obviously on friendly terms. I reminded myself to telephone her.

Viv had stuffed a few slips of paper in with the folders: doodle-covered telephone numbers, lists of items like water, Q-tips, and "bas?" I didn't know what "bas" stood for, and the question mark made it that much more intriguing. I put these scraps in with the letters.

The receipts were not surprising, though I hadn't realized quite how expensive Viv's cashmere undershirts were. I was still thrift-store shopping for my wardrobe, but then again, I had only two pairs of trousers that were not paint-spattered, including the black chinos I wore when working for Elaine's Eats-to-Go Catering Co.

I poured a bowl of cereal and flicked through Viv's Idea Book clippings. Lots of fashion shots, most of which looked recent to me. She'd also saved a bunch of decorating ideas that were at odds with the masculine, stark feel of the house. She'd collected pictures of small, fussy, cottagey-looking rooms, full of floral patterns and color. Shelves with doily paper edging holding delicate cups and saucers. Overstuffed mismatched chintz chairs with tasseled pillows and small tables strewn with leather-bound books. Perhaps she and George were going to get a cottage. Or maybe—the idea slipped into my mind—maybe Viv was planning a house of her own.

I put my bowl into the dishwasher and tried not to imagine my sister collecting ideas for her new dream home: a cozy, cluttered place with no room for large dogs or a basketball-playing neat-freak husband.

The same manila folder of magazine clippings also held a handful of baby items: a deluxe folding stroller, another mural (dancing rabbits on a field of green), a monogrammed white receiving blanket, a lace-rich christening gown. I put these papers aside with Viv's journal and sat for a moment before deciding where to start.

If I were my sister, where would I put my old journals? Into a bonfire? Lined up on a shelf? Boxed and put into storage? Stacked in the back of a closet?

Tomkin followed me into the garage as I scanned the big translucent storage tubs. George had labeled things in his neat, mechanical handwriting: "Christmas lights," "Christmas ornaments," "Fourth of July stuff," "RC plane parts." Nothing of Viv's.

The dog and I surveyed the mudroom, the utility closet, the telephone nook, the cupboards above the washing machine. Viv and George had so much *stuff*. Stores of cleaning supplies, toilet paper, paper towels, extra sets of sheets still in their plastic wrapping.

Back in the study Tomkin watched as I started with the bookshelves. A quick look didn't reveal the plain black spines of Viv's journals, but I did spot the *Emily Post's Etiquette* and the tattered old collegiate dictionary that Viv had considered essential during all our childhood moves. We used to consult *Emily Post* for hints on how other families approached the world; I was tempted to revisit those authoritative pages with those declarations about table-settings and thank-you notes, formal introductions and the art of conversation, but I resisted. Instead, I riffled through the pages quickly, in case Viv had slipped anything into the book. Aside from a slip of blank paper—random, surely—tucked into the section entitled "The Code of a Gentleman," the book was empty.

Reluctantly putting the friendly blue spine back into place, I took a methodical approach to my search, beginning at one end of the wall and looking at each shelf. Where there was room to hide something behind the stacked volumes, I pulled out chunks of books and searched the pockets of space.

When I heard Dad Rowan start the shower, I stopped searching and went to the kitchen to brew a fresh pot of coffee. Someone from St. Bart's had left a batch of blueberry muffins earlier in the week. I popped a couple into George's big oven to warm.

The dogs greeted Dad Rowan in a knot of big feet and wagging tails. "There's coffee and muffins in the kitchen," I called to him. His hands were busy patting the dogs as they churned around him. He looked up and nodded. His eyes were bloodshot.

"Can I make you an egg or something?" I said.

He shook his head and then straightened. "No, thanks, I'll just have some coffee. Looks like you are busy."

I shoved the papers from Viv's room farther along the counter to make room for him to sit. He poured coffee while I took the muffins from the oven and fixed a plate for each of us.

He said that he had meant to save his appetite for lunch, but even as he said it, he was tucking into a blueberry muffin. He told me that he and Artie were going to meet after he went to the hospital to see Viv. Did I mind if he took the car?

Of course I didn't. "I stopped by the hospital this morning," I said. "There's no change yet. She's still unconscious."

Dad Rowan nodded, the corners of his mouth drawing in carefully.

I wanted to ask if he knew if Viv was pregnant, but what if he didn't? It seemed heartless, given how wrecked he looked. I groped for the least painful way to approach the topic.

"I'm grateful that your sister and the baby survived," he said, answering my unspoken question. "From what Artie told me, it's been touch-and-go."

A fresh wave of worry rose in my chest at his words. "Her doctors say we just need to give her some time."

Dad Rowan pursed his lips and looked even more grave. His plate was empty.

"Can I fix you something else?" I said.

He patted my hand. "That was delicious, my dear. Thank you."

The dogs watched from the mudroom as he backed the Saab out of the garage.

I put the dishes in the dishwasher and ran Viv's files back up to her bedroom. While there, I searched George's side of the bed as well and then looked at their closet again. I took a quick survey of the other upstairs closet: luggage, more stacks of linens, a tangle of sports equipment. No stack of black journals. No composition notebook labeled "English."

Back in the study, I used the heavy wooden stepstool to reach the top shelf. A row of magazine boxes— embossed to look like leather with an oval opening that doubled as window and pull-ring—took up a longish stretch of shelving. The first box was empty, but the second held a lone familiar black notebook. A quick look showed Viv's handwriting.

I let the diary slap to the floor, startling the dogs. The other magazine boxes revealed three plain black notebooks. After glancing inside the covers to confirm that these were Viv's, I dropped each onto the floor without further investigation. Tomkin whined from the doorway.

"It's okay," I told him. "It's just books."

I opened one of Viv's journals at random. "*June 21, 1990. Atlanta.*" She was doing her residency then. "*34 hours on call and nothing doing. Unbelievable. Caught up on my sleep—first time in years. George back from Arizona Tuesday.*" I flipped a few pages along.

On July 2, Viv made a list, probably injuries she'd helped treat: "*Compound fracture/femur. Resect lower bowel assist. Misc. sutures.*" Each item included a brief description. Viv used symbols I recognized: the circle with an arrow for male, circle with a cross for female, and mostly obvious abbreviations—"*12yo circle-arrow*" was a boy twelve years old, followed by "*Grn eyes. Scared.*" My attention snagged on "*17 u/blood. Rotten cabbage smell.*" I didn't want to investigate those details.

The next page had this: "*So hot outside. Went to the movies to cool off. Saw Days of Thunder, Die Hard 2. How tall IS Nicole Kidman?!?*"

I turned to the back of the book. She had a list of "Books to Read" that covered three pages in various inks. The journal's last entry was dated January 1991. She had written a long page about where she hoped to work, with pros and cons carefully noted in columns. San Francisco, Tampa, Nashville, Dallas. Nashville's pros included "*DG's work.*"

I put the notebook down and picked up another. The cover was battered, and a water-stain held half the paper in a permanent wave. The book opened on a section of stuck pages.

"*March 4, 1987. National Military Day. Went to hear live jazz last night on the West Side.*" A list of homework assignments followed. She had been in her third year of medical school in Manhattan. Then Viv wrote, "*Merde!*" in black marker, with an arrow pointing at the stain. The ink had melted and smeared, gluing pages together. Viv's handwriting was even more forceful on July 24, 1987, on the other side of the stuck pages. "*Merde au troisième degré! Serves me right, trying to write and take a bubble-bath and drink champagne all at the same time w/DG.*" She had inserted a few more symbols: a swirly heart for "love" and the hobo symbol for "a good road to follow," which was probably a comment on how things were going with Dear George, plus a coy little shooting star, repeated twice.

I could fill in the blanks about the shooting star: a sort of personal scorecard on George. Discomfort—the idea of my wise sister, giddy and playful, frolicking in a bubble-bath with her boyfriend—made me drop the notebook and pick up another. It too was from her residency years in Atlanta. It contained much the same: lists of various surgeries, descriptions of patients, book titles, comments about movies and outings with Dear George dotted with swirly hearts and shooting stars.

Out of curiosity, I turned to the autumn of 1989, Viv's first year in residency, when I'd driven through Atlanta and visited. Viv wrote, "*September 12, N here for three days. Wanted to do a ton of stuff w/her. She ended up cooking for us and helping shop for clothes I didn't need. N seems directionless, lonesome, tired. Her hair looks awful.*"

My hand, seemingly of its own accord, was reaching up to check my hair. I tugged the elastic loose and shook my head. It wasn't awful, I told myself. I smoothed it back into a ponytail and resumed my place in the notebook.

"Wish I could fix her up—but who?" Then, underscored heavily, she'd added, *"I ruined her life."*

What is the expression about eavesdroppers? They seldom hear any good about themselves?

Chapter 24

ONE OF the dogs began sneezing behind me. I looked over the edge of the couch at the animal. Dwalin's expression was all intensity and anticipation, held for a moment in suspended animation as the next explosion came to him. A line of slobber, what Dear George told me was officially known as a "slinger," appeared on the wall next to the dog.

"Blech," I said. Dwalin rubbed his face on a forepaw, paying no attention to me. I got a towel and took a quick swipe at the dog and the wall. The dog wagged his tail and scratched himself a spot to curl up.

Back on the couch, I took a breath.

My sister thought she ruined my life? I reread the entry and then tried to think. In September of 1989, things had been going fine.

But she thought she ruined my life.

I put the idea aside, though it nagged at me. I reached for another notebook. January 1982. The second half of Viv's freshman year at SUNY Potsdam.

VIV's SAT scores had earned her a deluge of mail from colleges all over—even Harvard sent a packet. Reaching for a world-weary air as she flipped through the glossy crimson booklet, Viv had said, "They have a geographic requirement in the Ivy League. They have to recruit from places like the North Country and Wyoming." But we were both impressed.

After pestering the high school guidance counselor for more information about student loans and scholarship applications, Viv took me to the Flower Memorial Library in Watertown and we both researched how to pay for college.

As a result, the week my sister turned eighteen in the summer of 1981, we packed up for Potsdam, New York.

"The SUNY system is great. I'm going to end up spending big bucks on med school anyhow, so I might as well get a bargain undergrad degree."

We moved into a pokey little duplex near the Potsdam library, where we stayed for the next four years. It had two tiny bedrooms ("We'll have to go outside to change our minds," Viv quipped) but the utilities were included in the rent. During the winter, we kept the thermostat pegged at 80, luxuriating in the smell of burning dust as the baseboard heaters fired up.

Viv had one job ready for her when we got there, waiting tables at Rocky's, a diner that might have been the twin of The Pit Stop. She even had some of the same truck-driving customers.

At first, she spent all her free time scaling a mountain of paperwork.

For three days in a row, she camped out in the financial aid office at the university, stubbornly working through the extra forms and bother involved when a student does not have parents. She was energized by getting the better of the labyrinthine regulations. She marched off to Canton, the county seat, to get herself named as my adult guardian.

"The good news," she announced, after one of her bureaucratic siege-days, "is, once I get this guardianship paperwork finalized, we can get a housing subsidy—after all, it's not like I can move you into the dorm with me. Plus, I get bumped up on the financial aid matrix."

I understood Viv's sense of victory. She'd earned it. But truth be told, the better news for me was the relief, finally, from having to worry the people from Social Services would swoop in, put us into care, separate us.

In January, Viv wrote: "*Started work-study job in the bio lab. Ms. Skinner (!) is the manager. Other student workers: Lynda w/the black eyeliner, plaid-pants Sean, and funny Sanjeev who grew up in Indiana.*"

I remembered those people. I let myself be drawn into the journal entries, as if Viv were talking to me.

My sister had blossomed in Potsdam. Despite a full course-load and two jobs, Viv threw herself into the social life of college. She joined groups and went on date after date.

"I don't understand," Ben LaBreara had told me when he and Viv broke up right after high school graduation. "I thought we were doing fine."

It was a refrain I heard often in the next few years. "I guess Viv is right," another one told me. "But it seems like we were just starting to get to know each other."

I felt bad for the boys she ditched so adroitly. They seemed bewildered at how it had come to an end.

"*Film society toured the Roxy, talked about screening a silent film w/live-music accompaniment, the way they were originally shown to the public. Wonder if Etienne from SdcF plays piano? Should have asked. Quel instrument jouez-vous? Bet it means something obscene.*"

The SdcF was the Societe de club Français, which Viv refused to call "French Club." Instead, she would tell me, "I have es-dee club Français tonight, *chérie.*"

I remembered making some crack about sherry or going clubbing with the French. Stupid jokes, but they made Viv smile.

"*It's snowing. Again. Left the Datsun in the driveway. Aced the homework set in Chem. Professor B. stopped me after class to see if I was planning to take her summer seminar. Hmmm.*"

In February, she wrote: "*Went to lunch w/Sanjeev at school cafeteria. Endless mounds of food. Smelled just like high school. Sanj said take Western Thought & Civilization next year, good professor.*

"*Graham from Bio last semester asked me out.*"

Graham from Bio's wasn't around long. He gave her a copy of Kahlil Gibran's *The Prophet*. As far as I knew, she never once opened the book. I'd probably spent more time on the phone with him than Viv had.

I skipped past the list of Viv's homework assignments. A week later, she wrote, "*Got a C on English Comp paper for 'not following the assignment.' Merde! Should have dropped this class after Professor Shilton made the crack about my hair. Asked to re-submit the paper. Due next Monday. Out w/dull Graham from Bio again.*

"*Had tea w/Marie Chou after class—she said to file a complaint about Shilton w/Dean of Students, but worth the time? Too crybaby? I'm smarter than that.*"

I thought about that one for a while before I started to remember. There had been a professor who kept calling Viv "Carrot-Top" or "Little Red Riding Hood." Something inappropriate. Viv was indignant.

"I pay that jerk to teach, not mock me."

"He probably just likes you," I said, because it was the kind of thing she'd tell me when I was in grade school.

She thrust a middle finger into the air. "He can pound sand."

I laughed, but she didn't.

I flipped pages, searching for *what* I didn't know. Then my own name caught my eye.

"*N's first track meet this week. Probably the only kid without parents standing on the sidelines. Probably the only kid w/no one to cheer for her at all. Pitiful. But God knows they wouldn't be cheering for her even if they were around. Make sure she signs up for typing.*"

Starting high school had felt like a genuine fresh start. Our family unit might be a little outside the norm, but Viv and I didn't have to worry about keeping our cover stories straight or traveling in a pack for safety.

When I told Viv I wanted to play sports, she voted for the one least likely to send me to the emergency room. My first choice, volleyball, was fraught with broken fingers and soft-tissue injuries. We agreed that field-hockey was too rough—in Cape Vincent we had ridden the bus with a forward whose magnificent black eye faded only to be replaced by a split lip during her championship season. And while the coaches might have liked having another tall girl for basketball, my sister predicted concussions and knee injuries.

So I ran track. Straight lines, minimal contact, cheap equipment, and less chance to hurt myself than traditional team sports. I never found any particular turn of speed, but I liked the way running long distances took me out of myself, like dreaming, and I had stamina. Additionally, I felt comfortable as part of a team. We had only one track coach, so I was thrown together with a mixed group of other runners—varsity and junior varsity, boys and girls. We all practiced together, doing our sit-ups and push-ups, circling the track, riding the bouncing school-bus to meets at other schools, complaining about wind-sprints, and gossiping about our teammates and schoolwork.

Running was not exactly the most glamorous of spectator sports. I don't remember other kids' parents yelling from the sidelines. The runners used to cheer for each other when the announcer called our names at the starting line. It hadn't seemed pitiful at the time.

In March, Viv found a solution to the problem of the English professor: *"Hope Shilton dies of something lingering. Handing out papers, he goes, 'Girl w/red hair?' I didn't even look up. Then he goes, 'Here you go, Red,' and drops the paper on the edge of my desk. Like my name wasn't on the paper (got an A, thank you very much!).*

"Maybe should have waited until the end of the semester, but really – Red?? What an ass. Waited until the rest of the students cleared out, then: 'Professor Shilton, I'm not sure if you mean to, but when you make remarks about my personal appearance in front of the other students, it seems like it takes away from the learning environment of class.'

"Then silence. Just like Jahn used to do, I let it sink in. Ass-face. It was a sweet touch to quote the student handbook. Marie Chou might be a genius."

How like Viv to score her points without giving up her dignity.

I skipped to the end of the semester, where she had listed her grades: Chem II A, Chem Lab A, Bio II A+, French Conversation A, English Comp A-.

Flipping through the book, my finger stuck on a page in May. *"200 in the mail, plus breakfast shifts next two weeks: rent paid through August!"*

That exclamation point—Viv was proud of her efforts to secure subsidies and scholarships and all manner of financial aid. But "200 in the mail"? She hadn't used a dollar symbol, but she had to be referring to money. I wondered where it had come from. We had both worked as much as we could, Viv always aiming to pick up the heavy-tipping breakfast shift and me sometimes going straight from one babysitting gig to another.

I didn't know how much we paid in rent for that duplex apartment, though I did remember that having the utilities included was the main reason we stayed there for all four years in Potsdam.

It seemed like the finances just chugged along once Viv got to college. I was pretty sure things were easier in Potsdam. Our phone never got turned off, though we didn't always pay the whole bill at once. Then, too, since we didn't use envelopes of cash to organize our finances, it might have just *seemed* less iffy.

Viv took us both to the bank when we moved to Potsdam, where she started a checking account for herself and made sure I put something aside in a savings account of my own each week. We still had oatmeal weeks, but financial aid or a student loan or something always trickled in. I remembered not worrying about money so much during those years, but based on that exclamation point, I bet Viv did.

At the end of the journal, in August of 1982, before classes started, she wrote: "*N babysat this weekend—she washed, dried, & folded every sheet we owned, every towel, the blankets, & all our clothes. No laundromat run until who knows when!*

"*Cracked me up. Totally serious N goes: Put the laundry money toward new underpants. In another life, she would be telling the servants, Arrange for the ball-gown to be delivered by noon.*"

I didn't remember that particular weekend. I spent a lot of time babysitting.

When we got to Potsdam, I looked into setting up at the farmer's market, but it already had table after table of organic produce and preserves. At fourteen I was still too young to work at the usual fast-food restaurants, so babysitting was my only option.

We'd picked up a cheap bicycle at a yard sale, and I mastered it—barely—by grim effort. I had skinned knees and scuffed palms to show for it all summer, but with the bike, I could circle town in thirty-five minutes or so.

I made up a flier with a fringe of tear-off tabs with my name and phone number and the words "experienced babysitter" printed neatly along the bottom. I rode around town and posted fliers at the country-club end of town, in the larger, cleaner grocery store, and in the prosperous-looking hardware shop.

The phone was ringing by the time I got back to the apartment.

I was good at babysitting. I could keep a group of youngsters busy and happy and take the odd fifteen minutes here or there to run the vacuum or do the dishes. Some of my regulars, like the Bebernes family, would hire me for whole weekends at a time.

"Anybody can take care of kids," Viv said. "It's essential to get some kind of trade, make decent money."

Decent or not, babysitting money kept us in food in Potsdam—plus I signed us up for the food cooperative, which made Viv grumble, but which meant we a few cheap staples each month in exchange for working a shift in the back room of the patchouli-scented co-op store. I learned to cook even more variants of chili, most without meat.

SELF-indulgence tempted me to keep reading, but I suspected that I wasn't learning anything useful—nothing essential, as Viv might say—from these old journals. What *was* interesting was that these four books each represented a year or less of Viv's history. By rough estimate, I'd say there had to be at least a dozen journals missing, including the composition notebooks from when we were kids. She was not the kind of person to throw away her journals. It looked as if Viv or maybe someone else had removed most of her journals from the leather-look cardboard files on the shelves.

She'd hired a private detective.

If she'd hired Ed Maynard to investigate something from our past, then my sister might have handed over her diaries to prove something or another. And it stood to reason that if she had given the private detective the diaries that included important clues or facts or whatever—these remaining diaries were, obviously, not important. Great.

Torn between why and where and who, I sat staring at the black books until the sound of paper dropping through the mail slot woke the dogs. Balin remained curled on her rug, but the other two trotted to the foyer to investigate.

The telephone rang just then. I got to the phone before the answering machine picked up. The gatehouse was calling to tell me that the housekeeping service was here. Did I want them to come in?

I did.

While the cleaning crew—four women in blue polo shirts and puffy vests carrying buckets and brooms—did their usual, I sat outside on the picnic table with my sister's black notebooks and watched the dogs as they snuffled their way around the lawn.

Okay, I thought, *these* notebooks got left on the shelf. Of the whole bunch of journals, *these* were not useful. They must not have contained some specific information. About our parents? About Viv wanting a baby?

I looked at the house. Electric light shone into the gloomy day from windows upstairs and down. The cleaning crew was running the dryer, the hot air a domestic waft of scent across the open lawn.

I opened Viv's journal from 1982.

"*Midterms this week. Half shifts at the diner. All I want to do is go clothes shopping. A London Fog trench-coat lined in sable. LaPerla underwear. New socks. & a set of wings for the pigs flying around me.*"

This I understood. This was the Viv I knew.

"*Went to kegger at Clarkson w/Charlotte to celebrate. Smart boys, stupid party. Too much cigarette smoke & too many beers.*" She used the circle-arrow symbol for boys and on the next page, the swirly heart in place of the word "love": "*Saw Breaking Away at the Roxy w/Steve Z. Love that movie. Steve Z is a bad kisser.*"

Chapter 25

I PAID the cleaning crew with cash from the neat stack George had left in the telephone nook and marked the calendar when they were scheduled to return. As I looked at the date, I hoped that Viv would be awake by then. I didn't dare calculate how long after *that* until I got back to Sarasota.

My stomach clenched. I'd left behind a half-finished wall mural in Sarasota. The architect must be tired of looking at it in the living room. I'd already had to skip out on catering events where my friend Elaine had planned on my help. I hadn't talked to Gabrielle, the friend who had offered wall-space in her swanky gallery on St. Armand's circle for my paintings in the coming spring.

I was missing a second week of classes at the New School. The beach-volleyball team was playing without me. That careless circle of friends was eating boisterous meals that I hadn't cooked, talking about art, and laughing about everything without me.

INSIDE the house, the dogs patrolled, huffing a little at the smell of lemon before settling down. Looking at the neat piles of mail the cleaners had left on the desk, I sat myself down.

"Sorry, Viv," I said aloud as I used the letter-opener on the first of the envelopes with windows.

Then I said, "Whoa."

Balin opened an eye from her perch on her dog-bed and shut it again.

I could cover the electric bill from my own checkbook, but it would wipe my account clean in less than two months. I plunged into the rest of the pile. Maybe it was a matter of scale—add a couple of zeroes, and it wasn't that different from my own finances. They were doing all right.

The bottom of the pile came too quickly. I toyed with the idea of cooking something for lunch, but I wasn't hungry. I told myself to stop avoiding. Back to the search.

I spun the chair to look around at the study again. A whole row of three-ring binders stood on a shelf within easy reach. I pulled out the oldest binders, the ones with the seams beginning to split. They were fat with schoolwork and endless pages of Viv's class notes from college and med school. Organic Chemistry, Cellular Biology, Physical Chemistry.

In the newer binders, Viv had saved the scientific programs from conferences entitled things like, "Topics in Gastroenterology" and "Abdominal Wall Reconstruction." A messy chunk of paper for each conference—and she had gone to the effort to three-hole punch it and save it.

The last binder under my hand was the color of red licorice. It smelled industrial and new. The first section, marked with a neatly typed label, "Admin" held a safe-deposit agreement letter from Marine Midland Bank. This bank was located in midtown Manhattan, which made it inconvenient for snooping. I supposed that explained one of the small bank envelopes with the key I'd found in Viv's bedside table.

The next section, "Vitals," opened to a familiar document in a non-glare protective sleeve. My own birth certificate.

The sight of it was like a cold draught on my skin.

When we were little and moving, sometimes with only a day or two's notice, Magda and Jahn had often squabbled about family documents. One or the other of them would have stuck the birth certificates and other important papers in a different spot and then they would have to tear things apart to find them.

My sister put herself in charge of our birth certificates around the time I started first grade. It was Viv who always brought them with us to the first day at a new school and it was my sister who made sure that the embossed forms were stashed close to hand in every new house when we moved.

The thing was, I'd taken over responsibility for my own birth certificate as a teenager. At any given time, I could have said precisely where the yellowing form was stowed. This was a crisp new photocopy inside the plastic sleeve. My sister must have made a copy the last time I stopped to visit her in Tennessee.

She must have, I thought was a lurch, *filched* the document from my backpack. She would have had to look through everything I carried in my luggage until she found the plastic file case tucked into my portfolio.

I wouldn't have said no if she'd asked. She had to know that. I'd never say no to my sister for anything. I'd give her the blood in my veins. In fact, I *had* given her blood from my veins.

Last spring, taking the long way back to Brooklyn from Florida, I'd stopped here at my sister's house. After parking the truck, I'd run upstairs to the guest room with my backpack so I could brush my teeth and splash water on my face.

The dogs were sniffing around the room when my sister came in. They gave her a wide berth. "Roll up your sleeve," she had said, slotting several paper-wrapped packets from her blazer pocket. "I want to check something."

She swabbed my arm with an alcohol wipe. "I'm going to extract some blood," she said. "Look out the window while I do this."

I didn't. I watched dark red blood fill the plastic cylinder. I asked her what she was doing, but I didn't really expect an answer.

"Oh, I'll tell you if it comes to anything," she'd said, her airy tone making it obvious that she didn't think my blood would amount to much.

"You're not concealing a nameless malady that only I can cure?" I tried to sound like one of those earnest young people from one of her Victorian books. "Tell me, tell me, do—is it consumption? The gripe? A galloping case of the vapors?"

She snorted. "Not hardly." Her hands on my arm were quick and professional. "Say 'Ha!'" she said.

I did, and the blood flowed a little faster.

"Cool, huh?" she said. "The beauty of blood pressure."

"Yay, blood pressure," I said. After a moment, she pressed a cotton-ball over the spot, removed the needle, and bent my arm around the cotton. I nodded at the vial in her hand. "So?"

"Sew buttons." Viv used a childhood in-joke, but her tone suggested that the conversation had reached a dead end.

I let the whole topic go. Since medical school, she had rarely explained herself to me. She made decisions and moved on. I thought it was mostly a doctor thing—

her native bossiness encouraged by having whole staffs of support people waiting for her command. If she made up her mind not to tell me why she was doing something, what was the point of arguing? She would tell me, or she wouldn't—I couldn't force her to explain.

But now, with a copy of my birth certificate tucked into a plastic sleeve and filed neatly inside this red binder, I wondered.

She'd taken a sample of my blood and—here was proof—she must have snuck into my things to get hold of my birth certificate. Viv had *snooped* through my things. This was hard to believe. My sister despised snooping. I'd never known her to be sneaky. She believed in privacy. I didn't think she would ever have stooped to pawing through someone else's private things.

But she had.

Instead of asking to look at my birth certificate—she must have guessed I wouldn't have pressed her for an answer. If nothing else, she had to know that—she'd rooted around in my bag on the sly. It was so unlike her. Maybe she'd hired someone else to do it.

That thought made me stop and realize how crazy it sounded. Not like my birth certificate was top secret anyhow. Who cared if she copied it? What would I think next—that my big sister had hired an operative to make off with the top-secret microfiche? I was an idiot. I opened the binder again. There must be a good reason she hadn't told me.

Over the years Viv must have looked at my birth certificate a thousand times, same as me, waiting outside all those principal's offices in the new schools, sitting on a hard chair while the inevitable secretary pecked at a typewriter. The birth certificate was nothing special: the ornate crest of Bridgewater Township in the State of Pennsylvania, the hospital and attendant at birth, three dates: date of birth, date filed (three days later) and date issued. There was my name, Nicola Maria Jones, the names of John and Mary, and the word *female.*

Why did it make my blood drop a degree or two to see this sharp-edged copy, with the grayed colors rendered clear and black on the fresh white paper? It was the same old information. The raised seal from the original had bent the light so it showed crisp as a coin on the photocopy.

I wanted to put the cover back over the paper and not touch the binder again until my sister was awake next to me, explaining everything.

I gritted my teeth and turned the page. Viv's own birth certificate followed, issued by the Commonwealth of Pennsylvania in the township of Cannalega. John and Mary A. Jones, the name of an attendant, the various dates, and Viv's tiny footprint, almost square, with the arches leaving tiny crevasses like the topographical map of a wee badlands.

Something caught my eye.

I flipped back to my own birth certificate. Date issued: October 8, 1968.

I looked at Viv's certificate. Date issued: October 22, 1968.

I'd been captivated once by a wonderful Art-Deco etching in a book. It showed Pandora in the act of lifting the lid of the forbidden box. All stylized 1930s curves, she knelt with her long fingers still holding the lid ajar as a river of evil spirits flowed out. The bend of Pandora's round knees echoed the waves of her hair. Her face turned away from the box—the smooth and elegant lines of her expression distilled the very essence of regret. I hadn't thought of the picture for years, but I felt the parallel.

I dug a fingertip into the sharp, heat-sealed edge of the binder. It didn't matter if my birth certificate had been issued before my sister's. What did it even mean, *issued*?

Pandora's box? I was being stupid. And melodramatic. These were photocopies of the same old official documents that had been part of my life forever.

I turned the plastic page and found another document marked by the crest of the Commonwealth of Pennsylvania in Cannalega. I read it twice before I could begin to understand.

It was my sister's death certificate.

Vivian Marguerite Jones, daughter of Mary Alice and John MacKenzie Jones of Nathan, Pennsylvania. Issued August of 1964. W.P. Bilden, MD, Cor., had scrawled the words "pneumonia," across the small line for cause of death, and for her age, he had filled in "13 months."

I flipped the page, my heart beating so hard that I watched my fingers tremble with the rhythm of it.

There was no death certificate for me, just a small note on the Obituary page of the *Montrose Independent*, November 17, 1966.

"Infant Nicola Maria Jones returned to heaven. Daughter of Mary Anne and John Jones of Montrose, sister to Robert and Scott and granddaughter to Alice and Robert Jones, Sr. Her uncle, the Reverend Simon Hamelin will officiate at a private service for immediate family at Holy Mary on Thursday at 11 am."

Something was wrong. Something had to be untrue, or a mistake. I didn't understand. My sister might have enjoyed the macabre joke of finding a tombstone with her own name on it. After all, what could a person expect, with a name like "Jones"? But this was too much. Why document these coincidences? These unlikely birthday-twins? I didn't even know what to call these two dead baby girls with the same names as us.

The same names and the same birthdays, only they didn't grow up to become my sister and me.

My fingers were turning the page before I could think to command them. The phrase "returned to heaven" kept repeating in my mind, and I didn't want to let my eyes trace the words again.

The next transparent page contained a lab report summary dated from last spring. The computer printout was smudgy with carbon and but had copied clearly enough. *This* was the reason for the blood Viv had taken from my arm.

The laboratory had tested two blood samples. Sample one, which Viv had labeled with a tiny arrow and her own initials, and sample two, which had its own arrow and my initials. Both blood samples belonged to the A-positive group. Viv had scribbled "35% of pop = A+. Most likely sibs."

There was nothing else in the binder.

Most likely siblings? People were forever mistaking the two of us for twins. We had the same long feet and long hands, the same overlapped wolf-teeth, identical fat eyelids. We had similar voices and we often said the same thing at the same time. We laughed at the same things. We were both really tall. Of course we were siblings. Had she truly doubted it? She must have doubted it enough to make sure.

The phrase came back to me: *returned to heaven.* The two little girls who didn't grow up to become Vivian and me. And my sister's careless jotted note: "Most likely sibs."

The two little girls who didn't grow up to be Viv and me—it occurred to me painfully late, like a hammered thumb finally transmitting the hurt: *those* girls were not sisters.

Viv and I were not those little girls. The little Nicola Maria Jones who returned to heaven was *not* the sister of that Vivian who died of pneumonia. And neither was I.

What's more, Viv had known this for some time and kept it to herself.

Very gently, I put the licorice-red binder back down on my sister's desk. Pandora herself couldn't have wished more than I did to close it up again. My sister's doubts—now mine as well—pouring out of this binder.

I was not Nicola Maria Jones. She was not Vivian Marguerite Jones Rowan. My palms felt clammy. Someone's life was getting ruined. A cool sweat started on my back. Darkness feathered the edges of my vision.

I pushed the cushy leather chair away from the desk and leaned over my knees. Recite the alphabet, I told myself, as my sister would have suggested. Go like this, take deep breaths. I put her advice to work. One of the dogs, Balin, lifted her head and looked across the room at me, our eyes on a level. "E F G," I told her, and the dog turned her head to the side, considering me from an angle as I continued, "H I J K."

IT took longer than it should have—years of practice at not thinking about things finally paying off—but the thought came to me before I got to the end of the alphabet.

"If we aren't Nicola and Vivian Jones," I said to Balin, sitting up fast enough to feel dizzy all over again. "Who are we?"

Which was the question I needed to ask Ed Maynard, because *that's* what Viv had hired him to find out.

Chapter 26

I DON'T recall the exact circumstances of why I didn't finish second grade. We moved in April before school was out. Viv enrolled and completed her sixth grade, but I stayed home with Magda. I wasn't ill. Perhaps I had already finished my classwork for the year—I was reading before I started school, so those first years weren't a big challenge.

Maybe they kept me from school to stay with Magda because Jahn was away. It was a blank to me. Viv would be bound to remember it all better than me.

I spent the long days of that May at home with our mother. I helped her put in a little flower garden. She let me stir eggs into a batter. She made us cinnamon toast for a snack. Each morning full of promise, as if the day was an untouched pad of paint in a new box of watercolors.

To sit next to my mother on the back stoop in Rossie as she drank a glass of hot black tea meant that I, too, noticed the squirmy brown weasel bounding around the broken-down hay wagon next to the barn. "*Mustela nivalis*," she said, barely moving her lips to speak. "The least weasel. 'Mustela' is the family of weasels and mink and ferrets. 'Nivalis' is 'wintery,' because it changes coats into white for the winter."

The bright mustard-colored goldfinches dipping from perch to perch were looking for tiny seeds, she explained. "They are *Carduelis tristis*. 'Carduelis' means 'thistle,' and they eat the seeds. 'Tristis' means 'sad.'"

"But why call them sad?" I asked, forgetting to hold still. The birds retreated to the trees in a bright swoop.

"Maybe the scientists judged yellow an unhappy color."

"Or maybe," I said, trying to be clever, "maybe because the finches make the *thistle* sad when they eat the seeds."

My mother didn't seem to hear. She focused her gaze back over the neglected farmyard. "Hold still," she said. "And listen."

I held still and listened. Birds sang and the grass rustled, from wind and, maybe, from something else.

She set the tea on the stair and rose to her feet. She cocked her head, listening, and then stepped neatly across the grass. She held a finger to her lips and beckoned me to follow. She stopped where the lawn met the field. At the sagging barbed wire fence, last year's unshorn hay was exposed from pale green growth at ground-level up to the towering blonde tips.

She pointed. A flash of silvery-brown velvet showed in a tiny path at the roots of the hay.

"*Sorex araneus*, the common shrew. Eats twice its weight in slugs and insects every day. 'Sorex' means 'shrew-mouse.'" She shrugged, as if to say that the early scientists lacked imagination. "But 'araneus' means 'spider.' Back then, they thought shrews had a poisonous bite."

The shrew flashed by again. My glance met my mother's and we both smiled.

"Shrews aren't poison, but they are the fiercest little things you'll ever see," my mother confided. It felt as if she was presenting me with a gift-wrapped box of treasure.

"*Sorex araneus,*" I repeated.

Before I could think of a good question to keep my mother talking, the phone rang, and she crossed the yard and nipped into the house.

The shrew rustled noisily at my feet. I heard the juicy, unmistakable sound of chewing. I bent to the pathway and saw the tiny animal holding still as it devoured an earthworm. It had started in the middle, pinning the hapless ends of worm to the ground with both forepaws.

The worm wiggled even as the shrew wolfed it down. It was over in an instant, before I even had the chance to wish someone else had seen it with me.

Chapter 27

PERCHED on the elegant cream-colored sofa in the small reception area outside of Artie's office, I didn't pick up a glossy magazine from the neat arc on the coffee table.

A fuzzy-looking print of a quaint fishing village, hung on the wall behind his assistant's desk, kept drawing my attention. Though it was expensively matted and framed, the print itself was just slightly out of register, the colors misaligned so that a tiny hem of yellow showed along the lower edges of the huts and boats. The blurring was visible even from across the room.

After five minutes or so, Artie flung open his office door and bounced into the reception area. After an indecisive moment of greeting, we settled on a brief hug hello.

"Come in, come in."

We sank into chairs on opposite sides of Artie's big desk.

"Nicky, what can I do for you?"

I retrieved a folder and Viv and George's big checkbook. "First, I need to write a couple of checks for these—" I held up a fan of bills. "And—"

Artie held out a hand and leafed through the bills. He gave me a blank look.

"I need to have you sign checks for these," I repeated. It didn't seem all that complicated. "They are due next week."

Artie's expression cleared, and then he squinted at me. "You know the standard way to write a check, right?"

I felt my eyebrows climb. I wondered how he imagined I lived, how I paid my own bills. I felt heat in my face as I thought about what Viv might have said about her irresponsible little sister.

"Yes, Artie, I know how to write a check. I just need to have someone sign for Viv. And since you are their lawyer, I thought you should probably do it." It seemed to me that I was being patient.

Artie scooted himself closer to the desk. "In point of fact—ah. Well. Legally, I cannot. Your sister assigned power of attorney to you."

"But, power of *attorney*?" I said, with a sinking sensation.

"That means you are her legal representative and that she made you responsible for looking after her affairs." He didn't sound exactly condescending, but his explanation seemed to be aimed at a rather slow student. "Among other things, you can write checks for any reasonable expenses. Just sign your name along with the initials 'POA' in place of her signature."

"That works?"

Artie nodded and leaned back in his chair. He smiled. For a moment I was reminded of Dear George and his dogs after they'd been very good. Artie seemed genuinely happy that I'd understood.

"It's not a complicated matter at all. It's a common arrangement for legal representatives. I also informed the hospital that you are your sister's next of kin, as per her and George's will."

I felt my face stiffen.

"It means that you are legally the person to make medical decisions for your sister and her child," Artie continued. "I sent—ah—a copy of the power of attorney paperwork to your sister's bank. There shouldn't be any delay in processing the checks. I'll have a notarized copy sent to the house in case you need it for anything else."

I nodded. "Thanks."

"What else can I tell you?"

I flipped through the check stubs in the big ledger checkbook. "Do you know Ed Maynard?" I asked.

"Sure do. Ed does quite a bit of work for us."

"And for Viv?"

"Ah, well. That's something I meant to approach with you. I'm glad you brought it up."

"Why's that?" I asked, keeping my eyes on the checkbook. I tried to make my face smooth and untroubled.

"When we were drawing up the paperwork for your sister's will—it's customary to identify all living relatives." His voice took on the practiced cadence of a lecture. "I understood from George that she was an orphan, but she explained to me about your parents."

"They left," I said. "When Viv was in high school." I thought for a moment about the various ways Viv had explained our childhood to people over the years. I didn't think Artie needed to hear details from me. Besides, who knew what my sister had told him?

Artie cleared his throat. "Right. Vivian said she hadn't heard from them in something like five years."

I thought I must have misheard. "I'm sorry. What did you say?"

"Ah—Viv said it had been a few years since she'd heard from her parents. She said she had no wish to contact them, but we agreed that it would be sensible to at least locate them. I gave her Ed's number and she said she would have him look into the matter."

"Yes," I said. My voice sounded almost normal, even to myself. "I met with Mr. Maynard earlier this week."

"Ah," Artie said. "How's it going?"

"He wants to give the full report to Viv."

Artie plucked a pen from his desk-drawer and twisted it in his fingertips. "Maynard is a good investigator. Very thorough."

"And discreet," I said.

"Absolutely," Artie agreed, with another happy smile for his slow student making such strides. "Wouldn't use him otherwise."

I DIALED Ed Maynard's telephone number and when the receptionist asked for a message to give to Mr. Maynard, I kept it brief.

"Tell him it's Nicola Jones. Tell him I know what my sister—Dr. Rowan—hired him to do. Ask him to please call me when he has time to talk."

He phoned within an hour. I wondered, with a malicious little start, if it had taken him all that time to work up the nerve to call me back. My skin was prickly with irritation.

"I just got your message from my service," he said. "They told me your sister explained what she hired me for. I'm pleased as punch to know she's—"

I interrupted. "Actually, I was talking with Artie Slate. He told me Viv hired you to find our parents. My sister is still—" I struggled with the sentence. "She's still unconscious."

"Oh. I am sorry."

"Will you tell me what you've learned so far? Since I am her legal representative and it's not a secret anymore?"

"Nicola, I don't think this is the sort of thing you want to hear over the telephone."

I didn't answer. In the pause, I heard him fire up his Zippo lighter and take a sharp breath of smoke.

"Hello?"

"I'm here."

"This is not easy. You understand this is an unusual situation. I don't want to—" He stopped and sighed. Then his voice sounded firmer, as if he had come to a decision. "You understand that your sister asked me to locate your parents?"

"Yes."

"She provided me with notes and dates and various information. Diaries, letters, addresses and so forth. She explained how she had been hearing from them regularly by mail up till the spring of 1988."

He stopped to take a breath of cigarette smoke. My thoughts raced. 1988. Go figure. 1988 was eight years *after* they drove into the sunset. Eight years, and Viv had never said a word to me.

In 1988, I was in Rome, and Viv was finishing up medical school. Eight years of missed birthdays and graduations and Viv had known where they were the whole time?

Ed's drawl brought my attention back to the telephone. "I did some research, made some calls, and then I took a trip to Malone, New York, the last address Vivian had for them."

"Malone," I repeated.

"It's a little town right next-door to the back of beyond. On the edge of the Adirondacks—"

"I know where it is," I said.

"Right. Well, I went to their last address and found out—I'm very sorry to tell you this. Are you sitting down?"

I told him I was.

"This is not the kind of thing you should hear over the telephone, but I found out that John and Mary—Jahn and Magda—Jones passed away in January of 1989 of accidental carbon monoxide poisoning. From a kerosene space heater in their apartment." Ed gave me a moment. "I'm so sorry."

"You're sure it was them?"

"Yessum. I spoke with their landlord, their neighbors. People who worked with him described him and his wife, his accent, his working habits."

I wasn't surprised, somehow. Jahn and Magda were dead. Really dead. It would probably hit me later.

Ed's voice was gentle. "Do you want me to give you a minute? I'm preparing a written report. You may find it's easier to take in on paper—"

"No. Just tell me. What did you do next?"

"Well, naturally I phoned your sister."

"But she had been in a car accident."

"Not exactly. This was earlier in the summer. I spoke with your sister, and she told me to keep looking."

"Keep looking?" I repeated, stupidly.

"Are you sure you want to hear this now?" Ed asked. "I'll be back in Nashville by the end of the week. We could meet—"

"No. Just tell me."

"During our initial consultation, your sister explained that she harbored suspicions about her—your—parents."

I made a noise of agreement. I'd heard all about my sister's suspicions. She'd had a dozen contradictory theories about Jahn's possible mob connections or criminal activities. I think she enjoyed making up histories for our parents.

When they'd left, I'd tried not to think about why. As a kid, it was enough for me that they'd left us. That was the most important thing. They were gone. Anyway, I had *thought* they were gone.

Now they really were.

Ed continued, "Vivian told me that she thought that Jahn and Magda might not be your birth parents."

"Wait. What?"

"When I first met with her—" Ed spoke carefully. "Your sister asked me to locate her parents. She said that she was not convinced that Magda and Jahn were her biological parents. She explained the estrangement with Magda and Jahn and the circumstances under which they left. On top of that, she told me that she had recollections that didn't seem to fit her family history."

"Recollections?" I said.

"Yessum," Ed said. "She explained that, over the winter, a couple of unsettling memories had resurfaced that made her want to find out about Magda and Jahn."

Last winter, I thought. I felt my head bobbing at the end of my neck. The pencil in my hand was tracing the word "Malone" on a piece of scrap paper.

Ed continued, "So, after Malone, I paid a visit to Cannalega township in Pennsylvania."

"To investigate Viv's birth certificate," I said. I had nearly forgotten about Viv's red binder with its official documents.

"That's right," Ed said. "And it looks as if your sister's birth certificate—the one she has been using? It rightly belongs to a child that passed away of crib death back in 1964."

"What about mine?"

"Are you okay, ma'am?"

"You looked at my birth certificate as well?"

"Yessum. Your birth certificate belonged to a baby girl who didn't live more than a week. That was in the next town over from Cannalega."

I took a breath. Ed puffed on his cigarette.

"How does—why do we have the wrong birth certificates?"

"That's the question, isn't it?" Ed said. "I'd have to say that it's very *very* unlikely that this was some kind of mistake. Someone had to look high and low for a pair of birth certificates with these particular similarities. Whoever it was—and, frankly, anyone with a little knowledge and a lot of patience can create a whole identity starting with a birth certificate like this—"

"So someone *found* these birth certificates?"

"Manner of speaking only," Ed said. "I expect someone spent a good while combing through vital records until they found two children with the right ages and genders, with the same parents' names. Then they simply requested the birth certificates, paid for them, and went on from there. Unfortunately, the county doesn't keep records of who has ordered copies of the certificates."

"But we've always had these birth certificates. "

"Not quite always," Ed's drawl sounded kindly.

My shoulders squared up. "So, Mr. Maynard, who are we really?"

Ed coughed over a laugh. "Isn't that just like your sister? She said the very same thing."

When I didn't answer, he continued, his voice more professional.

"That's what I'm looking into. Proceeding with the assumption that someone—maybe Jahn and Magda Jones, maybe not—wanted to create a new identity for you and your sister. A couple of scenarios present themselves as to why, but it's all speculation until I can—as you might say—get a line on where Jahn and Magda come from."

"Are you getting a line on that?" I spoke mechanically, thinking that I already felt distant from the moment, as if this conversation had already happened a long while ago.

"That remains to be seen," Ed admitted. "I drove out to the places your sister told me you two lived as kids: Rossie, Vergennes, Massena, Cape Vincent, you know the towns, I think. Talked to neighbors and such. There's a woman your folks used as a reference in Maine—"

"In Maine?" I said. "I'm pretty sure we never lived in Maine."

"Right," Ed said. "Short story: in 1969, John and Mary Jones signed a lease agreement on a house in Vergennes, Vermont. They listed two references— standard stuff. By chance, the landlord still had that lease on hand. I managed to track them down."

"So what did they say?"

Ed sighed. "The one, an electrician, had retired to North Carolina, and passed away last year. The other is a woman named Penny Hardiwick."

"Penny Hardiwick?" The pencil in my hand had written "Maine" in an acrostic from "Malone."

"Yessum. She was one of Magda's classmates at the University of Pennsylvania from—" Ed paused, perhaps to read his notes. "1962 through '64. Only it wasn't Mary Jones back then. It was Marsha Ranklin."

"Wait."

"Yessum?"

"Viv was born in 1963. Or, wait—"

Ed's voice was very gentle. "Your sister and I reckon that those birth certificates are pretty close to your physical ages—give or take six months or a year."

I watched the pencil trace perfectly round numerals: 1966. The year I was born. The year I'd *thought* I was born.

"Nicola? Would you like me to give you a moment? Call you back?"

All the truth you want to pay for.

"No," I said. "What else did you find out?"

"Last week after we spoke, I took a drive up to Three Churches over in West Virginia to speak with a woman, name of Bethany Ranklin." Ed cleared his throat. "This would be the paternal aunt of Marsha Ranklin—of Magda Jones."

I nodded, and then made a noise to indicate that I was still listening.

"Miss Ranklin is seventy-eight years old; she raised Marsha from a little girl. She's a sharp country woman. I'm pretty certain that Marsha—Magda—would not have been able to conceal a pregnancy from her school friends, as well as from her aunt, during the timeframe when your sister would have been born."

Ed lit another cigarette.

"Miss Ranklin had not heard from her niece since 1988, though up until then they had been in contact regularly."

He paused to take a sip of something.

"She said she'd never met her niece's husband, Jahn. There was some bad blood between Marsha and Miss Ranklin's brother—that would be Magda's uncle, who has since passed away—regarding the marriage. The quarrel was that she married outside the church, and to a foreigner.

"I showed her the photo your sister provided of Magda Jones. Miss Ranklin identified her as Marsha Ranklin.

"Miss Ranklin allowed me to look through the family photo albums—there will be copies of those in the written report I'm preparing—and we discussed the family a little. The Ranklins don't have a history of red hair. And as far back as Miss Ranklin can recall, no one in the family has stood even close to six feet tall."

"Wow," I said, for lack of anything else.

"I'm sure it's a lot to take in."

I agreed that it was. After a longish silence, I said, "What next?"

"You want me to keep looking?"

"Yes," I said. "Of course. She wants to find out who we are."

Ed told me that he had a few days' work back here in Tennessee, and then he'd probably go to Kansas City to catch up with another one of Marsha Ranklin's college roommates. Was there anything else he could tell me?

"Do you have—did you say that Viv gave you some journals?"

He sure did.

"Do you need them still?" I said.

"No, ma'am. That is, I don't have them with me. They are at the office. I can have my assistant box them up, if you like."

I said I would.

"Would it be convenient if I had them left at the hospital for you?"

I told him that would be great. We said our goodbyes, and I sat in the telephone nook with my hand pressing the receiver to the cradle for a long time.

Chapter 28

I PUT my chilly fingers against Viv's neck, the way she used to rouse me in the middle of the night. I called her name with goofy exaggeration. "Oh Viiiiiiiv-ian." I spelled GOOD MORNING SLEEPYHEAD into her palm. She did not stir.

I was flipping through the notes on the clipboard at the foot of her bed when Dr. Wilsey and a gaggle of others in white coats—Viv's OB/GYN team—filed into the room.

Feeling oddly furtive, I surrendered the clipboard, but Dr. Wilsey didn't even glance at it.

"We're somewhat concerned," she began.

My stomach dropped.

"There is very little precedent to judge, but we're worried that the baby's growth is not advancing as vigorously as we'd hope to see." Dr. Wilsey nodded gravely and added, "We think it's time to insert a feeding tube."

I pressed a hand against my side, willing my guts to settle as the team explained how it would be done. They told me that it had been ten days since the accident, a number that surprised me, and that while the initial trauma care had focused on Viv, ongoing care would address the needs of Viv's baby as well. A feeding tube would benefit both Viv and the baby.

"And when Viv wakes up?" I asked.

Dr. Wilsey gestured to one of the other doctors, who piped up. "Removal of the endoscopy peg is very straightforward, with almost no risks of side-effects. It will leave a tiny scar."

I asked what Viv would be eating, imagining dinner poured from a blender. Dr. Wilsey tagged another doctor to answer: "A polymeric formula that includes vitamins, protein, fats, sugars, minerals—similar to a protein shake."

When I ran out of questions, Dr. Wilsey said, "Someone will stop by with paperwork for you to sign." When I nodded, she said, "We'll do the insertion later today."

Dr. Wilsey was the last to leave, and she stood with a hand on my sister's arm before following the group down the hallway. I didn't expect to ask, but the words were out before I could stop them.

"Is she going to be okay?"

Dr. Wilsey's little smile heightened her resemblance to a Renaissance Madonna.

"We don't know," she said. "We just have to give her time."

Chapter 29

"IF YOU need to go to Florida," Dad Rowan said over dinner, "I can hold down the fort here."

As I hesitated—I knew I couldn't continue to leave my friends and my work and my roommates in limbo while I waited for Viv, but I wasn't sure what he meant—he added, "You must have things to do there."

"But," I said. "Don't you have to get back to Arizona?"

Dad Rowan smiled a little sadly. "There's nothing that can't wait."

"I have a painting job to finish—it might take a few days." Or a week, I thought.

"Aren't you enrolled in school?" he said.

"I can't go back—I'll take a leave of absence," I said, though I was pretty sure it was too late to get a reimbursement. "If you can stay to look after the dogs and keep an eye on Viv, I'll drive back as soon as I wrap things up in Sarasota."

IN A burst of hectic fourteen-hour days, I finished the big mural commission. I gulped a celebratory drink with the clients and cashed their check before the paint was dry.

My housemates used my departure as an excuse to throw an impromptu bon-voyage party. It was a big, boozy blow-out, with my beach volleyball teammates and people from the local art scene. I told my friend Gabrielle—the one with the ritzy gallery in St. Armand's Circle—that I didn't know if I'd be able to leave Nashville any time soon. She insisted that it didn't matter where I worked. She reminded me that I had been working with a broken wrist when we'd first met.

"You keep painting," Gabrielle said, gesturing with her goblet of wine. "I'll keep saving space for you."

My eyes felt hot with emotion, but before I could embarrass us both, Elaine from Elaine's Eats-to-Go arrived. She was carrying a big tray of cream-puff swans and shouting over the general brouhaha at Bryon, the sculptor, to please fetch the black beans from the back of her van, and where the hell was Nicola?

EVEN groggy and hungover late the next morning, it took me no more than a couple of hours to stow all my possessions into the covered bed of the little pickup. For once it gave me no joy at all to be able to pack up so quickly.

Leaving Sarasota felt like being erased. I didn't even want to imagine how much I was going to miss these people.

I had the truck radio blasting and the window down as I drove north on I-75. The air was incredible: clear and bright, making the muted colors look as super-saturated as a 1950s musical.

As seen from the highway, the view was like a microscope slide: the Florida scrub landscape sliced into cross-section, all palmettos and tall pine trees with chestnut-colored or fire-blackened bark. Without the highway, a person would never penetrate this thick undergrowth, or see the tree-trunks from this peculiar, side-on angle.

As I drove, radio stations faded in and out. I crossed through the rolling hills of horse country in Ocala. One of my volleyball buddies had slipped a going-away present into the truck: a handful of mix-tapes she'd recorded for my drive north. I popped one in at random. It started with the Fabulous Thunderbirds.

I sang along with the bell-clear voice of Kim Wilson, shouting to the world outside my window, "*I'd put out a fire with a shovel and dirt/and not even worry about getting hurt/ain't that tough enough?*" and for a moment, I couldn't wait to tell Viv about this band, this great song.

I'd been keeping a lid on my thoughts about Viv in her hospital bed. I talked with Dad Rowan each evening to check on her and make sure they were okay. He had no changes to report, which made me even more uneasy.

Now, with the wind tugging at the twist of hair at the back of my head and the brassy music filling the cab, a wave of unhappiness crested and crashed through me. My voice cracked in the middle of a word, and I had to clench my hands around the steering wheel to keep from crying out loud.

No one could say when my sister would wake up. I might not have the chance to tell her about this music. I might not get to show her my latest paintings. She might never explain what she was thinking and how we had drifted so far apart. We might never talk about the baby. We might not ever be able to talk at all.

Chapter 30

I FUELED up at an enormous gas station in Gainesville and went inside for a fountain drink. I eavesdropped on the various conversations of tar-flecked road construction workers around me as we waited for the cashier.

One of Viv's boyfriends had gotten me a job as a painter's helper on a construction team the summer of 1983 after I finished tenth grade.

"That's what I've been telling you," my sister had said. "It's essential to get a trade. People always want their houses worked on. It's not a bad way to put yourself through college."

I didn't bother pointing out that people always needed someone to look after their kids, too.

The work was actually pretty good. At first, I was shy around the crew, but they didn't treat me much differently than they did one another. The men often forgot about me as they worked in the next room or down the hall. I had expected their conversation to turn macho, brutal even.

Up until that summer, I'd never observed ordinary guy-talk, never followed the masculine conversational give-and-take about sports, never before recognized the mild teasing between elder and younger men. They didn't talk over one another the way girls at school did. They took turns, but once they'd started, they'd keep telling stories for hours. I tried to explain to my sister about how, while quietly rolling paint onto a wall, I was getting a glimpse into the workings of a foreign culture.

"The land of men," my sister said. "Great. Send me a postcard."

My sister broke up with the house-painter boyfriend at a picnic concert that summer. He related the news to me with surprise, having not expected it, but he took the situation with good grace. He didn't hold it against me—though he did talk about my sister more than I wanted.

I'd be stuck up a ladder, cutting in Navaho White paint along a crown molding, while he rolled it onto the walls and tried to work out what had happened with my sister, going over the details again out loud. I don't suppose it mattered whether I was listening or not. He just needed to talk.

To my sister's disappointment, I continued to babysit for the Bebernes family a couple of nights a week all that summer. Viv never remembered the name. "You're going to be at what's-her-name's tonight?"

"Bebernes. Yes. I'll be back late." After a long day with the construction crew, I'd get dropped off at the curb in front of the Bebernes' house.

I told Viv I was saving up for a school trip, but in all honesty, I just liked spending time in that crowded and sloppy household.

The kids were funny, and Cath Bebernes was open-handed with her time and attention. She would sit down to ask me about how my day went before she and her husband went out. She remembered the names of the people I talked about. She recommended books to read—

she was a big fan of British writers like Dick Francis and Dorothy Sayers and P.G. Wodehouse.

It was easy to overlook her little quirks. She often looked down her short nose at something just over the other person's shoulder as she talked. She dotted her s with perfectly round circles, which, as Viv pointed out, "Most people get over by the time they get out of middle school."

She studied catalogs closely and sometimes referred to things around the house by their marketing descriptions: an espresso cotton tee, nubby woven-silk toss pillows, sheer charmeuse curtain panels.

After looking at the pictures I'd made of her children one afternoon, Cath Bebernes had signed me up for life drawing class. "I think you should try it for a couple of weeks, see if you like it. I'll cover the fees for the first month. You can pay me back with a drawing."

After the first month, Cath Bebernes said that if I enjoyed the class, I should keep going, and she'd continue paying. She said it made her feel like a patron of the arts. She was generous that way, buying the kinds of snacks she knew I liked and including me when she took her kids clothes-shopping. For Christmas one year, she ordered me a Fair Isle sweater from L.L. Bean that matched her family's.

My sister wasn't especially thrilled about the drawing class. She couldn't complain, since it didn't cost us anything, but she thought I could do better with my Saturday mornings. "Take an AP course," she advised. "Get some of your core requirements for college out of the way."

But I kept going to the studio. I liked the other students. I liked the seriousness of it. At first, I could barely look at the models. Each week it was someone different, naked in the middle of the room: skinny, chubby, lumpy, tall, beautiful, ugly, scarred, short, muscled, lopsided, male, female. It was unsettling to see an ordinary-looking person drop her bathrobe and find a pose to hold for ten minutes. But then, one Saturday, I don't remember when, the naked body standing in the middle of the room was just something to sketch.

The two hours always passed in a flash. Simply moving my pencil or charcoal over paper in the company of other artists was pure joy. Everything except the work of my hands faded away, and even when the picture did not turn out, I never doubted that I had been doing real art.

For that, if for no other reason, I would have kept babysitting for Cath Bebernes, but it was an appealing household, with its worn oriental rugs and ecru flokati throws and the shearling-lined slippers in five sizes pointing in every direction in front of the mushroom velveteen loveseats.

I could have slipped into the Bebernes family without a ripple. I sometimes daydreamed that, instead of leaving at the end of the night, I'd tuck myself into the trundle bed in the girls' rooms. I wouldn't take up much room, and I loved the children. I could blend right in, a quiet older daughter who was good with the kids and cleaned the house without being nagged.

But after an evening of babysitting, with its measured amount of television, popcorn, and homework, after I ran the dishwasher and tidied up the children's toys, folded a load or two of laundry, and fell asleep in front of the television, I'd leave. Cath or her husband would drive me back to the duplex apartment near campus, watching from the car until I unlocked the front door and turned to wave goodbye.

"Has he ever—you know—made a pass at you?" my sister asked as I let myself into the apartment late one night.

"What?"

"Mr. What's-his-name, happy family guy, has he put the moves on you?" Viv was curled up on the couch with a textbook, a blanket tucked around her legs against the damp air.

"No—jeez. No!"

"I wouldn't be surprised if he does."

"Because you think he's a perv?"

"No," she said, slowly. "Because you look good."

"Yeah, right. String-bean good?" My sister rarely talked about how I looked unless I asked for her opinion about a specific outfit. I was still wearing my paint-splattered overalls and a baseball cap. At nearly six feet tall, I could only hope I had reached my full height. I suspected she was teasing.

"Shut up. Seriously. You're not cute like a kitten or a cheerleader or—"

I snorted, pulling off my work-boots with a manly clunk.

"But," she continued unbothered. "I think you are going to be hard for them to resist."

I lifted my eyebrows, skepticism incarnate.

Viv nodded. "Men start looking at you and see this—object. They don't know what you are thinking or where you come from. They just see this collection of qualities: a skinny girl, long legs, big blue eyes. Thank God you don't have a big chest."

"Yeah, I'm always grateful for that." I kept the sarcasm piling up so that she might continue telling me about myself.

"Don't be stupider than you have to be," Viv said, without heat. "No joke. Since you are quiet, men are going to fill in the blank with whatever they like—they'll be all, 'Ooh, you're so mysterious! You're such a good listener.'" Viv put her head to the side and gave me a sickly, puppy-dog look, "'Nobody understands me the way you do!'"

I wanted to laugh, but Viv didn't really seem to be making a joke. She looked disgusted. For once, I was pretty sure it wasn't *me* that had irritated her.

"But—"

"No." Viv spoke quietly, a bitter edge to her voice. "This is how it is: they'll look at you and just see you in relation to what *they* want. You'll just be something pretty, something that listens, something that waits around for them."

I didn't answer. As far as I knew, her boyfriends hadn't ever been serious—or at least my sister hadn't been serious about them. I didn't think her heart had been touched, never mind broken.

Viv sighed, her mood lightening. She squinted at me. "So that's what you have to look forward to!"

"Sounds wonderful," I said.

She smiled. "Hard work being a girl."

"So?" I prompted. "Any idea when this all is going to happen?"

Viv picked her watch up from the table, held it to her ear and spoke with a straight face. "Any minute now. You should be able to hear it coming."

"What?"

"Yeah. There's a distinct noise it makes as it starts. It sounds like—" She made a wolf-whistle, fighting to purse her lips against her smile.

"Great," I said. "I'll listen for it."

Viv winked and settled herself back in her book.

I headed toward my own room to get ready for bed, but a thought made me turn back.

"So what should I do?"

Viv's face was blank. Evidently, she had forgotten what we were talking about.

"What should I do about the, you know, impending doom with men?" I said.

"Oh God, I don't know. Don't be surprised when they start acting like jerks? Don't buy into it. Be your own person."

"But—" I started to say. Viv cut me short.

"Whatever you do, don't turn out to be one of these stupid little girls who comes to school goo-goo-eyed with hickeys all down her neck." Viv shook her head and sniffed. "Some ass-face tells her she's so special, she's so beautiful—and she ends up flunking out of school, living in a crappy rented trailer with a handful of snotty-nosed brats and bad teeth. Or worse."

"Worse than a handful of bad teeth?"

My sister rolled her eyes, but her expression was bleak. "Yeah. Plenty worse: rotten teeth, no money, and no options."

I was tired and had to be up early the next morning to paint houses, but I didn't want to leave my sister alone. I hefted the teapot from the orange-crate we used as a coffee-table.

"Want some more tea? I could whip up a batch of scones if you are hungry."

My sister closed the book over a scrap of paper and set it down on the table. "No," she said, standing and stretching. "I don't know why I stayed up so late."

"Because you missed me, and you longed more than anything to impart your worldly wisdom about men to me?"

Viv smiled then. "Fool. We don't have enough time in this whole week for me to tell you what I know about men." She crossed to me and bumped her shoulder into mine. We rested our heads against each other. After a moment, she lifted her head and said, "Go to bed."

I put both my arms around her and after a pause— we weren't huggers as a rule—she squeezed me back.

Chapter 31

AN eighteen-wheeler honked, the sound combining with a big *whoof* of air pushing through my open window as the truck shot past me. I looked down to see that I was doing forty-five miles per hour on the open highway. I checked my mirrors and stomped on the accelerator.

My driving had always made my sister crazy. She took me to Canton to get me a driver's permit when I turned sixteen. She had me circle a big empty parking lot, her face expressionless as I haltingly got the hang of the clutch. After the Datsun bucked to a standstill from the third gear, again, she said, "Alrighty then. Practice makes perfect, but that's enough for now."

It took three tries, but I passed the driver's test a few weeks later.

It was me behind the wheel of the orange Datsun when we first got to Manhattan. Viv was starting med school on the Upper East Side, while I was going to start college at SUNY Stony Brook, out on Long Island. We had been studying guidebooks from the library in Potsdam all summer. We were going to explore New York City for ten days before school started. There were ethnic foods we wanted to try and dozens of stores and tourist sites to visit. I had a long list of museums for me to explore, including a museum of fashion that I thought we might both enjoy.

Viv and I had sold all of our worldly goods except for what we carried with us in the car. We were so excited we'd been finishing each other's sentences all the way downstate from Potsdam.

It was Viv's turn to navigate while I drove. She was frustrated by my caution. Buses and taxicabs honked and swerved around us. But she was unwilling to give me the map and risk my getting us lost. "Oh my God, you are a bad driver!" she said at a stoplight.

She piloted us into a parking garage midtown near the Allerton House, where we were going to stay. "Remind me never to let you drive again," she said as we got out of the car in the cool, dimly lit garage.

The two of us had never been in a car together with me in the driver's seat since.

Getting to college that fall was one of the hardest things I'd ever done. It wasn't that I didn't want to attend school—I had no other idea of what to do with myself than to go to college. Viv certainly expected me to go. I was prepared. I'd sent four applications out and got four acceptances back. That wasn't the problem.

But it was almost impossible for me to decide. I tried to picture myself in the context of the glossy photos in the prospectuses that came in the mail addressed to me.

Could I see myself walking through an autumn-colored college town that was not Potsdam, New York? Me in the stands, like the students in these pictures, cheering for some sports team? What would it feel like to be me, wearing a college-logo sweatshirt, listening raptly in a lecture hall? How would it feel to be me, laughing in a snowball fight on a strange snow-covered quad?

It was the imaginative leap that had me teetering on the edge of this new life. I couldn't see myself away from Potsdam, away from home, away for the first time—though I didn't say it—from my sister.

The prospect of moving into a dorm and being transformed into a college student seemed unreal. So I'd stalled and dithered. Viv grew impatient. "If you want to go to Rochester, go to Rochester," she told me.

Did I want to go to Rochester? Or did I want to go to University of the Arts in Philadelphia? Or did I want to go to SUNY Stony Brook?

"If you can't decide," my sister advised me, "choose the one with the best financial aid package. Pick one. It's just undergrad. You'll probably end up getting your masters and *that* degree will be more important."

That had been her own strategy—and of course Viv was accepted at her top choice for med school. Her ambitions worked like that: she decided on her goal, made a plan to get there, and carefully followed each of the steps she'd outlined. She hadn't had to wait long for the heavy envelope from Cornell Med to show up in the mailbox.

She insisted that it shouldn't matter to me which school she chose. "Never mind where I end up. You don't have to drag around after me anymore," Viv said. "You should go to the best school for you."

I picked Stony Book finally—a state school with a good art department that offered me a generous student-aid package. It had a nice campus, interesting course offerings. And it was only an hour or so from Viv.

AFTER a whirlwind ten days of playing tourist in Manhattan, we retrieved the Datsun from the parking garage and Viv took me to Long Island. The streets were nearly empty on the weekend morning. We got to campus early.

Keeping a distracted eye on the road, Viv snatched the paperwork from my hands to double-check the schedule. "The dorms should be open," Viv said, glancing from the papers to the campus outside the windshield. "It's ten o'clock already. Where's the welcoming committee?"

I didn't answer. My stomach was tied in knots, whether from the drive, anxiety, or from Viv's prickly mood, I didn't know.

Viv pulled the Datsun half off the road to paw through the packet of papers the college had sent. "Well," she said, extracting a page. "Here's the map. Let's see if we can find your dorm and unload this stuff."

There wasn't much stuff to unload, as it happened. Cath Bebernes had found a little steamer trunk at an antique store over the summer. For a going-away present, she'd packed it full of things she thought I'd need for my dorm room: an electric kettle, pretty sheets, my favorite tea. She'd offered to ship it to me at school, since it was an inconvenient size to fit into our little car. It would be waiting for me somewhere.

The rest of my belongings amounted to a pile that half-filled the backseat: a duffle bag, a couple of cardboard boxes, a plastic sack of toiletries and two tubes of pictures and posters.

Viv and I located the parking lot closest to the dorm and we carried my things across the wide grassy space to the entrance. A plump girl in a *Stony Brook!* T-shirt held the door for us. The back of her shirt said, "Resident Advisor 1985-1986."

"You're early!" the advisor was shouting with enthusiasm. "Hi! I'm the resident advisor for Barnes Hall this year."

"Hi," I said, and introduced myself.

"Looks like you are ready to move in, Nicola Jones from Potsdam!" she said.

I nodded.

The girl gestured around. "This is the lobby. I'm setting up a welcome table—but let me get you started with this packet. Here's your key. And this reference sheet, it shows the numbers for emergency, the library, and so on, see?"

I did. I didn't trust myself to look at my sister as the resident advisor kept pointing out the obvious.

The advisor indicated the stairway (directly in front of us) and the elevator (under a sign that said "Elevator") and told me my room was on the second floor ("One flight up.")

Viv and I trotted up the stairs. I struggled for a minute with the key in the door, but once the door thunked shut behind us, my sister put down the suitcase and said, "This is a light-switch. It works the lights. See?" Her face was utterly blank.

I let my own face slacken in amazement, "No! Reeeeeealy?"

We both sniggered.

"Is that a window?" I pointed. "And that—could it be a bed?!"

"People sleep in beds!" Viv said, echoing the cheery tones of the girl downstairs.

Then, in a more normal voice, she said, "So, which bed?"

I looked. "I like the windows over that one, but maybe I should wait for my room—"

Viv interrupted me. "Or you could do the normal thing and just pick the bed you want. God! Be nice later, after you figure out whether your roommate is going to be a nightmare. You got here first. Take the bed you want."

I picked, and Viv tossed the duffle onto the bare, striped mattress. She watched me unbuckle the straps and then said, "Oh, I forgot something. I have to go back to the car. Which is parked in the parking lot." She gave me a sly look.

"Is the parking lot, um, outside?" I offered.

She grinned. "I'll be right back."

I'd put my clothes away in the little closet and stacked my books onto the shelves in the compact desk area before I thought to wonder what Viv might have forgotten in the car. It occurred to me that she might have left already.

She might have decided to avoid a long good-bye scene. She still had to deliver the Datsun to its new owner—she was selling it for the same $600 we'd paid for it—and take the train back into the city.

I ran to the other window, which overlooked a slice of the parking lot, but I couldn't see the familiar orange shape of the Datsun. I flung open the door and there she was, one hand raised to knock while the other held a narrow brown cardboard box.

For a long, *long* moment, we looked into one another's faces. I don't know what she saw in mine—panic maybe—but she looked a little wary.

"Well," we both said, the word ringing in stereo between us.

"Jinx," we both said, still in stereo as we stepped out of arm's reach of each other.

"Double jinx." Viv managed to get the words out a fraction of a second ahead of me.

She gave my arm the gentlest of pinches.

"You want to get going," I said.

She shrugged. "I can stay if you want."

I said no, though I suddenly really did want her to stay.

"Here," she said, holding the box out. "Open this."

"What is it?" I asked.

"A present. Duh. Don't get me started."

I opened the box. She hadn't taped it the way she liked to do at Christmas, so that each package was in effect its own practical joke. The top lifted off easily to reveal a battered wooden case.

The wooden case opened to a lustrous black velvet bed filled with beautiful old drawing tools: French curves and drafting compasses, a metal ruler, triangles, and protractors. The mechanical pencils had matching X-Acto knives with rich emerald-green enameled details on the fancy handles. I picked one up and hefted it.

"Pretty, isn't it?" Viv said.

"It's X-Acto what I needed," I said.

Viv winced but came back with, "My, what a sharp wit you have!"

"But it's a double-edged sword."

We smiled at each other. The elevator dinged in the distance. Viv looked at her watch and then shook it. "I should go," she said.

"Give us a hug then, guvnor," I said, in my best Cockney accent.

She squeezed me so tight it hurt, but I squeezed her right back.

"You do good," she commanded in a fierce whisper. Then, in a more regular tone of voice, she said, "You'll have them eating out of your hand in about a week."

"Who?"

My sister gripped my upper arms in her hands and pushed herself away from me. "Duh," she said, "Everyone."

She took the two steps to the door and then turned back. "You have my number. We'll talk on Sunday. Okay?"

I nodded.

"Bye. Love you."
"Love you too."

Chapter 32

BY THE END of the day, I felt as if the road was never going to end. Nothing existed except the drone of pavement under the wheels, the roar of air past the window and the white dotted line verging to the vanishing point on the horizon. The dirt next to the road was the color of pumpkins. A sunburned left arm made me sensitive to the temperature dropping.

A herd of white-tailed deer stood in the trees on the side of the road. The sight barely registered. I saw their oddly squat tan bodies held up by slender legs. They were close enough for me to see that their noses were black and shiny. I noticed antlers. Their ears pivoted toward the road like hairy saucers.

A mile or more later, I put the elements of deer, trees, and cars together and remembered how my sister had landed in her hospital bed. My foot eased itself back from the accelerator pedal. I found a place to stop for the night at the next exit.

I parked the truck under a buzzing neon sign for the Sandman Hotel. A pink-and-orange sandman stood on one pixyish tiptoe, holding a wand that poured twinkling specks into the twilight. I paid cash for a room and then re-parked my truck on the crackling gravel in front of my own pink concrete-slab porch.

The room was cold and damp, but the heater glowed orange after I cranked it up. I called Tennessee. Dad Rowan answered on the third ring. No, there were no changes in Viv's condition. She was holding steady. He had a lot to talk about, but nothing important to say.

Ed Maynard had said he'd be out of touch on another investigation. My Florida friends were busy. Trisha was traveling on business, but I had forgotten to bring her hotel phone number. It was still taped to my old door in Sarasota. She'd probably be staying at one of the Fairmont hotel properties, all thick towels and deluxe in-room bars, great soaps, piles of fluffy pillows stacked on the bed with her cosmetics and gear strewn around the large bathroom. I'd tagged along with her and had seen how the other half lived.

My bathroom at the Sandman was tiny, tiled in vintage acid yellow and sage green, the chipped yellow tub icy to the touch. A plastic-wrapped wafer of soap sat on the sink. The water ran rusty for a moment when I started the shower. I was too tired to bother, suddenly, and I turned the water off.

Noises from the parking lot woke me. I twitched the curtains from the edge of the window to see if my truck was safe. The parking lot was full. It felt late. Two people were leaning against their cars next door, having a perfectly normal conversation at a volume that suggested they spent their days shouting over machinery noise.

A distinctly scratchy feeling had started at the back of my throat, and although I drank two glasses of water, I felt dry and hot. The bedside alarm clock glowed red: 3:57. I was bone-tired, but I knew sleep was not going to return. The loud conversation continued outside.

I went back to my warm nest of covers. The slippery bedspread slid and caught against the sheet.

THE winter our parents moved us all from Vermont to New Hampshire, my sister and I stayed in a room just like this one in a little roadside motel built of cinderblocks. It was so cold I felt the heat sinking like a river through the thin carpet into the concrete slab floor. Viv and I were sharing a bed. The television was on with the sound turned off. A shaft of too-bright light from the streetlamp shot through a gap in the curtains.

Perhaps it was the first night Jahn and Magda had left us alone. I don't think I had started school yet.

Awake next to my sister in that motel bed, I was suddenly sure that there had been a mistake: I did not belong in this cold motel room. There was something wrong. I didn't belong with this family moving again and changing Viv's school. It was like looking down at the cat on your lap only to discover you've been petting a porcupine or a mink.

I was five and I knew, I *knew* that something terrible had happened. A huge mistake had been made. Even the sister sleeping next to me seemed remote and unconnected to me. I was alone in a terrible place.

Just then Viv started to snore in earnest, inhaling one huge, exaggerated, snuffling snort like a cartoon character. The farcical noise broke the spell. I don't remember telling myself to forget—but I had not thought about that night, that panicky certainty, from that moment until this one.

Had Viv ever felt that? When she told Ed Maynard that she suspected Jahn and Magda were not our parents, were *these* the sort of unsettling recollections she'd had? What did she remember that I didn't? A cardboard crate full of Viv's journals was waiting for me in Nashville.

I glanced at the radio-alarm clock: 4:19. The conversation outside seemed to be wrapping up, the two people shouting goodnight to one another. My throat was sore. I had another solid chunk of driving ahead of me. I was catching a cold and wanted to pull the covers over my head and pretend nothing was wrong. How pathetic.

I got up for another glass of water. I dressed and looked out the window. The parking lot was quiet, the row of cars shining under a pristine film of dew. I couldn't just sit here and think. I had to move. I had to get back to Tennessee.

Chapter 33

I UNLOCKED the front door of Viv's house with her hidden key. The dogs stopped barking when I called, "*Mellon!*" through the door. They were already wagging their tails and turning heavy-footed circles as I looked inside. They bumped gently into me, bending so that their knobby sides swept along my legs and then plunging their big skulls against me so I could rub their ears. Balin looked stiff, but she wrinkled her snout in a kind of canine grin, her head low and her old spine curved in a coy, happy crescent.

It felt like an honor to have them surging around me, their eyes bright with welcome, their thick toenails sometimes landing on my sneakers, their bony tails whacking into my knees.

I walked through and let them out the back door, noting the signs of Dad Rowan in the kitchen: a row of dishtowels hung unevenly on the oven door, vitamin jars and prescription bottles and packages of crackers scattered on the black countertops. The sort of clutter Dear George cleared before you even noticed. He hadn't learned it from his father. The thought gave me an uneasy pang.

Dad Rowan had left a note on the fridge. His handwriting was tidy, like George's. "At hospital. Back later. Will bring dinner."

My sore throat had melted into a faint burn, but my head was throbbing. For the past hundred miles I had been sneezing in long, body-shaking fits. I needed chicken soup and a good night's sleep.

The answering machine had the usual hang-ups and one wrong number. I debated for a moment whether to phone back. My sister sometimes played along when someone mistakenly called her line. It was a funny but cruel habit. I left them for another day.

I flipped through the pile of mail. A small package was addressed to me from Brooklyn Heights. Trisha's mom had sent a Tupperware dish of my favorite almond biscotti and a pink floral card printed with an insipid motto about love. Inside she had written her phone number with the words, "Just a reminder."

I went directly to the telephone and dialed Sophia Cutillo's number. I didn't need to look at the greeting card to remember the digits.

"What? Who is this? Nicola? That name sounds so familiar," she said, her voice a rougher version of Trisha's. The Cutillo family believed in sarcasm for every occasion. "Are you going to tell me about Sarasota, or do I have to wait for my daughter, Patricia Beatrice Too-Busy Cutillo, to give us the news second-hand?"

It was pointless to argue when she was in this mood. I *had* skipped calling her since going back to Florida.

"I got everything done," I said. I heard Sophia stir milk into her ever-present cup of coffee. I pictured her settling down at the kitchen table for a long chat, one scuffed slipper dangling off an elegant foot as she crossed her legs and put her elbows on the table.

"So what about that sister of yours?"

The Cutillos had never spent much time with my sister, though they had tried to include her for holiday dinners when she lived in the city.

"I haven't been to the hospital to check on her, but there's been no change."

"Something like that happened to a cousin of mine," Sophia began. "She had a car wreck, and she lost the baby. It was terrible. Tragic. She sued the hospital."

In the short silence that followed, I expected Sophia to continue with the tragedy of her cousin. To be fair, the Cutillos had a large extended family, but no matter how bizarre an incident, some cousin or another could always be counted on to have had nearly the same thing happen.

But Sophia didn't finish the story. "And now you are going to stay with your sister until she is well," she concluded, her voice gentler, not quite making a question of this statement.

"I guess that's right," I said, feeling suddenly heavy and exhausted.

"And what about you? Your show in March?" she asked. "Will you be able to paint? Don't you need a studio or a gallery or whatever?"

"I don't know," I said. "I haven't even started to think about that."

"I'm sorry, baby girl," Sophia said. She meant it, despite her bluster. She took a breath. "Papi and I are right here if you need us, you know that. We'll figure it out."

I mumbled a reply and she laughed.

"You sound terrible. Eat something and phone me when you've had some rest."

ONE of the dogs scratched at the back door and I swung it open for them. They trooped into the steamy kitchen and stood near me as I adjusted the flame under the pot of chicken. I set the oven timer and then took myself to the living room couch.

I snagged a blanket from a hassock footstool and then, in a sort of automatic reflex, I emptied the hassock to see what else was to be found. Another blanket, a couple of old *Vogue* magazines. I reloaded the hassock and tumbled onto the black leather couch. In minutes the dogs, sprawled on the carpet in lumps, lulled me to sleep with their snoring.

The buzz of the oven timer roused me. I had been dreaming of my first job as an au pair in Rome. Probably the animal scent of chicken stock reminding me of how the two soccer-crazy boys in my care exuded this same smell as their body odor. I could never figure out how it happened. I made sure they got to school smelling of soap, in clean clothes, but by the afternoon, when they came home sweaty and impossibly grimy, they were as fragrant as good chicken stock.

"You stink," I'd tell them. We would chorus together, "Stink, stank, stunk!" Nevertheless, I liked sniffing the chicken-soup smell of their heads. It made me less homesick somehow, that first year in Rome, even as the act of palming their small, hot scalps with my hands— like a mother bear cuffing and rolling her cubs— squeezed my heart.

In the kitchen, I skimmed the broth clear and pulled the drumsticks out. I turned up the flame under the pot and waited for the chicken to cool.

Tomkin had followed me into the kitchen. He sat in his Egyptian-cat pose, tall and straight. His nose winked black and shiny in the afternoon sunlight. I pulled a drool towel from its drawer and rummaged through the refrigerator until I found some American cheese. Dad Rowan seemed to put things back wherever he found space. He'd left half a Sara Lee cake on the top shelf, so everything was crowded. Tomkin's tail banged against the floor a few times and he waited politely for me to hand over the cheese.

I sneezed four times in a row and then dragged myself upstairs to raid Viv's closet for wool socks. I chewed a couple of orange baby-aspirin from Viv's medicine cabinet—she had once told me that the chewable kind worked fastest—and poked around for the emerald-green jar of Vicks. She'd sworn by the power of the stuff.

Back in the kitchen, I picked the chicken clean while the stock boiled down. I squeezed half a lemon into a bowl, added a scant handful of shredded chicken, and ladled broth over it with a pinch of sea-salt. I slurped it down while standing over the sink.

After putting the rest of the meat into the stockpot and turning off the gas, I rinsed my bowl and discovered the dishwasher was full of clean dishes. Too tired to do better, I left the bowl in the sink. I took a box of tissues to the couch and barely heard the dogs snoring before I fell asleep.

The simultaneous racket of the dogs, the garage door opening, and the musical roar of the Saab woke me.

I met Dad Rowan in the kitchen. He carried a handful of white paper bags—garlicky takeout Italian that I smelled even with my clogged nose. The dogs sniffed and milled around his legs.

"No," I said. "You don't want to hug me, I've got a cold."

Dad Rowan backed away with a sympathetic grimace and began putting foil take-out boxes on the counter. "Well, I brought us some supper. I didn't know when you'd get here and I didn't know what you'd like, so I chose a smorgasbord." Dad Rowan took clean silverware from the dishwasher and said, "I hope you're hungry."

When I said I might stick with soup for now, he said, "I hope you don't mind if I go ahead and eat," he said. "These medications of mine—"

He shook his head and slid a multi-compartment pill box closer to his plate and started telling me about them.

As he talked, I slid one haunch onto a stool. I wanted to go straight to bed, but Dad Rowan kept up a steady flow of talk.

I let the dogs out and filled their dishes, garnishing the kibble with a few bits of chicken fat. My sinuses pounded as I bent to put the bowls onto the floor.

"You look awfully tired," Dad Rowan said. "You don't need to stay up on my account, my dear. Why not call it an early night?"

I admitted I was ready for sleep again.

"It's good to have you back," Dad Rowan said as I started toward my room. His round face was turned toward his plate, so I saw the white semi-circle of hair around his freckled bald spot.

"Thank you for looking after Viv," I said.

"Nothing I'd rather do." He looked up at me and then ducked his head back over his food. He might have had tears in his eyes.

"I appreciate it anyhow."

Dad Rowan bobbed his head again without looking up. Definitely tears. After a long moment of silence, we said our goodnights and I went to bed.

Shortly afterwards, Dad Rowan turned the television on in the living room, loud enough that I could almost make out what the announcer was saying as I drifted off. Later, Dwalin nosed open my door and stood by the bed, gazing at me with concerned, droopy eyes. I gave him a pat and got up to shut the door. He circled a few times before dropping with a thump and a sigh.

Chapter 34

DAYLIGHT streamed through a gap in the curtain. I'd dozed feverishly through a whole day, but my sore, hollow-feeling bones felt itchy. I was awake and impatient.

Dwalin watched me from his bed, eyes limpid with sleep. One velvety black ear had flipped over his head. He looked like a pouty Hollywood actress with an artfully mussed hairdo.

"We've got stuff to do," I told the dog. "Lots to do and who knows how much time." He whacked his tail against the fluffy bedside rug and smacked his lips in preparation for a yawn. His eyes closed slightly as the stretch travelled up his shoulders and along his big front legs.

I put on Viv's wool socks and a sweater over my pajamas. The dogs watched me curiously as I padded into the kitchen. They flinched as I broke into a fit of coughing. Dad Rowan had left a note on refrigerator. He had gone to church and would visit Viv afterward. He hoped I was feeling better.

The teakettle was full already. Dad Rowan admitted that he liked to keep the pot topped up so he was less liable to scorch it . He'd chuckled about it at the time, but the idea worried me. I'd twice found water bubbling merrily away to nothing while he watched television in the other room.

WHEN I got stalled on a painting project, I'd learned over time to resist the impulse to tackle the creative problem head-on. Maybe because I always had a second or third job to keep me occupied, I'd gotten into the habit of letting my thoughts percolate. Instead of worrying about the problem directly, I'd stop thinking about it, put it to one side. Some other part of my brain would work on it and a solution would present itself as if it had been there the whole time.

I was going to scour Viv's journals to find out what I could about our past, maybe even why she thought she'd ruined my life, but the important thing—the idea that had bubbled up sideways while I was balling up tissues and drinking plenty of fluids—was what would happen next. What needed to be done. What I needed to do.

I didn't know how long it would take Viv to get back on her feet, but no matter how soon it would be, I needed to get the house ready. I needed to figure out what she wanted from me.

What had she planned to do when the baby arrived? I was pretty sure she meant to keep the baby. Even if the only evidence was a couple of paperback books and some pictures torn from a magazine.

Had she planned to call me and have me fly up to decorate the baby's room? Did she mean to move to a new house? Were she and Dear George okay? Who might she have talked to about these things? When I considered the visitors who had come to her room, I couldn't picture her having a heart-to-heart with anyone I'd seen.

The thing was, from the very start, my sister and Dear George had been a self-contained unit. They did everything together. George accompanied her to medical conferences, and she often went with him on the odd golf junket or investment seminar. They hiked and spelunked and bought pottery together. Once they had started seeing one another, I rarely saw Viv alone.

Viv used to say that she could depend on George to be reliable: reliably good-looking, reliably responsible, reliably reliable. He chatted with everyone at parties, he liked to have guests over for dinner. He was neat. He made sure the cars were serviced. His hair was always well-cut, his clothes always seemed appropriate to the occasion.

He was perfect for Viv. She was elegant and he was handsome. They were the kind of couple who was always talking when you came into the room. If Viv had a heart-to-heart talk with anyone, I couldn't imagine it being anyone but George.

I ate toast and poured a second mug of tea while trying to imagine what my sister would have planned, what she would have thought. But honestly, I had never known.

Maybe she had left a letter or something with Artie. I half rose to go to the phone before I reconsidered. If Viv had a plan, Artie would have passed it along already.

Then I thought again—maybe Viv had specified that Artie could tell me only when I asked. Maybe she had left instructions for me someplace that only Artie could access once I said—I stopped myself, recognizing the irrational turn my thoughts were taking. This situation wasn't some sort of test Viv had designed for me to pass or flunk.

Still, I *would* telephone Artie.

I reached Leora, who told me that she was on her way out. Artie had left early to meet Dad Rowan for breakfast. She didn't expect to see him until suppertime. I should call her later in the week; we should meet for lunch when I felt better. I hung up and felt the energy draining out of me.

The toast popped up with a cheerful chime. The dogs looked at me expectantly. "Yeah," I said. "I'm going to brace up and plan. But first I'm going to go snoop through my sister's journals and figure out what she's been doing. Who's coming?"

With a blanket draped over my lap and throw-pillows piled around me, I gazed at the messy and haphazard pile of notebooks. I decided to start by sorting them by year and go from there. The composition notebooks started in fourth grade. There were five of them, and I arranged them chronologically on the coffee-table.

Riffling through the pages of one of the later black notebooks for a date, I discovered that someone had left sticky notes throughout the book. Viv? Ed Maynard?

A bright yellow note marked April 10, 1989. Viv's entry was short: "*No letter. No check. Statute of limitation?*"

This made me pause for a long time. Eventually I closed the notebook and slipped it onto the side.

After I arranged the notebooks in order, it seemed important that I gather the rest of Viv's journals from the study to complete the set. There were fourteen of the journals by the time I'd finished. The trouble was, I saw, there were gaps. The latest journal, aside from the one I'd found in her bedside table, was nearly three years old. I didn't think she'd just gone back to keeping a journal the week before the car wreck, and she obviously hadn't thrown the old notebooks away.

At least two journals from the 1980s were missing too. I'd need to ask Ed Maynard about them. Perhaps his assistant had forgotten to include them. I made a neat note at the top of a fresh sheet of paper. I sipped at the tepid cup of tea, stalling. For now, I told myself, I'd work through the ones I had. From the start.

The oldest notebook said, "Social Studies" on the battered cover. It was as bent as a boomerang and spread itself open on my lap. Viv's backward-slanting handwriting was younger and rounder and large on the page. She had pressed the pen deeply into the paper, doodling a curlicued box around a sentence.

The words leaped from the page: "***Nicola Maria Jones, if you are reading this, you are in so much trouble I pity you!***"

"Oh, sis!" I said aloud, startled into laughing. "You don't know the half of it!" This must have been the same diary that Viv had caught me reading when I was a kid. Instinct made me glance over my shoulder. When I realized what I was doing, I said, "I hope you *do* catch me, sis."

Chapter 35

VIV WROTE every few days to start, usually just a couple of sentences.

The first entry, dated January 1972, set the tone. "*Read Little House in the Big Woods by Laura Ingalls Wilder. Mrs. Rose said there are seven other books in the series.*"

She mentioned events from the school-bus. "*Mrs. Gamble stopped the bus to yell at Matt.*" And she detailed the actions of Jahn and Magda: "*M asleep all day but got up to make fried chicken for J. He drank six beers and yelled about the furnace.*"

A yellow sticky note marked a page that recounted an argument between Jahn and Magda: "*Fight today. J shouting about the truck and then he said, 'You had to get those g.d. kids!' M said, 'Don't you use that language in front of me! They are your kids as much as they are mine!' and J said, 'THAT's true, anyway!' They kept screaming at each other and I took N to the woods to wait for it to stop.*"

I didn't remember that fight, but Viv's diary entry left me with an itchy, uncomfortable feeling. I closed my eyes, trying to bring the memory into focus, but it slipped away from me. Okay, I thought, it will come back. My head felt heavy on my neck when I opened my eyes.

I skimmed the rest of the journal. Viv wrote often about her teacher, Mrs. Rose, that year. We moved from Lancaster, New Hampshire to New York State in late March. A yellow sticky note marked the page: "*Moving again. Mrs. Rose gave me a box of Whitman chocolates and said, 'You will be an excellent student at your next school, but I'm sorry you are not going to be in my classroom for the rest of the year.' Not fair! Don't know how I did on the reading tests—won't ever know.*"

The next entry said, "*New teacher is Mr. DellaRocha. Ugh. Penmanship drills all morning, flashcards after lunch. Twelve weeks until summer vacation.*"

A final sticky note flagged the back cover. Around the printed table converting English measurements into metric ones, Viv had written a series of addresses. The names seemed distant and dreamlike, though Ed Maynard had mentioned them only a few weeks back: *Purdy Loop, Massena, NY, RD #2 Dumas Road, Lancaster, NH. Miller Road, Vergennes, VT, County Road 334, Fairfax, VT.*

IN THE next composition notebook, Viv's handwriting grew smaller and more hurried. In 1973, she'd started using more abbreviations. She made perfect little ampersand symbols instead of writing out "and." She shortened "with" to a W and a slash. She referred to her classmates by initials. ("*BK tripped DL & went w/Mrs. B to the office.*").

She sprinkled the pages with hobo symbols, like the flattened loop for "mean man." In fifth grade, Viv had taught me a dozen or so of the hieroglyphs from a library book about hobos and the Great Depression. She'd kept the book out of Magda's sight. The mean man loop was obviously Jahn. Obvious, anyway, when paired with Viv's clever little pictograph of a sheep—three ovals and two dots that looked unmistakably sheeplike—that stood for Magda.

A sticky-note pointed to a description of Jahn's truck and the license plate, as well as two long strings of letters and numbers. Driver's license numbers? One for Jahn and one for Magda. What in the world had compelled Viv to write this down in sixth grade?

No sooner had I thought the question than I had my answer: *what if?*

Each and every one of Viv's plans began with a "what if?" All this information was protection against the possibility of an accident back then. She must have gone into their wallets to get these numbers. Evidently, I wasn't the only one working hard to stay prepared for a disastrous phone call in the middle of the night.

HALFWAY through the notebook, Viv had written the address of the big house in Rossie along the inside margin of the notebook. She also wrote, "*George Alberry, landlord.*" This page was flagged with a yellow sticky-note. She must have looked through these notebooks herself before passing them along to Ed Maynard. She must have marked passages that held information that he could use in his investigation.

Pages of Viv's observations from 1973 and 1974, when she was in fifth and sixth grades, followed: "*Jahn & Magda gone five days. Out of milk.*"

"*Jahn drunk. Magda told me to take N outside.*" Viv hadn't created a pictogram for me. I found myself scanning the pages for that elegant "N."

"*N cut her thumb today, not badly, but a lot of blood. She was so proud not to bleed on the food.*" My index finger slid across the knuckle of my thumb by habit to find the old scar. Viv had bandaged it up and gone back to her book, as I remember, with the comment that I was lucky to miss nicking the bone.

"Report cards in. N has all A's & B's except for art. How can this be? All she wants to do is draw & play with her dolls. N says teacher doesn't like the way she draws. Should get Magda to parent-teacher conference."

I wondered if Magda had ever talked to the teacher. Probably not. I didn't remember anything changing. I remember talking about Mrs. Jarzof with Viv. She told me it wasn't that the teacher didn't like me or my drawings, it was just a personality difference.

I spent a lot of time at the school library that year. Mrs. MacMillan was the librarian. She shared root beer barrel candies from her desk drawer.

A few pages later, Viv wrote, *"Read Island of the Blue Dolphins by Scott O'Dell. Maybe read all the Newbery Award books? Starting My Side of the Mountain by Jean Craighead George."* I remembered that book, too. Mrs. MacMillan had helped me send away for a list of the Newbery books for Viv, and when the big envelope came in the mail, Jahn's face had stilled. The vein in his forehead bulged.

"Who said you could use this address?" Jahn had demanded.

"It's our address," Viv had answered for me.

"It's just a school project," Magda had said, though I hadn't told her about it. "There's no harm done."

He hadn't said anything else, but he'd watched with narrowed eyes as I'd opened the envelope and showed Viv and Magda the poster. I'd loved that poster: the tiny images of the book covers as clear as stamps, each promising a wonder.

VIV marked the day we moved from the big brick house in Rossie to the awful trailer in Carthage with a yellow sticky-note. "October 20, 1975. Fight w/Jahn. Moving again. Not fair—starting midterms at the new school. He told me I was lucky to go at all. As if he was the big man allowing me to attend 7th grade.

"*N & I rode in the back of the truck w/the stuff down the interstate. Is that even legal? Magda slapped my face when I asked. She looked scared. She told me to shut my mouth. She didn't want Jahn to hear.*" Viv had doodled a star next to this sentence in a different color of ink.

I wondered if Viv had wanted Ed Maynard to read this passage as evidence that Jahn and Magda were afraid of drawing the attention of the cops. Still, at the end of a long day moving house—maybe they were on the lam, as Viv used to theorize, but I could just as easily see Magda simply trying to prevent Viv from upsetting Jahn.

Sitting on the couch all these years later, I shrugged. The movement reminded me of my physical surrounding, and I wondered if I had been muttering aloud. The dogs were still sleeping, so perhaps not. My tea was cold. I gulped it down.

I looked back at Viv's notebook. "*MJ & ALJ came up at recess and asked if I was Amish or if I just liked weird clothes. 'Weird clothes,' I told them. 'What's your excuse?' If they don't think you care, they don't keep teasing you.*"

We stayed in Carthage for about six months. I remembered the exact smell of the trailer. The tang of mouse plus the chemical smell of the adhesive holding the carpet down and the paneling up, overlaid with the stink of sulfur-water from the well. A heavy, hopeless smell.

"*Teachers don't really care about the Newbery Award books here. Read A Tale of Two Cities by Charles Dickens over the weekend.*

"*In gym MJ & ALJ asked all nicey-nice if I got the curse yet. I said, 'Do you mean have I menstruated?' All* afternoon they were hissing, 'Mennn-strooo ate him. Mennn-strooo ate him.' I ignored them.

"Spent Saturday in Watertown. Magda dropped us at the Flower Memorial Library & drove off. Karmel Korn at the Arcade for lunch. Wish we could live at the library like in From the Mixed-Up Files of Mrs. Basil E. Frankweiler."

I riffled through the remaining pages. No sticky-notes. I reached for the next journal, the one marked "Geography."

Viv had started this journal at the beginning of ninth grade in Carthage. "September 10, 1976. ALJ got married over the summer. She is fifteen. MJ went around telling anyone who listened that ALJ planned it on purpose—that she wanted out of the house, so she got pregnant. It's the only thing people are talking about.

"English teacher said we'll be reading The Scarlet Letter & To Kill a Mockingbird this year. Ha ha. Wonder if she'll discuss irony?"

We moved to Cape Vincent three weeks later. "Exact same classes, no comments about the clothes. Funny Algebra teacher. Strawberry milk at lunch—yum."

Viv used her journal to keep track of schoolwork assignments, often writing about what she was learning ("Mendel's theory of heritability came from his work as a gardener in a monastery") She also listed the books she'd read. As time went by, she described what she liked or didn't like about the books she was speeding through. For instance, Viv reread The Untouchables several times in 1977. She noted that it was Eliot Ness' autobiography—focusing on how he'd put away the gangster Capone.

A yellow tab and darkly inked star stood next to the following entry: "Eliot Ness chose to be incorruptible. His goal was to get Capone off the streets. It wasn't Capone's worst crimes that did it: it was carelessness & sloppy accounting that all added up. Ness never gave up being *able to catch Capone. He stuck by his plan even when everyone else thought it wouldn't work."*

Viv made the occasional comment about me, which I couldn't help but read: *"N made friends w/the Ramesy kids next door. Mrs. R asked if she could babysit but Magda said N was too young."* And later, *"N didn't wake up when Jahn came home last night. Thank God. Big fuss, Magda crying, furniture tipping over. They made up the usual way. Wish I could turn off my hearing."*

Again, I had an elusive sense of something I nearly remembered. It was like the memory of a scent before the smell returns. I closed my eyes and tried to let it come back: something about fighting, something maybe late at night? Magda and Jahn making up from a fight? No, not that—something out of the ordinary. Something—my memory refused to set it loose.

My temples throbbed in time with my heartbeat. After a moment, I put the notebook down and ran upstairs to Viv's medicine cabinet. More baby-aspirin and back to the kitchen to make another cup of tea.

On the couch, I flipped straight to Viv's sticky notes in the next journal.

"What's leverage against Jahn? Magda is weak; Jahn is the one who has to be moved. Eliot Ness?" In a different color of ink, she added, *"If Jahn went to jail, Magda would fall apart. We'd end up in foster care. If Jahn went away, could we live w/out him?"*

One of those dark, over-scored stars stood next to this entry: *"Civics class special project. Asked to profile Eliot Ness, but Mr. G said, Why not try something a little more modern, like the Chicago 8? Me: Who was that? Mr. G: How soon they forget. It's one of the most important modern legal struggles in this country—you should know about it. Everyone should. Me: Okay."*

She listed reference books to order at the Flower Memorial Library in Watertown, then jotted this: *"When*

I said I was writing a paper about Chicago 8 for Civics, Jahn went nuts. Couldn't figure out if he was mad at the US Govt, protesters, politicians, cops, or lawyers. Didn't seem to matter that it was me doing the research, he just started ranting. Remember to put paper covers on the books." A week later, she wrote, *"Abbie Hoffmann might be my hero. Fearless & incorruptible in his own way. In court, he used the rules for his own purposes."*

Years later, Viv told me about him. She found it amazing that Abbie Hoffman—founder of the Youth International Party, jester, and one of the FBI's most wanted outlaws—had been hiding in plain sight in the North Country while we lived there.

I turned pages, my attention catching on random entries: *"Got Magda to take me to JC Penny for a bra. Would have been humiliating except Magda was twice as uncomfortable. Why? Not like they were measuring HER chest."* A week later, *"Johnny Sykes kept staring at me on the bus. Like somebody poking me with a stick. I'd rather be invisible, but I turned around & said: Didn't your mother teach you it's rude to stare? His face turned so red it was purple. Offense = the best defense."*

Poor Johnny Sykes—everyone knew his mother had been sent away to "the 'burg," the mental asylum in Ogdensburg. Bet he hadn't pestered Viv again after that.

"Finished Bleak House by Charles Dickens. Found $5 bill in the book. Makes $223 in the piggybank."

And there was the familiar sloping "N." Even though not marked by one of Viv's yellow sticky notes, I read it anyway. *"N learning to cook w/Magda. They looked up from the kitchen table at me w/the same expression when I came in after mowing the lawn. Both wearing aprons. N goes: Don't track grass through the kitchen. Sounded just like Magda. So I turned around & walked back outside. Wanted to break a window or scream. Instead, climbed onto the shed & let myself into my bedroom window, did*

31 chin-ups, took a shower, went to sleep. Woke up later when N brought dinner to me."

I yawned, then tried to shake off the sleepiness. I drank my tea and focused on Viv's journal.

We had moved to Natural Bridge the summer of 1978 after school ended, but we only stayed there for a month or so, changing houses again before the start of the schoolyear. The journal ended with a list of addresses that Viv flagged with the familiar yellow sticky-note: *Slough Road in Carthage, Frontenac Springs Road in Cape Vincent, RFD #3 in Natural Bridge*, and, penciled in later, *Star School Road in Dexter*, where Viv and I stayed after our parents left.

I leaned my head back onto the sharp corner of the couch. My eyes closed. Sleep for just a little while, I told myself. Everything will still be here.

Chapter 36

VIV RESENTED Magda, but it wasn't fair to say Magda was forever asleep or unavailable. Though she rarely spoke of herself—rarely told stories about people at all— she instead offered up the names of things and facts about them. She pointed out the first unsteady skein of Canada geese crossing the sky while summer still seemed strong ("Autumn's on its way."). She was the one who woke us up to watch a luna moth emerge from its drab cocoon in the middle of one dark summer night.

After Viv read about a schoolboy who lives off the land, Magda said she knew some of the wild foods from the book. She offered to find us some of the plants, and she said she could cook a meal of wild food if we wanted her to. For once my sister let down her reserve.

That whole spring, the three of us went on walks where we gathered cattail tubers and boiled them in a coffee can over an open fire. We brought home dandelion greens and cooked wild onion soup and made dry, crunchy pancakes from acorn flour and cattail pollen. Magda showed Viv and me how to distinguish wild carrot from water hemlock. In her quiet, soft voice, she told us that we were apt to find crowns of asparagus springing up near the foundations of old farmhouses, and when we *did* find the pale green spears in a tangle of brown brush near a jumble of rocks from an old fireplace, even Viv was impressed.

Jahn joined us once, driving us along the narrow old farm roads past leaning barns and empty wooden buildings polished bare and silver by wind.

"Lilacs only grow where they are planted." Magda pointed to the big purple clusters of bloom. "This is a good spot," she told Jahn. He pointed the truck across a dented culvert, following the faint tracks of an overgrown driveway to an open meadow that had once been a front lawn.

Magda fussed over Jahn, re-positioning the picnic blanket and opening a Mason jar of iced tea for him. Viv struck off across the open space, heading, I could tell, for the trickling sound of a stream. She was looking for crawfish, which we had yet to find.

I waited for Magda, and she watched Jahn as he flopped down and tried to make himself comfortable. He complained about the unseasonable spring heat, but waved her away as she hovered, ready to move the blanket again. Magda was reluctant to leave him, but Jahn himself got up and wandered into the shade of the birch trees. She raised her voice as he walked away, "Mind where you step. I expect there's an old well around close by." He lifted a hand in half-hearted acknowledgement.

Not very long later, Magda and I were kneeling over wild-strawberry runners, examining the green nubs that would grow into fruit. The meadow was full of the racket of birds chirping.

"Did you hear that?" Magda asked me.

"A bobolink?" I asked, because even though I hadn't heard a bobolink, she loved the crazy cheerful song of those black-and-white larks.

"No, a sort of 'jar-jar-jar.'" Many years later, I learned that most birders put the songs of the birds into human words. At the time, however, I thought it was something unique to Magda, a way she translated the songs of the birds that she knew so well into something that I could understand.

At that moment, Jahn shouted, "Look!" He came leaping through the meadow, his face lit by some unusual emotion.

"Look!" he said again. "Magda, look!"

As he rushed toward Magda, I studied him. It took a moment to identify his mood: he was happy. Really happy. No sarcasm in his voice, no mockery in his dark eyes. He held out hands filled with a pile of what looked like smooth white balls.

"Puffballs. Puffball mushrooms," announced Magda.

"You must cut them like this," Jahn said, gesturing across his palm and nodding, "to be sure of them."

"Because they have to be white all the way through," Magda finished for him, triumphant. She and Jahn stood looking at one another, hands touching, smiling into one another's eyes over the clutch of mushrooms.

"What are puffballs?" I said, but neither adult answered me.

Viv trudged back across the field to see what Jahn had been shouting about. The front of her dress was wet. Grey clay mud spotted her arms. She gazed at the two grown-ups for a moment and then rolled her eyes at me. "C'mon. There's a stream."

When we got out of earshot, Viv said, "I thought a snake might have gotten him. I was kind of hoping for a rattlesnake."

"Magda says there aren't any poisonous snakes in this region—"

Viv stopped and pinched my bicep with cold fingers. "No duh."

"Ouch. But Magda says—"

"*Everyone* knows there aren't any poisonous snakes here anymore. God. I was just *saying.*" She dropped my arm as if it had burned her.

We didn't find crawfish that afternoon, though Viv kept us flipping rocks and looking for fossils past the hour when both of our stomachs were growling. When we returned to the picnic blanket, Magda and Jahn had eaten most of the sandwiches already. They'd tucked a dishtowel into the belly of the basket and then filled it to the brim with puffballs. Jahn was impatient to get back to the house to cook them.

The four of us went exploring a few more times, but Viv's interest turned away from the search for wild food. Maybe because we never did find crawfish big enough to eat, she started collecting leeches and freshwater clams and clear little minnows that she caught with her hands. She secreted them home in jars and then replaced the pond-water with some of Jahn's vodka. When the adults were away or busy, she'd dissect a jar or two of her specimens, mining Magda's sewing kit for tools and taking neat notes in her composition notebook on what she found.

By the end of that summer, Viv had moved on to other pursuits—although one jar of leeches, looking like dried slugs in a soup of their own grayish slime, came with us from house to house all the way until high school. Viv excelled at biology, naturally, and the biology teacher must have been happy to have a student as motivated as she was. He suggested books for her to read and ordered a baby shark and then a fetal pig for her to dissect. She probably gave the specimen jar of leeches to him. He wrote recommendation letters when Viv applied for college.

I kept up the habit of hunting for wild foods for years, gathering milkweed greens and wild asparagus every spring, harvesting feral apples and hickory nuts in the autumn. After Viv and I were on our own, I discovered Euell Gibbons. I cooked batches of fiddleheads and day-lily buds, which I prepared with the same thin egg-batter Magda had used for frying puffballs.

If I needed her to, Viv would come foraging, but her heart wasn't in it. She didn't much care about food, as long as there was something to eat. She might not notice that we had had oatmeal for breakfast and dinner for days in a row when the budget was tight—school cafeteria lunches never tasted so good as during an oatmeal week—but I appreciated having a handful of dried apples or wild plums to change things up.

I WOKE on my sister's uncomfortable black leather sofa with a kink in my neck and the longing for a mixed green salad – the tender, bitter kind with arugula, cress, baby spinach, young chicory, and the first leaves of dandelion.

I took my teacup to the kitchen and scavenged for something green while the water heated. I found a solid rectangle of frozen spinach and some slightly wizened celery. I replaced the spinach and rustled up some peanut butter for the celery.

Fortified by my snack and bearing a fresh cup of tea, I went back to the black leather couch. I turned to the next journal and flipped directly to the yellow sticky-note.

November 1979. We lived on Star Road then.

"Told them I wanted to finish high school here. Outrage & shouting. Jahn stormed out. Magda wept. Time for a brilliant plan."

Flipping past my birthday (a disappointing *"Mr. G said the Iranian hostages will never get out. N made her own birthday cake."*) I saw this in early December: *"I signed up for the SATs this spring. I HAVE to be here for them."*

Months passed before Viv marked another passage with a sticky-note: "*The other waitresses were talking about W2s & taxes. I didn't make enough to file, but: What does Jahn fear most? The authorities. Or getting caught for something. They should have been filing income taxes. That = lever.*"

The next entry Viv had marked was not dated. Her handwriting was shaky: "*Huge fight with Jahn before N got home from school. Like usual, but I said it: Told them I would report them to the IRS for tax evasion if they didn't let me go to college. He started punching me. She dragged him off me. Stood up, said if he ever did that again, I would kill him in his sleep. Think I scared him. Scared myself. Icepack on my face. Think I have a cracked rib. Hurts.*"

I flipped pages until I found the nearest date: April 6, 1980. Jahn and Magda had lit out later that same month.

Did I remember anything like this? Jahn and Magda were slappers; Jahn was especially quick with a backhand, but they weren't punchers, were they? Rib-breakers? I'd never deliberately pushed them, but to threaten Jahn with the IRS? Reckless wasn't even the word. It would have been like tossing him a live grenade. It would have been like declaring war. It would have been like suicide. She must have known how badly he would take it.

I was hugging the open notebook to my chest. Even at this distance, I still felt frightened for Viv.

I lowered the book to my lap and read on. She skipped a line between days, so the next day went like this: "*Stayed home from school. Told Magda what I wanted from them. Told her I had left a letter w/a friend at school w/all the details. Said if I didn't show up in* school the next day, the friend would put the letter into the mail to the IRS. Recited address for IRS.

"Pointed to my black eye & the bruise on my face & said: You are a bad mother. You can't even keep us safe from him. You should go.

"Feel like Becky Sharp by way of Abbie Hoffman & Eliot Ness."

I reread the page. My sister had driven our parents away.

They hadn't just left one day. She'd forced them—blackmailed them—to leave us. The audacity of her plan made me nearly sick to my stomach.

I looked at the stack of her journals bristling with bright yellow sticky notes. Sweat prickled along the backs of my knees.

She hadn't told me anything about this. She'd looked genuinely shocked when I'd said, "They are gone." But she must have already known they would leave. "No joke."

She'd made it happen, and never said a word. No joke—except maybe the joke was on me.

I extracted myself from the cocoon of blankets and pulled off the wool socks. I blew my nose, took a deep breath, and turned back to the notebook.

Chapter 37

I WORKED my way through the pile of journals, trying to keep my attention on the pages Viv had flagged. I got up for scrap paper to mark passages that I meant to revisit later.

By the time Dad Rowan got back, I was almost finished. The dogs roused to the sound of the garage door and Dad Rowan walked into the kitchen telling the dogs to simmer down. His cheeks were pink with cold.

"Have you smelled the air out there?" he said, pulling off his gloves and hooking the keyring onto its shelf. "Snow's coming. Don't get much of that in my part of Arizona."

He told me about his day. He'd gone with Viv to the lab where a technician had performed an ultrasound.

"Technology they have is a miracle." Dad Rowan kept shaking his freckled head and then patting his fringe of hair back into place. "You could see the baby's tiny feet and—" He checked himself in the middle of his amazement, his voice going flat as he finished saying, "—everything."

He pulled off his coat and hung it in the mudroom and said yes when I asked if he wanted soup for dinner.

As we set the table and sat to eat, the conversation limped along. At each pause, I saw the sagging of weariness and grief on his face, but he kept pulling himself together to say something or answer my questions. It was hard work for him.

"I think I'm almost over my cold now," I said, as Dad Rowan cleared the dishes, rinsing them and putting them into the dishwasher. "I'm ready to head into the hospital, probably tomorrow."

"Yes," he said. "I was wondering about that." He grimaced. "Wait, that sounds funny. I was wondering about your sister and the situation. That's what I meant."

I let him continue.

He rubbed a hand over his bald spot. "I don't know—I don't—I just think it's not fair to expect you to handle everything—these decisions—without help. You are just a young girl."

"I'm not sure about 'fair.'" My voice sounded stiff. But I was thinking, just a young girl? *Just*? I wasn't even that young anymore. I hoped he was speaking from a different generation.

"I didn't mean to imply you couldn't handle this and more besides," Dad Rowan said. "My son George—" He stopped, looking surprised and lost. He sat and after a moment, he continued, softer. "George always said you and your sister were extraordinary people."

We were quiet for a moment. It seemed as if he was making an offer, but I wasn't sure what it was. If there was something I was supposed to say, I didn't know what it was. The silence pulled on us.

"Well," he said finally. "Well. I suppose it's time for me to head back to Arizona."

"It's good having you here," I said, surprised to find it true.

He smiled, though he looked sadder than before. He eased himself off the tall chrome barstool. Lifting two bowls from the cupboard, he said, "Care for dessert?" He went to the freezer for the carton. "We have ice cream."

Plain vanilla—what Trisha called sweet butter masquerading as ice cream. She was strictly a chocolate fan.

"There's chocolate sauce," Dad Rowan added with a wheedling note.

"Just a small bowl," I said, not wanting to turn him down.

As he pried open the ice-cream container, the front doorbell chimed, startling all of us. The dogs raced to the front door barking their deep, reluctant barks. I dashed after them and told them to sit. They complied, but barely, crouching on their hocks around the entryway.

I opened the door to a pair of tiny witches wearing tall pointed black hats. "Trick or treat!" Adults hovered in the shadows by the road.

It was Halloween night already and I'd lost track of the date. Though I'd seen the orange-and-black displays at the drugstore, I hadn't thought to buy candy. And in a neighborhood like this we were bound to have trick-or-treaters.

I was just telling the little girls how frightening they were when Dad Rowan reached the front door, a small, crumpled bag of butterscotch candy in hand. "Oh, my! I hope these are good witches," he said.

"We are!" they chorused back.

Dad Rowan handed out orange disks and waved as the two skipped back down the stone walkway, where, prompted by their parents, they shouted, "Thank you!" over their shoulders.

Other small groups of costumed children and their adults trailed from porch light to porch light along Viv's street.

"Close the door and turn off the lights, quick," said Dad Rowan. "No candy on Halloween. What a disgrace! They'll TP the lawn for sure!"

We hurried around shutting off the lights. We were breathless and giggling, trying to be quiet. The dogs followed, galloping at our heels from room to room. We met back in the kitchen, where Dad Rowan dished out ice cream for us and I gave each dog a piece of yellow cheese.

I WOKE coughing the next morning, with Tomkin shifting his eyes reproachfully at me from his perch on a throw-rug as I honked into a tissue. "I'm getting better," I said.

He wasn't buying it.

"Fine. I won't take my germs to see Viv."

Seeing me up and dressed, Dad Rowan smiled and offered breakfast. "Can I sell you some waffles?"

He told me how he was going to spend the day, including some maintenance on the Saab.

I started to object, but the expression on Dad Rowan's face stopped me. "I'll reimburse you from Viv's checking account," I said.

He smiled wryly as he wrapped his scarf around his neck. "No need. I'd like to do this for you and your sister."

I had the sense again of an offer being made—followed by the sense that I was putting a foot wrong somehow. "I appreciate it," I said. "It's kind of you."

He shrugged and fumbled with the buttons on his coat. His collar was folded under.

"Here," I said. "Turn around, let me get that." He turned obediently and I straightened the collar around his scarf. He looked dapper. His freckled head, with its fringe of white hair looked neat as a dinner bun above his shoulders. I had the impulse to hug him, the way you catch a kid on his way out the door to school. Instead, I smoothed the fabric over his shoulders.

"Thank you, my dear," he said, settling his hand over mine and giving it a squeeze. "All right. I'll be off, then. Nothing I can do for you while I'm out? How about I pick up some dinner on the way home—Chinese food? Artie told me about a Szechuan place..."

Dad Rowan left more or less still talking as he closed the mudroom door behind him.

Chapter 38

I WAITED on the low couch at Artie's office staring at the out-of-register print of the quaint fishing village. It nagged at my attention like a hangnail. Artie emerged after less than five minutes, shooting his starched cuffs and settling the lines of his suit coat over his shoulders. He asked his assistant to bring us coffee and ushered me into his office.

From across his wide desk, Artie steepled his fingers together and asked, "How's it going?"

"It's okay," I said, and then wondered how to begin.

Just start asking, I supposed.

"To start with," I said. "I'm wondering if you know where Viv might have put a box of her journals."

He gave me a doubtful look.

"Maybe Viv left a note or something for me?"

"Ah—a note?" Artie looked almost stupid, with his handsome head turned to the side and his mouth not quite closed.

"I was hoping she left something with you, a note, or some sort of directions?" My voice trailed off weakly.

"Their *will* is a kind of directive," he said, seeming to grope around for the idea. "And the fact that she chose you as her medical guardian implies that she expected you to carry out her wishes."

I interrupted, "Yes, but *what* wishes?"

Artie adjusted the edges of the notepad on his desk.

After a moment, I said, "So—no note from Viv."

Artie shook his head.

"And no journals?"

His forehead wrinkled. "Journals?"

"That would be a no, then, huh?" I sighed.

"I don't know," Artie said, ignoring my sarcasm. "George's assistant boxed up his effects from the office. Naturally, I haven't opened it—I've been meaning to bring it to the house. Or perhaps the safe-deposit box at the bank—have you found the key for that?"

"Is it small and odd-shaped, with a plastic top?"

"That sounds like the right one."

"There are two, actually."

"Two?"

"Yeah. One from a bank in New York and one from here, I think. They kept them inside those little deposit envelopes from the bank."

Artie looked curious and guarded at the same time. "I didn't know about any out-of-state account. It seems irregular."

"Do you know what's in the safe-deposit boxes?"

"No. I'd expect George to have stored copies of their important papers and perhaps some valuables, such as jewelry or a watch." His expression was troubled. "But I don't have a record of a second safe-deposit box—"

"Maybe it's an old key," I offered.

The assistant tapped on the door and came in with a tray of coffee and treats. Artie's pale eyes lit up at the sight of the chocolate-chip cookies. Tough guy had a soft spot.

"Artie, what happens if someone discovers—oh, never mind."

Artie finished his first cookie and bit into another, the expression on his smooth face neutral, listening.

I meant to change the subject, but instead the question seemed to burst out on its own. "What if I found out that—since I was very little—I've been using someone else's birth certificate?"

Artie took a careful sip of coffee and spoke cautiously. "As—ah—an officer of the courts, I am sworn to uphold the law." He held up a hand to stop me from interrupting. "If one of my clients told me her identity was based improperly—on false documents, for instance—the important thing is whether the client knew or did not know about the improper documents."

"If I just found out?" I said.

"If my client—ah—began to entertain suspicions about her documentation, I would recommend a professional investigate the matter."

"Am I your client?"

"In point of fact—yes."

"Does Ed Maynard count as a professional?"

"To a certain degree, yes." Still holding the crescent-moon-shaped remnant of cookie, Artie said, "If Ed uncovered something of this nature, he'll probably advise that you talk to a lawyer."

He *has*, I thought, and I *am*, but my annoyance was mild.

"And he is looking into the matter further?" Artie asked.

I nodded.

"We can discuss it more thoroughly when we have his findings."

It was comforting that Artie, an officer of the courts sworn to uphold the law, wasn't freaked out. If he wasn't worried, maybe I shouldn't be either.

We finished our coffee. Downing another cookie as he spoke, Artie explained how to access the safe-deposit box downtown. His frown returned at the mention of the safe-deposit box, but he didn't have any other suggestions as to where Viv might have stored her journals. He told me if I'd tell him the bank name and the number on the second key, he'd do some checking on the box in New York.

MS. WALSINGHAM, the office manager at Viv's office, unlocked a heavy wooden store-room door and gestured me in.

"These are Dr. Rowan's things. We stuck her furniture here because Dr. Singh—who's filling in for her—needed the office space for her own things."

She stepped back and shrugged at the windowless back room where Viv's things were stored. A pair of open-topped cardboard cartons on the desk held black-framed diplomas and certifications and a pair of watercolors I had done in Italy, along with various knick-knacks—I could identify a jar of pens and a desk clock among the jumble. The office manager used the set of keys to unlock Viv's desk and filing cabinets. "We keep patient records separately, but if there's anything like that mixed in with Dr. Rowan's files, please treat it as confidential."

I assured her that I would.

She asked if I wanted a cup of coffee and told me she'd be in the outer office should I need anything. I thanked her and watched her leave.

At a glance, it seemed obvious that Viv's black journals wouldn't fit into the cardboard cartons, but I sorted through them anyhow and then shoved them to the very edge of Viv's desk, leaving room in case I found anything that looked promising.

I scooted a stepstool over to the filing drawers and sat down to flick through the files. Someone had neatly typed labels for Viv's monthly billing records and on-call schedules. Likewise, somebody had transcribed her daily rounds notes. It hadn't been my sister typing, I was certain.

Viv had signed me up for typing in high school. "You can always get a secretarial job," she'd said. "It's the kind of thing you can fall back on if you need to." She herself had gotten the only C grade in her life in typing class. She'd fumed at her inability to pick up the skill and worked doggedly and unsuccessfully to raise her grade.

Viv's familiar handwriting, slanting and dramatic, scrawled across the tabs of files in the big desk drawer. "Bills," she'd written in red marker. "Bank Misc" and "Maynard" in blue ball-point. "Notes" in pencil. I stacked these folders on the desk and topped it with Viv's appointment book and Rolodex.

I meant to read the files at Viv's house, but curiosity got the better of me. I opened the "Maynard" folder. Viv had scotch-taped one of Ed's familiar business cards (*All the truth you want to pay for*) to a page of notes. She'd jotted down his rates and the dollar amount for the retainer she'd given him. She'd also photocopied her letter to him. I settled more comfortably on my perch and read it:

June 21, 1993

Dear Ed Maynard,

Thanks for agreeing to take on this investigation. As we discussed, I am enclosing photos and documentation that may be useful. I marked pertinent passages from my childhood journals. Also, as you suggested, I've written up some of the things that recently raised my suspicions about Jahn and Magda Jones.

Look forward to speaking with you soon.

Dr. Vivian Marguerite Jones Rowan

Viv hadn't had the letter typed, but her careless handwriting was clearer than usual, as if she was mindful that someone had to be able to read it.

Stapled to the letter, she'd made a list describing the things she'd sent to Ed Maynard: *Graduation photos of N & me. Photo of Jahn & Magda* (she used the little pictograms) *in Rossie. Copies birth certs, passports, essay, estimate of payments from Jahn & Magda 1980-1988, notes, journal pages about Goodnight Moon.*

Following the letter were a couple of pages photocopied from Viv's journal—one of the missing ones I hadn't seen yet. She'd indicated with an arrow what she meant for Ed to see. She'd made copies of several hand-written pages, one entitled "Earliest memory?" and another with the heading "Imaginary friend." I kept flipping through the papers.

My sister had saved an old-fashioned computer print-out, the kind that came out on one long continuous sheet folded over and back again with scraps of paper clinging to the slightly yellowed edges. The dot-matrix ink had faded. She must have kept it since Potsdam, from when she'd applied to med school. I knew she'd sweated over her admittance essays, though she'd never asked for my help proofreading or typing.

My sister tailored her personal history to suit her audience—as everyone does from time to time. She sometimes recycled the tales of other people's parents or placed us in a different setting when retelling the events of our childhood.

Still, it made me almost cringe to see how Viv had used our Cocker Spaniel story on the medical school application:

I went to the emergency room once when I was a child. A dog bit me. It was not a big dog—a Cocker Spaniel— but it attacked me as I pushed my sister in her stroller on the sidewalk. I ended up with several puncture wounds in my leg and a jagged laceration on my upper arm.

The trip to the hospital is a blur, but I can remember exactly how the examination room became calm and quiet as soon as the doctor walked through the door. At first it was chaotic—a dozen people rushing around and the nurse kept asking me if I didn't want to be a good little girl. I remember thinking it was a silly question to ask me.

Then the doctor arrived. He was a tall man—although all adults must look tall to a child—with thick glasses and messy hair. Unlike the nurses, he didn't try to convince me that I should look away from the wound on my arm. He didn't tell me to be brave.

Instead, the doctor asked me what happened. When one of the adults in the room started to explain, he stopped her and said that he wanted me to tell him about it.

When I said that I wanted to see what he was doing, the doctor didn't argue. He didn't seem surprised by my curiosity. He talked me through the process of using a dissolving suture to join the muscle tissue, and then he explained how he would realign the sides of the wound as neatly as possible.

By the time he tied off the first stitches, I knew what I wanted to do when I grew up: I wanted to wear a white lab coat like his. I wanted nurses to listen to me and do as I asked. I wanted to have his kind of certainty as he explained how to treat puncture wounds. And most of all, I wanted to repair injuries the way he closed up the laceration on my arm, so calm and confident. It was like watching a magician do a magic trick, making the injury disappear, except that the magician explained how the trick worked.

I wish I could thank him. The wound healed neatly, but more than that, he told me I could become a doctor when I grew up. He said it would take years of hard work, but if I really wanted to, I could be a doctor like him. It has been my goal ever since.

Viv had an impressive collection of pharmaceutical giveaways in her desk: nice pens, leather notepads, tiny office kits and an all-band radio, each imprinted with the name and logo of a drug company. She had stuffed a wad of canvas totes bearing the names of surgical seminars into the back of a drawer. They probably matched the seminar materials she'd put into the three-ring binders at home.

I found one the right size to hold the stack of things I'd gathered and went to find the office manager to lock everything back up and to get directions to the nearest bookstore.

AT THE bookstore, I sat down on one of the diminutive chairs in the children's section and looked at *Goodnight Moon*. It was a classic. I knew it from babysitting. Most of the families had a copy—chewed and tattered perhaps, but still good for a quieting read before naptime.

I was sure I hadn't known the story myself as a child. Or had I? I opened the book to a bright spread and let the focus of my gaze relax so that the green walls and striped curtains blurred into blocks of vivid color. I kept my attention still, just feeling the four simple colors: blue, red, yellow, green.

Nothing.

But Viv had known *Goodnight Moon*. She hadn't told me. Not when she first remembered it last winter, according to Ed Maynard. Even after brooding over it for months, she never mentioned it during our weekly phone conversations.

Instead, she'd photocopied pages of her journal so that Ed Maynard—a complete stranger—would know about it. She'd even drawn an arrow for Ed to the important paragraphs:

December 2, 1992. Went to bookstore w/DG this afternoon. Odd thing: a picture book stuck on the end of a bookshelf in the mystery section. Picked it up & had to sit down on the floor. It was spooky: I recognized it. Goodnight Moon by Margaret Wise Brown. Reading it, I knew what was going to rhyme next, even though I didn't remember ever reading it.

By the end of the book, when the picture gets dark, I could almost hear the voice of the person reading the story, putting lots of expression into the little mice & the old lady whispering hush."

"If a patient told me about an experience like this, it wouldn't make an impression on me. I probably wouldn't believe it meant anything. But someone from before Magda & Jahn used to read this book aloud to me. I know it. I really liked the book, but I never read it to N. And that seems significant.

I rubbed at the chill-bumps that had risen on my arms. Significant? I would have said impossible, a picture book that she knew but which I did not.

Chapter 39

AT THE hospital, I found Viv looking larger. Her belly made a sizable hump under the covers. One of her feet was uncovered; it seemed inflated, the toes like smooth round pebbles. The bruises on her face had paled to shades of yellow, green, and rose.

An oily, sweetish scent—the concentrated essence of Viv—rose from her. The shaven side of her scalp had grown a plush stubble of new hair. The row of black stitches had been removed from the long cut on her face, leaving a scar that was pink and shining, like plastic. Additional sacks of fluid hung above her bed.

Someone had left a bright bouquet of silk chrysanthemums by her bed. I shivered at the sight of them—Viv had told me once that they were known as *les fleurs de morte,* flowers of death—and I put them on the floor outside the door.

I touched Viv's warm arm, telling her about the trip to Florida and back, about getting a cold, about Dad Rowan and me sneaking around in the darkened house hiding from the trick-or-treaters.

I picked up her hand, the square-tipped fingers shaped just like mine. Her broken finger was still splinted, though it was only barely swollen. When we were kids, she would wake me by tickling my nose with the end of her hair, putting cold fingers on my neck, tapping the skin behind my ear, or squeezing a fingertip.

I stretched my index finger to the spot behind her good ear and tapped twice. I knew it was being unrealistic, but after a moment, I tapped a quick SOS and then pulled my hand away. I watched her face, listened for a variation in the rhythm on her monitors. Nothing changed. I timed my breathing to the steady machine noise and tried to suppress the urge to pinch the pink pad of her thumb, as if I could startle her awake.

"I've been reading your journals, sis," I said. Not a flicker to indicate she heard. "I'm finding out stuff you probably wanted to keep secret. I guess you know I have to."

I picked up the green leather *Nicholas Nickleby* and found the bookmarked page. Dad Rowan must have done a lot of reading, as only a small section of the deckle-edged pages remained. It came to me with a sinking sensation that the novel had a second volume, just as fat and—I suspected—just as much fun to read. My mind wandered as I spoke Dickens' sentences.

A paragraph later, the realization came to me: I didn't have to read this. I could pick any book—I could even read Viv's own diaries aloud to her. Maybe outrage would bring her back.

"Hey, Viv," I said. "I just bought this great kid's book. It's called *Goodnight Moon*. Ever hear of it? I'll bring it in tomorrow. We can read it together."

AT A tapping at the door, I looked up to see Viv's surgical team—minus Dr. Pete—trouping in. The doctors ran through the routine with the pen and the flashlight, checking her reflexes. The process went quickly. No one seemed surprised when Viv's foot gave only a tiny twitch.

The short, freckled one stood across Viv's bed from me. "We've scheduled a tracheotomy for your sister later today."

"A what?"

"It's a bedside procedure. Because a throat tube like this one is not the best long-term solution." He touched the clear plastic tube taped into place on my sister's face. "So what we'll do is, we'll remove it and then we'll make a small incision just here—" He pointed at his throat with a pen. "For the tube."

He asked if I had any questions.

"What happens when she wakes up?" I said. "Will she be able to talk?"

"When the patient is able to breathe without the trache," he said, "we simply remove the tracheostomy collar and tube, and the hole closes back up."

Pushing aside the gruesome image, I managed to ask, "Is there any other option?"

"We could continue with the throat tube, but it's not optimal: over time, a certain amount of damage to the soft tissue is almost guaranteed."

They left with the promise that they'd send along some paperwork for me to sign.

I HAD only a few moments to fidget and worry before the usual parade resumed. I discovered that Dad Rowan had been busy. Each time a nurse or a technician came through the door, they asked after Mr. Rowan.

"Charm must run in the family," I said to Viv when the room was quiet.

I made myself read to the end of the full chapter of *Nicholas Nickleby* before going to the ICU waiting room to phone Trisha at work. She sounded harassed.

"Should I call you back?"

"No," she said. "It's just one of those weeks. They flew me back from San Francisco overnight."

"And man, are your arms tired!"

"Wow! Funny *and* original. So, you made it back to Nashville and you had a cold, and you are at the hospital now."

"Yes, yes, and yes. You've been talking to Sophia."

"Sophia has been talking to me," Trisha said. "Everything is okay there?"

"Everything is pretty much the same." I didn't want to get into the details of Viv's various tubes with Trisha.

"Ma said you sounded terrible. Not just the cold."

"I've been reading Viv's diaries," I said.

"Ooh. Juicy?"

"She blackmailed our parents into leaving."

"They weren't your parents—" Trisha started to correct me automatically. She had been thrilled when I'd told her Ed Maynard's discovery about our birth certificates. Her voice jumped an octave. "Blackmailed? How blackmailed?"

"Told them she'd sic the IRS on them."

"Holy crap. And it worked?"

"Signs point to—yeah."

"Whoa."

I said, "Viv never mentioned that she was the reason our parents left."

"Your parents who weren't actually your parents—"

"Yeah, yeah. But she never told me. Don't you see? She let me think Jahn and Magda just dropped us on the side of the road like a couple of kittens in a box. And then she let me think she was like some kind of superhero to get by without them."

"I can't believe I'm saying this," Trisha said, taking a sip of something and sounding like a younger version of her mother. "But she kind of was."

"Yeah, but they sent money—like hush-money!—to her, every month or so. And she could probably have contacted them if something really awful happened."

Trisha sighed. "But she didn't contact them, did she? She was, what, sixteen, and she shoved your parents out of the picture? At sixteen? She managed to get you both through high school and into college. Not exactly easy, and you didn't end up—excuse me for saying it—suffocated in your sleep."

I couldn't argue with that. I circled back. "She never told me."

"Maybe she was just trying to protect you."

"Hmm."

"Look, I have to go look at the boss' daughter's friend's portfolio—you know *that's* going to be a treat—but let's talk tonight. Okay?"

"Okay. Thanks."

"For what? Loser."

"Bye."

I returned to my sister feeling better. I told Viv that I had just been talking to Trisha. I signed into her hand, spelling each word for her in case she was paying attention. Viv had never warmed up to Trisha and her family.

"That roommate of yours," she'd say. "That roommate and her family. What are *they* up to these days?"

From the very beginning at Stony Brook, Trisha had taken me in. She'd hauled me along to Cutillo family events and helped me remember which of her uncles was which. After welcoming me into the family, Sophia and Papi Cutillo had made a point of trying to include my sister as well. They invited her for Sunday dinners, for birthday celebrations, for holiday get-togethers. "I'm catching up on my sleep," Viv would say as an excuse for not taking the train out of Manhattan. "I've got research to do."

In turn, this made Trisha resentful. "Not for nothing, but you'd think she could say 'yes' once in a while. What's the big deal—supper every now and again? Make Ma happy."

When I did manage to persuade Viv to join me and the Cutillo clan, the visits didn't go well. My sister's presence made everyone uneasy. Trisha's brothers—who normally moved around in a sort of impenetrable bubble of physical confidence, self-interest, and cologne—grew awkward when Viv directed her attention toward them.

Papi often tried to engage Viv in discussions about non-traditional medicine. He'd speculate about chiropractic and folk remedies, and Viv would close the topic by saying something dismissive, like, "And for hundreds of years, people believed they could cure warts by eating mercury."

Papi would laugh, as if Viv had said something clever, but I was uncomfortable with my sister's bad manners.

I think it was Sophia who made the biggest effort. Sophia remembered Viv's course-load from previous conversations. She always asked about Viv's housing arrangements and dating life—questions that Viv found intrusive, but which meant that Sophia was genuinely interested. That's where Viv's reserve seemed especially hurtful. I tried explaining each side to the other, but it never really worked out.

"THEY are different from you." I said the words slowly as I spelled them into my sister's palm. "But it doesn't make them wrong."

Chapter 40

RETURNING to Viv's room after lunch, I found the door shut. Several loaded medical carts were parked along the hallway. The technician standing by the nurse's station—she had adjusted one of Viv's machines earlier—said, "They'll be finished in ten minutes or so."

Settling myself into the ICU waiting room, I listened for the rattle of carts and noise of feet in the hallway before going back to her doorway.

I was not expecting Viv to look worse. But when the person leaning over her moved aside, I saw my sister flat on her back on the bed, her legs splayed, and her neck arched uncomfortably over a roll of toweling. A sort of necklace made of white tape held a hard plastic knob—for a shocked moment, I thought it was a shower-rod holder—against the base of her throat.

My hand was pressing against the base of my own throat. It was an effort to make myself step toward my sister's body.

A white cloth stained with red had fallen to the floor at the head of her bed. Flecks of blood had dried on the white skin of her neck. But the slow rasp of the ventilator matched the rise and fall of her chest, and her hand was warm in mine.

"Nicola. Nicky?"

I heard Dr. Pete's voice, the faint accent giving my name an extra twist.

"Nicola, come away for a moment."

Dr. Pete steered me away from Viv's room with a wiry grip on my elbow. He hustled us down the hospital corridor. A handful of people filled the ICU waiting room, and Dr. Pete barely paused before sending me farther down the hallway. He led me through the door of an on-call room across from the bank of elevators.

"Sit," he said, indicating the straight chair. "Put your head down and breathe."

But I didn't. The muscles in my chin pulled at my lips. Tears felt like acid in my eyes.

He looked at me for a moment and then held out both arms. "Come on," he said. When I hesitated, he waved his fingers impatiently, pulling air toward himself.

"It's okay," he said. "I think you need to have yourself a good cry."

I let my forehead drop to his shoulder. He kept his warm palm on my spine while I sobbed, murmuring now and again that it was okay.

When I was merely snuffling, he said, "There. Better?"

I nodded without raising my head.

He put paper tissues into my hand. "Will you tell me?"

Speaking into his lab coat, I tried to explain. "She looked like she was dead. That thing in her throat—"

"The trache."

I blew my nose. "It looks terrible."

He made a sound of agreement.

"It looks like she's getting worse."

He lifted me away and looked into my face. "Is that it?"

"Yes."

He snuggled me back onto his shoulder. "Okay. You're right. It looks worse. We don't like to put in a tracheostomy tube because there can be some complications. But also—mostly—because we are optimists, surgeons. Her brain activity still gives us reason to hope. We hoped that Viv would not keep needing the ventilator. But she does."

After an easy pause, he said, "Does that make sense?"

"Yes."

"And they told you that when she doesn't need the ventilator anymore, this incision will just close up?" At my nod, he added, "And that's not so bad."

I repositioned my forehead on his bony shoulder. My hair caught on the roughness of his chin. I took a deep breath. He smelled good. "Mm," I said.

"I regret to say it, Nicky, but I have to go."

"Do you?" I said, pushing my nose into the crook of his neck.

He chuckled. "Yes, I do. I am working, and you are my friend's sister. Attractive as you are—" He gave me a dry, quick peck on the forehead, firmly sealing the rejection. "I wouldn't like to explain to Viv for taking advantage."

It had been the impulse of a moment, but I couldn't help feeling a little hurt at his dismissal. Then he added, "I must ask for a rain check."

"A rain check?"

"Is this not a phrase?"

"It *is* a phrase," I said, trying not to laugh, "It's just not something anyone *says.*"

"But I do." He was twitching his clothes into order as he spoke. Without ceremony—and with what had to be the ease of long habit—he gave my appearance a quick, impersonal survey, straightening my shirt collar and patting my hair into place.

"And this smooth talking works for you, Romeo?"

Behind the glasses, his gaze was uncertain for a moment. When he saw that I was teasing, he had the grace to look a little embarrassed. He shrugged and reached for the doorhandle.

"Oh, God," I said, struck by the mortifying thought. "Tell me you aren't in love with my sister."

He turned away from the door. He was grinning. "No. Not in love with anyone. And no." He held up a finger to stop my question. "Viv and I, we were never together that way. Viv is my friend." His grin faded. "Perhaps my best friend."

ON THE way back to Viv's room, I caught up with Dad Rowan and Artie Slate as they stood talking outside the ICU waiting room.

"There she is," Artie said when he caught sight of me, which made me wonder briefly what he'd been saying.

Dad Rowan greeted me with a bear-hug.

"Have you been in to see her?" I asked him.

He nodded.

"It's been good seeing you, Dad," Artie said. He gave me an inquiring look. "If—ah—Nicola can give you a ride home?"

I told him I could.

"I'll head back to the office. Call me if I can do anything." These last words were directed to us both, and we waved as Artie left.

When Artie stepped into the elevator, Dad Rowan sighed. "The weight of the world on his shoulders, poor kid."

At my expression, he said, "It's never just simple, is it? He lost a brother to cancer. Spent too much time in the hospital himself as a youngster. He's having a hard time all the way around."

He tucked my hand into the crook of his arm and gave me a sad-eyed smile.

I thought, *this* is why George was so reliably reliable and kind. He got it from his dad. I wondered if Viv—after having offered advice and warnings to me about men for all those years—understood this truth about George and Dad Rowan.

We started toward Viv's room, and one of the nurses waved from the nurse's station.

"Good morning, Lily-Ann," Dad called, his voice cheerful. "Hope your son is feeling better!"

"Dad Rowan?" I said when he'd finished chatting with the nurse.

"Yes, my dear?"

"Thank you."

He pressed my hand with his elbow. I didn't trust my voice to say anything more, and once we got to Viv's room, he made for the box of tissues and blew his nose before suggesting that he read a little Dickens for us.

DAD Rowan went back to Arizona later that week, looking brave but fragile, hefting his neat black suitcase and slipping into the hurrying crowd of people at the airport. "After all this time, I'd be surprised if my neighbors are still talking to me. The lawn will be a shambles."

He insisted I drop him at the curb. He didn't want me to wait for his plane to board. "There's no call to spend a minute longer here than necessary. I've flown more than my share of miles and I know it's no fun waiting in an airport."

He telephoned when he arrived home and I was grateful. The house felt even more empty and unwelcoming without Dad Rowan's clutter and the too-loud television.

Chapter 41

ACCORDING to the one of the hand-written notes Viv had shared with Ed Maynard, she had once had an imaginary friend named Mermalaude.

Viv noted exactly how the imaginary friend looked: Mermalaude kept her hair in two braids, with a feather in her beaded headband. She lived inside Viv's shoe at night. She wore moccasins and a deerskin dress. Mermalaude was a warrior and a Cherokee princess. Viv wrote, *"Mermalaude was tall and very strong and smart. I knew she was make-believe, but I missed her when she went away. I didn't tell Jahn and Magda about Mermalaude, but I know that she had not been a secret before them."*

When I put the paper down and said the name aloud a few times, "Mermalaude, Mermalaude," it seemed faintly familiar. Then, surprisingly, I had a clear vision of the fringed hem of a soft leather skirt brushing against a smooth tan leg. The buckskin fringe would have made a little pattering noise as the wearer moved.

I shivered, reminded of the Gina Davis movie *Beetlejuice,* where a ghost was summoned by calling his name three times. I was tempted to cross my fingers and spit against a possible haunting by Viv's long-ago imaginary Cherokee friend.

The next handwritten page contained a bare paragraph that started, "*My sister and I were hiding under the kitchen table. I was wearing footed pajamas— the kind with the papery soles and the metal snaps that go up the insides of the leg. A tablecloth hung down like a tent. We had hidden there before. The linoleum tiles on the floor were worn. The place, the apartment, felt urban— maybe the air smelled like a city, or maybe it was the sound of a train or traffic. I was keeping my sister quiet and safe.*"

Another photocopied piece of paper was labeled "Earliest Memory?" Viv described the bright sunshine pouring in through a window, which made her think it was summertime. She wrote, "*I was listening to something mechanical clack and thump behind me. Several adults were there. They weren't paying attention to me. I saw their feet. Someone might have been playing the guitar, but that wasn't interesting to me. I was squeezing a gob of dough while my sister slept in a wicker basket on the braided rug next to me. She was little, in a diaper. I liked the way the dough was sticky and rubbery at the same time.*

"*One of the adults said something about me looking after my sister. Someone else said that I was really good at taking care of her and it made me feel very grown-up and important.*"

Viv had never mentioned any of this to me.

WHEN Ed Maynard telephoned at the end of the week, I had a few questions ready for him. Did he have time to talk? He said yessum, that he had just finished his supper. He lit a cigarette with his Zippo. We inhaled at the same time across the telephone line.

"So, my sister contacted you when she started to remember things from before Jahn and Magda?"

"Something like that. She said she'd been troubled by some 'anomalies' in her memory."

I laughed.

Ed continued, "My understanding is that your sister's first memories of Jahn and Magda start at about the same time she would have attended first grade. In 1969."

It still felt like a boot in the gut. I'd have turned three years old that November. Three years old—give or take.

"But," Ed continued, his voice slow and careful. "Before then, no memories of Jahn and Magda."

"Right," I said. "And Viv never asked Jahn and Magda about it?"

"As she explained it to me, Vivian hadn't thought about the significance of her memories until recently."

I felt a pang. I was still searching for the rest of Viv's journals. I'd been combing the ones I'd found for insight about my sister wanting to start a family. So far, not one word about family, pregnancy, or the longing to have children.

Ed continued, "When she wrote to them in 1989, the letter was returned by the post office. She suspected that Jahn and Magda had fled, having, as she put it, 'fully discharged their responsibilities' to the two of you."

I didn't answer. I wondered how it could be that Viv was so certain about what Magda and Jahn owed us.

"Still there?"

"Yeah, just thinking." I looked down at the notes I'd taken in the middle of the night before. "You tracked down Jahn and Magda to Penn State?"

"University of Pennsylvania, actually. I spoke with one of Magda's roommates and she told me about a man." The sound of rustling pages came from Ed's end. "During the spring of her sophomore year, Marsha started seeing a Hungarian fellow, name of Jahn Kiraly. He worked in the engineering department as a laboratory tech of some kind. The roommate described him as 'unpleasant and domineering,' with an accented voice and a distinctive red scar on his right forearm. Sound familiar?"

I told him it did. Hungarian, I thought, *that* makes sense.

"Looks like this Kiraly fella got fired and he and Marsha left town. Before the University, there's not much trace of him. It's a common name, and it might be that he was using an alias even then. A lot of young Hungarian immigrants came through Philadelphia and Cleveland after the Soviet invasion of 1956."

Ed sighed before continuing.

"Boys as young as sixteen coming to the States all by themselves, with no family, no friends. I didn't find any record that this Jahn Kiraly had any family connections here in the States. It wasn't at all unusual for these young guys to leave everything behind to escape the regime over there. A lot of them fell right off the radar once they realized how tolerant the authorities were over here—and this Kiraly guy was lucky to only get himself fired from the University. He'd gotten into a fight in the lab where he worked, knocked out a co-worker and busted up a bunch of equipment."

"I think he did that kind of thing more than once."

Ed lit a cigarette. The crinkle of cellophane proclaimed that it was a new packet. "I told you he'd had his driving license suspended, didn't I?"

"I don't think so."

"I put the details in the written report, but there was a series of DUIs in the 1980s. According to his last employer, Kiraly had been pretty volatile at work, complaining that the other guys were talking about him. The wife drove him to and from work. In any case, this Jahn didn't file taxes as Jahn Kiraly, or as John Jones, so far as I can tell."

"No," I agreed. "That's how Viv got them to leave. She threatened them with the IRS."

"Yessum."

"But she never confronted them about where we came from?"

"She didn't mention it. You don't mind my saying, but it seems your sister confronted them about a lot of other things."

"Does it sound like I am accusing her of something?"

Ed paused a long moment, and I heard the noise of ice clunking into a glass during the pause. "Not my place to judge, frankly." He inhaled smoke. "The way your sister explained it, she wanted to get the two of you safe back then. She wanted to stop changing schools and settle down. I don't think she spent much time speculating about Jahn and Magda's motives until just recently."

"Because of the baby," I concluded.

"I'd guess so. She didn't say to me. But I guess it's natural when a baby is coming, looking back and looking forward."

I made a noise of agreement.

"The future starts in the past, my old grandma used to say." He coughed out a laugh. "I might be turning into an old geezer. Sorry."

"And you don't have any other material Viv gave you?"

"Just the photographs, and it sounded like you were familiar with them."

"No other notebooks?"

"Just the ones we returned to you. As I said, your sister gave us a selection of journals. Just the ones she thought we could use. You haven't found the rest of them?"

"No," I said. "I wonder—"

"Ma'am?"

"Nothing. I just wish Viv could tell me what she was going to do."

"You mean—what was she going to do with the information I found for her?"

Not exactly, I thought, but it was close enough. I said, "Yeah."

"Oh, I'd imagine it would all depend on what she found out," Ed said, lighting another cigarette. Ice clinked. "You'd be surprised how often my clients never do a thing with the information I find for them."

"So why bother hiring you?"

"To confirm their suspicions, maybe. I'm sorry to tell you, but sometimes—domestic investigations mostly—clients keep the information in their back pocket. For a weapon, so to speak."

I did know what he meant, or anyway I could imagine. I didn't tell Ed that I was pretty sure my sister didn't need another weapon in her back pocket. On the other hand, she *did* like to be prepared.

Ed told me that he was working on finding Sara Banner, Marsha Ranklin's second roommate from college.

"And so—?" I said, trying to connect it with the rest of Ed's investigation.

Ed explained. "My strategy is to narrow down where Jahn and Magda were, geographically. I've got a researcher combing the records for two missing little girls, but you can imagine—needles in a haystack."

I could imagine, at least a little.

Ed continued, "Marsha Ranklin's aunt thought that Marsha had kept in touch with this roommate." Ed paused to take a sip from his clinking glass. "But Ms. Banner recently relocated from Michigan to Toronto. As far as I can tell, she's been traveling for business for weeks. But I'm confidant I'll catch up with her before long."

I nodded.

Not hearing me, Ed put his glass down with a thump. "As long as you want me to keep going?"

"Yes," I said. "Keep going."

Chapter 42

I SLEPT badly in Viv's house after Dad Rowan left. Awake at night, I scoured the big rooms for Viv's missing journals, but didn't find them. I made myself tea and carried the mug through the empty-feeling rooms. Tomkin padded along with me, seeming confident that a slice of cheese would reward his vigil. I'd done a lot of house-sitting over the years, but Viv's house didn't grow more welcoming over time. The edges stayed sharp. It never seemed cozy to me.

Some nights, I'd sit on the chrome barstool at the black kitchen counter and listen to the central heat cycle on and off. I decided that the wee smalls were hatched from nights like this: they swarmed from a small, still pool of yellow light in the middle of this strange dark night-time country. Not a single light shone inside of any of the houses nearby. Nothing moved but the bare branches of the trees.

After stopping by the hospital one morning, I took myself into Nashville proper to investigate the safe-deposit box at Viv and George's bank. It was a disappointment. The boxes didn't resemble little combination safes, as I had expected. Instead, a wall of enameled metal cabinets held surprisingly small compartments.

Viv and George's shallow drawer contained roughly what Artie had predicted: a copy of their wills, the insurance policies, bank and brokerage statements, titles for their cars. It was a tight squeeze to remove everything, including a small flannel sack that held a heavy silver pocket-watch.

An envelope marked "Identification" gave me a brief thrill until I read the contents: just George's birth certificate and baptism record, their wedding license, and their passports. Nothing about two little girls (most likely sisters) who weren't actually named Jones.

I considered making a quick trip to New York to investigate the other safe-deposit box, but Artie had said he could make arrangements for a "designate" to visit the bank and access the contents of Viv's other safe-deposit box. Trisha had agreed to be the designate. They had gotten going, but the process seemed ponderous—evidently, there was a lot of notarized paperwork and registered mail involved in getting into a safe-deposit box in Manhattan.

IN THE second week of November, the baby team announced that they were currently—cautiously—pleased with Viv's progress.

"We feel there's no need to perform a cesarean section at this time," Marilyn Wilsey told me. "And we are very—*very*—happy about that. To be completely honest, we are feeling our way along here medically with a maternal head trauma like this."

The group all nodded agreement.

Dr. Wilsey prompted the team to share the more certain good news. One of the doctors said, "The baby seems to be back on track, and of course having the mother unconscious should not be a barrier to a successful natural delivery." The relief on their faces made me frightened all over again.

"Oh," said Dr. Wilsey. "Did you want to know the gender?"

AFTER the team left, I looked at my sister. Hair fanned around her head on the pillow, a frizzed and messy half-circle like a broken halo. Her eyelashes inky against her pale skin. The trache collar with its tubes like a pastel blue scuba set.

I could trim her hair short while she slept, I thought. I could make the two sides even. That would make it easier to keep neat as she slept. A gamine cut—it would look cute. Surely she'd understand once she woke up. She'd be peeved, no question.

I'd explain to her that it was just hair, that it would grow back. I felt a deep squeeze of tenderness for my sister, as if for once I were the older, wiser one with the advice and consolation to glide her through this fashion emergency.

I got the nurse Lisa to help me. She thought to make a neat lasso of dental floss to tie off the braid, suggesting that we save the hank. I scissored off Viv's ponytail and then snipped and snipped until we had filled the wastepaper basket with loose bits of curl. The two sides didn't quite match – the short side was really too short after the surgical buzz-cut, but it looked better.

We went to work on the remaining hair with wet washcloths and powdery dry-shampoo and Viv's favorite boar-bristle brush. The hair quickly sprang up and circled Viv's face with a bright cap of auburn. It looked cute.

Several of the other nurses came in to admire our handiwork, and though I offered to help, I only watched as two slim little nurses expertly changed Viv's sheets. They shifted Viv in stages, barely speaking to coordinate their efforts as they untucked and tucked and eased fresh sheets on her bed. Their actions were smooth, confident, and so kindly with her inert limbs that I felt tears start in my eyes.

When they left, I pulled myself together and told Viv about her new haircut, about how with a bit of gel she could spike her hair like a rock star if she wanted to. I picked up *Nicolas Nickleby* and put it back down. I pressed "play" on one of Viv's jazz tapes.

As DeeDee Bridgewater noodled away, I got my pencils and pad and sketched my sleeping sister. Her face as smooth and soft as sand, her neck long and white without the heavy ponytail, the dark of her eyebrows and hairline bringing shape to the white page. She looked like a different person on paper and in the bed, a young girl, perhaps, someone delicate and vulnerable. Someone fragile as an eggshell—with a baby inside.

Even then, with the baby looming like a cloud, its heartbeat blipping on the monitor, a C-section just barely averted (for now, for now at least), it still seemed unlikely.

Of course Dear George loved dogs and kids. He would have been a great dad. But—the thought came back around to my stubborn sister. Viv wouldn't have decided to have a child simply because her husband wanted one. Too much like Magda being a sheep.

And to have kept trying to have a baby after a miscarriage, a second miscarriage—a third? How difficult that must have been. Could my sister have continued trying to have a baby because of George? Would George have asked her? I didn't know, but it seemed me that it could only have been her own heart making her keep trying.

I knew what made *me* feel all gooey about babies: sharp little gums, dimpled knees and tiny tapered fingers moving like seaweed in an unseen tide. The smell of them, the way my hand curved around the solid, humid heat of them.

But what made my sister weak? Surely it wasn't logic. Was it the smell of baby or the fleshy squint of a fat cheek? A Don King hairdo rising off a tender fontanel? Triple-rolled plump thighs? Wiggly block feet and toes the size of peas? I imagined that some detail had gotten inside her heart, pried a crack in it, and pulled it open to make room for wanting a baby.

That question was one of the things I looked forward to asking her. I was going to tell her how scared she had made me and how angry. I was going to demand answers to more questions than I had ever thought of asking before.

I wasn't going to respect our taboo subjects. I was going to ask whether she and George were really happy, and I was going to demand to know why she had kept all these secrets in the first place.

"When you wake up, Viv," I said to my sister, "you have a boatload of explaining to do."

Chapter 43

WE HAD never been very good at arguing with each other, my sister and me. A few weeks before I graduated from high school, I came home to the duplex apartment in Potsdam to find Viv sorting the mail. She held an opened letter out to me and announced, "I got you a job."

"But I already have a job," I said, not taking the letter.

"A better job," my sister said, shaking the paper at me. "A real job. Working in a medical office."

"I don't want to work in a medical office."

"Don't be stupid." My sister dropped the letter on the table in front of me. "You want to make a nice chunk of change this summer, right?"

"I'll make a nice chunk of change painting with the crew again." Not to mention—and I wasn't going to bring it up—I planned to keep babysitting the Bebernes kids.

Viv made a visible effort at patience. "But with *this* job you'll have time in the evenings to get a head start on some of your classwork."

I looked at my sister without speaking. Did she think I needed to get a head start on my classwork? Did she think it was going to be too challenging for me to handle academic work during the semester? She couldn't believe that I was stupid. I was in the Honor Society. I'd done well on my SATs. Not as well as she had done, but I'd put up a decent score.

Viv said, "Really, it's an easy job and the money is great." She pushed. "All summer in a nice cool office building. You should take it."

"If it's so wonderful, why don't *you* take it?"

"There's a typing test." Her voice was colorless. She was frowning at the table. I knew it still bothered her that she couldn't get good at typing.

My resistance melted. I felt bad for her. She'd found an ideal job and she just wanted one of us to get it. No big deal. I wanted her to be happy.

I interviewed for the job and passed the typing test. But when I calculated the hourly rate and the schedule of the office job—only thirty-seven hours a week—over the course of the whole summer, the house-painting gig worked out better.

My sister shrugged when I showed her the math. "Yeah. That makes sense. I just wanted you to get some good job experience under your belt."

I didn't tell my sister that I thought working with the painting crew *was* good job experience. Or that I didn't mind hard work. Or that—no matter how easy and nice or how well air-conditioned it was—I didn't want to sit in an office all summer. Plus, I enjoyed working with the same crew each summer. I liked putting on my paint-splattered work clothes and packing my lunch and accomplishing something.

AT THE end of June, I told Viv that I would be away for the Fourth of July holiday. The Bebernes family and their best friends—another family with kids—were going down to Lake George to share a cottage, and they wanted to have a live-in babysitter for the long weekend.

Viv looked up from the TV set. She was addicted to a French-language sitcom called *Les Brilliant* that played on the Quebec television station. I should have waited for the end of the show before telling her, but I was headed straight to bed, and I knew that she'd already seen this episode.

Her shoulders slumped dramatically, and she spoke as if she couldn't believe what I was telling her. "Four days, seven kids, no break? Are you crazy? There's not enough money in the world to make that worthwhile."

I told her how much they were paying me.

"Wow," she said. "What's that per hour?"

Stung, I retorted, "A lot more than I'd make sitting around the apartment doing nothing."

My sister had a *Vogue* magazine open in her lap. The pages crinkled as if her hands had involuntarily stiffened. Her eyes got squinty, and she spoke through clenched teeth. "I'm working at the diner that weekend."

"I meant *me*," I said. "I meant more than *I* would make sitting around the apartment."

"I guess it's all about you," Viv shot back. Her voice was nasty. She turned back to the television with the magazine on her lap. She dismissed me and my distress with a contemptuous flick of one glossy page.

Heat flooded through me. I was scared and angry at the same time. Later on, I thought of half a dozen or more things that I should have done right then. I should have mimed yanking the invisible dagger out of my heart. I should have faked a full-on Victorian fainting spell. I should have blown an enormous raspberry of derision at my sister.

Instead I stood like a spooked farm animal, blowing and snorting. I couldn't find a single word to answer her. My head filled with angry tears. As I stumbled off to my room, I could barely see.

I tossed and turned over how bitter she had sounded and how quickly she had sparked to temper. She must have been brewing on those feelings for a long time, yet I had no idea what I'd done to make her so furious. I resented the injustice of it, because it certainly wasn't my intention to irritate my sister. It frightened me to know that she was angry with me. It was alarming to see how cruel she could be over almost nothing.

I left for work the next morning before she got up. She was at the diner when I got home. What with one thing and another, we didn't run into each other again until I got home from the weekend in Lake George. I unlocked the front door and let myself in, sunburned and tired, with a pocket full of cash. Viv was sitting in front of the TV in our little apartment, again watching *Les Brilliant* with a magazine open in her lap.

When I stepped through the doorway, she looked up and said hello as if she'd forgotten all about the fight. So I pretended it had never happened. I said hello. It felt awkward, but my sister seemed untroubled.

"How was the weekend?" I asked. "No firework incidents to report?"

"Nope. Potsdam survived another weekend of hooliganism," my sister said with a smile. "How was yours?"

"Good," I said.

"Good." After a moment, she gathered up her things, stood, and said, "Well, I'm opening the diner tomorrow, so I should hit the hay. Sleep tight."

"Goodnight." I took myself to bed, even though it was early, and I'd wanted to tell her about the cottage and Lake George, about the food and the bonfires at night, about this colorful other world I'd visited.

I consoled myself by thinking how little she liked hearing about these small adventures. They probably bored her. If she didn't want to know, I wouldn't bother her with the details.

A MONTH or so later, I was unpacking my bags at college. I'd thought it would be harder to live away from my sister that first semester at Stony Brook. I'd expected it to be difficult to share a room with a stranger. I didn't know if I'd adjust to dorm living. I wasn't sure about eating all those cafeteria meals. And what if my roommate, as Viv suggested, turned out to be a nightmare?

The girls in the room on the opposite side of the shared bathroom almost had me convinced that I would have a room to myself, but Trisha arrived late in the afternoon. I heard the Cutillos before they reached the door of the dorm room. Trisha, surrounded by a flying wedge of family. Sophia and Papi and each of her brothers carried things for Trisha: big suitcases, bulging Bloomingdale shopping bags, a stereo and a mini-fridge, and a hanging bag of clothes for her closet.

They squeezed in and introduced themselves, everyone talking loudly at once. They unloaded everything onto Trisha's bed. Sophia told them to clear Trisha's bed, that it was unsanitary to leave suitcases and things on the mattress. Then they argued cheerfully about where to put everything. At one point, both of Trisha's parents started to cry while Trisha's brothers hulked around uncomfortably.

I would have left them to their privacy, but I was pinned in my corner of the room by the crush of Cutillos. Trisha pulled away from her parents' collective hug, patting their shoulders and giving me a harassed look. "Ma, Papi, come on, you're embarrassing my roommate."

"What? She's never seen parents saying good-bye to their baby girl?" Sophia Cutillo's gruff voice was spirited. She kept an arm hooked around Trisha.

Papi wiped his face with the palm of his hand, a gesture so unstudied and graceful that I felt my own eyes start to water. I looked out the window and stretched my jaw in the way my sister taught me to ward off tears. "It's okay," I said. Then, pointing, "Ooh, is that your car?"

They all rushed to my window to see a tow-truck moving into place at the direction of the campus police. It wasn't their car, but the automotive drama spurred them to finish unloading and say their goodbyes.

"Thank you," Trisha mouthed to me as she left to walk them to their car.

Because I'd had the morning and most of the afternoon to learn my way around, I showed Trisha to the dining hall and gave her a tour of as much of the campus as I knew so far. We started talking that afternoon and didn't stop until we fell asleep that night.

I called Viv on Sunday and told her about Trisha and her family. She listened, but then asked, "What about your classes?"

When I asked Viv about how it was going for her, she said, "People here were all at the top of their classes, but I'm still pretty smart." Her voice was excited and confident. She admitted it was a relief, for the first time in six years, not having to work during the schoolyear. Overall, so far, medical school was better than she had hoped.

On the first long weekend break, Trisha invited me to come home with her to her parents' place in Brooklyn Heights, but it seemed disloyal.

I went instead to see Viv in Manhattan, where I slept curled up on the loveseat in Viv's tiny student apartment. She studied all Saturday while I wandered the Frick Collection. We met up at Viv's new favorite Szechuan restaurant. Afterward, we met with a blur of her fellow medical students over glasses of wine. We went to a late-night set of jazz in the Village.

On Sunday, Viv and I walked around and looked at things. We talked and tried on clothes and browsed open markets and ventured into every store that looked remotely interesting.

It stung a little when Viv suggested that we finish the long weekend early.

"You should probably take an early train back to Long Island. That way we can both rest up for school."

I left her apartment at dawn, detouring to the Museum of Modern Art sculpture garden and the museum store. I went to the public library on Fifth and sketched the lions before catching an afternoon train back to Stony Brook. Trisha got to the dorm late with a Bloomingdale's bag of leftovers from home.

"The house seemed the same but smaller. My brothers seemed bigger. It was good to have real food again," said Trisha. "But I'm glad to be back here."

"Me too," I said.

I went to Brooklyn Heights with Trisha for the Thanksgiving break. My sister suggested it. "If you are going to be busy over Thanksgiving..." Her voice had trailed off expectantly.

I had been reluctant to mention it, but I said, "I got invited to the Cutillos." I'd actually hoped my sister would join us.

"Good, then," my sister said. "I'm going to go on a road-trip with some friends."

Viv came back from vacation with sunburned shoulders and feet, she later said on the telephone. She'd had a great time, enjoyed traveling with her classmates. She loved the ocean and the sand and the smell of seaweed just washing in from the sea.

She asked if I'd had a good Thanksgiving feast with "that roommate of yours."

I said yes. Because I thought she would say something belittling about Trisha's family, I asked Viv for more details about her vacation. She seemed happy to tell me.

THE following spring, my sister and I were walking north on First Avenue into the teeth of the late-winter breeze. I was going to be spending a few days on Viv's loveseat during the March break. Viv had just met my train and we were stopping to pick up soup on our way to her apartment.

"I got it!" my sister announced. "I got the fellowship. I'm going to spend the summer on that project I was telling you about."

I didn't remember her telling me about any project for the summer, but I nodded anyhow, amazed to see my sister so bubbly with excitement. She was practically skipping. Her face had a glow that made passers-by look twice at her.

"I didn't want to get my hopes up—*you* know. But the letter came this week, and I will be one of the four research fellows. They are going to fly me to Argentina."

"Argentina?"

"I know. I'm glad I took eight years of French." She pulled a face at me, but her grin came back almost instantly.

"You're going to be away all summer?" I said.

"The fellows fly out the week after finals," she said, "and we'll be back in August." She looked over at me and added, "This is huge."

"I know. I'm glad for you."

My sister bumped me gently with a shoulder as we walked.

"No—I'm glad." I said. "I just wasn't sure what we were going to do over the summer."

"Have you thought about summer school? Give you a leg up on next year. Stay in the dorms, maybe, get a part-time job near campus?"

Of course she had mapped out a plan for me. This was Viv, after all.

I made a non-committal sound and then said, "So, Argentina?"

She tossed her hair. "It's going to be amazing," she said. As she talked about it, I tried to understand why I felt so burned. Was I jealous of her research project? It was exactly the kind of thing she'd worked for and earned. And I wanted her to be a success.

But I wasn't happy for her.

I didn't like the way she was ready to park me someplace for the summer without her, like someone tying a dog's leash to a telephone pole while she goes inside for ice-cream. It was silly to feel this way. I wasn't a kid. I had lots of friends and plenty of options. It wasn't like I was going to be alone.

I reminded myself that Viv wasn't frightened. And *she* was the one flying thousands of miles away from home. And then I thought: *home?*

She was finally getting away from me.

It was stupid and babyish and selfish, but I had been holding onto the idea that things would return to the way they were. Come summertime, I had thought it would be me and my sister against the world again. Not that we would return to the North Country, but I'd thought we would share an apartment someplace. I'd thought that my life hadn't really changed.

Of course my sister was moving on. She had ambitions. I knew that as well as I knew anything. And after all, she had maneuvered us through years of struggle to get us here, to get herself into one of the best medical schools in the country. And this research fellowship was exactly the sort of thing she'd dreamed about.

And after all, I was nineteen. A grown woman. I was registered to vote. I had a checking account. I was in college. Realistically, I could pick any one of a dozen different ways to spend my own summer. I could find a contractor who needed a wall painter. I could exercise my typing skills. I could sub-let an apartment in Stony Brook. I could join my friends working at a summer camp in the Adirondacks. I could even put on the salmon-pink grown-up outfit Viv had found for me and get hired as a shopgirl at a gallery in the city. The possibilities were endless when I thought about it.

As it turned out, I spent that summer with a wealthy family on Long Island working as an au pair ("Wonderful! You'll be a *glorified* babysitter," was the way my sister reacted). Trisha took my steamer-trunk of winter clothes and books back with her to Brooklyn and I went straight from the dorm to the Olivers' big house in East Quogue.

Au pairing was easy for me—it *was* like babysitting, but without going home at the end of the evening. I stayed in a small guest room near the kids. The pay wasn't great, but there were virtually no expenses and the Olivers were a pleasant family. I read a lot of paperbacks and played countless hours of beach volleyball that summer. Mrs. Oliver and the children drove me to my dorm at the end of August. We looked like just another suburban family in a station wagon.

Viv returned from Argentina with a dozen stories and a suitcase of alpaca scarves. I went into the city to spend the day with her, one of those perfectly clear Saturdays in Manhattan when everything looks like a movie set. We wandered around Central Park, and she told me about her adventures, and then George Rowan met us for lunch. And that was kind of that.

MY second year at Stony Brook was awful. Trisha said that I was just stretching my wings, but I felt more like Icarus, falling.

That semester brought some really bad decisions about sleeping with people. Followed by the pregnancy and the abortion. I dyed my hair fire-engine red and then had to dye it back to black. I drank too much. I didn't eat enough.

I kept up a decent GPA—heaven knew Viv had taught me how to stay on top of academic challenges—but I lost respect for most of my teachers and the classes I was taking. I had the sinking feeling that I had chosen the wrong school, the wrong curriculum, or maybe even the wrong approach to becoming a working artist. I wanted practical instruction on technique; instead, I listened to endless critiques about style. The professors sounded biased and pompous.

One professor suggested that I needed to "postmodernize the aesthetic" of a landscape painting I'd submitted for review. He told me, very seriously, that real art is not pretty, nor is it supposed to be pretty—a statement that irritated me then and still continued to rankle. Had he never looked at the great works of the past five thousand years?

I didn't challenge him, since the point of the review session was to listen to the opinion of others. And I did try to see his point of view, as my sister had advised. But after he was finished, I couldn't help asking whether by "postmodernizing the aesthetic" he meant "to ugly it up." He told me I didn't yet "fully understand the discipline."

When I recounted the story on the phone to Viv that weekend, she told me I was being stupid to challenge the professor, no matter how subtly, unless I had some specific strategy for getting ahead. I said I wasn't sure I *wanted* to get ahead.

Viv said, "God! It's just undergrad. Brace up. Deal with it. Get through it and then get your masters so you can get a decent job teaching or something."

Over dinner in Brooklyn Heights, I told the Cutillos about the postmodernizing thing. Sophia Cutillo was indignant on my behalf. "What are these professors teaching you—fashion or art?" I thought she totally got it.

I withdrew from Stony Brook four days into the second semester of my sophomore year. My reasons were not very original: I felt stifled, miserable, trapped. I might have changed majors or even just switched classes, but I couldn't face another mean-spirited week of school. I was itching to put some miles under my feet. I wanted a fresh start. I wanted to do something that made me feel good about myself again.

I took Trisha and Sophia up on their offer of shelter. Papi and one of Trisha's brothers drove out to Stony Brook and picked me and my things up from the dorm. They took me home to Brooklyn Heights, where Sophia led me straight to the spare room and told me to sleep until I was ready to get up.

I called Viv at the usual time that week and told her I was in Brooklyn Heights. I told her I had withdrawn from college. I thought she would just hang up on me, but she said, "Do you need rainy-day money?"

I told her I didn't.

"What are you planning to do now?"

"I am going to think about that."

"Fantastic!" she said. "I needed something else to worry about right now."

"I'm fine," I said.

"Obviously. What next? How about you find a nice Italian boy and settle down? Maybe you can sit around and eat pasta all day?"

"I'm going to paint," I said.

That's when she hung up.

She called back to tell me I needed to get back to school. I told her that I would be okay. She insisted that I wasn't going to be okay until I got myself back to school. I hung up on *her* that time.

I didn't tell my sister about my new au pair job until I had signed the contract and had the airline ticket for Rome in my hand.

Chapter 44

I WAS sitting next to Viv in the hospital, filing her fingernails and chattering about the trip I'd made to the veterinary emergency room with Balin that morning.

"And do you know how much doggie prescriptions cost?" I asked her. I imagined she didn't. It was roughly as much as we used to spend on groceries each month in Potsdam.

Balin would be fine, I told Viv. Her arthritis had flared up, but the vet had given the dog a shot and explained Balin's daily medications to me.

A rap at the doorway announced a tiny woman in a plum-colored suit. She carried a clipboard into Viv's room.

"Hello," she said. "I'm Tamara Plaise. I'm with Social Services."

I put down the emery board and looked at her.

As a kid, I'd lived in dread of social workers. They were the people who would discover that Viv and I needed to be rescued. They would separate us and put us into foster care. These were the people who would ruin Viv's careful plans.

Tamara Plaise was a firm, neat person, with ivory-colored shoes that might have been lifted from a 1940s pinup poster: all curved heels and perky bows. When I stood, she would barely reach my waistband.

"Your sister's surgical team asked me to stop by."

We shook hands and I introduced myself. She repeated that she'd come at the suggestion of Viv's surgical team.

"But my sister's condition hasn't changed."

"Yes. Exactly." She looked at her clipboard for a moment, letting the silence draw out. "They suggested that it might be time for us to discuss long-term care options for your sister."

"What are we discussing?"

"Over the long term, if your sister's condition doesn't improve, you'll probably want to explore a more appropriate care setting."

It was as if Tamara Plaise were shoving me over the edge of a cliff. My paint-spattered sneakers were no match for her wee Betty Boop pumps. "But the baby—" I managed.

"Until the baby comes, your sister should probably stay right here," she said, keeping the clipboard pinned to her neatly buttoned front with a skinny elbow while making calming gestures with her small hands. "But if she continues to remain unconscious, then of course it makes sense to move her to a skilled nursing facility."

"A nursing home?" I asked, feeling the earth begin to slip out from under me.

She gave me a long look from behind her glasses. "Of course, this can be a difficult decision for families to make. We have a transition counselor who might be useful. If you like, I—"

A rush of righteous emotion pounded through me. Heat flamed up my neck. I was angry about a lot of things. I didn't want to be here in Nashville, waiting for Viv to wake and explain what she'd been up to. I didn't want Viv and me to be some little girls lost in the woods. I was angry that Viv had left me in charge without enough direction, but this was too much.

Some busybody in a purple suit clickety-clacking into the room and grilling me about my plans to put my sister into a nursing home—right in front of Viv? How dare she?

I stood up and Tamara Plaise took a tiny clattery step backwards. She spoke quickly. "Perhaps this is a bad—"

"Let's talk outside," I managed to say in a level voice.

She minced ahead of me into the hallway. I concentrated on breathing and looked over my shoulder at my sister for a moment. What would you do, I wanted to ask Viv, but I knew. I took a deep breath. If she were dealing with this moment, my sister would figure it all out. She'd keep calm and make a plan.

I felt my cheeks cooling as Tamara and I walked down the hallway. When I pointed toward the waiting room with the vinyl chairs, she sidled away from my arm like a shy lapdog.

"Let me start over," Tamara Plaise said as we got to the waiting room. "I apologize. I didn't mean to sound insensitive. I'm here to help."

We sat and she began again, hesitantly at first. She mentioned support groups for caretakers like me. She explained the specifics of my sister's health insurance and disability benefits, the range of care available after my sister's baby was born.

"We have a lot of very good options right here in the Nashville area." Her voice took on a satisfied note.

"How about options outside of Tennessee?" I asked. To the extent that I had thought about it, I really wanted to get myself back to Sarasota, to my friends, to Gabrielle's gallery show. I needed to be back in Florida.

Tamara Plaise looked down at her paperwork and then gave me a brief smile. "Your sister's benefits package is very generous, compared to some. However, her employer is connected to the university, so her benefits are tied into the state of Tennessee."

I reached for the correct vocabulary. "Do they transfer?"

"Not entirely." Tamara leaned forward over the clipboard. "But it depends on the level of care your sister needs." She went on to describe the levels and I concentrated on her words, rather than the stark Hopper-esque images they conjured: full-time nursing facility, long-term care, rehabilitation, speech therapy, counseling, physiotherapy, group housing. She mentioned things like "persistent vegetative state," and "impairment," and "disability."

Even though Dr. Pete and the surgical team had never used this terminology in describing Viv's situation, I felt the phrases sink through me like indelible ink marking a glass of clear water.

Eventually, Tamara Plaise moved onto the subject of neonatal support, naming incredible sums of money available should Viv's baby be born prematurely. Or if it had birth defects. I felt the urge to cross myself, or knock wood, or spit between my fingers to ward off the possibility.

Tamara re-crossed her legs tightly and settled her clipboard back onto a pointy knee. She summarized with confidence. "This is a lot of information, I know that. There's no need to make any decisions today, but we find it's helpful for the patient's advocate to become familiar with the options."

"Just be ready, right?" I asked, thinking my sister would approve.

Tamara looked at me with sympathy. "Preparation helps, of course, but situations like this are simply very difficult."

She handed me her card, told me to phone should I have any questions, and then said she'd be contacting me again in a week or so. My fingers dwarfed hers when we shook hands.

I went back to Viv and didn't tell her about my conversation with the social worker. I was tired, though it was early still, and I thought about the dog having her nice nap to recover from the visit to the vet. I pictured myself curling up next to Viv's hospital bed, scratching one of the thin white hospital blankets into a nest before circling and thumping down and tucking my hind legs up under me.

"You're looking cheerful," Lisa the nurse commented, slipping into Viv's room. "I saw you chasing Tamara Plaise out of here earlier."

I spoke without thinking. "She's a yappy dog."

Lisa snorted. "That may be. But she gets things done."

I nodded, and then the dreary weight of the things the social worker had told me settled on my shoulders again.

Lisa bustled from IV to catheter and smoothed the thin blanket over Viv's feet. She said, "Just to let you know, we're planning to move your sister in the next day or so."

Anger poured over me. "Move her where?"

"It's nothing drastic—really. She's not leaving Intensive Care. We're just going to change her room."

"Why do that?"

Her face was serious. "We think Dr. Rowan might benefit from having a little more quiet. As you know, this spot is probably the busiest and noisiest in the ICU."

I thought for a moment, and then said, "And there are other patients who deserve front-row seats?"

The nurse shrugged, not quite apologizing. "That may be. She'll still be getting the best care."

"What if I don't want her to be moved?"

Lisa nodded. "You can object, of course. If you want, talk with the nurse-supervisor and she can bring it up with administration. I'm not sure the decision will change."

Someone down the hall was calling for a nurse.

"I have to go," she said, walking.

The sound of my sister's machinery swelled. I looked down at Viv's warm, pink palm, which I cradled in my hands. Did it look as if her hand were drawn in just a little? Were her long white fingers forming a hint of a claw shape? Were they becoming the hands of someone who would never wake?

Were these the hands of a comatose person in a long-term nursing facility? Someone permanently impaired? Someone nearly forgotten in a room at the end of a long hall?

I placed her arm back down on the bed, as gently as I could, and lifted my jacket from the hook by the door. I shrugged it on as I began walking, faster and faster, until I reached the stairway.

I hopped down the stairs, crossed the lobby at a trot, and banged open the hospital exit doors. The outdoor air was raw. I heard breath whistling at the back of my throat.

I began to run. My feet slapped the pavement. Dirty puddles of rainwater splashed up the legs of my jeans.

I ran on the sidewalk, through intersections, across the street and back onto the sidewalk, block after block. A stitch pulled on my side. I coughed and spat but kept running, leaping over puddles. I ran on my toes at first, sprinting, with my fists pumping near my chin. The stitch eventually gave up trying to stop me.

My chest began to burn, but I kept running. My heels started hitting the concrete. My hands splayed open and flopped. The arches of my feet burned, and each step jarred.

I felt my own ridiculousness: it was the wrong time of day for exercise, and I wasn't even wearing real running shoes.

I was an idiot in a heavy wool jacket, sopping wet blue jeans, and high-topped canvas sneaks. But I could no more stop my legs running than I could make the rain stop falling.

Nothing registered as I ran. I didn't care where I went. I covered distance, turning only to avoid stopping for cars or groups of pedestrians or where highway overpasses blocked my way. Another stitch pulled in my chest, but I kept pounding my high-tops against the ground, propelling myself forward.

I didn't stop for a very long time.

The rain continued and the afternoon stretched toward sunset. By the time I slowed to a walk, I felt the blisters on my feet beginning to squish.

Several of them had burst by the time I found my way back to the hospital parking lot. I went straight to my truck and drove to Viv's house.

Getting into the shower, I held up a foot. The sole was flushed as red as my sister's palms. Clear pillows of blister tipped each toe. The two smallest toenails on each foot were throbbing. They'd probably be purple before long.

Along the hinge of each foot, from the round ball all the way across to the outer edge, a blister had grown and then torn open. There was no blood, but the jagged pieces of yellow skin looked revolting. Another layer of blister waited under the raw wound.

I knew the pain would get worse, but part of me wanted to push my tender feet against the ground and still be running.

Chapter 45

MY FEET kept me awake. I stayed under the covers with the lights out. The dogs snored gently, like surf rasping against three different shores around the dark room. The central heating cycled on and off.

For once, I didn't reach for my sketchbook or get to work on the watercolors for the show at St. Armand's Circle. I didn't daydream about returning to Europe. I didn't plan how I was going to catch up with friends in Sarasota.

If only, I thought. If I could change just one thing—if I could change things by wishing—I'd wish my sister and George had never crashed their Volvo.

Then I thought: I wish George had somehow kept the car on the road that night, missed the tree, and gotten them home safe. Or better yet, I wished that they hadn't gone into the hills that weekend at all, never visited that particular pottery studio on the other side of the mountains. I wished they had never started driving around the state collecting ugly dishes. I wished that she and George had settled in San Francisco instead, where they *couldn't* have been driving through these mountains at night.

It was like tugging on a hanging piece of yarn and unknitting a sweater.

Since I was wishing and unraveling history anyhow, I went ahead and wished I'd visited Viv on my way to Florida this past September, so she couldn't have avoided telling me about the baby coming. I couldn't even remember why I'd been in a hurry to get to Sarasota.

I wished that I could go back and force her to tell me what she was really doing—all those Sunday afternoon phone calls when she must have decided *not* to say anything. I should have known. When Viv suggested that we catch up over the winter instead, I hadn't given it a second thought.

I should have come to see her. There were cheap flights to Nashville. It was ridiculous that I hadn't seen my sister in more than six months. I wished I could take back that time and do it over again.

Looking further back, I wished I'd insisted that Viv come see me in Florida the year before. Or if she'd come to Italy, *that* would have changed things. The two of us could have traveled together.

Better yet, if only I had skipped that idiot boyfriend my sophomore year in college—I should never have slept with him. Or at least, since I had been so determined to behave badly, I should have doubled up on protection, like Viv used to advise.

If I could do it over, I wished I had skipped that entire semester.

Which took me back to the summer with the Oliver kids in East Quogue when I could have made up my mind *not* to resist the charms of the handsome young George Rowan, back before he became my sister's dear, Dear George.

Ah, I thought, stopping like a stubbed toe, *that's* when she ruined my life.

I felt a rush of certainty, identical to the popped-cork realization of what, *finally*, to leave out or add to the composition to make a painting right. *This* was what she was writing about in her diary when she said she'd ruined my life.

I savored the insight. I hadn't seen it before, but here was the truth: she had ruined my life. Yes, I thought. My sister Vivian had ruined my life. It was all her fault.

Forgetting the state of my soles, I stretched my legs. My feet pressed against the covers with a shocking jangle of nerves. I flinched and rolled over carefully.

I tried saying the words out loud: *She ruined my life.* It didn't sound convincing. Trying to regain the sense of certainty, I said, "She ruined my life the day she met Dear George. My sister ruined my life."

The furnace cycled on. The dogs continued to snore. Before long, I began to think I had painted myself into a corner.

If I wished that it was me and not Viv with George, if he was *my* Dear George, this would have been *my* ugly house. It would be *me* living in Tennessee in the middle of this suburban maze. Artie and Leora would be my best friends. I'd have been collecting blah-colored pottery.

Would I have quit school to marry George? Maybe. If it had been George and me who had fallen in love. More likely, I would have stayed in school, painting junk I didn't like, trying to earn the approval of my professors—and Viv and probably George—and get the degree. Viv would have been happy for me to finish college, but if I had, I would have probably hated painting altogether by now.

If I had gotten together with George in East Quogue that summer after freshman year, I probably would never have painted that first wall mural. I probably wouldn't have met any of my artist friends, or those girls from the loft apartment, or Elaine. I certainly wouldn't have gallery space in St. Armand's Circle for the show in March.

George hadn't been a visual person. He didn't mind ugly things as long as they were neat. He didn't notice colors—might even have been color-blind, now that I thought of it. That would explain the bland, tan color-scheme of this room. And it would explain his preppy uniform: Brooks Brothers shirts in either blue or white—soft and frayed on the weekends over denim, crisp and starched with neat khaki trousers or grey suits for work. No wonder he hadn't spent more than a moment looking at the pictures I'd painted for them.

If it had been George and me in love after that lunch with Viv, I wouldn't have behaved badly my sophomore year. And that would mean I wouldn't have gone to Rome. I wouldn't have come home to the attic bedroom Trisha's parents fixed up for me. I might not even be friends with Trisha. No almond blossoms in the hills in Italy, no winter in London, no beach volleyball on the gray sand in Brighton Beach and the white sand of Siesta Key.

The sweater started knitting itself up again.

When it came right down to it, I wasn't sure a life could be ruined just like that, with a single wrong step. People back-track all the time, make mistakes, try over, start again, right? Could someone else, after all, truly ruin your life? People talked about ruined lives, but had I ever seen someone whose life was ruined?

I thought about the grimy homeless guys dozing on the subway gratings in New York. I thought about the high razor-wire fence surrounding the prison in Cape Vincent.

Maybe I didn't know from ruined, as Sophia would have said.

And to be fair, that one lunch when they'd met and fallen in love—was that Viv's fault? It wasn't like she had forced me to let George go. Not like she took him away from me. The flashbulb didn't go off when he met me.

I'd never told anyone, let alone my big sister, that George was even in the running to be my boyfriend. Of course, Viv might have guessed, since I'd never brought anyone to meet her before. But I hadn't stopped her, hadn't said, hey wait, I have dibs on him. So if anyone was doing the ruining, it wasn't Viv.

Chapter 46

TRISHA woke me early the next morning, calling to sing me a hoarse, throaty version of "Happy Birthday" before she went to work. I'd genuinely forgotten the date. Trisha was chewing something as she spoke.

"We sent your present after I got back from this last trip, so it's late. It's from Papi and me both." She barely paused, "And what's up for your day?"

I felt my shoulder lift in a shrug. I was hunched over the telephone, my feet twisted to keep the throbbing soles from touching the cold tile floor. I stood straight and talked into the phone, "No plans. I'll be at the hospital."

"Okay, but tonight?"

"Probably staying in." As soon as I said it, I realized how pathetic it sounded.

"Come on, nothing special for your birthday?" Trisha's voice faded. She'd probably squeezed in the call between eating her breakfast, drinking coffee, ironing her clothes, and drying her hair all at once. "Didn't one of those cutie-patooties from George's office call? Don't you have like a string of admirers yet?"

"Yeah, right."

"Don't sell yourself short." Trisha's mouth moved away from the phone.

"Have you seen me lately? I couldn't sell myself short if I tried."

"Lucky you. *You* try being short." Trisha's voice creaked, and I heard her take a bite of something. She crunched. "But what about the love-life? What's the deal?"

"Not a lot of opportunity." I said. Then, thinking about the awkward moment with Dr. Pete, I added, "Not a lot of appropriate options."

Trisha drew breath to start listing people I should be dating and why, but I made a pre-emptive strike. "What about you? What's new with the Jersey Wonder?"

"Funny you should ask." She smiled. I could hear it even in the silence of the telephone connection. "I walked him to the bus. Might be a Mr. New Boyfriend on the horizon."

"Dish!"

"Not yet." Chewing muffled her words. "I don't want to wreck it. I haven't told anyone else yet."

"You don't want to talk about it? I find *that* hard to believe."

"This is me, not talking." Trisha held the silence for a long beat.

I heard her take a small, quiet bite of something. "What's for breakfast?"

"Cold pizza."

The conversation moved on to food until her time was up.

"I've got to catch a train," she said. "Promise me you'll do something fun today. There's gotta be, I don't know, like a *museum* down there, right? Take the day off, okay?"

The idea seemed absurdly pleasant. It was my birthday, after all. Why not? I hobbled to the back door and let the dogs out. I dished up their kibble, and while they crunched and gobbled, I got out the yellow pages and pulled the city map from my truck. I could take myself out for breakfast and then have my choice of museums. Not including the attractions devoted to country music and local history, there were a handful of possibilities.

I was toweling Balin's face when the phone rang. With Tomkin still standing patiently for his clean-up, I let the machine get it. I paid little attention to my own voice on the new outgoing message, anticipating more cheerful birthday wishes.

After the beep, Ed Maynard's voice spoke. "Nicola, this is Ed Maynard calling. I've got some—"

"Hey, hey—I'm here."

"I'm calling from a little town called Snake Tree, Pennsylvania. Do you have a minute?"

I told him I did.

He asked about Viv and then got straight to his news.

"I found Marsha Ranklin's other college roommate— the one in Canada."

"Okay."

"She—Sara Spenser is her married name—was in touch with Marsha regularly, with only a few gaps in their correspondence."

It sounded like Ed was getting ready to light a cigarette, his Zippo lighter snapping open and closed.

"Long story short, Ms. Spenser told me that Marsha had episodes when she became 'unhappy and religious' from time to time.

"Summertime, 1967 or '68, Marsha Ranklin was 'ranting about unwed women having babies out of wedlock left and right.'"

Ed sighed. He was still fiddling with his lighter.

"Ms. Spenser wrote back right away, concerned because Marsha had never sounded 'so bitter and intolerant.' Her letter was returned by the post office, marked 'No longer at this address.' The next time Ms. Spenser heard from Marsha, it was probably six months later."

Papers rattled.

Ed cleared his throat and said, "I'll read from my notes: 'She told me to call her Mary Jones and that Jahn's name was John. She didn't explain why—but you know those were dramatic times, with the draft and the student protests. It seemed better not to ask.'"

"That's weird."

"Yeah," Ed said, "Obviously something happened with Jahn and Marsha. Ms. Spenser didn't keep any of this correspondence. But she did remember the name of the town that returned her letter."

"Which was?" I said, because Ed seemed to be waiting for me to ask.

"Snake Tree. It's a little farming community in northeast Pennsylvania. Just a few miles down the road from Bridgewater Township. Less than an hour by car from Cannalega."

"Oh."

"So I drove to Snake Tree. And, well, here's where things get a little squirrelly. I checked business permits, licenses, that sort of thing for Mary and John, or Marsha and Jahn, for 1967 and 1968. Got nowhere. Then I went to the newspaper morgue."

"The morgue?"

"That's what they call their back-issue library."

"Ah."

"I found out that Snake Tree had just the one big local news story in the summer of 1968. A fire killed a handful of young people living on a farm just outside town. I don't have proof of anything, and it's just a hunch—"

In the pause, his Zippo snapped several times in rapid-fire succession.

"Ed?"

"The newspaper printed photos of those young people, and one of them looks an awful lot like Viv."

"But—okay. 1968? My sister?"

"That's what I want to follow up on. This woman and her two little girls disappeared in the fire."

"What woman?"

"I'm sorry. Let me back up. A woman named Naomi Anderson from Philadelphia is who I mean. According to the newspaper accounts, she perished in the fire. She's the one who's the spitting image of your sister, and in 1968, she had two little daughters."

"Oh. Okay."

"I'm thinking I want to send this newspaper clipping down to you. I think you'll want to see it."

"Okay."

Ed paused and said, "Are you all right with this?"

My head nodded, and then my mouth caught up, "Yes, I'm okay. I don't know what to tell you."

"You want me to keep investigatin'?"

"I do." And I did—it mattered to Viv.

"Since I am near the end of your sister's retainer, are you comfortable with sending another check to the agency?"

I asked how much of a check he needed. When he explained how much more of my sister's money was going to be required, I gulped. But I reminded myself about the scale of Viv's budget (what looked like a car to me was the equivalent of a month or so of upkeep on the house to Viv) and I jotted down his address.

He told me he'd have his assistant drop a copy of the newspaper article at the hospital and ask them to hold it for me at reception. We signed off, and I wished I hadn't picked up the telephone.

I limped to Viv's desk and wrote the check. Without having to spare a second thought about where to find them, I extracted an envelope from the bottom desk drawer and stuck one of Dear George's neatly coiled stamps onto it.

I DIDN'T get to the museum that day. I'd already decided that I'd worry about Ed Maynard's newspaper article later, but then Artie called. Again, I picked up the phone thinking that it was birthday news, but Artie wanted to have a lunch meeting to discuss "the disbursement of George's life insurance settlement, especially as it pertains to provisions for their child."

Over pasta, Artie started by talking about George's life insurance. "You'll—ah—want to consult an investment advisor," he said.

"But I can wait for Viv, right?" I said, thinking about the hefty balance of their checkbook.

He folded his lips in disapproval. "It's a sizable amount of cash," he said.

"Can we just park it in their savings?" I knew the difference between stocks and bonds, but I wasn't going to risk making a bad investment with my sister's money. "Wouldn't that be the safest option?"

"Yes. But there are—well, I suppose it depends on what happens with the child."

I put my silverware down. "What *happens* with the child? What are you suggesting?"

Artie spoke carefully. "I think we should consider writing up adoption papers—ah—should it be born healthy."

I knocked the underside of the table against bad luck. "What are you talking about, adoption?"

"I think we'd be remiss if we did not fully consider the best interests of the child."

Heat washed over me. "You want me to give her baby away?"

Artie shot a look over his shoulder at the other diners. "I'm—that's not what—" He held his palms up. "I know it's difficult, and I understand how this must sound."

My face felt stiff and hot.

"And, honestly, it's not about what I want," he said. "It's about what's best for the child, if Viv doesn't—"

"No." I cut him off. I couldn't bear to have him finish the sentence.

Artie held my gaze with an expression that mixed weariness and nervousness with something like compassion. He pitied me.

"Nicky," he started. "We don't have to discuss the issue right now, but believe me, adoption is a sensible option to consider."

"Sensible?"

Artie gave me a level look. "If Viv is unable, do you honestly think that you are ready to be a good surrogate parent?"

Before I could even begin to answer—because even Viv would have to admit I had the skills—he continued, "And, surely, your sister wouldn't have expected you to sacrifice your future."

He said it with such sincerity it could have been the truth.

"Why don't we let my sister tell us what she wants when she wakes up?" I said, gritting my teeth.

Artie didn't meet my eyes. "But we should be prepared. In case she—ah—doesn't."

He'd said it. I felt anger and strength fall away from me.

Artie's voice continued, even more gently. "At least—keep it in mind, Nicky. As a possibility. For the baby, if not for yourself."

After lunch, I got lost driving across Nashville. Trying to take myself to the Vanderbilt University campus and its art gallery, I found myself on the other side of Viv's hospital. Despite my plans to spend the day away from Viv, I ended up easing my truck into its usual parking spot. I limped up the familiar flight of stairs to Viv's floor.

I sat and put both of my hands around Viv's.

"Please be there," I said. "Please come back."

I fell asleep in the visitor's chair with my sore feet propped up on the bed next to Viv, waking only when the nurses came to turn my sister in her bed.

I'D VISITED Viv and George right after they first moved into the house in Nashville. They hadn't even finished unpacking.

Viv led me through the house while Dear George started making dinner on his fancy new six-burner stove. Opening all the doors to show me closets and rooms and hallways, she'd said, "Look how much space there is!"

The house smelled of fresh paint and sawdust. "No one has ever lived here before," she told me.

"Do you remember moving house when we were kids?" I said.

Viv rolled her eyes. "All those houses full of junk! One time, I found somebody's stash of porn. Ugh!"

"Where?" I said, not remembering anything about it.

"Oh, I don't know. It might have been the place in North Sheldon."

"That had to be a shock for you. In fifth grade? Yuck."

Viv shrugged and kept walking. "Whatever."

"But what did you do with it?" I persisted.

"I snuck the bag into the closet in Jahn and Magda's room."

I laughed out loud in a burst of admiration. "Nice one, sis!"

She stopped and faced me. Her voice was exasperated. "Well, not like they were going to notice, and I certainly didn't want you to find it. You probably would have brought it to Magda, and been like, 'Mommy? What are these people doing?'"

I laughed again, less comfortable. Viv's imitation of me was harsh, as if she was still irritated at my childishness.

"And God knows," she continued with a spirited toss of her hair, "it would have ended up with Jahn smacking you or smacking me and sending someone to bed without supper for freaking Magda out."

"Well then," I said, carefully, thinking about what she meant. "Thank you for doing that."

She made an uncomfortable face. "It was my job."

"You were good at protecting me," I added. It was true. I was thinking about how she continued trying to protect me, even now we were both grown women, but I kept quiet.

"It wasn't that much fun back then," she told me. She didn't shake an index finger at me, but I understood that this was a lecture. "Living like that. People don't really *choose* to live like that."

I didn't answer.

"It wasn't a good way to grow up." She sighed and folded her arms over her chest. "It wasn't nearly as fun as you seem to remember, Nicky."

Before I could answer, before I could protest that I had plenty of bad memories too, or that she wasn't the only one with a hard job to do in childhood, Dear George yelled for us. His voice stretched the word "girls" like the twanging note of a steel guitar.

Viv and I looked at each other, startled for a frozen moment. Dear George sounded eerily like Magda calling us indoors for supper.

Maybe we remembered some things differently from our childhood, but this? We both remembered *this* the same.

"Just a min-nut!" I sang back to George, just as Viv and I had done as kids. Viv giggled at me. Then we turned together and jostled along the hallway, racing downstairs to the kitchen.

Chapter 47

WHEN Leora invited me for Thanksgiving dinner with the family, I asked her what I should bring.

Her voice on the telephone was breezy, busy. "Nothing, hon, just yourself and your appetite."

"I'd be happy to bake a pie," I said. "Or maybe some oyster stuffing?"

A too-long pause. "There's no need. My mother and us girls have been doing Thanksgiving for ages and I can't think of anything we leave out."

"How about wine?" I suggested.

Leora took a sharp breath. "We don't serve alcohol with my family at the table."

"I can't show up empty-handed."

"Oh, there's no call to fuss. Just come on over. Around one. We'll have the parade and then the football games on. It'll be fun."

Leora's dining room sparkled: white tablecloth and candles, silver flatware and Noritake china, chairs lined up around the long table like well-behaved kids. A buffet table was crowded with crystal pickle dishes, stacks of dessert plates, steaming bowls of potatoes, sweet potatoes, green beans, corn stuffing, baskets of pecan-studded dinner-rolls and—it struck me as odd—a galvanized metal tub full of chipped ice and curved bottles of Coca-Cola.

The men, Artie among them, trooped in from the living room, where the television was blaring. The women carried even more food from the kitchen as we seated ourselves around the table. Someone was dispatched to turn the television down.

They all talked at once and the introductions were haphazard and confusing: Uncle Jimmy, Uncle Clayton, Uncle Yuley, the cousins Jimmy Junior and Shayna, Aunt Sarah, Aunt Celia, Great-Aunt Sarah, an elderly man named Peaches, Leora's sisters Rubonia and Tattie, and Leora's very fat mother, Diana. Everyone sat and then Diana rearranged the seating, her contralto voice as rich and powerful as a stage actress'.

When the family was situated as Diana wished, everyone joined hands for the prayer. Diana spoke.

"Thank you, dear Lord, for this wonderful feast. We hope to honor you and praise you in every deed and thought through the sustenance you have seen fit to give. Please bless us and keep us close to the side of righteousness. Through this and every thing, amen."

Conversation started immediately after the answering "amens." Serving dishes were handed around the table. Leora and her sisters, the youngest women at the table, talked as they carried the bowls and platters back to the kitchen to be refilled, words tossed over their shoulders careless and comfortable. How certain of one another they seemed. No surprises, no fabricated histories, no hidden agendas.

Artie seemed diminished among Leora's family. He sat next to Leora, serving them both when the dishes circled the table. She didn't speak to him, and he kept his attention on his plate. They seemed unconnected to each other. Trisha had said she thought their marriage was in trouble.

Uncle Clayton interrupted my speculation. He asked how I was getting along in Nashville. Aunt Celia, across from me, silenced the room with the flat-toned voice of the hearing-impaired. "Sheep? What sheep?"

Diana shook her head and projected her powerful voice. "For the Nativity, Celia. The living manger. At the church, remember?"

I watched Leora and her sister exchange a laughing look. "Remember when Tattie made the pecan rolls?" Leora said.

Everyone remembered. And then they talked about a famously burned bean casserole and the year the turkey never thawed. Leora and her two sisters had nearly the same tinkling, feminine laugh, like crystal chimes in a small wind. All the women in the family moved their heads the same way when they laughed.

Unbidden, the thought came to me: were Leora and Artie planning to have children? There were no youngsters at the table. What would it be like to grow up surrounded by this much family? What if Artie and Leora wanted to adopt? I tried not to think about it. So what if they did? I told myself. It had nothing to do with me and Viv. It wasn't like they wanted to adopt Viv's baby. Or maybe they did.

The casserole I'd brought reached my end of the table. Someone had taken a single small, polite spoonful. It had looked golden and good in George's kitchen, but among these elegant mountains of food, the pottery dish looked puny and casual.

Voices grew subdued as plates began to fill. Diana looked down the table and caught my eye. Her rich voice rang out. "Let's ask our guest about *her* Thanksgiving traditions." She looked at me expectantly.

I felt my face lifting into a public expression, and I wondered if I had been glowering at the ring of faces around the table. With the miserable thoughts I had running around my head, I was failing at the most basic level of *Emily Post's Etiquette*. I tried to gather my wits to say something pleasant.

"There weren't enough of us to make it festive like this," I started. They looked at me with politely interested faces. I added, "My sister and I served at a soup kitchen one Thanksgiving."

I didn't say: sometimes we went to the movies, or: we often bought our feast supplies on sale the week after Thanksgiving. I didn't tell them about the time we plucked and cooked a wild turkey my sister had hit with the Datsun on the road on her way home from The Pit Stop. It had been dreadful, all flavor but with the texture of a dog's chewie toy.

Leora announced, "Nicola and her sister grew up in New York City!"

My mouth snapped shut.

Diana's deep voice rang out. "A city girl! I took my girls to the city when Tattie was fifteen. Glory, what an adventure that was!"

As I collected myself, Leora's sisters recalled their youthful shock at the whole duck carcasses in the restaurant windows in Chinatown, their astonishment at the number of languages spoken, and the wonderful shopping. Leora nodded in agreement while Diana looked on indulgently. The conversation surged along without me. I barely tasted the food on my plate.

I wondered what version of our childhood Viv had told Leora. I wondered if Leora had simply inferred that Viv and I had always lived in New York, or whether my sister had invented a glamorous youth for us. Were we Greenwich kids? Upper West Siders? Had we attended private school? Taken ballet lessons? How did that story work with Viv's cardinal rule about lying—"lie to keep us out of trouble"? It didn't bear thinking about.

When the green beans came my way again, I held the dish for Uncle Clayton and asked which teams he liked for the afternoon's football games.

Leora and her two sisters cleared the table, still talking, gracefully palming the Noritake. They shooed me back to my chair when I tried to help. "Company doesn't need to bother with those things,"

I felt like a grim reaper among these people, sitting at their table, but with a big rusty scythe held at the ready. I would have traded any one of them for my sister.

They had so much and there were so many of them, and I had nothing.

I *ached* with the wish to swap one of their lives for my sister's. I would have mowed any one of them down to get my sister back. Honestly, I would have sacrificed the whole house of them. They'd offered me nothing but kindness and I was thinking, *I'd trade you for my sister.*

Leora poured coffee while her sisters dished up wedges of pie and distributed them around the table, knowing without asking which uncle preferred which flavor of pie. Leora suggested the chocolate for me, and I almost took a bite before I noticed that the table was still. No one lifted a dessert fork until Leora and her sisters returned to their seats, unfolding snowy napkins across their laps.

Diana looked around the table and the last murmur of conversation died away. Her voice was as rich as the gravy. "Let us thank the Lord and pray now for Nicola's sister."

ON THE way back to Viv's house, I bought clove cigarettes, the turquoise package a reminder of the nights out in the big cities I'd known. I poured a glass of whiskey from Dear George's cabinet and sat on the cold, damp flagstone steps as the dogs patrolled the back lawn in the afternoon gloom. I concentrated on the warmth of alcohol in my stomach and the rush of dizziness from the smoke.

The clove cigarette smelled strange and sweet, like air from another planet. The scent made the dogs sneeze as they circled me. When I'd first tried one, my sophomore year in college, I loved the way the clove tingled on my lips.

My sister had lectured me about how clove cigarettes were even worse than simple tobacco: each breath brought not just tar and carbon monoxide but hot clove oil sinking through the pink tissue of the lungs. This smoke seared the lining of the throat, she'd said, and burned tiny perforations into the sponge of the lung like leaf mosaic eating through the tender leaves of a plant. Good, I thought now, drawing in another spicy chestful. Fine. Burn away.

I poured the rest of the glass of whiskey onto the dead grass, shooed the dogs inside, and took myself to the hospital.

AT MY sister's bedside I sat without touching Viv.

When I was a very little girl, my first good picture was a recognizable portrait of her. It got left behind in a cardboard carton in an empty bedroom somewhere when we were kids, but I could reproduce it even now from memory. Her pointed chin, like a triangle pasted onto her square jaw, and the dark eyebrows above her direct, gray-eyed gaze. For her hair, I had used three crayons from the jumbo box: not just the candy-apple red, but orange and brown, blending the strokes to re-create the color I knew better than my own. When I finished, I was proud of it, but I remember wishing my own hair were complicated like hers.

That picture gave me an ambiguous feeling for years afterward, whenever I thought about it. Nothing as simple as envy about Viv's hair or simple pride for the picture. The feeling was tainted by a mixed sense of ownership. My sister's auburn hair and my own success in making a picture of it blurred together.

As if, in a way, we both owned that hair—she by possession, me by catching it on paper. And there was more: my sister's brilliant brain, her nerve, her clever plans and determination were all partly mine. Just as my artwork, my travel, and every decision I'd ever made was always partly hers. It had never been just me alone. Until now.

In the washroom, I glanced up into my own reflection. The skin looked thin and tight across my forehead, the bone too close to the surface. I pulled the neck of my sweater away from my throat. The mechanical workings of the shoulder showed at the collarbone, a series of levers and cords just under the skin. I had lost padding. My shoulders were knobby, the muscles across my upper body turned stringy, chickenish. Tendons pulled like bowstrings when I raised my shoulders in a shrug.

Good, I thought, Good. Let me be as hard and white as bone.

I lifted my sweater and the sight of my ribcage as I inhaled, the bones bumping under the skin, made me furious. I wanted to scribble the image out. I stared into my own eyes, thinking about chopping off my hair, dying the stubs platinum, becoming as sharp as an icicle.

I hated my sister and I hated myself.

I could not separate the two of us. The impulse to pinch or slap my sister's serene face as she rested only poured back into me: it was my own face I could not stand. My too-long nose, the fat eyelids, the blue eyes staring from their darkened sockets. I was revolted by the freckled belly, the clenched fists, those same long white limbs as my sister.

I wanted to lose myself. I wanted to forget. No more me, no more her. I was weary and I wanted to stop seeing this face, these hands, these eyes, her face, her hands, her eyes. My own eyes shut in response to the thought.

The dark of my eyelids carried me away. I imagined falling into sex. Just some nothing sex with another person. The way it felt to have someone else touch my skin, the kissing and the blurring of shapes into blocks of dim color, the smell of someone else's breath, skin, sweat. The way thoughts un-focus into just that moment when your stomach drops and your fingers feel eight times more sensitive, the skin lit with nerve endings. That unspooling moment of inevitability. It was possible to feel the power of it radiating from my skin as I stood with my eyes shut in the hospital bathroom, irresistible and strong as gravity or a wildfire.

I could go to a bar and go home with a stranger.

I could telephone Dr. Pete—never mind that he had told me he was out of town this week. With this certainty on me, like a black lace dress, I could have knocked on anyone's door and ended up in bed. Hell, I could probably seduce Artie. I could call one of the cute guys from Dear George's funeral.

And just like that, the lights of my skin—the million shimmering specks of feeling—extinguished. Power out. Stones thrown at a streetlight.

I remembered the funeral and the morgue and George's face, blurred and softened, the color of green alabaster.

I was ashamed. Awash in shame. My eyes opened but I couldn't meet my own gaze in the mirror. I didn't want to have sex with anyone. I could barely stand to feel my own skin, let alone someone else's. My stomach turned over and I vomited into the toilet from shame and misery.

I wanted my sister back. I wanted her to be sitting up next to me in her hospital bed, reading a magazine in the bad fluorescent light, a cup of perfect hot cocoa beside her, patting the covers next to her legs and inviting me to sit down for a chat, listening calmly while I told her what was bothering me. But she was frozen, asleep, perhaps just holding on somewhere, her breath regulated, her every electric twitch recorded on a bank of instruments.

There was nothing to do but wait, wrapped tight in my cocoon of evil thoughts, wishing I could make a deal with the devil to get Viv back. I wished there were a devil to make a deal with. I wished *I* were the one holding on someplace in the dark, while *she* paced helplessly around *my* hospital bed.

I WENT back to Viv's house at midnight that night, to the usual big-footed dance of the dogs as they welcomed the car and then, with just a touch less animation, greeted me. They had all been sleeping, their eyes hooded, comfortable warmth radiating off their fur. Balin rubbed by, pausing to look up at me with her side pressed against my leg for a moment, and then the three hurried ahead of me, back to their beds.

I stood in the kitchen, trying, as I often did, to pinpoint what exactly about this room felt so unwelcoming. The cool gleam of stainless steel? The isolated puddles of yellow from the can lights reflected on the dark wood and the black countertops? I missed the chipped and messy cabinets of the shared kitchen in my sublet in Sarasota. My stomach growled hugely.

The refrigerator held a motley assortment of shriveled leftovers, so I brought out eggs, milk, parmesan, and the limp remains of a bag of spinach. I'd scramble it into a sort of frittata and have hot cocoa with it. Tomkin joined me as I rattled the fork in the mixing bowl. He made it clear that a sliver of parmesan would provide an acceptable substitute for his usual slice of sticky American cheese. He gulped it gently from my fingers and then evidently drooled it loose from the roof of his mouth a few moments later, chewing and bobbing his head like a horse eating oats.

The eggs bubbled, the rich smell coming off the skillet in a steamy puff, and I kept the heating milk whisked to avoid scalding it. I put the pan of eggs under the broiler to finish. The cocoa just filled one of Viv's ugly pottery mugs. The frittata slid whole from the pan onto my plate, picture-perfect.

I got a fresh fork from the drawer and picked up my late dinner, meaning to carry it to the end of the bar. Somehow it slipped. The plate hit the edge of the black counter, flipped, and smashed onto the tile floor.

Rough tan pottery shards shot to every corner of the room. After a split second when I might have begun weeping, I felt anger boil like molten lava under the pumice shell of my skin.

Hideous, ugly pottery.

I swore and dropped the cup of cocoa onto the tiles. It went off like a bomb. I returned to the cupboard and pulled three plates down in each hand. My wrists trembled with the weight of the horrible things and the weakness of my hands made me angrier yet. Stupid dishes! I slapped them across the counter-edge and big pie-slice pieces fell onto the floor and mixed with the downed food.

I threaded my index finger through the handles of a pair of mugs and let them fall, reaching for more without looking at the mess they made.

A big platter followed.

"You and your stupid dishes!" The yowl of my voice reverberated in my own tear-clogged head.

I broke all the dishes in the cupboard while the dog cowered in the corner.

When I stopped, I was too tired to be horrified.

The floor was a gritty, Jackson-Pollock carpet of cold scrambled eggs, splattered cocoa, and chunks of heavy pottery the color of oatmeal. Tomkin paced in the mudroom, with his long tail tucked up under his hind end. The other dogs peered through the doorway, whining just at the edge of my range of hearing, their sad eyes looking even more anxious than usual.

I imagined one of them stepping on a piece of broken pottery, the sharp edge of it cutting into a rough black pad, and I winced. My own tender feet cringed inside the soft slippers I'd borrowed from Viv's closet. I picked up the mess, swept, mopped, and then led the dogs outside.

I smoked another clove cigarette as they squatted and lifted legs. I wanted to kick the dinky little maple tree to splinters. "I hate this place," I told the dogs. "I hate it here."

They stopped sniffing the lawn to look at me. Balin walked slowly up the stone steps and then leaned against my leg for a moment, as if to confirm to one of us that the other was there. She sneezed and stood looking at the back door. I opened it and warm air poured out on my feet as she went inside. The other two dogs followed her, leaving me shivering alone outside.

Chapter 48

EVER since my first airplane flight, departing JFK on a raw blue February afternoon and arriving the next morning in the golden roar of Rome, I've loved traveling by air.

Every possibility exists in an airport: so many destinations to pick and the potential to see anyone you've ever known hauling a suitcase across wide shining floors.

At an airport it seems like there's better chance of love at first sight. A person can be transformed into someone better and more interesting during the sure swoop of a plane across an ocean. Coincidences are more common at an airport, where people from any corner of the world might be going to the very same place.

Nearly everything about air travel appealed to me: the neat uniforms, the number of gatekeepers and passwords on the way to the tiny, snug nest where you incubated across the distance. I even loved the thin lap blankets that never quite covered my cramped legs. The taste of the hot coffee they served meant nothing weighed against the height above the surface of the earth and how many hundreds of miles from dry land you were, and that the temperature outside was negative fifty degrees. It was magic.

If the Nashville airport had had a flight to anywhere the day after Thanksgiving, I would have taken it.

I was all set: passport, cash, credit card, those few essential things my sister taught me to grab when a person needed to make a dash for it, plus my sketchbook and pencils.

Had Viv inspected my duffel that afternoon, I think she would have almost approved. I thought for sure I was ready. All I could think about was escape.

But out west, an arctic cold front was beginning a cascade of delays and cancellations. Standing in front of the rows of orange blinking monitors I watched my options narrow to Memphis, Cincinnati, Raleigh—small American cities I could just as easily reach by driving. Which made the whole idea of flying someplace seem pointless.

If I was running, I ought to end up someplace farther away than that.

I sat in the airport with my sore feet propped on my own luggage, gazing around the shining public space, idly eavesdropping on family conversations as the airport slowly shut down. The little stores closed their rattling mesh gates, the smell of barbeque faded, and the cleaning crew took over the wide hallways. Before long, even the nearest potential destinations disappeared from the monitors.

I felt like a fish swimming around in muddy water as a net slowly closed in. As if I didn't already know I was trapped.

I drove back to Viv's ugly house where the dogs met me at the door, stretching and stepping their big paws onto my toes.

In my defense, I must say I hadn't forgotten about the dogs when I plotted my escape. I'd planned to call Artie just before getting onto the plane so they wouldn't be left to starve to death or anything.

The dogs milled around the kitchen as I checked the answering machine. Sophia Cutillo, three messages from friends, a check-in message from Viv's classmate, Marie Chou, plus a long, forlorn-sounding ramble from Dad Rowan about nothing at all.

I asked the dogs if they wanted to go outside. They wiggled, wagged their long tails harder, and stomped their big feet faster on the floor. I walked outside with them, where they adjusted to the drop in temperature by sneezing and shaking their heads, so their ears sounded like limp hands clapping.

After a quick circuit of the lawn, Tomkin sat gingerly, crouching above the cool stones at my feet. He didn't quite look up at me. He glanced past my shoulder, flattening his ears in apology for the world, and scooted a fraction of an inch closer to me.

I rubbed the back of my hand in the hollow of his skull behind his ear. He leaned into it, forgetting to crouch. His entire energy focused on the sensation of my knuckles moving the gristle of his ear. If I took my hand away, he might have tipped over, but I kept rubbing. When I stopped, he came out of his transports gradually, giving himself a mighty shake that made his jowls snap. Then he thumped his tail vigorously on the cold ground.

His perpetually worried look had smoothed out. "Silly old bear," I said to him. He surprised me by bowing over his forelegs like a puppy and flashing the whites of his eyes at me. He shed his usual calm and began to caper with slow abandon. The other two joined in, weaving around in a rare celebration, snuffling at one another and cavorting like underwater creatures.

They boxed as they leaped around, their mouths open, smacking and chomping the air as they passed one another. Even Balin felt lively enough to rear up and bat her big paws at the other two.

Chapter 49

MY EARLIEST memory was of my sister. Though I had not remembered it for years, the feeling of anxiety and then relief tangled up with the memory was utterly familiar and comforting. As I sat in George's kitchen with my sore feet soaking in a pan of Epsom salts, it came back to me: the memory and the history of the memory all at once, like a rock that you find again after throwing it into a pond.

When I was babysitting, I'd hunted a hundred times for a lost scrap of tattered old blankie for one child or another who couldn't rest without it. That's what this scene must have been to me: a worn scrap that gave me comfort over and over until the day I just stopped thinking about it.

The memory goes like this: I am waking up on the wide blue vinyl backseat of a car. I'm small enough that I don't quite fill my half of the bench seat and I am lying down. It's warm. One hand is pins-and-needles from being under my head. I have the thumb of the other hand plugged into my mouth. The only sound to be heard over the engine noise is the air rushing past the window. The sun is low in the sky and the shadows of tree-trunks stipple the light as the car rolls along.

I'm almost frightened, waking with the noises and sensation of movement, but then I see my sister. Viv is sitting up very straight, with her sharp chin almost resting on the blue metal windowsill. She's paying attention to whatever she can see out the window, but perhaps I make a noise, or she sees me move from the corner of her eye, because she turns toward me with a smile, and although I don't know I had been about to cry, I am suddenly *not* going to cry.

The sight of her familiar face, her hair glowing red in the off-and-on flickering stripes of sunlight, is as reassuring and comfortable as the sensation of being tucked into bed. Having seen her, I can smile and stretch and slip back into slumber once more. Before going back to sleep, however, I watch the sunlight flickering, bright enough that it shows orange and then green-black on the other side of my eyelids, and when my sister presses her bare foot against mine, gently, I waggle my foot back against hers. And then I do fall asleep again.

EVERYTHING started with my sister. Once upon a time, before that telephone call I'd been dreading forever, I would have said that my sister and I were incredibly close, that we knew each other better than anyone, that we had raised one another and that we had been through so much together that no one could ever be as close as the two of us.

But without her awake to explain, I had no idea what she wanted me to do. I couldn't guess what dreams she had. And yet she had put me in charge of taking care of her life. It was ridiculous. She was my whole family, and I barely knew her.

Still, I was determined that my sister wouldn't be a stranger after she woke. No matter how Viv woke up—

even if she woke up just fine—I wasn't going to let things slide back to the way they had been going. That much I knew for sure.

Doing is easy if you know what you want to do, Viv had told me time and again. Still, there are plans and there are plans. It's one thing to plan your way into medical school. But honestly, who could have planned for this particular eventuality? Who might have thought, what if there is a car accident and a long hospital stay and the big house is left empty? Who anticipated a baby on the way and a slightly tottery old dad and four hundred pounds of assorted English mastiff? No one could think that way. No one could make a plan for all that.

But in the same way the smell of turpentine seeps through the air and gets your attention, an idea occurred to me. I realized that someone *could* plan for such an eventuality. My sister, for instance. She had made a big back-up plan that had covered even this specific, unexpected future. That plan was me. What if everything went wrong? Nicky would be there. I was myself my sister's emergency plan.

And in that case, I thought, things were really going to change around here.

I TELEPHONED Arizona that evening. Dwalin sat as close to me as possible, his pelvic bones framing my foot. He looked coquettishly over his shoulder at me as I dialed the phone, like a friendly, lumpy sea-lion. I was still smiling when Dad Rowan picked up the telephone. I figured I'd ask for money advice. He'd retired from a career in banking, and I could really use his opinion. And I hoped the topic would give me a way to stay connected to him. But we never got around to the subject.

He sounded tired. When I asked, he told me that one of his neighbors had had a stroke the night before. "It's not so much that I knew him. We only started golfing together when I got here. We weren't that close, really. It's just the shock. He was nine years younger than me."

"Is there anything I can do?" I asked.

"No," he said, "No. I'll be fine. It's just the way things go. One of the hazards of living in a retirement community."

In the short silence that followed, with Dwalin sitting on my foot and the two other big dogs snoring gently in the stark, spacious kitchen, I pictured Dad Rowan in his lonesome condo kitchen. He'd have a stack of magazines piled on the table and the television turned up too loud. The over-filled teakettle would be steaming away because he'd forgotten about it. He'd have leftover take-out heating in the microwave, and he'd probably forgotten to remove the plastic wrap.

"So, when the baby comes, will you come visit?" The words crossed the telephone lines before I realized what I intended to say.

Silence answered, and I said, "Hey, are you still there?"

"I'm here."

"When Viv's baby is born, will you come to stay here in Nashville with us?" I repeated.

His voice came hoarse and solemn. "I'd be honored. Truly." Then, after a juicy sniff, "I didn't mean to pry, but I understood from Artie that perhaps—I wasn't sure whether you would keep the—or if—well. This *is* something to celebrate."

As he began to tell me about how much he was looking forward to his first grandchild, his voice regained some of its usual cheer, and the words started to flow like water. He explained that he could hardly wait to see what the baby looked like, whose features it would favor. He said he had been thinking about his family history and how he meant to dig out the old picture-albums.

When he stopped, his voice grew lower and more serious. "Still and all, your sister might not appreciate having an old fart like me hanging around."

I had the phone pinned to my ear with my shoulder so I could use both hands to rub Dwalin's chest, which made the dog extend his wide chin to the sky in a heavy-muzzled coyote silhouette. I made a noise of disagreement, though honestly, I couldn't begin to imagine Viv's response.

"I don't know whether she'll want me there," he said. "But there's nothing I'd rather do. Believe it or not, I took care of George quite a lot when he was a baby. My wife Dorothy had the postpartum blues. Couldn't get out bed some days. Of course, I was a young man then, healthy as an ox."

He laughed, perhaps at the idea of being like an ox. While he took a breath, the phone line crackled. I heard hope mixed with sadness as he continued, "But what I'm getting at, is—I could be of some help."

It occurred to me that Dad Rowan was orphaned from both directions now, from top and bottom. His parents had probably been gone for a while, but he was old, and with his wife and his only child both dead, he was completely alone. And he was far more isolated than I was, because George would never wake. *Could* never wake. Emotion squeezed high in my sinuses.

"Once she's up and about, Vivian can tell us exactly where to get off—and you know she will!" My words came out strange and jolly, but Dad Rowan laughed with me. "But until then, let's do as we see fit."

We agreed that he would come around Christmastime and stay for some weeks. He could get an open-ended ticket, or maybe he would drive over. He would think about it before deciding. After I hung up, I had a moment of doubt, but I pushed it aside. If Viv didn't want him around, then *she* could be the one to send him back to Scottsdale.

Chapter 50

ED MAYNARD'S assistant had left an envelope for me at the front desk of the hospital. When I stopped by the reception area, the two elderly volunteer ladies behind the big desk looked into every nook and cranny before they located the big manila envelope. One spoke disapprovingly. "This has been here for days. We can't be expected to hold things forever, young lady."

I agreed, apologized, and scurried off with it to my sister's room. I told Viv that Ed had sent a surprise for us while I straightened a bouquet of silk flowers and scotch-taped the fallen get-well cards back onto the wall.

When there was no more fussing to be done, I sat on the visitor's chair and slid a finger under the taped flap of the envelope. A half-dozen slippery fax pages slid out. The print was grainy, but the headlines came out clear enough: "Fire Claims Lives Overnight," "Drug Use

Suspected in Fatal Hippie Fire," and "Ten Perish in Hippie Fire."

I shuffled the pages, looking for pictures. The photos seemed to be lifted from high-school yearbooks: the women each wore one of those dark V-neck drape tops. My eye barely registered the men—boys, really, with nerdy plastic glasses and knobby necks above their ties. Instead, I studied the face that Ed must have meant: a stubborn-looking girl with a pointed chin at the tip of her square jaw.

The caption named her Naomi Anderson. She had the thin-skinned look of a redhead. If I teased Viv's hair into a big helmet with little flippy ends pointing away from her neck and plucked her eyebrows into dramatic arches, Viv and this girl would look similar. Like sisters, maybe.

As I stared at the pixelated image, the differences seemed to outweigh their similarities: Naomi Anderson had rounder eyes than Viv, and a shorter nose. Her mouth was smaller, and her lips looked fuller, pouty. Though Naomi wasn't wearing any jewelry, she had an undeniable look of privilege.

Then I considered one of the other victims, Melinda Nussman. A different species: the barrette holding back her dark hair revealed wide, boneless temples and a soft jawline, utterly unlike Viv. I shook my head. It was probably just the grainy quality of the newsprint by way of the facsimile machine. I looked at the dates on the newspaper stories and shuffled the faxes into order before reading them.

The fifth of July was a Friday in 1968. The weather unseasonably cool but fine. The first story came in the morning edition of the paper, with a short report that the fire department had been called to the scene of a house-fire outside Snake Tree overnight. A dozen or more people were thought injured or killed in the conflagration.

The evening edition of the paper put the story on the front page and gave it a name, the Hippie Fire. According to the neighbors, the farm on Dry Spring Road hosted as many as two dozen residents, "long-hairs and Yippie-types," during the summer.

Along the margin, Ed had noted that Yippie stood for Youth International Party, but I remembered the term from Viv talking about Abbie Hoffman. I found my place and continued reading.

The fire chief suspected that fireworks—or possibly an oil lamp—had set the wooden house structure alight sometime after midnight on Thursday night. An unnamed volunteer firemen described arriving at the scene: "It was chaos, half-dressed people running around, and cars parked every which way in the driveway and lawn." The inhabitants of the farm—goats, chickens, pet dogs, as well as their human caretakers—had to be chased away from the burning buildings.

The reporter described the empty wine jugs and the sleeping bags abandoned in the singed hayfields.

Several bodies had been found in the half-burned outbuildings, but the fire-marshal's job was complicated by the nearly complete destruction of the farmhouse. Of this wooden structure, only a blackened cellar remained. The owners of the property had been away at the time. Police were investigating the possibility of hallucinogenic drug use.

Within the week, reporters had obtained photographs and background information about the victims of the fire. John and Holly Fairwether, both age twenty-five, and their three children (five-year-old Jeremiah, three-year-old Joshua, and four-month-old Jacob) came originally from Hershey, Pennsylvania. Electrician Steve Davin, age twenty-eight, and his girlfriend Melinda Nussman, age twenty-six, came from Cincinnati, Ohio. Twenty-one-year-old Naomi Anderson and her daughters Meshella, age four, and nineteen-month-old Lavinia had moved to Snake Tree from Philadelphia earlier in the summer.

I turned the names over in my mind. I looked at my sister.

"Hey, Viv? Listen. How does 'Meshella' sound to you? Familiar? Yeah, me neither. How about 'Lavinia'?"

It stopped me cold.

Baby Vinnia.

I trotted out of Viv's room and stood in front of the triptych-style telephone booth, trying to decide which number to call first.

I left a message with Ed Maynard's answering service, and then hesitated before calling Trisha. What could I tell her? That the detective had found someone who looked like my sister and who had a child with the same oddball name as the doll I'd carried throughout my childhood?

I stopped myself. I needed to speak with Ed first and Trisha later. That would give Ed a chance to track down some more details about Naomi Anderson and her daughters.

I TOOK my restless feet back to Viv's room. The OB/GYN team was huddled around Viv's round white belly.

"How's it going?" I said.

One of the doctors looked up and smiled. Another spoke up. "The latest ultrasound looks good. The baby is tracking well for thirty-three weeks. We're not out of the woods, so to speak, but we are very pleased to reach this milestone."

I asked which milestone.

"Well, of course, every week toward full term means a better chance for a healthier baby, but we're pretty confident that this baby could thrive even if it were born today."

"Today?"

The group smiled at my expression.

The doctor said, "Let's not get ahead of ourselves. We're just saying that this baby has a much better chance four weeks before full term, rather than six or eight weeks ahead of time."

"So, four weeks to go?"

They all nodded, like a shelf full of bobble-headed dolls. One said, "Four weeks, give or take." And they all nodded some more. They left shortly afterwards.

BEFORE Viv and the baby came home, I thought, giving the words a trial-run in my mind. When Viv and the baby come home. Once Viv and the baby settle in. Then I thought about Viv's house. Where was the baby going to sleep?

"Make a plan," my sister had always said. "Figure out your goals and you're halfway there."

I tucked the covers loosely around my sister's legs and finished the advice. "Start with a list."

I took a pen and paper with me back to the payphone in the waiting room, making a list even as I dialed the number for Sophia Cutillo. She began with, "You're calling from the hospital. Do you want to call back, reverse the charges?"

"No, I put it on the credit card."

"You want to be careful with that, sweetheart." She took a sip of something. "Tell me what's happening down there."

I passed along the update from Viv's obstetricians.

She *tsk*ed in sympathy. "My cousin Marina's sister-in-law had a baby five weeks premature, weighed four pounds. Can you imagine? Like a little bag of rice and covered with fur."

Sophia told me about the premature baby—currently playing Little League—and then said that she and Papi were ready to come to Nashville to help with the baby.

"We won't stick our nose in where it isn't wanted, but you know you are like another daughter to us." Her voice grew rougher. "Not that Miss Patricia Beatrice Big-Britches doesn't keep us worried enough as it is. What is she thinking with this Jersey Wonder boy? Is she serious about him? *Can* she be serious about him?"

I couldn't get a word in edgewise for ten minutes. It was great. She gave me her sardonic opinion of the girls her sons were dating—she always pretended to disapprove of her boys' swashbuckling ways and constantly changing cast of girlfriends, but Trisha and I agreed she got a kick out of the drama.

Then Sophia brought the conversation back to babies by asking if my sister had a baby registry, or if any of "Vivian's girlfriends," a phrase that startled me, had planned a baby shower.

"Not that I know," I said. "I'm going to go shopping for things today."

"What are you going to get?"

I pulled out the notebook and said, "Everything."

"Wash the baby clothes, but don't bring them into the house until it's nearly time," Sophia said. "It's bad luck."

"Is it okay if I paint the baby's room?" I was only partly teasing.

Sophia snorted. "Of course, you can paint the baby's room now. Do you want to fumigate the poor thing? Just don't put new clothes away, you know, or make the bed. Not until the baby is born safe, God willing." I could almost hear Sophia making the sign of the cross. I wondered if the grandmother on the Via Bionchi Vecchi in Rome, the one who spat through her fingers to ward off bad luck, would tell me the same.

"What about a crib?" I said.

"Doesn't your sister already have one?" she asked.

I told her no, and she told me not to buy until she had read up in *Consumer Reports* and discussed it with her cronies. "And hold off on getting a collapsible playpen and a bouncy swing. Let Papi and me ask around. But you'll need a car seat first."

She began telling me about a crib recall and got off the phone only when one of the boys—Papi or one of Trisha's brothers, she didn't differentiate between them in conversation—came home.

ARTIE Slate was my second call. Luckily no one seemed to need the phone in the waiting room. "Nicole?" he said, when the receptionist put him through. "Is everything alright?"

"Yeah," I said. "No change at the hospital, but I just wanted to update you on what I'm planning."

"Go ahead," he said.

"Regardless of whether Viv recovers fully," I hurried through this part. "Or not. I plan to bring the baby home."

"Okay," Artie said.

"And help her raise it." It? According to Dr. Wilsey, Viv didn't want to know ahead of time, and I'd been more than happy to follow her lead, but maybe I should find out the baby's gender.

"Okay," Artie repeated.

"That's it?" I said.

Artie sounded a little tired as he answered. "Viv and George were expecting the baby when they wrote their will. They put you in charge. I can offer advice, but the decision is ultimately yours."

I'd been bracing for some kind of fight. I wasn't sure for a second whether it was relief or disappointment I was feeling.

"Are you still there?

"Yeah," I said. "I just—sorry."

"No need to apologize."

I wasn't sure that was true. "Hey, Artie," I said. "I probably should have said before, but thanks for looking out for them."

I SHOPPED that afternoon, piling a bassinette and padding, a sturdy and complicated car-seat, and oversized containers of Johnson & Johnson baby potions into a shopping cart. I hesitated with several packages of soft cotton onesies in my hand: preemie size or age 0-3 months? Blue or pink? Would it have red hair or dark blonde, blue eyes or grey?

I put both packages of the little clothes back on the shelf and tried to clear my mind. Stick to the list, I told myself. Stick to the plan.

I selected a changing table and a pair of miniature nail clippers. I paused in front of the bales of disposable diapers. We don't need them yet, I thought. I hefted a short case of bent glass bottles and perused the shelves of formula. Had Viv planned to nurse? The thought jabbed me in the lung. I turned away from the formula and gently set the bottles back.

Time enough for that later, I told myself. It could wait until after the baby was born.

I pushed my shopping cart back to the aisle of soft little receiving blankets, picking green and yellow things and a bedding set with cheerful embroidered fishes swimming along the edges. I piled handfuls of cozy pale burp-cloths on top. I got a week's worth of tiny knit caps and pair after pair of miniature socks that barely fit over the top joints of my thumbs.

Chapter 51

"HOLY crap on a toasted bun, what did you say to my mother?!"

"And hello to you, Patricia Beatrice Too-Busy Cutillo."

"She is on a complete tear. I stopped by yesterday and she's working the phone banks like a freaking maniac."

"I asked her for help getting ready for the baby," I admitted.

"Praise the Lord."

"What?" I put down the baby bedding I'd been folding.

Trish's voice was sincere. "It's the first time in years she hasn't bugged me about my love-life."

"She thinks you're still dating the Jersey Wonder."

"Bite your tongue!"

"So?"

"So tell me what's going on down there—" Trisha peppered me with questions. "How's Viv? How are you? Has your private detective found anything new and exciting?"

"Viv is the same. I'm okay." I turned back to the laundry and tucked the phone into the crook of my shoulder. "I was going to wait and tell you when I knew more, but—have you ever heard of Snake Tree, Pennsylvania?"

"No. Should I? What happened there?"

"For one thing, it *might* be where Marsha Ranklin turned into Mary Jones and picked up a couple of daughters."

"As in adopted them?" She framed the words carefully.

"Maybe. Maybe not." I told her about the Hippie Fire and Ed's hunch about Naomi Anderson, who had two little girls the same age as Viv and me.

"Did I ever tell you about the baby-doll from when I was little?"

"Do tell!"

I snorted. "My doll was named 'Baby Vinnia'—"

"Weird."

"I know. But I had her since before I can remember, and it turns out that this hippie chick, Naomi, had two daughters: Meshella and Lavinia."

"As in Baby Vinnia?!" Then she said, "Hang on, there's the doorbell."

I heard the indistinct rumble of Trisha's feet thumping across the floor and an excited greeting. I folded the last of the tiny bedding and gave the pile a satisfied pat.

I looked around George's kitchen. I was going to make orange-cranberry bread to bring to the hospital, but the corded telephone didn't quite reach across the room to the oven. I didn't hear footsteps coming back to the phone, but Trisha returned with a clunk and, "Still there?"

"And where else would I be?"

"On your way here?"

"I wish. Who was at the door?"

Trisha's voice was matter-of-fact as she answered, "Mr. New Boyfriend." She continued loudly over my interruption. "That's a whole other conversation." Then, conspiratorially, "I might have to send a diagram."

I told her I was looking forward to it.

She said something to Mr. New Boyfriend and then, "So back up: Did you see the newspaper? Does the hippie chick look like Viv? And how come Ed thinks her girls didn't die?"

"It was a hot fire," I said. "I guess the remains were—well, I don't know exactly. I didn't ask."

"Oh. So—okay. So maybe the hippie chick is alive too?"

"No, they identified her body." My tone of voice came out all wrong.

"Nicky! For crying out loud. But you maybe had a hippie mom, once upon a time. Maybe you have grandparents? Aunts and uncles? Cousins? Brothers?"

"Maybe. Maybe I have grandparents. Or maybe there's someone out there whose dead daughter looks a lot like Viv."

That shut us both up. I heard a deep voice asking Trisha something on the other end of the line.

"Hang up," I said.

"No—wait a sec." She muffled the phone and had a brief conversation. She was laughing when she uncovered the receiver. "He just got back from Japan," she started to explain.

"Hang up," I repeated. "There's no other details yet. Seriously. We can talk later."

"I'm being a jerk," she said. "You discover that you're like this milk-carton kid and I have a thousand questions, but I'm going to hang up because of some boy. I am a bad friend. Hate me."

"Nope. You'll have to try again. Bye!"

"I'll call you from work tomorrow."

I hung up smiling.

Then I rooted through the cupboards, searching through the neat stacks of baking gear for Dear George's loaf pans. I knew he had a pair of them, because the last time I'd come through Nashville, I'd made banana bread.

Sniffing the steam rising from the bread, my sister had said, "Have you ever thought about opening a bakery?"

"Does that mean you like the banana bread?" I'd said.

I'd always tried to cook at least a couple of times whenever I visited Viv and George. It felt homey to me, the meals that I cooked for them in their kitchens over the years. More often than not, however, my sister preferred to go out to eat. "I want real Italian," she'd say, or, "Let's let someone else do the dishes after."

On the second morning of my visit last time, I'd taken myself downstairs early to cook, before Viv could suggest that she wanted to go out for breakfast. I was mixing in the last bit of cheese for the omelet casserole when Viv padded into the kitchen.

Viv lifted a corner of the banana bread from the loaf and popped it into her mouth. "Yum," she said. "Seriously, you could start a business."

"Or I could just make banana bread every now and again." I kept my tone light. It was too early in the morning to start this discussion with my sister.

I didn't bother mentioning that I'd already started a business. I'd painted half a dozen wall murals over the winter and had taken myself to London for a month on the proceeds.

"Even if you started by just catering breakfasts..." My sister's voice was contemplative. I suspected that she was calculating profit-loss ratios.

"I work with a caterer," I said, placing the casserole dish into the oven with more attention than it deserved. "It's not really a good full-time job for me."

"Well, you'd hire someone to do the grunt-work—" Viv started.

George breezed into the kitchen just then, smelling of toothpaste mint and piney aftershave, his worn Oxford shirt starched smooth but hanging untucked over his blue jeans. He managed to give Viv a squeeze with one arm while cutting banana bread with the other. He extracted the slab single-handedly without tearing the rest of the loaf.

"I was just telling Nicky she should start a bakery."

"Or she could move in, bake for us," George said, releasing Viv and using both hands to tackle the challenge of working a pat of butter across the hot surface of the bread.

I opened my mouth, about to play with the idea of moving into the house, but my sister spoke first.

"No way." Her voice was serious. She wasn't kidding.

George and I both stopped to look at her.

"I mean, no way that would work." Her voice limped over the statement, making it even less convincing. No one spoke for an awkward moment. George was frowning at Viv. Viv was giving George a complicated look that might have meant anything.

When Viv spoke, it sounded like an apology. "Nicky knows what I mean," she said, without looking away from her husband.

"Sure I do," I said.

Now they both turned and looked at me. My face felt hot. I opened my mouth. There were terrible things I would have said, about moochers and loser baby-sisters and moving on, but George piped up.

"So, hey, did you guys catch the game last night?" George's voice was bright and impersonal. Over the years, I'd heard him do this in conversation. He'd occasionally offer up a random query that derailed an argument before it really got going. Keeping a straight face, he'd wait politely for an answer. The effect was so goofy and distracting that it almost always worked to nudge the discussion away from an unsavory topic. He'd never used the technique on me.

A long beat of silence followed. George kept his eyebrows raised in an expression of anticipation and interest. It was unnerving. I forgot entirely what I'd been about to say. My fury drained away, leaving me empty and chilled.

"Sorry," Viv said to the room. And then, more sincerely, to George, "Sorry."

His expression didn't change.

Viv spoke to me. "Sorry. George is right. *What* a game!"

"Probably the best play was in that fifth quarter," I offered, weakly, only because George was still giving me that expectant look.

"Yeah," Viv said. "The fifth quarter's always full of surprises. So, what else is in the oven?"

Chapter 52

I HAD finally given up hope of finding them when Viv's missing diaries turned up.

Trisha called me from the bank in Manhattan to tell me that my sister had *not* left journals in the safe-deposit box. "There's some banking statements, some little trinkets, and a letter marked 'In Case of My Death,'" she said.

"Don't open it!"

"I wasn't going to."

"It's just—" For a moment I thought I might choke on dread and superstition.

"I know," Trisha said. "I didn't even touch it."

I was grateful that she understood without my having to explain. After a moment, Trisha continued, "But—no notebooks. Do you want me to mail this stuff down to you?"

"Is it important—I mean, does it look like anything I need to see?"

"No, not really. Just some of her personal stuff." Trisha sniffed. "You know, after all this bother, I thought the bank would be a little more glamorous, but it was like being inside of a filing cabinet."

I was clearing out the extra upstairs bedroom, getting ready to paint it for the baby. After studying the magazine pictures Viv had saved of babies' rooms, I'd decided not to paint an elaborate mural for the nursery. If the baby turned out to be a boy, it was well within my skill to make a field of sunflowers and daisies like the one she'd saved look boyish, but I wanted to wait for Viv and talk it over with her.

In the meantime, a swirling band of yellow, like a sash or a playful streamer of sunshine, would circle the room. I'd make the ceiling bright blue with a scattering of fluffy white clouds. I'd start by putting up a fresh coat of white paint over the whole room, even inside the closet, so I had to shift the daybed and the moving boxes and miscellaneous junk—orphaned lamps and overflow clothes—out of the room.

I reached into the closet and tried to hoist the suitcase, but it was heavier than it should have been. I tipped it over and unzipped the lid to find a matching smaller suitcase tucked inside. It was also quite heavy. That one unzipped to reveal a stack of black notebooks, bricked together with fat rubber bands. No yellow sticky-notes. There were more than a dozen of the black books. Viv's journals.

I zipped the small suitcase back up and hauled it downstairs to the living room. I made a bargain with myself: I could look at one of Viv journals after I prepped the room to paint. I could read a second one after I got the walls primed, and I could have a third one the next morning at Viv's bedside.

I ORGANIZED the journals by date, but I didn't read them in order. The first entry I read was from her junior year in college.

"*Watched N cut Paul's hair. He came by to take me to the jazz ensemble practice at the Crane School, but stayed in for dinner (lentil thing, spicy) and TV and a haircut. Out of nowhere, N can cut hair. Please please please don't let her want to go to beauty school."*

It was an effort not to fling the book across the room. I wanted to shake the twenty-year-old Viv and say, "What's so wrong with being a hairdresser?"

Viv's later diaries were thick with information about her work and what she and George did on the weekends. She wrote nearly every day, detailing all sorts of information. Only rarely did she mention how she felt about things. I tried to skim the descriptions of surgery. She wrote about her occasional squabbles with other doctors or administrators at the hospital. She was careful to keep her temper at work, and it didn't really surprise me to see how much energy she spent on planning her way through these conflicts. She tackled them like a crafty general on a military campaign.

After trudging through her journal of 1990, when she was a resident in Atlanta—and more than once gagging at the kind of surgical detail she found worth noting—I came across this: *"Pregnancy ended this morning. DG also taking it very hard. Howl. Want to crawl under covers & sleep until I forget."*

Where was I in February of 1990? Why did I not know how unhappy she must have been? How could she have gone through it without me? My poor sister.

I READ every page of her journals. I figured out that she tracked her menstrual periods with a little crescent moon symbol, but I couldn't interpret the two or three little squiggly lines that sometimes accompanied the crescent moon. After the moon didn't appear the previous spring, she wrote, *"June 16, app't w/Marilyn. Crossing fingers. Crossing toes. Maybe due date first week January."*

She recorded only a few details of her own condition. *"July 12. Can't get enough canned corned beef hash but can't stand smell of steak. No morning sickness." "August 3. Vomited twice before surgery yesterday, but fine today."* And then in September, *"Felt the little butterfly fluttering today. Would have grabbed anyone to feel my belly but was solo in the scrub room."*

I'd never before felt so much like an excluded younger sister.

She'd have welcomed any random stranger to share this miraculous little moment, but she couldn't bring herself to mention it to me when we talked on the phone?

In case I didn't feel bad enough, the following Sunday's entry bore out my suspicions: *"Great brunch after church. LOVE bacon this month. Weird... N leaving Brooklyn for Florida again this week. I don't know how she does it. Wish she would just get a job & settle down someplace. Told her we'd catch up over the winter."*

I wondered, for the hundredth time, when Viv had planned to tell me about her pregnancy, or if she had meant to tell me at all. How would it go? Would she have dropped it casually—"Hey Nicky, guess what?"

I would never have guessed.

Maybe she would have squealed the news to me like a girl. "I'm going to have a baby!"

Or maybe she meant to show up with the baby in her arms and say nothing at all. I shivered.

Although—what if she'd planned to spring it on me all at once? Perhaps she'd use Ed Maynard's investigation as the other half of the news that she was having a baby.

She wrote: *"Hired detective. Hope he can track Magda & Jahn before Christmas. Wonder how he got into the business? Former cop?"*

That would have been an enormous gift. Surprise! A family! Sort of like getting a past and a future delivered to me in a neat—or anyway neat-*ish*—package.

Though, honestly, it was probably like so many things I'd learned about Viv's life: nothing at all to do with me. Even when you know it's self-pity, it still stings a little.

Chapter 53

"NICKY? It's Ed Maynard. I'm calling from New Jersey."

I listened to the answering machine messages as I let the dogs outside. Ed's voice sounded animated.

"Just a quick update with some news. I located Naomi Anderson's family. I've got to catch a train to Long Island, but I expect to call you tomorrow after dinnertime with more information. Hope to catch you then. Okay, bye-bye."

I wasn't expecting my heart to thud so hard.

If Ed had found something out, I told myself, maybe I'd just let Viv deal with it. Whatever Ed Maynard discovered, it could wait until Viv got better. It had already waited for decades. I had enough to deal with just trying to get ready for Viv's baby.

"Nice try," Trisha said when I told her my strategy. "You really think you can just put this on the back burner?"

"*If* they turn out to be related to us."

"If they are," Trisha agreed, "You kind of have to contact them."

"But—"

"I know. What would Viv do?"

"WWVD?" I said.

Trisha ignored the quip.

"I don't know," I said. "Honestly, I have no idea."

"Okay, and what would *you* do? If it was just you deciding?"

"Always with the hard questions, huh?"

Trisha let me think about it.

If it were just me by myself, curiosity would drive me.

I didn't want to step on Viv's toes, but if the Anderson family turned out to be related to me, I'd want to know what they were like. And wouldn't I want Viv's baby to know about everything? Even if the Andersons were horrible and mean, I wouldn't want to try to conceal the truth.

Unless Viv woke up and told me differently, I'd plan for her child to never feel as alone as I had in the past few months in Viv's big sterile house.

"If these people turn out to be related to Viv and me," I said, "and if they are not just awful, where to start?"

"You could have Ed tell them that you have been looking for them."

"Sounds a little creepy."

Trisha thought for a moment. "You could go see them—or maybe accidentally sort of run into them someplace."

"Creepier," I said.

"You could call. Or write."

"Write what?"

"You know letters, right? Stamps, envelopes, Hello Kitty stationary?"

"Ha ha."

"I know you've been saving those note cards for a very special occasion." Trisha had once discovered my (very modest) collection of Hello Kitty stationery supplies. She enjoyed bringing up the topic whenever she needed to give me a good jab.

"Yeah, I *was* saving it up for something really good," I said. "Now that you mention it, maybe I should use it when I write to your mom and tell her a little bit about Mr. New Boyfriend."

Trisha choked on whatever she was sipping or nibbling. When she stopped coughing, she said, "Go ahead. You want to kill me already, tell my mother all about my love life. That's a great idea!"

"You still haven't mentioned that you let the Jersey Wonder go?"

There was a considering pause on the other end of the line. "No," she said finally. "I'm just not ready to, you know, share him with everyone."

"Ooh! Honeymoon phase?" I said, with an obnoxious kissing noise.

"No. Well—not just that," she said. "I don't want to scare him off. You know."

"So you're saying he's shy and skittish, easily frightened?"

"God, no. Skittish? No. But my family—" Trisha stopped herself, and I felt protective, suddenly, of the noisy, nosey Cutillos. For a minute I remembered the exact smell of their brownstone in Brooklyn Heights: the mixed scents of floor polish, sausage cooking, men's cologne, and coffee that flavored the air on that first step inside the heavy front doors. The hallway lined with posed family photographs—Papi grinning and Sophia in a black turtleneck with her hair caught up tight in the same ponytail in each picture, while Trisha and the boys sprouted up around her.

"You don't want him to meet your family?" I said.

"Just not yet. Not until—well, I really like him."

"And you're afraid he won't get along with them? Or that he'll be all freaked out by them?"

"You know how they are." Trisha's voice was almost apologetic.

"I do," I said. "They're great. If he's going to get scared off or freaked out by your family, then he totally doesn't deserve you."

Trisha gave a bitter gust of a laugh. "Since when does that stop me?"

"But family is—" I paused, struck by my own argument.

Trisha didn't let it go. "Family is—what? You're going to say it's more important than some new boy?"

"I was going to say, 'Family is family.'"

Trisha didn't laugh.

We both let a long moment pass. When Trisha spoke again, her voice was gentle.

"Better to find out for yourself what these people are like than to keep wondering, huh?"

Chapter 54

IN DECEMBER, after the first real snow came and then melted overnight in Nashville, I finally talked to Nellie Greenspan. She told me she was a rental agent for vacation properties across the U.S.

"You left a message for my sister, Dr. Vivian Rowan?"

"Yes, Dr. Rowan asked me to call back this week so that she could tell me which property she meant to take."

"Property?"

"Crested Butte or Siesta Key."

"Beg pardon?"

"Dr. Rowan left a deposit with the agency in October. She told me that she couldn't decide whether she wanted to go skiing in Crested Butte, Colorado, or sit on the beach in Florida this winter, so she asked me to call her back this week."

"Did she—can you tell me about the properties?"

Nellie Greenspan didn't hesitate. "The Crested Butte property is a ski-in ski-out condo, just a short walk from the main street of Crested Butte. Wonderful spot. Great skiing.

"The house in Siesta Key is one of our most attractive locations. In-ground pool and—best of all—a wide-open view of the Gulf of Mexico for spectacular sunsets."

"What were the dates?" I said.

"Three weeks, checking in January 20 after 3 pm, checking out February 9 at twelve noon."

I calculated quickly in my head. January 20 would be a bit more than two weeks past her due date. February 9 was a month before my show was scheduled to take place on St. Armand's Circle, not that it mattered.

"Ma'am?"

"Sorry," I said. "I'm trying to take care of things for my sister while she is in the hospital."

"Oh, I hope it's nothing serious," the rental agent said, pausing with anticipation.

No one wants to hear that it's serious. "Thanks."

"I have the rental agreement in front of me, and I'm sorry to say, it looks like it's a non-refundable deposit."

"I wonder where she wanted to go?"

"My notes only say that she wouldn't be ready to decide until now. Either property would make a wonderful vacation destination."

"If she can't make the trip this year, can we put that deposit toward something next year?"

"Yes, of course. Being that it's more than 30 days out, the agency can credit the deposit toward another rental agreement."

After a few minutes, Nellie Greenspan and I agreed that it would be a good idea to postpone Viv's trip. The rental agent would be mailing a new agreement and a catalog of vacation rental properties across the U.S.

Before going to bed that night, I worked on a mobile of colorful fish using watercolor paper and some copper wire from Dear George's neatly organized garage shelves. The fish would match the bedding that was waiting—washed and folded—in a big shopping bag in the garage.

I thought of sprinkling in a few pairs of skis among the fish. I tried not to trace the logic of my sister's vacation choices: Had she really planned it so that if she lost the baby, she would go skiing? Because who would bring a newborn to a ski-in, ski-out condo in Colorado in January? On the other hand, Colorado would probably be a good place to distract yourself and your husband if you'd lost a baby.

Another baby.

It had to be some consolation to think that she'd planned to come see me—Siesta Key was the next beach south from Sarasota. I'd have to think she had meant to bring the baby. She *must* have meant for me to be part of her life with the baby.

"STOP ME any time you like," he reminded me. "Sometimes it's easier to hear just a little at a time."

Ed Maynard kept the thick spiral-bound report clamped under his arm. When he removed his tan canvas jacket, he passed the report from one hand to the other. He hitched his chair closer to my sister's hospital bed, speaking to both Viv and me.

"As you know," he said, without consulting his notes. "I believe your mother—your biological mother—was Naomi Porter Anderson, originally from Orange, New Jersey."

He reiterated his findings. My sister and I were almost certainly Meshella and Lavinia Porter. Lavinia and Meshella Porter had maternal grandparents in New Jersey and possibly a paternal grandmother in a nursing home in Cocoa Beach, Florida. We'd need blood tests to confirm.

There was an aunt, Ellen Gustenhaus, in Huntington, New York. She was Naomi Anderson's identical twin. She looked a whole lot like Viv, tall, with the same red hair.

"What I believe happened is that, on the night of the Hippie Fire in Snake Tree, Lavinia and Meshella were separated from Naomi in the confusion. There were a lot of scared people, and the police chief told me that some folks cleared out of the farm in a hurry. He figured they didn't want to get busted for marijuana or whatnot. I'm guessing Marsha Ranklin felt that she was rescuing the children when she and Jahn left the farm with the two little girls that night."

Ed stopped to check if I was okay.

I was okay.

"For the next twelve years, Magda and Jahn lived as Mary and John Jones with their daughters Vivian and Nicola. As far as I can determine, Jahn Kiraly and Marsha Ranklin never attempted to make a legal connection to you and your sister. They were—more or less—kidnappers."

At my nod, he continued his summary.

"Jahn was a drinker whose belligerent outbursts frequently cost him his job. Aside from dodging income taxes, there's no evidence that they were involved—as Viv suspected—in anything else of an illegal or underhanded nature."

I stifled the impulse to nudge Viv, to see how she was taking this news. "So, no Mafia hits? No communist plots?"

Ed took the question seriously. "Not so far as I can tell. And I have made inquiries about that. The details are in here." He tapped the bound report against a thigh. "Was there anything else you want to ask?"

It took me a longish moment, but I asked if Naomi's family had ever suspected that the children might have survived.

"No. The Porters have mourned and buried a son, a daughter, and two granddaughters. They focus on their remaining daughter, Ellen Gustenhaus, and her two sons."

"Do we have a father?"

"Best guess says that he passed away in 1980. A student, friend of Naomi's brother. Not married to Naomi."

I found I was chewing on a cuticle. I put my hands in my lap and thought about how to phrase my question. Then I just asked. "Are the Porters nice?"

Ed nodded. His expression was kind. "They seem like solid citizens. He held an executive position in the pharmaceutical industry before he retired. He golfs now. They live a comfortable life in a prosperous neighborhood. She volunteers at the children's hospital, seems pleasant, has a wide circle of friends."

"If I wanted to contact them—?"

Ed grinned. "Ellen Gustenhaus. The aunt. I think you'd like her. She's sharp. Looks a lot like Vivian, runs a math tutoring business out of her home. She was happy to talk about her sister and the nieces she knew way back when."

I nodded.

"After you read the report—it's pretty thorough—and if you have any other questions, give me a call."

Ed Maynard shook my hand firmly and handed me an invoice. He slid the thick report down gently on the curved orange seat of his chair. He touched Viv's hand, told her he hoped she'd feel better soon, and loped off.

I opened the envelope and read over Ed's invoice. It held a final accounting, complete with a detailed list of expenses and a check to reimburse the difference between the retainers and the bottom line on the invoice. When I noticed his train-fare from Philadelphia to Penn Station to Huntington I had to laugh. I'd used the Long Island Railroad line myself to go to back and forth to Stony Brook when I visited Viv in Manhattan.

Then I pulled the chair up to my sister's bed, peeled my shoes off, and pushed my sock-footed toes into the gap between the hospital bedframe and Viv's mattress, and turned to the private detective's written findings.

The bound report looked like a low-budget textbook, with a flimsy clear cover and a wide black binding. It smelled of sweet fresh ink. The pages fought the plastic spine as I tried to turn them.

"All the truth you want to pay for," I told my sister. I wrestled with the pages and began reading.

The report included duplicates of old photos—a whole set of sepia images of the Ranklin family, whose pale eyes gleamed eerily from the page, along with several of Naomi Anderson and her twin sister Ellen, looking like children themselves with a bald little baby propped between them. Ed had included a copy of a graduation photo of Nathaniel Porter, the older brother of Naomi and Ellen, who had the family's pointed triangle chin and a big Adam's apple like a knuckle bulging over a narrow tie.

There were a handful of action shots of a lanky and pale basketball player named Christopher Lacey whose long puffy eyelids were half closed in one photo as he concentrated on shooting the ball. In another, a familiar wide grin transformed his sulky face. His mouth was all big teeth, with heavy, wolfish canines that overlapped up front. On the following pages were black-and-white school portraits of pair of skinny, freckled girls, aging from six up to about twelve. At first glance, the girls looked quite a bit like Viv. I kept turning back to the pictures. As I studied them, these girls with their matching braids and short bangs gazing up seemed to look more and more like me.

I wished Viv could see them.

I slid my shoes back on and took the report with me to the cafeteria while I fetched hot water for tea. I'd remembered to restock the teabags in Viv's bedside table, and at least this one big ceramic mug had escaped the pottery massacre.

On the way back, I looked up from the report just in time to avoid colliding with a group of doctors in rumpled surgical scrubs standing around and chatting in the hallway.

Ed had photocopied legal notices, articles about the Hippie Fire from the newspaper in Pennsylvania, and smaller pieces from several New Jersey papers. There were a depressing number of newspaper obituaries, including the notice of Nathaniel Porter, Naomi's older brother, who had been killed in Southeast Asia at nineteen. In his service picture, Nathaniel looked about twelve years old, playing dress-up as a soldier.

As well as visiting each address where Viv and I had lived as kids, Ed had spoken with virtually everyone who had known Marsha Ranklin. He'd talked to former co-workers of John Jones, and he'd interviewed nearly all the survivors of the Hippie Fire and both the retired police chief and fire marshal of Snake Tree. The conversations were transcribed in full on light pink paper, which distracted me only for a moment. I read them avidly.

He'd interviewed Naomi's mother, Mrs. Gregory Porter, quite briefly ("least said is soonest mended," is how Mrs. Porter responded to his questions about the Hippie Fire and her daughter Naomi). He'd talked extensively to the sister, Ellen Gustenhaus; she'd had plenty to say about Naomi and her kids.

Ed had visited the assisted living facility in Cocoa Beach where Elizabeth Lacey was living. Elizabeth Lacey was the mother of Christopher Lacey, college basketball star and—this theory from Ellen

Gustenhaus—the most likely candidate for father to Naomi's children.

"This might be your grandmother," I said aloud to my sister. I held up the page. "We might have grandparents."

The last section of the report cited a scientific paper about ears. According to the research, there were specific points of reference in describing ear-shape. One could use the shape of a person's ears for identification, and further, ear-shape was heritable. Families tended to have similar ears. Ed compared a photo of Viv's right ear with that of Ellen Gustenhaus—and enumerated the points of similarity. Ed concluded that there was a high probability of relation.

I glanced up from the report. Viv's ear peeped through her short hair, pink and delicate as the petal of a poppy. I traced the matching whorls and dents of my own ear. How had I never noticed?

Chapter 55

"SO, WHAT does it mean to you if someone says 'Oh, her? She likes to party'?" I had the phone pinned to my ear by a shoulder, talking to Trisha while I assembled a tray of cannoli on the wide marble countertop in George's kitchen. I was making the pastries to bring to the hospital.

"Is that a trick question?" Trisha's voice was matter-of-fact.

"Not really. I'm just checking."

She sounded doubtful. "Did someone say that about you?"

"No. I'm trying to decode it from the private investigator's report." Trisha tried to interrupt, but I kept talking. "I am trying to figure out if it means that she smoked pot, or if she slept around, or if she, you know, enjoyed attending parties."

"'She' meaning Hippie Mom?" Trisha managed to get the words into the conversation.

"Yup. Naomi Porter Anderson. She'd just turned twenty-two when she drove a beat-up Oldsmobile sedan from Philadelphia to rural northern Pennsylvania with her two daughters in 1968. She was thinking about going to live in an ashram out West."

"How very groovy of her."

"I know," I said. I walked back to the phone nook to quote from Ed Maynard's open report. "But listen to this. She 'liked to party,' but she 'had a temper to go with that red hair.' This is from the guy who owned the Hippie Farm. He said, 'One of the guys made a pass or something and she wasn't cool with it. She hit him with a frying pan. She was a hard worker, but she created a lot of friction.'"

"She sounds like a sparkplug."

I wiped my hands on a dishcloth and flipped a page. "Her sister Ellen said that 'she was the kind of girl that other girls hated and boys couldn't stay away from.'"

"You have an aunt."

I continued to pour out Ed's findings. "'After the death of her brother Nathaniel in the Southeast Asia conflict.' That means Vietnam, I guess. 'Naomi began staying out late with boys, drinking.'"

I took a sip of orange juice and summed up the rest of the page. "Hippie Mom got pregnant at sixteen, refused to name the father, ran away to Greenwich Village."

"How?"

"Small trust fund from Grandma, plus money from her sister, plus maybe support from one of brother Nathaniel's friends."

"That sounds promising. Hippie Daddy?"

"Daddy maybe, hippie not so much. Basketball player in school. Economics major at Columbia, business school in Philadelphia, married twice, no kids, died of an accidental overdose in Burbank, California in 1982."

"Oh, Nicky, I am so sorry."

"Want me to read more?"

"You want to tell me more?"

"Would you rather I just mail the report to you? That way you can read it and know as much as I do."

"Just talk!"

"Hippie Mom told people at the farm that she had been disowned by her parents."

"But they didn't disown her." Trish spoke with assurance.

"You're sure?"

"Absolutely. You lose a son in a war and one of your daughters runs a little wild? No big."

I considered this for a moment. "Okay. In New York, Hippie Mom got involved with the student activism movement, got arrested at a 'be-in' protest. After the birth of her second daughter, she moved to Philadelphia—"

"Did she name the father?" Trisha said.

"Nope. But her sister said that she went to Philadelphia to be near this guy Christopher Lacey, her brother's best friend, who had gone to business school in Philly."

"Okay."

"But then Christopher Lacey married someone else."

"Ouch."

"Yeah," I said, switching ears for the telephone. I rolled my shoulders and continued. "Hippie Mom started seeing a guy named Steve Anderson and got married shortly after that. Here, let me read. 'Naomi could give as good as she got, but this guy was bad news.' That's according to her sister."

"Nice."

"So this Anderson guy beat her up and she grabbed the girls and came back to Jersey for a few months. The marriage was dissolved, and Naomi hit the road again 'looking for a good place to put down roots with her girls.'"

"That's ironic. Leave home to find a place to put down roots."

"So she ended up meeting the owners of the Hippie Farm at a concert. She told her sister that she was looking forward to living in the country. "

"Her sister, your aunt."

"*Most likely* my aunt," I corrected. I clamped the phone between my shoulder and ear and went back to the fussy process of making cannoli.

"Have you written to her yet?" Trisha said.

"Nope." I hadn't, but I was getting used to the idea of her. "Have you told Sophia about the Jersey Wonder?"

Trisha hissed at me, a sizzle of derision. "So, what about Hippie Mom's parents—you have grandparents?

"*Maybe* our grandparents." I piped a line of cannoli filling into a pastry. "Retired people named Porter. Apparently, he golfs. She volunteers at the local hospital. They live in Jersey."

"What exit?"

"Oh, are we allowed to mock Jersey now?"

Trisha laughed. We stayed on the phone until she had teased every detail of Ed's report from me.

Chapter 56

IT TOOK a few tries, but I wrote a letter to Ellen Gustenhaus. I mailed it the same time as my Christmas packages. I told her that I was interested in knowing about her sister. I told her I thought my parents might have been at the Hippie Fire. I also said that, because my parents were dead, I hoped to find out what had happened back then. I imagined Viv would approve of my neat use of partial truth.

One marathon day early in December took care of all my shopping and wrapping. Nashville had some serious malls. And a lot of people wearing fur coats, even though it didn't feel winter-cold to me yet.

As I inked address labels for the packages—to friends I'd made in Brooklyn, Sarasota, London, Denmark—I imagined the packages shooting off in every direction from Nashville, leaving a starburst pattern of paths across the map.

The line to Ellen Gustenhaus in Huntington, New York glowed red.

ARTIE called with a question about something financial from Viv and George's files, and I asked his advice how much I should tip the guy at the security gate of Viv's housing development. We ended up agreeing to meet for lunch at his favorite Italian place the next day. Over lunch, I told him about Ed Maynard's report. I explained about the possible kidnapping that might have happened on the night of the Hippie Fire and the probable other family that Ed Maynard located.

"According to this report, my sister and I might be Meshella and Lavinia Porter."

Artie made a non-committal noise as he worked his way through the piping-hot dish of baked ziti. Perhaps he meant to indicate that he'd heard me. Or maybe he just liked the ziti.

"When I was little, I had a doll named Baby Vinnia. It's not the kind of name you hear every day," I said.

Artie chewed for a moment, wiped his mouth carefully with a big white napkin, swept a few breadcrumbs under the edge of his dish, and took a sip from his goblet of ice water. "As far as documenting and establishing identity," he started. "I—ah—would advise that we start the process after your sister's child is born."

"I've written to Ellen Gustenhaus."

"That's fine," Artie said.

"But—" I was momentarily at a loss. He didn't seem surprised. I said, "But what if we *aren't* those people's little girls?"

Artie nodded as he bent over his food again. "Of course, we would begin by investigating that connection."

I wondered if Artie had been specially trained not to show surprise at the things his clients told him. Maybe it was a lawyer thing.

Or perhaps he had been expecting news like this from me. Maybe he knew all about it already. I took a careful breath. "Have you talked to Ed Maynard?"

He shook his head absently. "No."

He glanced up from his plate. His bright eyes narrowed at me.

"No! Certainly not about a confidential matter between a client and—no. After you and I spoke last time, I—well, I looked into the matter."

He lifted a piece of buttered bread from his plate and examined it. "I drafted a preliminary legal strategy in case you needed to—" He shrugged. "In case you had an identity issue."

I laughed. An identity issue.

Artie smiled, for once seeming to understand exactly. "But in any case, I think the matter should wait until your sister's baby comes." He pinched a small wedge of bread from the slice and popped it into his mouth.

"Yes," I said. "I'd like to make sure Viv has a say in it."

After a moment of stillness, Artie nodded and said, "Ah—in point of fact. Yes. There's no real hurry."

Chapter 57

I CAN recall the exact sequence of events the night of Daisy's birth. Everything has remained bright-edged and clear regardless of what I've wished I could forget.

The telephone rang at four in the morning when I happened to be awake anyway, standing in the middle of the room with the yellow sash, my feet bare on the thick carpet, thinking about whether I should switch the changing table with the crib to opposite sides of the room. I couldn't decide where the furniture really belonged.

Dr. Pete's voice on the phone sounded hushed and urgent, telling me that Viv was in labor.

"Is she awake?" I asked, a crazy flood of sunshiny color filling my chest. The relief was huge. I felt my face stretch into a smile.

"No," he said. "I'm sorry. You'll want to get here right away."

I drove through the dark to the hospital, my hands gripping the truck's steering-wheel so tightly that, when I pulled off my gloves in the lobby of the hospital, my fingers were reluctant to straighten. Yellow ridges crossed my palms. I was staring stupidly at them as I bumped open the stairwell doorway at my sister's floor.

Dr. Pete met me outside Viv's room. "They've taken her to surgery," he said.

We stood facing each other under the florescent lights. He waved at someone over my shoulder and pointed at me with a thumb. Blood pounded in my temples and throat. I was ready, but there was nothing to do.

Dr. Pete looked terrible. His whole body slouched onto itself, deflated, like a figure from an allegorical tale—Apology or Defeat.

I shook my head. Focus, I thought. I asked him what was going on.

He stood straighter and then sighed, sagging again, before saying, "I'm sorry. I don't really know. She started having contractions."

"But she can't have a baby without—" I shut my mouth suddenly, certain that I would jinx everything if I finished the statement.

He didn't answer. He didn't need to. He was looking at me with such pity that I knew, completely and utterly, that my sister didn't need to wake up.

I might be the last person in the world to understand, but Viv might never wake up.

Other people were not expecting her to wake up. Her baby might never be born. I understood then that things were going wrong, and this night was going to be the end of something—maybe the end of everything—one way or another.

We went into Viv's room. We stood holding onto each other. He mumbled about being on call for the past two days. He apologized for it, but said if I didn't mind, he needed to put his head down for a moment. He sat on the edge of the hospital bed and folded his glasses into the breast pocket of his white coat as he spoke. He leaned over and tucked his feet up onto the bed, neat as a cat. He laced his fingers together over his chest and after a very few minutes he was asleep. I dimmed the lights and closed the door behind me.

In the small ICU waiting room, I paced around the coffee table and said Viv's name to myself over and over.

A DOCTOR in surgical gear knocked on the doorframe of the waiting room. A paper mask hung lopsided around his neck. "Ms. Jones?"

I jumped to my feet.

"Your sister is still in surgery." His smile was wobbly. "Would you like to see the baby?"

I couldn't speak. I nodded and he led the way, the papery booties on his shoes *shushing* with every step.

He gestured toward a sturdy cart that had a clear dome of plastic protecting my sister's daughter.

Daisy was scrawny but long, with dark hair plastered to her head. Four pounds fifteen ounces, and just over seventeen inches tall.

She looked like a wise old man, frowning and wrinkled with a pointed little triangle of a chin. Her skin was the clear orange-red of cinnabar, spotted here and there with something pale and waxy. Her arms and legs were too slender, a frog's limbs attached to her tiny body, but she was so beautiful.

When I reached into the incubator, she wrapped her long fingers—the nails impossibly miniature versions of mine and Viv's—around the end of my pinkie. The tips of her fingers paled with the grip she put into them. She held on, not opening her eyes, and her frown lightened a little.

THERE'S a technical term for what happened to Viv, but the truth is I don't need to know anything more about that kind of thing.

It's bad enough to understand about beneficiaries and investment returns, stone monuments, and funeral services, but aneurisms and hemorrhages and heroic measures? It's pointless to remember the names and processes by which my sister stopped being alive, even though I knew I would have to explain it all to her daughter one day.

In the quiet time in the dimness of Viv's bedside, after the *whoosh* and *bleep* of the machines keeping her alive had hushed, the still body of my sister became just that unimaginably tiny bit more still. I held her hand, our long fingers intertwined as hers chilled.

Of course I talked to her, said what I could in hopes of helping her soul make its way elsewhere. I told her that the baby was beautiful. I couldn't even describe how beautiful.

I said that the doctors assured me a few days in the incubator were all it would take for her daughter to be ready to come home with me. I promised my sister that her baby would be fine. I told her I'd be fine, too. I wasn't sure of it, but it was a good promise to make.

I wished her good luck next time and told her that I hoped she'd land on her feet. I said I hoped we'd have the chance to try this again, and maybe not miss each other the next time.

I suspected she was miles ahead already. Probably out of earshot and not wanting to listen anyhow. Swimming fast through dark water or climbing a rugged trail, looking back at me weeping beside her bed, with a snort of impatience, tossing that thick head of hair and insisting that there was no point in crying.

Chapter 58: Brooklyn Heights, 1997

IT'S A surprise to me that I've never forgotten that my sister is dead. I kept expecting it to slip my mind. I've imagined I'd say to myself one day, "Oh, I've got to tell Viv about that," as if she were only a telephone call away. I'd thought I might misplace the fact of her death for a moment or two.

I miss her, but not a day goes by when I've stopped remembering that Viv has died. I used to worry that I got it backwards somehow, in missing her this way. Didn't people normally get ambushed by remembering that a beloved person is gone? Although, to be honest, it seems even more unnatural to imagine that *I* have gone on without *her.*

I am here and she is gone.

Years have passed.

How can *that* be? Not just that I can't tell her things, but I continue to have things that I cannot tell her. She persists in not being someplace where I can find her.

I didn't know it, but somewhere in my imagination I'd treasured a vision of the future where we'd end up as old ladies in hats together. And yet I am here, and she is not.

I also thought that eventually my memories of Viv would merge with my memories of Daisy: the stubborn set of her jaw and that pointed chin, the lanky white limbs, even the complicated mixture of reds that made up her hair would come to mean Daisy to me, not Viv. Still, whenever Daisy has done anything noteworthy, I wish Viv were around to offer her opinions and plan her contingencies.

DAISY came home from the hospital the Monday after Viv's funeral. Viv's house had never seemed so welcoming: the entire Cutillo clan was staying with me, and Dad Rowan had arrived with a little U-Haul trailer towing behind his Volvo station wagon. The rooms were full of cheerful discussion and minor arguments and the scent of cooking. One dog always stayed within eyesight of Daisy.

Sophia remained in Nashville after the rest of the Cutillos went back to Brooklyn. She muscled Dad Rowan aside often as not for Daisy's baths and diaper changes and the marathon baby-walking sessions required for Daisy to fall asleep the first months. Perhaps she was making up for holding still for so long. Daisy was never a colicky baby, but when she was awake and unhappy, only a good walk or a bumpy car ride allowed her to sleep.

In the months after Viv died, I managed to finish the watercolor paintings for the show in St. Armand's Circle. Despite the midnight feedings and all the meals I cooked for my odd-shaped new family, I produced a dozen pictures. The gallery owner, Gabrielle, sold them all, only one or two to kind-hearted friends.

The whole gang of us left Nashville in the spring. After Papi Cutillo scouted prospects for us, Daisy and I bought a sturdy brick place in Cobble Hill, within easy walking distance of the Cutillo's house. We have a big backyard with a fence for the dogs, and a neat front yard with room to grow flowers. The house has always seemed like home, and I have kept it full of people and food and loud conversations.

With help from Papi and the boys, I made myself a long open white studio space along the attic of the house. It's full of skylights so that when I stand on tiptoe I can see a little sliver of the ocean—or the East River, anyway—through a gap in the trees and roofs.

I still paint—climbing up and down ladders just as Viv predicted—but the mural business has been good to our family.

We fixed up the ground floor with a suite of rooms for Dad Rowan. He sold his place in Arizona and settled comfortably into Brooklyn life. He took up gardening and he often plays cards and goes dancing with Sophia and Papi and their friends. He introduced the Cutillo boys to golfing—a passion that continues to puzzle Sophia—and he's the one who planted the row of cherry trees along the front sidewalk.

I bought a camera when Daisy started scooting and crawling. As soon as she was able to move, she was moving too fast for me to sketch.

I have taken some good photos of this family. The first one I ever sold showed Tomkin drinking water from a hose, all sparkling water-droplets and jowls, for what even my sister would admit was a "nice chunk of change." I think Viv would have appreciated Dear George's dog—the livestock—contributing to the household budget.

THE CITY was a different place with a baby. Strangers catching sight of Daisy in her cocoon of blankets often grinned at her and winked. Even people with worried expressions would take a second look, perhaps waving shyly to get her attention.

Dignified adults in business suits would make silly faces for her and then continue on their way, looking more cheerful.

Daisy accepted their tribute with the sweet, grave air of the Dalai Lama or the Queen Mum on parade. People often told me I had a beautiful baby and I never disagreed.

When we walked, the dogs flanked the stroller like a flying wedge of Secret Service people or an honor-guard of wise advisors to the young queen. Even Balin, who grew stiff and elderly enough to need a ramp to get up the back steps, became energized on these city walks. The three of them went *en garde* as we left the fenced backyard, alert and wary, not quite unfriendly, but serious.

If Daisy fussed, the dogs circled the wagon, sometimes blocking the whole sidewalk, but even the most impatient morning-rush-hour people had to smile as they squeezed past: the dogs all wrinkled frowns and steaming doggy breath in the cold air, attending to the whims of her Highness.

Most mornings, we'd stop twice on the walk to Prospect Park from the house. Once for my coffee, which I'd pop into the cup-holder on the deluxe stroller that Viv had marked in a catalog, and once to feed the mallards. I'd have the dogs sit and wait, but as soon as I opened the plastic bag and called the ducks, Daisy would begin to bounce in place, her legs kicking in rhythm to some martial air she heard.

Her eyebrows formed a solid russet line of concentration and she'd pull three long fingers out of her mouth and point, with a wet but imperious gesture, at the ducks. These minions pleased her.

All it took was for Papi Cutillo to walk into shouting range—"Hiya, Princess!"— for Daisy to lose her regal composure. When she was riding in the stroller, she'd squeal and wave both arms in the air until he released her from the seat and swung her around above his head. The two of them would laugh into each other's faces as if they were speaking a private language.

Even as it makes me smile, I feel a little pang, because Viv has not been here to marvel at Daisy's family. Between Dad Rowan and Nana Sophia and Papi—not to mention the Porters—Daisy has been rich in grandparents. Plus, of course, the aunts and uncles, her godfather Dr. Pete, and the extended aunts and uncles and cousins.

It has been a comfort knowing that if anything should happen to me, a wide net of family has been ready to catch Daisy and hold her safe.

Ed Maynard was right. Ellen Gustenhaus is funny and smart. My aunt—genetic testing eventually confirmed the connection—has a quick eye for what outfit will flatter. Like Viv, she adores *Vogue* and hates to feel a chill on her skin. She wears cashmere almost all year round.

We met on an overcast day of Daisy's first summer. Ellen had suggested I catch up with her in Huntington for lunch. She said, "I'll be sitting outside. I will wear a big straw hat."

I was carrying Daisy in a baby backpack, and I spotted Ellen reading at a café table. She looked up, scanned the street, and looked right past us. Then she looked back at me and frowned in just the same way Viv used to do.

I waved. The movement of my arm must have roused Daisy, because she began to complain. I hurried the last few yards and introduced myself, but between unpacking Daisy and getting her settled again, I barely glanced at Ellen.

When I did look, Ellen had pressed both hands to her mouth while she watched Daisy.

"She has just the look of her mother," she said, without taking her gaze from the girl. "Oh, Lavinia, I can't tell you how glad it makes me to see you again."

OF THE whole Porter clan, we have grown closest to Ellen. Mr. and Mrs. Porter—I've struggled with what to call them—are still in shock, I think.

I imagine it would have been easier for them to have red-haired Viv turn up on their doorstep. Even though Daisy looks like family, it has been a challenge for them to include me, especially after I told them I was keeping my name. I don't mean to be difficult, but I don't know how to be Lavinia Porter.

We've met a whole pack of Porter cousins. Every summer, there's a family reunion in the Adirondacks, with cottages and canoes and bonfires under the stars. Everyone has been very welcoming, and Daisy fits right in.

Soon after Daisy's first birthday, we went on vacation in Florida. We stayed in the beach place Viv might have rented if she'd had the chance, a few miles from the apartment where I'd been staying in Sarasota that last year before Daisy came.

We took a road-trip over to Cocoa Beach to meet Elizabeth Lacey. Daisy showed off her walking skills and her great-grandmother talked about Christopher Lacey as a mischievous young boy. I took dozens of photographs of them together.

TRISHA promoted Mr. New Boyfriend to Mr. Husband Man that next spring. When she finally got around to introducing him to the family, of course they loved him. And he loved them. As well he might. Daisy calls him Uncle Man.

Needing a dress for Trisha's rehearsal dinner, I took Daisy with me to Long Island to meet up with Ellen Gustenhaus.

Over the years, we've walked miles together, hunting for just the right thing. It's less like shopping and more like a hobby for Ellen, and we end up talking the whole time.

We were ambling past a pet store with a window full of puppies behind bars. One dish-faced cocker spaniel the color of butterscotch was chewing on a yellow plastic duck. It looked up and barked soundlessly behind the glass.

"A dog like that bit my sister," I told Ellen, pointing.

Ellen looked at the pet store and said, "I know."

We stopped to stare at each other.

"Your mother used to let Meshella push the baby stroller from one end of the block to the other. She wasn't allowed to turn the corner or cross the street, but she paraded up and down the block for hours at a time. This was in Philadelphia, the spring after you were born. Meshella loved pushing the stroller around."

"She loved pushing *me* around," I said without bitterness.

Ellen didn't respond, still gripped by memory. "The thing was, people kept an eye on her. She'd turned four, but she was so careful with her sister. When Naomi went inside—she wanted some more coffee, maybe, or the phone rang? I don't remember what she told me—it was for just a second. It was no time at all.

"Still, it only ever takes a second. No one saw it happen, but there was barking and screaming, and by the time Naomi got back outside, a dog had Meshella by the arm. There was blood everywhere."

I didn't interrupt Ellen to tell her about the essay Viv had written about the incident.

"Naomi said she flew across the lawn and ended up kicking and beating the dog to get it off Meshella. One of the neighbors drove them to the ER. Meshella spent almost a week in the hospital."

"That long?" I said.

"She'd lost a lot of blood. Of course, back then, people stayed in the hospital until they got better." Ellen made a snort of disgust. It sounded just like Viv. "Mom and I drove down from Jersey to be with Naomi. The doctors were thinking about starting with the rabies shots—it took ages until someone found the dog."

"It wasn't the neighbor's dog?"

"No. Or rather, as far as I remember, nobody claimed it." Ellen shrugged. "It was that kind of neighborhood—people clammed up when the cops came around."

"So they found the dog?"

"Yeah, someone caught it. It didn't have rabies."

"I think that hospital trip is what made my sister decide to become a doctor."

Ellen smiled. "That makes sense. And my sister was so embarrassed, because Meshella was just *smitten* with one of the residents."

"Really?"

"Well, she was four, but yes. I don't remember his name—maybe something Irish? Anyway, handsome guy. He told Meshella how brave she had been, protecting her sister from the big bad dog."

"And he was the one who stitched up her arm," I said, feeling myself back on familiar territory.

"No. Actually, that was lucky. There was a cosmetic surgeon who worked at the ER, a woman physician, who did the operation."

"Operation?"

Ellen nodded. "I can't imagine what it was like for Naomi, waiting all that time—hours—for Meshella to get out of surgery. By the time Mom and I got there, your sister had woken up and moved her fingers—they were afraid of nerve damage."

In the stroller, Daisy squirmed in her sleep, kicking off the blanket. After readjusting her covers, I said, "So, tell me about the cute resident."

"Sean O'Something?" Ellen shook her head. "Doesn't matter. He was assisting the surgeon, I guess. Is that what a resident does? Anyway, the morning after the surgery, he came in with the female surgeon to examine Meshella. Mom and I were there by then. The surgeon was pretty focused on business, but this resident started joshing with Meshella about how she ended up in the hospital. Well, Meshella piped right up about the dog, about her baby sister, about pushing the stroller, about how big and mean the dog was."

"*Was* it a Cocker spaniel?"

Ellen rolled her eyes. "Yes. Funny you ask that, because this four-year old baby girl kept elaborating on the story of the Monster Dog that Ate Philadelphia, you know, making it bigger and more dramatic—and it completely got under Naomi's skin.

"I swear, you could almost see steam coming out of her ears. I think it was the relief making Naomi a little crazy, but she couldn't stand it—she had to break into Meshella's story and set the facts straight."

Ellen clenched her jaw in imitation of her sister. "She was like, 'It was a Cocker spaniel!'" Ellen giggled. "You have to picture it: everybody bent over this little girl, trying to keep her distracted while they looked at this wound, nurses milling around—so much noise!—and there's Naomi screeching, 'She was protecting her little sister, yes, and she's very good about that, but it was a Cocker spaniel. A Cocker spaniel!'

"I thought I would pass out—Naomi was a skinny thing, not short, obviously, but wispy, with a wild head of frizzy red hair, yelling about which breed of dog had nearly taken her daughter's arm off. As if it was important."

Ellen sobered.

"Of course, as a mother—well, I guess sometimes it's easier to focus on details than to think about the big picture when your kid is in danger." She shrugged. "I don't know if the resident felt bad for Meshella with the crazy mother and all, or whether it was just part of his job, but he'd stop by Meshella's room and make a fuss about how brave Meshella had been to protect her little sister from the dog."

"It was a Cocker spaniel," I said.

"No," Ellen was smiling. "She said it more like: 'It. Was. A. *Cocker. SPANIEL.*'"

We both were startled into a burst of laughter.

"How many stitches did she have?" I said, thinking about the kernel of this story my sister had told me.

"Stitches? Oh, my gosh, it was—I want to say fifty. A lot. But the surgeon was meticulous. The nurses all told us how lucky we were to get her. A plastic surgeon in the Emergency Room. Oh, what was *her* name? Hartman? Harrison? Something with an H."

"We could look that up," I said.

"I guess we could," agreed Ellen. "Not that it matters."

"No," I said. "Not that it matters."

Chapter 59

I UNCOVERED what I think was the last of Viv's surprises from the safe-deposit box in Manhattan. My sister had secreted a packet of old love-letters from a college beau, along with a bank statement and an ancient Tiffany's box. The leather-covered box held a pretty, old-fashioned pink diamond ring. I certainly don't remember her getting the ring and I can't begin to imagine why she kept it. Maybe it would have meant something to Dear George. She might have bought it for herself. I haven't gone back through her diaries to see if she ever mentioned it.

I opened the envelope labeled *"In the event of my death."* Inside was a thick letter in that strong, backward-slanted handwriting. It was dated November 1992, eleven months before the car accident that sent me rushing to Nashville. The paper was ridged from the underlining she used for emphasis.

Dear Nicky,

Every year on your birthday, I re-write this letter and thank God that you haven't had to open it. If you are reading this, something bad has happened and I can't help you. I am sorry about that.

There's a lot to put into one letter. The goopy greeting card stuff you already know, but I'll say it again: I love you. You are strong and brave. You should be happy. I want you to be happy. *And though I should have found a way to say it more often, I am* proud of what you have done with your life.

I know I don't tell you often enough. Believe me, when the criticism about school or about your work comes out, I wish I could take it back. It's like there's a "play" button connected to my mouth and when it gets pressed, this stuff just comes out. I wrote this exact same thing last year, but I still mean it. Maybe next year we can skip the part where I say that I meant to be more supportive, less mean, a better sister. You deserve a better sister.

See, thing is, as long as I can remember, you've been my responsibility—but at the same time, for my whole life I've known what I wanted to do. Given a choice between what I wanted and what was good for you, I picked myself every time. I can tell you I'm sorry (I am) but what good does that do? Apologies don't help. You deserve an explanation of some of the selfish choices I made. Maybe it'll be like pressing the "rewind" button.

I should start with when Magda and Jahn went away. What you don't know is that Magda wanted to take you with them. I wanted them to go (you know how much I wanted them to just disappear) but they were going to take you away with them. I wasn't about to let that happen. The biggest fight ever. Jahn slugged me in

*the face. I had a black eye for a month. But no budging:
I was going to get myself into college (come hell or high
water) and I convinced them that the best thing they
could do was to let me go. But so help me God, I
couldn't do it all by myself.*

*I justified it by telling them they weren't fit, but that's
just an excuse. I told Magda she was useless as a
mother. You can guess how Jahn took that. When I got
back up on my feet, I said to her, "See what I mean?"*

*I told them you needed proper looking after, but it was
just an excuse. I couldn't bear the idea of you driving
away with them and leaving me alone. I said I was
worried about you, but that's not exactly true. I was
worried about me. I was scared to go on without you.
Some big sister, right?*

*Every time you move now, I know it's my fault. You
are adventurous, I know that. Still, when I watch you
living out of your car like a vagabond, I can't help but
think it's because I yanked you away from them. Even
though they were terrible parents (that's not just
making excuses, really, they were) I knew you loved
them. You were 13 years old. I know you missed them.
Missed Magda anyway. And yet it didn't stop me from
keeping you away from them.*

*I honestly didn't know if we could make it through that
first year. So much of life is luck. Let's say we were
lucky (bet you a dollar you can spot me justifying
myself this way too). What if, instead of spraining your
ankle in Dexter, you had broken your leg? Or what if,
God forbid, you ended up with a spinal injury? A house
fire, a car accident, a bad cut with a kitchen knife, and
then the jig would be up.*

Used to keep me awake night after night. But did it make me change my mind? No. I was going to college, and you were coming, like it or not.

I was so afraid of messing up. This is more justification, I know, but it used to haunt me: what if you ended up some stupid statistic (pregnant at 15, dead in a ditch from driving drunk, hooked on drugs, whatever) because of my selfishness? I didn't know if I could do any better than Jahn and Magda. Sure, I could take better care of you in a lot of ways, but having a big sister is not the same as having parents.

Something I get now. Or am starting to get now more than I ever did then. Because, Nicky, I want so much to have a baby. George and me and baby make three— though it looks like it's going to take time. Ugh. Hurts so much I could climb through broken glass just to feel better.

Remember how I used to tell you what a waste it was to spend your time babysitting? That having kids was like being a slave? I was so afraid you were going to get pregnant and it was going to be the end of the world...or, anyway, the end of MY world. Viv and Nicky and baby makes—well, even the most ruthless, cutthroat older sister could not keep hitting the books while you struggled to raise a child alone in poverty.

And since this is confession time, I was jealous of how easy it was for you. You just stepped into those people's houses. Remember how Mrs. Ramsey used to rave about what a natural you were with kids? God, it used to drive me nuts. Might as well give you an engraved invitation to the wonderful world of barefoot and pregnant. And the Beberneses—you even looked like them. I should have been thankful that you had a nice rich lady to take you under her wing, but I envied that too.

Bitter truth: I've been jealous of you, Nicky. You never lacked for friends. When we were little, every new school meant a fresh set of pals for you. Even in college my friends would tell me how cool my little sister was. There was always a nice family waiting for you. Did you know Cath Bebernes offered to pay your college application fees? I couldn't decide whether to be glad she cared or have a pity-party because nobody ever stood up for me with checkbook in hand.

Sure hope you aren't reading this. How awful am I?

Nicky, all these pages later and I haven't told you the half of it. Look, the most important thing I should have told you was that Magda and Jahn did not want to leave you. They kept in touch in their own way. They sent money (okay, I made them send money, but they always wanted to know how you were doing) and I should have told you that they hadn't just left. I should have. No excuses.

After George and I got married, I stuck the last of the rainy-day money into a CD in your name. The paperwork is in this safe-deposit box. It's the remainder of the money Jahn and Magda sent over the years (minus that check I sent for your IRA to get you started on your retirement planning). Most of the money got spent as soon as we got it, but I put aside a little for emergencies. I'm sorry that this is all I am leaving for you, but you have lots of skills to fall back on and you've never been afraid of hard work.

Also, the other really important thing is that I should have talked to you about George. When you were little, you would find something and you'd run up, going, "Here, look-at, here," as you put it in my hand. That time with George, it never crossed my mind that you hadn't brought him like a present for me. Later, you know, after that fall and then after you went to Rome, it occurred to me that maybe I had it all wrong. George says no, but still, I should have talked to you. Rude not to say thank you at least.

And yet despite everything I messed up, sis, you turned out really well. You are a good person. People like you. *Much as I have harped on you about getting a degree and finding a regular job, I admire your integrity. You keep sticking to the kind of work you love. It's never bothered you that the things you wanted to be good at aren't going to make you a lot of money.*

You aren't scared of new things. I mean, I wish you'd find a place to settle down, but you've got the knack for landing on your feet and enjoying what's around you, no matter how random. You didn't get it from ME, that's for sure.

Okay, that's enough for now. Maybe next year, when I re-write this letter again, I'll tell you about the tips I picked up from you. I should come hang out with you in Florida. Maybe get warm for once. If you are reading this and I haven't, I apologize for that too.

Love you—

It wasn't that Viv had a mysterious second life for me to discover; she just didn't talk about the one she lived. Not with me, anyhow.

Maybe she told Dear George everything. I'd like to think she did, because otherwise I was the closest bit of family she had, and I barely knew her. It's easy to assign blame. Her fault, my fault, both our faults: I turned my back on her when I ran away to Italy, and I never told her why I needed to run so far and so hard. But then again, she never asked. She didn't chase after me. She didn't offer to share her secrets, and she never asked to see mine.

I should have cornered her and talked about babies, about Dear George, about what sort of life she hoped to live. While I had the chance, I should have, and I didn't.

We never made it up. She's gone and we never talked. You can live with secrets and mysteries like that—of course you can. People live like that all the time—but it's a terrible way to leave things in the end.

My sister taught me everything, one way or another. Why not this, too?

The End

Acknowledgements

So many people helped in so many ways-—though above and through it all, my first, last, and most heartfelt thanks go to my favorite skipper. Thank you, darlin, for supporting my frequent mental absences from our shared life while I attend to those pesky imaginary friends of mine.

It's an odd choice of occupations, writing, and mostly a lonesome one, but for stalwart and boon companionship, writers Kathy Lacey, Cath Mason, Lisa Goodwin, and Jana Milosevich have made us a wonderful writing group. How many times have we met for coffee and to fend off such pigeons as want to alight and coo?

I owe a tremendous debt to early readers of the manuscript, who encouraged my stubborn will to get this book into the world. Thank you so very much for the time and generous feedback, Lois Raffel, Sasa, Wendy Reed, Lisa Hayward, Ned Johnston, Margaret Sutfin (we miss you, Aunt Margaret!), Mary Tone Rodgers, the gang at Scribophile (Kate Raync and Sarah Land, you rock!), Jen Holmberg, and my beloved aforementioned writing gang.

Deepest appreciation to my editor Katie Zdybel, whose insight and skill humbles me. She is, by the way, a lovely writer; if you are reading this, please go buy one of her books.

Thanks to Dr. Chad Christine for that one neurological answer and to the Tennessee State Police public relations department for their many answers to horrible questions.

Thank you Paul Utr and the folks at 99designs for the gorgeous cover.

Rodrigo Fuensalida designed the title font, Instrument Sans Font, while Philipp H. Poll designed the text font used in the printed book, Linux Libertine. Both are open-source fonts, and I salute the designers for making the world a more beautiful place.

Finally, and with an epic, Tommy Ramone-y drumroll: without a doubt, none of this story would have come to be without Sasa, my own charismatic older sister—Sarah Ellen Smith. While Sarah inspired the fictional Vivian Jones, my actual sister is a talented artist who does not—so far as I know—conceal dreadful secrets as Viv did. Sisters are our longest friends—if a person is really lucky. Which I am. Thanks Sasa.

About the Author

A rural childhood in the North Country, a lucky streak with standardized testing, and long practice with making ends meet helped AMY SMITH LINTON scramble through her undergraduate years at Cornell University.

After attending the Publishing Institute at the University of Denver, she worked at Farrar Straus & Giroux Books for Young Readers. She once carried a portfolio of Maurice Sendak's original artwork uptown via subway—only belatedly recognizing the risk of getting mugged with tens of thousands of dollars' worth of irreplaceable original art tucked under an arm.

A former sportswriter for the *St. Petersburg Times* and *Sail* magazine, she reviewed books for *The Tampa Tribune* and *Publisher's Weekly* magazine. Her fiction has appeared in *The Stonecoast Review, Halfway Down the Stairs, Rosebud, The Dead Mule School of Southern Literature*, and more.

She lives in Florida most of the time. When not writing, she races small sailboats with her husband, Jeff Linton. They have won several national championships and a couple of world championships together. She was once short-listed for the US Sailing Rolex Yachtswoman of the Year.

She's working on her next novel.

Updates and Bonus Material

Thank you for reading this story. I appreciate the time you've given to it and hope it served to entertain and perhaps pass the time more quickly through some real-life unpleasantness, like a long, crowded flight.

It would be a great kindness to this small publisher if you were willing to help spread the news about this (and any other) book you've enjoyed.

Personal book reviews and word-of-mouth recommendations are the lifeblood of authors in the new world of publishing. We appreciate your willingness to share your opinion with other readers and are glad to know about—and to amplify—social posts about the work.

To stay in touch, learn about our latest projects on and off the water, sign up for a newsletter, check the website: www.amysmithlinton.com

Bonus material especially for readers and reviewers of this novel can also be found on the website. Cheers!

Lifted Board Press, LLC

Printed in the USA
CPSIA information can be obtained
at www.ICGtesting.com
LVHW041543071023
760217LV00057B/1254